THE
HYMN

BY
THERON BROWN
AND
HEZEKIAH
BUTTERWORTH

PREFACE.

When the lapse of time and accumulation of fresh material suggested the need of a new and revised edition of Mr. Hezekiah Butterworth's *Story of the Hymns*, which had been a popular text book on that subject for nearly a generation, the publishers requested him to prepare such a work, reviewing the whole field of hymnology and its literature down to date. He undertook the task, but left it unfinished at his lamented death, committing the manuscript to me in his last hours to arrange and complete.

To do this proved a labor of considerable magnitude, since what had been done showed evidence of the late author's failing strength, and when, in a conference with the publishers, it was proposed to combine the two books of Mr. Butterworth, the *Story of the Hymns* and the *Story of the Tunes*, in one volume, the task was doubled.

The charming popular style and story-telling gift of the well-known compiler of these books had kept them in demand, the one for thirty and the other for fifteen years, but later information had discounted some of their historic and biographical matter, and, while many of the monographs were too meagre, others were unduly long. Besides, the *Story of the Tunes*, so far from being the counterpart of the *Story of the Hymns*, bore no special relationship to it, only a small portion of its selections answering to any in the hymn-list of the latter book. For a personal friend and practically unknown writer, to follow Mr. Butterworth, and "improve" his earlier work to the more modern conditions, was a venture of no little difficulty and delicacy. The result is submitted as simply a conscientious effort to give the best of the old with the new.

So far as was possible, matter from the two previous books, and from the crude manuscript, has been used, and passages here and there transcribed, but so much of independent plan and original research has been necessary in arranging and verifying the substance of the chapters that the *Story of the Hymns and Tunes* is in fact a new volume rather than a continuation. The chapter containing the account of the *Gospel Hymns* is recent work with scarcely an exception, and the one on the *Hymns of Wales* is entirely new.

Without increasing the size of this volume beyond easy purchase and convenient use, it was impossible to discuss the great oratorios and dramatic set-pieces, festival and occasional, and only passing references are made to them or their authors.

Among those who have helped me in my work special acknowledgements are due to Mr. Hubert P. Main of Newark, N.J.; Messrs. Hughes & Son of Wrexham, Wales; the American Tract Society, New York; Mr. William T. Meek, Mrs. A.J. Gordon, Mr. Paul Foster, Mr. George Douglas, and Revs. John R. Hague and Edmund F. Merriam of Boston; Professor William L. Phelps of New Haven, Conn.; Mrs. Ellen M.H. Gates of New York; Rev. Franklin G. McKeever of New London, Conn.; and Rev. Arthur S. Phelps of Greeley, Colorado. Further obligations are gratefully remembered to Oliver Ditson & Co. for answers to queries and access to publications, to the Historic-and-Geneological Society and the custodians and attendants of the Boston Public Library (notably in the Music Department) for their uniform courtesy and pains in placing every resource within my reach.

THERON BROWN.

Boston, May 15th, 1906.

INTRODUCTION.

Augustine defines a hymn as "praise to God with song," and another writer calls hymn-singing "a devotional approach to God in our emotions,"—which of course applies to both the words and the music. This religious emotion, reverently acknowledging the Divine Being in song, is a constant element, and wherever felt it makes the song a worship, irrespective of sect or creed. An eminent Episcopal divine, (says the *Christian Register*,) one Trinity Sunday, at the close of his sermon, read three hymns by Unitarian authors: one to God the Father, by Samuel Longfellow, one to Jesus, by Theodore Parker, and one to the Holy Spirit, by N.L. Frothingham. "There," he said, "you have the Trinity—Father, Son, and Holy Ghost."

It is natural to speak of hymns as "poems," indiscriminately, for they have the same structure. But a hymn is not necessarily a poem, while a poem that can be sung as a hymn is something more than a poem. Imagination makes poems; devotion makes hymns. There can be poetry without emotion, but a hymn never. A poem may argue; a hymn must not. In short to be a hymn, what is written must express spiritual feelings and desires. The music of faith, hope and charity will be somewhere in its strain.

Philosophy composes poems, but not hymns. "It is no love-symphony we hear when the lion thinkers roar," some blunt writer has said. "The moles of Science have never found the heavenly dove's nest, and the Sea of Reason touches no shore where balm for sorrow grows."

On the contrary there are thousands of true hymns that have no standing at the court of the muses. Even Cowper's Olney hymns, as Goldwin Smith has said, "have not any serious value as poetry. Hymns rarely have," he continues. "There is nothing in them on which the creative imagination can be exercised. Hymns can be little more than the incense of a worshipping soul."

A fellow-student of Phillips Brooks tells us that "most of his verse he wrote rapidly without revising, not putting much thought into it but using it as the vehicle and outlet of his feelings. It was the sign of responding love or gratitude and joy."

To produce a hymn one needs something more exalting than poetic fancy; an influence
"—subtler than the sun-light in the leaf-bud
That thrills thro' all the forest, making May."
It is the Divine Spirit wakening the human heart to lyric language.

Religion sings; that is true, though all "religions" do not sing. There is no voice of sacred song in Islamism. The muezzin call from the minarets is not music. One listens in vain for melody among the worshippers of the "Light of Asia." The hum of pagoda litanies, and the shouts and gongs of idol processions are not psalms. But many historic faiths have lost their melody, and we must go far back in the annals of ethnic life to find the songs they sung.

Worship appears to have been a primitive human instinct; and even when many gods took the place of One in the blinder faith of men it was nature worship making deities of the elements and addressing them with supplication and praise. Ancient hymns have been found on the monumental tablets of the cities of Nimrod; fragments of the Orphic and Homeric hymns are preserved in Greek anthology; many of the Vedic hymns are extant in India; and the exhumed stones of Egypt have revealed segments of psalm-prayers and liturgies that antedate history. Dr. Wallis Budge, the English Orientalist, notes the discovery of a priestly hymn two thousand years older than the time of Moses, which invokes One Supreme Being who "cannot be figured in stone."

So far as we have any real evidence, however, the Hebrew people surpassed all others in both the custom and the spirit of devout song. We get snatches of their inspired lyrics in the song of Moses and Miriam, the song of Deborah and Barak, and the song of Hannah (sometimes called "the Old Testament Magnificat"), in the hymns of David and Solomon and all the Temple Psalms, and later where the New Testament gives us the "Gloria" of the Christmas angels, the thanksgiving of Elizabeth (benedictus minor), Mary's Magnificat, the song of Zacharias (benedictus major), the "nunc dimittis" of Simeon, and the celestial ascriptions and hallelujahs heard by St. John in his Patmos dream. For what we know of the first *formulated* human prayer and praise we are mostly indebted to the Hebrew race. They seem to have been at least the only ancient nation that had a complete psalter—and their collection is the mother hymn-book of the world.

Probably the first form of hymn-worship was the plain-song—a declamatory unison of assembled singers, every voice on the same pitch, and within the compass of five notes—and so continued, from whatever may have stood for plain-song in Tabernacle and Temple days down to the earliest centuries of the Christian church. It was mere melodic progression and volume of tone, and there were no instruments—after the captivity. Possibly it was the memory of the harps hung silent by the rivers of Babylon that banished the timbrel from the sacred march and the ancient lyre from the post-exilic synagogues. Only the Feast trumpet was left. But the Jews sang. Jesus and his disciples sang. Paul and Silas sang; and so did the post-apostolic Christians; but until towards the close of the 16th century there were no instruments allowed in religious worship.

St. Hilary, Bishop of Poitiers has been called "the father of Christian hymnology." About the middle of the 4th century he regulated the ecclesiastical song-service, wrote chant music (to Scripture words or his own) and prescribed its place and use in his choirs. He died A.D. 368. In the Church calendars, Jan. 13th (following "Twelfth Night"), is still kept as "St. Hilary's Day" in the Church of England, and Jan. 14th in the Church of Rome.

St. Ambrose, Bishop of Milan, a few years later, improved the work of his predecessor, adding words and music of his own. The "Ambrosian Chant" was the antiphonal plain-song arranged and systematized to statelier effect in choral symphony. Ambrose died A.D. 397.

Toward the end of the 6th century Christian music showed a decline in consequence of impatient meddling with the slow canonical psalmody, and "reformers" had impaired its solemnity by introducing fanciful embellishments. Gregory the Great (Pope of Rome, 590–604) banished these from the song service, founded a school of sacred melody, composed new chants and established the distinctive character of ecclesiastical hymn worship. The Gregorian chant— on the diatonic eight sounds and seven syllables of equal length—continued, with its majestic choral step, to be the basis of cathedral music for a thousand years. In the meantime (930) Hucbald, the Flanders monk, invented *sight* music, or written notes—happily called the art of "hearing with the eyes and seeing with the ears"; and Guido Arentino (1024) contrived the present scale, or the "hexachord" on which the present scale was perfected.

In this long interval, however, the "established" system of hymn service did not escape the intrusion of inevitable novelties that crept in with the change of popular taste. Unrhythmical singing could not always hold its own; and when polyphonic music came into public favor, secular airs gradually found their way into the choirs. Legatos, with their pleasing turn and glide, caught the ear of the multitude. Tripping allegrettos sounded sweeter to the vulgar sense than the old largos of Pope Gregory the Great.

The guardians of the ancient order took alarm. One can imagine the pained amazement of conservative souls today on hearing "Ring the Bells of Heaven" substituted in church for "Mear" or the long-metre Doxology, and can understand the extreme distaste of the ecclesiastical reactionaries for the worldly frivolities of an A.D. 1550 choir. Presumably that modern abomination, the *vibrato*, with its shake of artificial fright, had not been invented then, and sanctuary form was saved one indignity. But the innovations became an abuse so general that the Council of Trent commissioned a select board of cardinals and musicians to arrest the degeneration of church song-worship.

One of the experts consulted in this movement was an eminent Italian composer born twenty miles from Rome. His full name was Giovanni Pietro Aloysio da Palestrina, and at that time he was in the prime of his powers. He was master of polyphonic music as well as plain-song, and he proposed applying it to grace the older mode, preserving the solemn beauty of the chant but adding the charming chords of counterpoint. He wrote three "masses," one of them being his famous "Requiem." These were sung under his direction before the Commission. Their magnificence and purity revealed to the censors the possibilities of contrapuntal music in sanctuary devotion and praise. The sanction of the cardinals was given—and part-song harmony became permanently one of the angel voices of the Christian church.

Palestrina died in 1594, but hymn-tunes adapted from his motets and masses are sung today. He was the father of the choral tune. He lived to see musical instruments and congregational singing introduced in public worship, and to know (possibly with secret pleasure, though he was a Romanist) how richly in popular assemblies, during the Protestant Reformation, the new freedom of his helpful art had multiplied the creation of spiritual hymns.

* But not fully established in use till about 1625.

Contemporary in England with Palestrina in Italy was Thomas Tallis who developed the Anglican school of church music, which differed less from the Italian (or Catholic) psalmody than that of the Continental churches, where the revolt of the Reformation extended to the tune-worship as notably as to the sacraments and sermons. Thisdifference created a division of method and practice even in England, and extreme Protestants who repudiated everything artistic or ornate formed the Puritan or Genevan School. Their style is represented among our hymn-tunes by "Old Hundred," while the representative of the Anglican is "Tallis' Evening Hymn." The division was only temporary. The two schools were gradually reconciled, and together made the model after which the best sacred tunes are built. It is Tallis who is called "The father of English Cathedral music."

In Germany, after the invention of harmony, church music was still felt to be too formal for a working force, and there was a reaction against the motets and masses of Palestrina as being too stately and difficult. Lighter airs of the popular sort, such as were sung between the acts of the "mystery plays," were subsidized by Luther, who wrote compositions and translations to their measure. Part-song was simplified, and Johan Walther compiled a hymnal of religious songs in the vernacular for from four to six voices. The reign of rhythmic hymn music soon extended through Europe.

Necessarily—except in ultra-conservative localities like Scotland—the exclusive use of the Psalms (metrical or unmetrical) gave way to religious lyrics inspired by occasion. Clement Marot and Theodore Beza wrote hymns to the music of various composers, and Caesar Malan composed both hymns and their melodies. By the beginning of the 18th century the triumph of the hymn-tune and the hymnal for lay voices was established for all time.

* * * * * *

In the following pages no pretence is made of selecting *all* the best and most-used hymns, but the purpose has been to notice as many as possible of the standard pieces—and a few others which seem to add or re-shape a useful thought or introduce a new strain.

To present each hymn *with its tune* appeared the natural and most satisfactory way, as in most cases it is impossible to dissociate the two. The melody is the psychological coëfficient of the metrical text. Without it the verse of a seraph would be smothered praise. Like a flower and its fragrance, hymn and tune are one creature, and stand for a whole value and a full effect. With this normal combination a *complete* descriptive list of the hymns and tunes would be a historic

3

dictionary. Such a book may one day be made, but the present volume is an attempt to the same end within easier limits.

CHAPTER I.

HYMNS OF PRAISE AND WORSHIP.

"TE DEUM LAUDAMUS."

This famous church confession in song was composed A.D. 387 by Ambrose, Bishop of Milan, probably both words and music.

Te Deum laudamus, Te Dominum confitemur
Te aeternum Patrem omnis terra veneratur
Tibi omnes angeli, tibi coeli et universae potestates,
Tibi cherubim et seraphim inaccessibili voce proclamant
Sanctus, sanctus Dominus Deus Sabaoth.

In the whole hymn there are thirty lines. The saying that the early Roman hymns were echoes of Christian Greece, as the Greek hymns were echoes of Jerusalem, is probably true, but they were only echoes. In A.D. 252, St. Cyprian, writing his consolatory epistle* during the plague in Carthage, when hundreds were dying every day, says, "Ah, perfect and perpetual bliss! [in heaven.] There is the glorious company of the apostles; there is the fellowship of the prophets rejoicing; there is the innumerable multitude of martyrs crowned." Which would suggest that lines or fragments of what afterwards crystalized into the formula of the "Te Deum" were already familiar in the Christian church. But it is generally believed that the tongue of Ambrose gave the anthem its final form.

---

*Περὶ τοῦ θνητοῦ, "On the Mortality."

Ambrose was born in Gaul about the middle of the fourth century and raised to his bishopric in A.D. 374. Very early he saw and appreciated the popular effect of musical sounds, and what an evangelical instrument a chorus of chanting voices could be in preaching the Christian faith; and he introduced the responsive singing of psalms and sacred cantos in the worship of the church. "A grand thing is that singing, and nothing can stand before it," he said, when the critics of his time complained that his innovation was sensational. That such a charge could be made against the Ambrosian mode of music, with its slow movement and unmetrical lines, seems strange to us, but it was *new*—and conservatism is the same in all ages.

The great bishop carried all before him. His school of song-worship prevailed in Christian Europe more than two hundred years. Most of his hymns are lost, (the Benedictine writers credit him with twelve), but, judging by their effect on the powerful mind of Augustine, their influence among the common people must have been profound, and far more lasting than the author's life. "Their voices sank into mine ears, and their truths distilled into my heart," wrote Augustine, long afterwards, of these hymns; "tears ran down, and I rejoiced in them."

Poetic tradition has dramatized the story of the birth of the "Te Deum," dating it on an Easter Sunday, and dividing the honor of its composition between Ambrose and his most eminent convert. It was the day when the bishop baptized Augustine, in the presence of a vast throng that crowded the Basilica of Milan. As if foreseeing with a prophet's eye that his brilliant candidate would become one of the ruling stars of Christendom, Ambrose lifted his hands to heaven and chanted in a holy rapture,—

We praise Thee, O God! We acknowledge Thee to be the Lord;
All the Earth doth worship Thee, the Father Everlasting.

He paused, and from the lips of the baptized disciple came the response,—

To Thee all the angels cry aloud: the heavens and all the powers therein.
To Thee cherubim and seraphim continually do cry,
"Holy, holy, holy Lord God of Sabaoth;
Heaven and Earth are full of the majesty of Thy glory!"

and so, stave by stave, in alternating strains, sprang that day from the inspired lips of Ambrose and Augustine the "Te Deum Laudamus," which has ever since been the standard anthem of Christian praise.

Whatever the foundation of the story, we may at least suppose the first public singing* of the great chant to have been associated with that eventful baptism.

---

* The "Te Deum" was first sung *in English* by the martyr, Bishop Ridley, at Hearne Church, where he was at one time vicar.

4

The various anthems, sentences and motets in all Christian languages bearing the titles "Trisagion" or "Tersanctus," and "Te Deum" are taken from portions of this royal hymn. The sublime and beautiful "Holy, Holy, Holy" of Bishop Heber was suggested by it.

THE TUNE.

No echo remains, so far as is known, of the responsive chant actually sung by Ambrose, but one of the best modern choral renderings of the "Te Deum" is the one by Henry Smart in his *Morning and Evening Service*. In an ordinary church hymnal it occupies seven pages. The staff-directions with the music indicate the part or cue of the antiphonal singers by the words Decani (Dec.) and Cantor (Can.), meaning first the division of the choir on the Dean's side, and second the division on the Cantor's or Precentor's side.

Henry Smart was one of the five great English composers that followed our American Mason. He was born in London, Oct. 25, 1812, and chose music for a profession in preference to an offered commission in the East Indian army. His talent as a composer, especially of sacred music, was marvellous, and, though he became blind, his loss of sight was no more hindrance to his genius than loss of hearing to Beethoven.

No composer of his time equalled Henry Smart as a writer of music for female voices. His cantatas have been greatly admired, and his hymn tunes are unsurpassed for their purity and sweetness, while his anthems, his oratorio of "Jacob," and indeed all that he wrote, show the hand and the inventive gift of a great musical artist.

He died July 10, 1879, universally mourned for his inspired work, and his amiable character.

"ALL GLORY, LAUD AND HONOR."
Gloria, Laus et Honor.

This stately Latin hymn of the early part of the 9th century was composed in A.D. 820, by Theodulph, Bishop of Orleans, while a captive in the cloister of Anjou. King Louis (le Debonnaire) son of Charlemagne, had trouble with his royal relatives, and suspecting Theodulph to be in sympathy with them, shut him up in prison. A pretty story told by Clichtovius, an old church writer of A.D. 1518, relates how on Palm Sunday the king, celebrating the feast with his people, passed in procession before the cloister, where the face of the venerable prisoner at his cell window caused an involuntary halt, and, in the moment of silence, the bishop raised his voice and sang thishymn; and how the delighted king released the singer, and restored him to his bishopric. This tale, told after seven hundred years, is not the only legend that grew around the hymn and its author, but the fact that he composed it in the cloister of Anjou while confined there is not seriously disputed.

Gloria, laus et honor Tibi sit, Rex Christe Redemptor,
Cui puerile decus prompsit Hosanna pium.
Israel Tu Rex, Davidis et inclyta proles,
Nomine qui in Domini Rex benedicte venis
Gloria, laus et honor.

Theodulph was born in Spain, but of Gothic pedigree, a child of the race of conquerors who, in the 5th century, overran Southern Europe. He died in 821, but whether a free man or still a prisoner at the time of his death is uncertain. Some accounts allege that he was poisoned in the cloister. The Roman church canonized him, and his hymn is still sung as a processional in Protestant as well as Catholic churches. The above Latin lines are the first four of the original seventy-eight. The following is J.M. Neale's translation of the portion now in use:

All glory, laud, and honor,
To Thee, Redeemer, King:
To whom the lips of children
Made sweet Hosannas ring.
Thou are the King of Israel,
Thou David's royal Son,
Who in the Lord's name comest,
The King and Blessed One. All glory, etc.
The company of angels
Are praising Thee on high;
And mortal men, and all things
Created, make reply. All glory, etc.
The people of the Hebrews
With palms before Thee went;
Our praise and prayer and anthems
Before Thee we present. All glory, etc.
To Thee before Thy Passion

They sang their hymns of praise;
To Thee, now high exalted
Our melody we raise.All glory, etc.
Thou didst accept their praises;
Accept the prayers we bring,
Who in all good delightest,
Thou good and gracious King.All glory, etc.

The translator, Rev. John Mason Neale, D.D., was born in London, Jan. 24, 1818, and graduated at Trinity College, Cambridge, in 1840. He was a prolific writer, and after taking holy orders he held the office of Warden of Sackville College, East Grimstead, Sussex. Best known among his published works are *Mediæval Hymns and Sequences,Hymns for Children, Hymns of the Eastern Church* and *The Rhythms of Morlaix*. He died Aug. 6, 1866.

THE TUNE.

There is no certainty as to the original tune of Theodulph's Hymn, or how long it survived, but various modern composers have given it music in more or less keeping with its character, notably Melchior Teschner, whose harmony, "St. Theodulph," appears in the new*Methodist Hymnal*. It well represents the march of the bishop's Latin.

Melchior Teschner, a Prussian musician, was Precentor at Frauenstadt, Silesia, about 1613.

"ALL PRAISE TO THEE, ETERNAL LORD."

Gelobet Seist du Jesu Christ.

This introductory hymn of worship, a favorite Christmas hymn in Germany, is ancient, and appears to be a versification of a Latin prose "Sequence" variously ascribed to a 9th century author, and to Gregory the Great in the 6th century. Its German form is still credited to Luther in most hymnals. Julian gives an earlier German form (1370) of the "Gelobet," but attributes all but the first stanza to Luther, as the hymn now stands. The following translation, printed first in the *Sabbath Hymn Book*, Andover, 1858, is the one adopted by Schaff in his *Christin Song*:

All praise to Thee, eternal Lord,
Clothed in the garb of flesh and blood;
Choosing a manger for Thy throne,
While worlds on worlds are Thine alone!
Once did the skies before Thee bow;
A virgin's arms contain Thee now;
Angels, who did in Thee rejoice,
Now listen for Thine infant voice.
A little child, Thou art our guest,
That weary ones in Thee may rest;
Forlorn and lowly in Thy birth,
That we may rise to heaven from earth.
Thou comest in the darksome night,
To make us children of the light;
To make us, in the realms divine,
Like Thine own angels round Thee shine.
All this for us Thy love hath done:
By this to Thee our love is won;
For this we tune our cheerful lays,
And shout our thanks in endless praise.

THE TUNE.

The 18th century tune of "Weimar" (*Evangelical Hymnal*), by Emanuel Bach, suits the spiritual tone of the hymn, and suggests the Gregorian dignity of its origin.

Karl Philip Emanuel Bach, called "the Berlin Bach" to distinguish him from his father, the great Sebastian Bach of Saxe Weimar, was born in Weimar, March 14, 1714. He early devoted himself to music, and coming to Berlin when twenty-four years old was appointed Chamber musician (Kammer Musicus) in the Royal Chapel, where he often accompanied Frederick the Great (who was an accomplished flutist) on the harpsichord. His most numerous compositions were piano music but he wrote a celebrated "Sanctus," and two oratorios, besides a number of chorals, of which "Weimar" is one. He died in Hamburg, Dec. 14, 1788.

THE MAGNIFICAT.

Μεγαλύνει ἡ ψυχή μου τὸν Κύριον.

Magnificat anima mea Dominum,
Et exultavit Spiritus meus in Deo salutari meo.

Luke 1:46–55.

We can date with some certainty the hymn itself composed by the Virgin Mary, but when it first became a song of the Christian Church no one can tell. Its thanksgiving may have found tone among the earliest martyrs, who, as Pliny tells us, sang hymns in their secret worship. We can only trace it back to the oldest chant music, when it was doubtless sung by both the Eastern and Western Churches. In the rude liturgies of the 4th and 5th centuries it must have begun to assume ritual form; but it remained for the more modern school of composers hundreds of years later to illustrate the "Magnificat" with the melody of art and genius. Superseding the primitive unisonous plain-song, the old parallel concords, and the simple faburden (faux bourdon) counterpoint that succeeded Gregory, they taught how musical tones can better assist worship with the beauty of harmony and the precision of scientific taste. Musicians in Italy, France, Germany and England have contributed their scores to this inspired hymn. Some of them still have place in the hymnals, a noble one especially by the blind English tone-master, Henry Smart, author of the oratorio of "Jacob." None, however, have equaled the work of Handel. His "Magnificat" was one of his favorite productions, and he borrowed strains from it in several of his later and lesser productions.

George Frederic Handel, author of the immortal "Messiah," was born at Halle, Saxony, in 1685, and died in London in 1759. The musical bent of his genius was apparent almost from his infancy. At the age of eighteen he was earning his living with his violin, and writing his first opera. After a sojourn in Italy, he settled in Hanover as Chapel Master to the Elector, who afterwards became the English king, George I. The friendship of the king and several of his noblemen drew him to England, where he spent forty-seven years and composed his greatest works.

He wrote three hymn-tunes (it is said at the request of a converted actress), "Canons," "Fitzwilliam," and "Gopsall," the first an invitation, "Sinners, Obey the Gospel Word," the second a meditation, "O Love Divine, How Sweet Thou Art," and the third a resurrection song to Welsey's words "Rejoice, the Lord is King." This last still survives in some hymnals.

THE DOXOLOGIES.

Be Thou, O God, exalted high,
And as Thy glory fills the sky
So let it be on earth displayed
Till Thou art here as there obeyed.

This sublime quatrain, attributed to Nahum Tate, like the Lord's Prayer, is suited to all occasions, to all Christian denominations, and to all places and conditions of men. It has been translated into all civilized languages, and has been rising to heaven for many generations from congregations round the globe wherever the faith of Christendom has built its altars. This doxology is the first stanza of a sixteen line hymn (possibly longer originally), the rest of which is forgotten.

Nahum Tate was born in Dublin, in 1652, and educated there at Trinity College. He was appointed poet-laureate by King William III. in 1690, and it was in conjunction with Dr. Nicholas Brady that he executed his "New" metrical version of the Psalms. The entire Psalter, with an appendix of Hymns, was licensed by William and Mary and published in 1703. The *hymns* in the volume are all by Tate. He died in London, Aug. 12, 1717.

Rev. Nicholas Brady, D.D., was an Irishman, son of an officer in the royal army, and was born at Bandon, County of Cork, Oct. 28, 1659. He studied in the Westminster School at Oxford, but afterwards entered Trinity College, Dublin, where he graduated in 1685. William made him Queen Mary's Chaplain. He died May 20, 1726.

The other nearly contemporary form of doxology is in common use, but though elevated and devotional in spirit, it cannot be universal, owing to its credal line being objectionable to non-Trinitarian Protestants:

Praise God from whom all blessings flow,
Praise Him all creatures here below,
Praise Him above, ye heavenly host,
Praise Father, Son and Holy Ghost.

The author, the Rev. Thomas Ken, was born in Berkhampstead, Hertfordshire, Eng., July, 1637, and was educated at Winchester School, Hertford College, and New College, Oxford. In 1662 he took holy orders, and seventeen years later the king (Charles II.) appointed him chaplain to his sister Mary, Princess of Orange. Later the king, just before his death, made him Bishop of Bath and Wells.

Like John the Baptist, and Bourdaloue, and Knox, he was a faithful spiritual monitor and adviser during all his days at court. "I must go in and hear Ken tell me my faults," the king used to say at chapel time. The "good little man" (as he called the bishop) never lost the favor of the dissipated monarch. As Macaulay says, "Of all the prelates, he liked Ken the best."

Under James, the Papist, Ken was a loyal subject, though once arrested as one of the "seven bishops" for his opposition to the king's religion, and he kept his oath of allegiance so firmly that it cost him his place. William III. deprived him of his bishopric, and he retired in poverty to a home kindly offered him by Lord Viscount Weymouth in Longleat, near Frome, in Somersetshire, where he spent a serene and beloved old age. He died æt. seventy-four, March 17, 1711 (N.S.), and was carried to his grave, according to his request, by "six of the poorest men in the parish."

His great doxology is the refrain or final stanza of each of his three long hymns, "Morning," "Evening" and "Midnight," printed in a *Prayer Manual* for the use of the students of Winchester College. The "Evening Hymn" drew scenic inspiration, it is told, from the lovely view in Horningsham Park at "Heaven's Gate Hill," while walking to and from church.

Another four-line doxology, adopted probably from Dr. Hatfield (1807–1883), is almost entirely superseded by Ken's stanza, being of even more pronounced credal character.

To God the Father, God the Son,
And God the Spirit, Three in One.
Be honor, praise and glory given
By all on earth and all in heaven.

The *Methodist Hymnal* prints a collection of ten doxologies, two by Watts, one by Charles Wesley, one by John Wesley, one by William Goode, one by Edwin F. Hatfield, one attributed to "Tate and Brady," one by Robert Hawkes, and the one by Ken above noted. These are all technically and intentionally doxologies. To give a history of doxologies in the general sense of the word would carry one through every Christian age and language and end with a concordance of the Book of Psalms.

THE TUNE.

Few would think of any music more appropriate to a standard doxology than "Old Hundred." This grand Gregorian harmony has been claimed to be Luther's production, while some have believed that Louis Bourgeois, editor of the French *Genevan Psalter*, composed the tune, but the weight of evidence seems to indicate that it was the work of Guillaume le Franc, (William Franck or William the Frenchman,) of Rouen, in France, who founded a music school in Geneva, 1541. He was Chapel Master there, but removed to Lausanne, where he played in the Catholic choir and wrote the tunes for an Edition of Marot's and Beza's Psalms. Died in Lausanne, 1570.

"THE LORD DESCENDED FROM ABOVE."

A flash of genuine inspiration was vouchsafed to Thomas Sternhold when engaged with Rev. John Hopkins in versifying the Eighteenth Psalm. The ridicule heaped upon Sternhold and Hopkins's psalmbook has always stopped, and sobered into admiration and even reverence at the two stanzas beginning with this leading line—

The Lord descended from above
And bowed the heavens most high,
And underneath His feet He cast
The darkness of the sky.
On cherub and on cherubim
Full royally He rode,
And on the wings of mighty winds
Came flying all abroad.

Thomas Sternhold was born in Gloucestershire, Eng. He was Groom of the Robes to Henry VIII, and Edward VI., but is only remembered for his *Psalter* published in 1562, thirteen years after his death in 1549.

THE TUNE.

"Nottingham" (now sometimes entitled "St. Magnus") is a fairly good echo of the grand verses, a dignified but spirited choral in A flat. Jeremiah Clark, the composer, was born in London, 1670. Educated at the Chapel Royal, he became organist of Winchester College and finally to St. Paul's Cathedral where he was appointed Gentleman of the Chapel. He died July, 1707.

The tune of "Majesty" by William Billings will be noticed in a later chapter.

TALLIS' EVENING HYMN.

Glory to Thee, my God, this night
For all the blessings of the light,
Keep me, O keep me, King of kings,
Under Thine own Almighty wings.

This stanza begins the second of Bp. Ken's three beautiful hymn-prayers in his *Manual* mentioned on a previous page.

For more than three hundred and fifty years devout people have enjoyed that melody of mingled dignity and sweetness known as "Tallis' Evening Hymn."

Thomas Tallis was an Englishman, born about 1520, and at an early age was a boy chorister at St. Paul's. After his voice changed, he played the organ at Waltham Abbey, and some time later was chosen organist royal to Queen Elizabeth. His pecuniary returns for his talent did not make him rich, though he bore the title after 1542 of Gentleman of the Chapel Royal, for his stipend was sevenpence a day. Some gain may possibly have come to him, however, from his publication, late in life, under the queen's special patent, of a collection of hymns and tunes.

He wrote much and was the real founder of the English Church school of composers, but though St. Paul's was at one time well supplied with his motets and anthems, it is impossible now to give a list of Tallis' compositions for the Church. His music was written originally to Latin words, but when, after the Reformation, the use of vernacular hymns, was introduced he probably adapted his scores to either language.

It is inferred that he was in attendance on Queen Elizabeth at her palace in Greenwich when he died, for he was buried in the old parish church there in November, 1585. The rustic rhymer who indited his epitaph evidently did the best he could to embalm the virtues of the great musician as a man, a citizen, and a husband:

Enterred here doth ly a worthy wyght,
Who for long time in musick bore the bell:
His name to shew was Thomas Tallis hyght;
In honest vertuous lyff he dyd excell.
He served long tyme in chappel with grete prayse,
Fower sovereygnes reignes, (a thing not often seene);
I mean King Henry and Prince Edward's dayes,
Quene Marie, and Elizabeth our quene.
He maryed was, though children he had none,
And lyv'd in love full three and thirty yeres
With loyal spowse, whose name yclept was Jone,
Who, here entombed, him company now bears.
As he dyd lyve, so also dyd he dy,
In myld and quyet sort, O happy man!
To God ful oft for mercy did he cry;
Wherefore he lyves, let Deth do what he can.

"THE GOD OF ABRAHAM PRAISE."

This is one of the thanksgivings of the ages.

The God of Abraham praise,
Who reigns enthroned above;
Ancient of everlasting days,
And God of love.
Jehovah, Great I AM!
By earth and heaven confessed,
I bow and bless the sacred Name,
Forever blest.

The hymn, of twelve eight-line stanzas, is too long to quote entire, but is found in both the *Plymouth* and *Methodist Hymnals.*

Thomas Olivers, born in Tregynon, near Newtown, Montgomeryshire, Wales, 1725, was, according to local testimony, "the worst boy known in all that country, for thirty years." It is more charitable to say that he was a poor fellow who had no friends. Left an orphan at five years of age, he was passed from one relative to another until all were tired of him, and he was "bound out" to a shoemaker. Almost inevitably the neglected lad grew up wicked, for no one appeared to care for his habits and morals, and as he sank lower in the various vices encouraged by bad company, there were more kicks for him than helping hands. At the age of eighteen his reputation in the town had become so unsavory that he was forced to shift for himself elsewhere.

Providence led him, when shabby and penniless, to the old seaport town of Bristol, where Whitefield was at that time preaching,* and there the young sinner heard the divine message that lifted him to his feet.

---

* Whitefield's text was, "Is not this a brand plucked out of the fire?" Zach. 3:2.

"When that sermon began," he said, "I was one of the most abandoned and profligate young men living; before it ended I was a new creature. The world was all changed for Tom Olivers."

His new life, thus begun, lasted on earth more than sixty useful years. He left a shining record as a preacher of righteousness, and died in the triumphs of faith, November, 1799. Before he passed away he saw at least thirty editions of his hymn published, but the soul-music it has awakened among the spiritual children of Abraham can only reach him in heaven. Some of its words have been the last earthly song of many, as they were of the eminent Methodist theologian, Richard Watson—

> I shall behold His face,
> I shall His power adore,
> And sing the wonders of His grace
> Forevermore.

THE TUNE.

The precise date of the tune "Leoni" is unknown, as also the precise date of the hymn. The story is that Olivers visited the great "Duke's Place" Synagogue, Aldgate, London, and heard Meyer Lyon (Leoni) sing the Yigdal or long doxology to an air so noble and impressive that it haunted him till he learned it and fitted to it the sublime stanzas of his song. Lyon, a noted Jewish musician and vocalist, was chorister of this London Synagogue during the latter part of the 18th century and the Yigdal was a portion of the Hebrew Liturgy composed in medieval times, it is said, by Daniel Ben Judah. The fact that the Methodist leaders took Olivers from his bench to be one of their preachers answers any suggestion that the converted shoemaker *copied* the Jewish hymn and put Christian phrases in it. He knew nothing of Hebrew, and had he known it, a literal translation of the Yigdal will show hardly a similarity to his evangelical lines. Only the music as Leoni sang it prompted his own song, and he gratefully put the singer's name to it. Montgomery, who admired the majestic style of the hymn, and its glorious imagery, said of its author, "The man who wrote that hymn must have had the finest ear imaginable, for on account of the peculiar measure, none but a person of equal musical and poetic taste could have produced the harmony perceptible in the verse."

Whether the hymnist or some one else fitted the hymn to the tune, the "fine ear" and "poetic taste" that Montgomery applauded are evident enough in the union.

"O WORSHIP THE KING ALL GLORIOUS ABOVE."

This hymn of Sir Robert Grant has become almost universally known, and is often used as a morning or opening service song by choirs and congregations of all creeds. The favorite stanzas are the first four—

> O worship the King all-glorious above,
> And gratefully sing His wonderful love—
> Our Shield and Defender, the Ancient of Days,
> Pavilioned in splendor, and girded with praise.
> O tell of His might, and sing of His grace,
> Whose robe is the light, whose canopy, space;
> His chariots of wrath the deep thunder-clouds form,
> And dark is His path on the wings of the storm.
> Thy bountiful care what tongue can recite?
> It breathes in the air, it shines in the light,
> It streams from the hills, it descends to the plain,
> And sweetly distils in the dew and the rain.
> Frail children of dust, and feeble as frail,
> In Thee do we trust, nor find Thee to fail.
> Thy mercies how tender! how firm to the end!
> Our Maker, Defender, Redeemer, and Friend!

This is a model hymn of worship. Like the previous one by Thomas Olivers, it is strongly Hebrew in its tone and diction, and drew its inspiration from the Old Testament Psalter, the text-book of all true praise-song.

Sir Robert Grant was born in the county of Inverness, Scotland, in 1785, and educated at Cambridge. He was many years member of Parliament for Inverness and a director in the East India Company, and 1834 was appointed Governor of Bombay. He died at Dapoorie, Western India, July 9, 1838.

Sir Robert was a man of deep Christian feeling and a poetic mind. His writings were not numerous, but their thoughtful beauty endeared him to a wide circle of readers. In 1839 his brother, Lord Glenelg, published twelve of his poetical pieces, and a new edition in 1868. The volume contains the more or less well-known hymns—

> The starry firmament on high,
> Saviour, when in dust to Thee,

and—

When gathering clouds around I view.

Sir Robert's death, when scarcely past his prime, would indicate a decline by reason of illness, and perhaps other serious affliction, that justified the poetic license in the submissive verses beginning—

Thy mercy heard my infant prayer.

*   *   *   *   *   *

And now *in age* and grief Thy name
Does still my languid heart inflame,
And bow my faltering knee.
Oh, yet this bosom feels the fire,
This trembling hand and drooping lyre
Have yet a strain for Thee.

THE TUNE.

Several musical pieces written to the hymn, "O, Worship the King," have appeared in church psalm-books, and others have been borrowed for it, but the one oftenest sung to its words is Haydn's "Lyons." Its vigor and spirit best fit it for Grant's noble lyric.

"MAJESTIC SWEETNESS SITS ENTHRONED."

Rev. Samuel Stennett D.D., the author of this hymn, was the son of Rev. Joseph Stennett, and grandson of Rev. Joseph Stennett D.D., who wrote—

Another six days' work is done,
Another Sabbath is begun.

All were Baptist ministers. Samuel was born in 1727, at Exeter, Eng., and at the age of twenty-one became his father's assistant, and subsequently his successor over the church in Little Wild Street, Lincoln's Inn Fields, London.

Majestic sweetness sits enthroned
Upon the Saviour's brow;
His head with radiant glories crowned,
His lips with grace o'erflow.

*   *   *   *   *   *

To Him I owe my life and breath
And all the joys I have;
He makes me triumph over death,
He saves me from the grave.

*   *   *   *   *   *

Since from His bounty I receive
Such proofs of love divine,
Had I a thousand hearts to give,
Lord, they should all be Thine.

Samuel Stennett was one of the most respected and influential ministers of the Dissenting persuasion, and a confidant of many of the most distinguished statesmen of his time. The celebrated John Howard was his parishoner and intimate friend. His degree of Doctor of Divinity was bestowed upon him by Aberdeen University. Besides his theological writings he composed and published thirty-eight hymns, among them—

On Jordan's stormy banks I stand,
When two or three with sweet accord,
Here at Thy table, Lord, we meet,

and—

"'Tis finished," so the Saviour cried.

"Majestic Sweetness" began the third stanza of his longer hymn—

To Christ the Lord let every tongue.

Dr. Stennett died in London, Aug. 24, 1795.

THE TUNE.

For fifty or sixty years "Ortonville" has been linked with this devout hymn, and still maintains its fitting fellowship. The tune, composed in 1830, was the work of Thomas Hastings, and is almost as well-known and as often sung as his immortal "Toplady." (See chap. 3, "Rock of Ages.")

"ALL HAIL THE POWER OF JESUS' NAME."

This inspiring lyric of praise appears to have been written about the middle of the eighteenth century. Its author, the Rev. Edward Perronet, son of Rev. Vincent Perronet, Vicar of Shoreham, Eng., was a man of great faith and humility but zealous in his convictions, sometimes to his serious expense. He was born in 1721, and, though eighteen years younger than Charles Wesley, the two became bosom friends, and it was under the direction of the Wesleys that

Perronet became a preacher in the evangelical movement. Lady Huntingdon later became his patroness, but some needless and imprudent expressions in a satirical poem, "The Mitre," revealing his hostility to the union of church and state, cost him her favor, and his contention against John Wesley's law that none but the regular parish ministers had the right to administer the sacraments, led to his complete separation from both the Wesleys. He subsequently became the pastor of a small church of Dissenters in Canterbury, where he died, in January, 1792. His piety uttered itself when near his happy death, and his last words were a Gloria.

All hail the power of Jesus' name!
Let angels prostrate fall;
Bring forth the royal diadem,
To crown Him Lord of all.
Ye seed of Israel's chosen race,
Ye ransomed of the fall,
Hail Him Who saves you by His grace,
And crown Him Lord of all.
Sinners, whose love can ne'er forget
The wormwood and the gall,
Go, spread your trophies at His feet,
And crown Him Lord of all.
Let every tribe and every tongue
That bound creation's call,
Now shout the universal song,
The crownéd Lord of all.

With two disused stanzas omitted, the hymn as it stands differs from the original chiefly in the last stanza, though in the second the initial line is now transposed to read—
Ye chosen seed of Israel's race.
The fourth stanza now reads—
Let every kindred, every tribe
On this terrestrial ball
To Him all majesty ascribe,
And crown Him Lord of all.
And what is now the favorite last stanza is the one added by Dr. Rippon—
O that with yonder sacred throng
We at His feet may fall,
And join the everlasting song,
And crown Him Lord of all.

THE TUNE.

Everyone now calls it "Old Coronation," and it is entitled to the adjective by this time, being considerably more than a hundred years of age. It was composed in the very year of Perronet's death and one wonders just how long the hymn and tune waited before they came together; for Heaven evidently meant them to be wedded for all time. This is an American opinion, and no reflection on the earlier English melody of "Miles Lane," composed during Perronet's lifetime by William Shrubsole and published with the words in 1780 in the *Gospel Magazine*. There is also a fine processional tune sung in the English Church to Perronet's hymn.

Oliver
Holden

The author of "Coronation" was Oliver Holden, a self-taught musician, born in Shirley, Mass., 1765, and bred to the carpenter's trade. The little pipe organ on which tradition says he struck the first notes of the famous tune is now in the Historical rooms of the Old State House, Boston, placed there by its late owner, Mrs. Fanny Tyler, the old musician's granddaughter. Its tones are as mellow as ever, and the times that "Coronation" has been played upon it by admiring visitors would far outnumber the notes of its score.

Holden wrote a number of other hymn-tunes, among which "Cowper," "Confidence," and "Concord" are remembered, but none of them had the wings of "Coronation," his American "Te Deum." His first published collection was entitled *The American Harmony*, and this was followed by the *Union Harmony*, and the *Worcester Collection*. He also wrote and published "Mt. Vernon," and several other patriotic anthems, mainly for special occasions, to some of which he supplied the words. He was no hymnist, though he did now and then venture into sacred metre. The new *Methodist Hymnal* preserves a simple four-stanza specimen of his experiments in verse:

They who seek the throne of grace
Find that throne in every place:
If we lead a life of prayer
God is present everywhere.

Sacred music, however, was the good man's passion to the last. He died in 1844.

"Such beautiful themes!" he whispered on his death bed, "Such beautiful themes! But I can write no more."

The enthusiasm always and everywhere aroused by the singing of "Coronation," dates from the time it first went abroad in America in its new wedlock of music and words. "This tune," says an accompanying note over the score in the old *Carmina Sacra*, "was a great favorite with the late Dr. Dwight of Yale College (1798). It was often sung by the college choir, while he, catching, as it were, the music of the heavenly world, would join them, and lead with the most ardent devotion."

"AWAKE AND SING THE SONG."

This hymn of six stanzas is abridged from a longer one indited by the Rev. William Hammond, and published in *Lady Huntingdon's Hymn-book*. It was much in use in early Methodist revivals. It appears now as it was slightly altered by Rev. Martin Madan—

Awake and sing the song
Of Moses and the Lamb;
Join every heart and every tongue
To praise the Savior's name.
*   *   *   *   *   *

The sixth verse is a variation of one of Watts' hymns, and was added in the *Brethren's Hymn-book*, 1801—

There shall each heart and tongue
His endless praise proclaim,
And sweeter voices join the song
Of Moses and the Lamb.

The Rev. William Hammond was born Jan. 6, 1719, at Battle, Sussex, Eng., and educated at St. John's College, Cambridge. Early in his ministerial life he was a Calvinistic Methodist, but ultimately joined the Moravians. Died in London, Aug. 19, 1793. His collection of *Psalms and Hymns and Spiritual Songs* was published in 1745.

The Rev. Martin Madan, son of Col. Madan, was born 1726. He founded Lock Hospital, Hyde Park, and long officiated as its chaplain. As a preacher he was popular, and his reputation as a composer of music was considerable. There is no proof that he wrote any original hymns, but he amended, pieced and expanded the work of others. Died in 1770.

THE TUNE.

The hymn has had a variety of musical interpretations. The more modern piece is "St. Philip," by Edward John Hopkins, Doctor of Music, born at Westminster, London, June 30, 1818. From a member of the Chapel Royal boy choir he became organist of the Michtam Church, Surrey, and afterwards of the Temple Church, London. Received his Doctor's degree from the Archbishop of Canterbury in 1882.

"CROWN HIS HEAD WITH ENDLESS BLESSING."

The writer of this hymn was William Goode, who helped to found the English Church Missionary Society, and was for twenty years the Secretary of the "Society for the Relief of Poor Pious Clergymen." For celebrating the praise of the Saviour, he seems to have been of like spirit and genius with Perronet. He was born in Buckingham, Eng., April 2, 1762; studied for the ministry and became a curate, successor of William Romaine. His spiritual maturity was early, and his habits of thought were formed amid associations such as the young Wesleys and Whitefield sought. Like them, even in his student days he proved his aspiration for purer religious life by an evangelical zeal that cost him the ridicule of many of his school-fellows, but the meetings for conference and prayer which he organized among them were not unattended, and were lasting and salutary in their effect.

Jesus was the theme of his life and song, and was his last word. He died in 1816.

Crown His head with endless blessing
Who in God the Father's name
With compassion never ceasing
Comes salvation to proclaim.
Hail, ye saints who know His favor,
Who within His gates are found.
Hail, ye saints, th' exalted Saviour,
Let His courts with praise resound.

Joseph
Haydn

THE TUNE.

"Haydn," bearing the name of its great composer, is in several important hymnals the chosen music for William Goode's devout words. Its strain and spirit are lofty and melodious and in entire accord with the pious poet's praise.

Joseph Haydn, son of a poor wheelwright, was born 1732, in Rohron, a village on the borders of Hungary and Austria. His precocity of musical talent was such that he began composing at the age of ten years. Prince Esterhazy discovered his genius when he was poor and friendless, and his fortune was made. While Music Master for the Prince's Private Chapel (twenty years) he wrote many of his beautiful symphonies which placed him among the foremost in that class of music. Invited to England, he received the Doctor's degree at Oxford, and composed his great oratorio of "The Creation," besides his "Twelve Grand Symphonies," and a long list of minor musical works secular and sacred. His invention was inexhaustible.

Haydn seems to have been a sincerely pious man. When writing his great oratorio of "The Creation" at sixty-seven years of age, "I knelt down every day," he says, "and prayed God to strengthen me for my work." This daily spiritual preparation was similar to Handel's when he was creating his "Messiah." Change one word and it may be said of sacred music as truly as of astronomy, "The undevout composer is mad."

Near Haydn's death, in Vienna, 1809, when he heard for the last time his magnificent chorus, "Let there be Light!" he exclaimed, "Not mine, not mine. It all came to me from above."

"NOW TO THE LORD A NOBLE SONG."

When Watts finished this hymn he had achieved a "noble song," whether he was conscious of it or not; and it deserves a foremost place, where it can help future worshippers in their praise as it has the past. It is not so common in the later hymnals, but it is imperishable, and still later collections will not forget it.

Now to the Lord a noble song,
Awake my soul, awake my tongue!
Hosanna to the Eternal Name,
And all His boundless love proclaim.
See where it shines in Jesus' face,
The brightest image of His grace!
God in the person of His Son
Has all His mightiest works outdone.

A rather finical question has occurred to some minds as to the theology of the word "works" in the last line, making the second person in the Godhead apparently a creature; and in a few hymn-books the previous line has been made to read—

God in the *Gospel* of His Son.

But the question is a rhetorical one, and the poet's free expression—here as in hundreds of other cases—has never disturbed the general confidence in his orthodoxy.

Montgomery called Watts "the inventor of hymns in our language," and the credit stands practically undisputed, for Watts made a hymn style that no human master taught him, and

14

his model has been the ideal one for song worship ever since; and we can pardon the climax when Professor Charles M. Stuart speaks of him as "writer, scholar, thinker and saint," for in addition to all the rest he was a very good man.

THE TUNE.

Old "Ames" was for many years the choir favorite, and the words of the hymn printed with it in the note-book made the association familiar. It was, and *is*, an appropriate selection, though in later manuals George Kingsley's "Ware" is evidently thought to be better suited to the high-toned verse. Good old tunes never "wear out," but they do go out of fashion.

The composer of "Ames," Sigismund Neukomm, Chevalier, was born in Salzburg, Austria, July 10, 1778, and was a pupil of Haydn. Though not a great genius, his talents procured him access and even intimacy in the courts of Germany, France, Italy, Portugal and England, and for thirty years he composed church anthems and oratorios with prodigious industry. Neukomm's musical productions, numbering no less than one thousand, and popular in their day, are, however, mostly forgotten, excepting his oratorio of "David" and one or two hymn-tunes.

George Kingsley, author of "Ware," was born in Northampton, Mass., July 7, 1811. Died in the Hospital, in the same city, March 14, 1884. He compiled eight books of music for young people and several manuals of church psalmody, and was for some time a music teacher in Boston, where he played the organ at the Hollis St. church. Subsequently he became professor of music in Girard College, Philadelphia, and music instructor in the public schools, being employed successively as organist (on Lord's Day) at Dr. Albert Barnes' and Arch St. churches, and finally in Brooklyn at Dr. Storrs' Church of the Pilgrims. Returned to Northampton, 1853.

"EARLY, MY GOD, WITHOUT DELAY."

This and the five following hymns, all by Watts, are placed in immediate succession, for unity's sake—with a fuller notice of the greatest of hymn-writers at the end of the series.

Early, my God, without delay
I haste to seek Thy face,
My thirsty spirit faints away
Without Thy cheering grace.

In the memories of very old men and women, who sang the fugue music of Morgan's "Montgomery," still lingers the second stanza and some of the "spirit and understanding" with which it used to be rendered in meeting on Sunday mornings.

So pilgrims on the scorching sand,
Beneath a burning sky,
Long for a cooling stream at hand
And they must drink or die.

THE TUNE.

Many of the earlier pieces assigned to this hymn were either too noisy or too tame. The best and longest-serving is "Lanesboro," which, with its expressive duet in the middle and its soaring final strain of harmony, never fails to carry the meaning of the words. It was composed by William Dixon, and arranged and adapted by Lowell Mason.

William Dixon, an English composer, was a music engraver and publisher, and author also of several glees and anthems. He was born 1750, and died about 1825.

Lowell Mason, born in Medfield, Mass., 1792, has been called, not without reason, "the father of American choir singing." Returning from Savannah, Ga., where he spent sixteen years of his younger life as clerk in a bank, he located in Boston (1827), being already known there as the composer of "The Missionary Hymn." He had not neglected his musical studies while living in the South, and it was in Savannah that he made the glorious harmony of that tune.

He became president of the Handel and Haydn Society, went abroad for special study, was made Doctor of Music, and collected a store of themes among the great models of song to bring home for his future work.

The Boston Academy of Music was founded by him and what he did for the song-service of the Church in America by his singing schools, and musical conventions, and published manuals, to form and organize the choral branch of divine worship, has no parallel, unless it is Noah Webster's service to the English language.

Dr. Mason died in Orange, N.J., in 1872.

"SWEET IS THE WORK, MY GOD, MY KING."

This is one of the hymns that helped to give its author the title of "The Seraphic Watts."

Sweet is the work, my God, my King
To praise Thy name, give thanks and sing
To show Thy love by morning light,
And talk of all Thy truth at night.

THE TUNE.

No nobler one, and more akin in spirit to the hymn, can be found than "Duke Street," Hatton's imperishable choral.

Little is known of the John Hatton who wrote "Duke St." He was earlier by nearly a century than John Liphot Hatton of Liverpool (born in 1809), who wrote the opera of "Pascal Bruno," the cantata of "Robin Hood" and the sacred drama of "Hezekiah." The biographical index of the *Evangelical Hymnal* says of John Hatton, the author of "Duke St.": "John, of Warrington; afterwards of St. Helens, then resident in Duke St. in the township of Windle; composed several hymn-tunes; died in 1793.* His funeral sermon was preached at the Presbyterian Chapel, St. Helens, Dec. 13."

* Tradition says he was killed by being thrown from a stage-coach.

"COME, WE THAT LOVE THE LORD."

Watts entitled this hymn "Heavenly Joy on Earth." He could possibly, like Madame Guyon, have written such a hymn in a dungeon, but it is no less spiritual for its birth (as tradition will have it) amid the lovely scenery of Southampton where he could find in nature "glory begun below."

Come, we that love the Lord,
And let our joys be known;
Join in a song with sweet accord,
And thus surround the throne.
There shall we see His face,
And never, never sin;
There, from the rivers of His grace,
Drink endless pleasures in.
Children of grace have found
Glory begun below:
Celestial fruits on earthly ground
From faith and hope may grow.

Mortality and immortality blend their charms in the next stanza. The unfailing beauty of the vision will be dwelt upon with delight so long as Christians sing on earth.

The hill of Sion yields
A thousand sacred sweets,
Before we reach the heavenly fields,
Or walk the golden streets.

THE TUNE.

"St. Thomas" has often been the interpreter of the hymn, and still clings to the words in the memory of thousands.

The Italian tune of "Ain" has more music. It is a fugue piece (simplified in some tune-books), and the joyful traverse of its notes along the staff in four-four time, with the momentum of a good choir, is exhilarating in the extreme.

Corelli, the composer, was a master violinist, the greatest of his day, and wrote a great deal of violin music; and the thought of his glad instrument may have influenced his work when harmonizing the four voices of "Ain."

Arcangelo Corelli was born at Fusignano, in 1653. He was a sensitive artist, and although faultless in Italian music, he was not sure of himself in playing French scores, and once while performing with Handel (who resented the slightest error), and once again with Scarlatti, leading an orchestra in Naples when the king was present, he made a mortifying mistake. He took the humiliation so much to heart that he brooded over it till he died, in Rome, Jan. 18, 1717.

For revival meetings the modern tune set to "Come we that love the Lord," by Robert Lowry, should be mentioned. A shouting chorus is appended to it, but it has melody and plenty of stimulating motion.

The Rev. Robert Lowry was born in Philadelphia, March 12, 1826, and educated at Lewisburg, Pa. From his 28th year till his death, 1899, he was a faithful and successful minister of Christ, but is more widely known as a composer of sacred music.

"BE THOU EXALTED, O MY GOD."

In this hymn the thought of Watts touches the eternal summits. Taken from the 57th and 108th Psalms—

Be Thou exalted, O my God,
Above the heavens where angels dwell;
Thy power on earth be known abroad
And land to land Thy wonders tell.

16

*   *   *   *   *   *

High o'er the earth His mercy reigns,
And reaches to the utmost sky;
His truth to endless years remains
When lower worlds dissolve and die.

THE TUNE.

Haydn furnished it out of his chorus of morning stars, and it was christened "Creation," after the name of his great oratorio. It is a march of trumpets.

"BEFORE JEHOVAH'S AWFUL THRONE."

No one could mistake the style of Watts in this sublime ode. He begins with his foot on Sinai, but flies to Calvary with the angel preacher whom St. John saw in his Patmos vision:

Before Jehovah's awful throne
Ye nations bow with sacred joy;
Know that the Lord is God alone;
He can create and He destroy.
His sovereign power without our aid
Made us of clay and formed us men,
And when like wandering sheep we stray,
He brought us to His fold again.

*   *   *   *   *   *

We'll crowd Thy gates with thankful songs,
High as the heaven our voices raise,
And earth with her ten thousand tongues
Shall fill Thy courts with sounding praise.

TUNE—OLD HUNDRED.

Martin Madan's four-page anthem, "Denmark," has some grand strains in it, but it is a tune of florid and difficult vocalization, and is now heard only in Old Folks' Concerts.

The Rev. Isaac Watts, D.D., was born at Southampton, Eng., in 1674. His father was a deacon of the Independent Church there, and though not an uncultured man himself, he is said to have had little patience with the incurable penchant of his boy for making rhymes and verses. We hear nothing of the lad's mother, but we can fancy her hand and spirit in the indulgence of his poetic tastes as well as in his religious training. The tradition handed down from Dr. Price, a colleague of Watts, relates that at the age of eighteen Isaac became so irritated at the crabbed and untuneful hymns sung at the Nonconformist meetings that he complained bitterly of them to his father. The deacon may have felt something as Dr. Wayland did when a rather "fresh" student criticised the Proverbs, and hinted that making such things could not be "much of a job," and the Doctor remarked, "Suppose *you* make a few." Possibly there was the same gentle sarcasm in the reply of Deacon Watts to his son, "Make some yourself, then."

Isaac was in just the mood to take his father at his word, and he retired and wrote the hymn—

Behold the glories of the Lamb.

There must have been a decent tune to carry it, for it pleased the worshippers greatly, when it was sung in meeting—and that was the beginning of Isaac Watts' career as a hymnist.

So far as scholarship was an advantage, the young writer must have been well equipped already, for as early as the entering of his fifth year he was learning Latin, and at nine learning Greek; at eleven, French; and at thirteen, Hebrew. From the day of his first success he continued to indite hymns for the home church, until by the end of his twenty-second year he had written one hundred and ten, and in the two following years a hundred and forty-four more, besides preparing himself for the ministry. No. 7 in the edition of the first one hundred and ten, was that royal jewel of all his lyric work—

When I survey the wondrous cross.

Isaac Watts was ordained pastor of an Independent Church in Mark Lane, London, 1702, but repeated illness finally broke up his ministry, and he retired, an invalid, to the beautiful home of Sir Thomas Abney at Theobaldo, invited, as he supposed, to spend a week, but it was really to spend the rest of his life—thirty-six years.

Numbers of his hymns are cited as having biographical or reminiscent color. The stanza in—

When I can read my title clear,
—which reads in the original copy,—
Should earth against my soul engage
And *hellish darts be hurled*,
Then I can smile at *Satan's rage*

17

And face a frowning world,

—is said to have been an allusion to Voltaire and his attack upon the church, while the calm beauty of the harbor within view of his home is supposed to have been in his eye when he composed the last stanza,—

There shall I bathe my weary soul
In seas of heavenly rest,
And not a wave of trouble roll
Across my peaceful breast.

According to the record,—

What shall the dying sinner do?

—was one of his "pulpit hymns," and followed a sermon preached from Rom. 1:16. Another,—

And is this life prolonged to you?

—after a sermon from I Cor. 3:22; and another,—

How vast a treasure we possess,

—enforced his text, "All things are yours." The hymn,—

Not all the blood of beasts
On Jewish altars slain,

—was, as some say, suggested to the writer by a visit to the abattoir in Smithfield Market. The same hymn years afterwards, discovered, we are told, in a printed paper wrapped around a shop bundle, converted a Jewess, and influenced her to a life of Christian faith and sacrifice.

A young man, hardened by austere and minatory sermons, was melted, says Dr. Belcher, by simply reading,—

Show pity Lord, O Lord, forgive,
Let a repenting sinner live.

—and became partaker of a rich religious experience.

The summer scenery of Southampton, with its distant view of the Isle of Wight, was believed to have inspired the hymnist sitting at a parlor window and gazing across the river Itchen, to write the stanza—

Sweet fields beyond the swelling flood
Stand drest in living green;
So to the Jews old Canaan stood
While Jordan rolled between.

The hymn, "Unveil thy bosom, faithful tomb," was personal, addressed by Watts "to Lucius on the death of Seneca."

A severe heart-trial was the occasion of another hymn. When a young man he proposed marriage to Miss Elizabeth Singer, a much-admired young lady, talented, beautiful, and good. She rejected him—kindly but finally. The disappointment was bitter, and in the first shadow of it he wrote,—

How vain are all things here below,
How false and yet how fair.

Miss Singer became the celebrated Mrs. Elizabeth Rowe, the spiritual and poetic beauty of whose *Meditations* once made a devotional text-book for pious souls. Of Dr. Watts and his offer of his hand and heart, she always said, "I loved the jewel, but I did not admire the casket." The poet suitor was undersized, in habitually delicate health—and not handsome.

But the good minister and scholar found noble employment to keep his mind from preying upon itself and shortening his days. During his long though afflicted leisure he versified the Psalms, wrote a treatise on *Logic*, an *Introduction to the Study of Astronomy and Geography*, and a work *On the Improvement of the Mind*; and died in 1748, at the age of seventy-four.

"O FOR A THOUSAND TONGUES TO SING."

Charles Wesley, the author of this hymn, took up the harp of Watts when the older poet laid it down. He was born at Epworth, Eng., in 1708, the third son of Rev. Samuel Wesley, and died in London, March 29, 1788. The hymn is believed to have been written May 17, 1739, for the anniversary of his own conversion:

O for a thousand tongues to sing
My great Redeemer's praise,
The glories of my God and King,
And triumphs of His grace.

The remark of a fervent Christian friend, Peter Bohler, "Had I a thousand tongues I would praise Christ Jesus with them all," struck an answering chord in Wesley's heart, and he embalmed the wish in his fluent verse. The third stanza (printed as second in some hymnals), has made language for pardoned souls for at least four generations:

18

Jesus! the name that calms our fears
And bids our sorrows cease;
'Tis music in the sinner's ears,
'Tis life and health and peace.

Charles Wesley was the poet of the soul, and knew every mood. In the words of Isaac Taylor, "There is no main article of belief ... no moral sentiment peculiarly characteristic of the gospel that does not find itself ... pointedly and clearly conveyed in some stanza of Charles Wesley's poetry." And it does not dim the lustre of Watts, considering the marvellous brightness, versatility and felicity of his greatest successor, to say of the latter, with the *London Quarterly*, that he "was, perhaps, the most gifted minstrel of the modern Church."

Charles
Wesley

Most of the hymns of this good man were hymns of experience—and this is why they are so dear to the Christian heart. The music of eternal life is in them. The happy glow of a single line in one of them—

Love Divine, all loves excelling,

—thrills through them all. He led a spotless life from youth to old age, and grew unceasingly in spiritual knowledge and sweetness. His piety and purity were the weapons that alike humbled his scoffing fellow scholars at Oxford, and conquered the wild colliers of Kingwood. With his brother John, through persecution and ridicule, he preached and sang that Divine Love to his countrymen and in the wilds of America, and on their return to England his quenchless melodies multiplied till they made an Evangelical literature around his name. His hymns—he wrote no less than six thousand—are a liturgy not only for the Methodist Church but for English-speaking Christendom.

The voices of Wesley and Watts cannot be hidden, whatever province of Christian life and service is traversed in themes of song, and in these chapters they will be heard again and again.

A Watts-and-Wesley Scholarship would grace any Theological Seminary, to encourage the study and discussion of the best lyrics of the two great Gospel bards.

THE TUNES.

The musical mouth-piece of "O for a thousand tongues," nearest to its own date, is old "Azmon" by Carl Glaser (1734–1829), appearing as No. 1 in the *New Methodist Hymnal.* Arranged by Lowell Mason, 1830, it is still comparatively familiar, and the flavor of devotion is in its tone and style.

Henry John Gauntlett, an English lawyer and composer, wrote a tune for it in 1872, noble in its uniform step and time, but scarcely uttering the hymnist's characteristic ardor.

The tune of "Dedham," by William Gardiner, now venerable but surviving by true merit, is not unlike "Azmon" in movement and character. Though less closely associated with the hymn, as a companion melody it is not inappropriate. But whatever the range of vocalization or the dignity of swells and cadences, a slow pace of single semibreves or quarters is not suited to Wesley's hymns. They are flights.

Professor William Gardiner wrote many works on musical subjects early in the last century, and composed vocal harmonies, secular and sacred. He was born in Leicester, Eng., March 5, 1770, and died there Nov. 16, 1853.

There is an old-fashioned unction and vigor in the style of "Peterborough" by Rev. Ralph Harrison (1748–1810) that after all best satisfies the singer who enters heart and soul into the spirit of the hymn.*Old Peterborough* was composed in 1786.

"LORD WITH GLOWING HEART I'D PRAISE THEE."

This was written in 1817 by the author of the "Star Spangled Banner," and is a noble American hymn of which the country may well be proud, both because of its merit and for its birth in the heart of a national poet who was no less a Christian than a patriot.

Francis Scott Key, lawyer, was born on the estate of his father, John Ross Key, in Frederick, Md., Aug. 1st, 1779; and died in Baltimore, Jan. 11, 1843. A bronze statue of him over his grave, and another in Golden Gate Park, San Francisco, represent the nationality of his fame and the gratitude of a whole land.

Though a slaveholder by inheritance, Mr. Key deplored the existence of human slavery, and not only originated a scheme of African colonization, but did all that a model master could do for the chattels on his plantation, in compliance with the Scripture command,*to lighten their burdens. He helped them in their family troubles, defended them gratuitously in the courts, and held regular Sunday-school services for them.

* Eph. 6:9, Coloss. 4:1.

Educated at St. John's College, an active member of the Episcopal Church, he was not only a scholar but a devout and exemplary man.

Lord, with glowing heart I'd praise Thee
For the bliss Thy love bestows,
For the pardoning grace that saves me,
And the peace that from it flows.
Help, O Lord, my weak endeavor;
This dull soul to rapture raise;
Thou must light the flame or never
Can my love be warmed to praise.
Lord, this bosom's ardent feeling
Vainly would my life express;
Low before Thy footstool kneeling,
Deign Thy suppliant's prayer to bless.
Let Thy grace, my soul's chief treasure,
Love's pure flame within me raise,
And, since words can never measure,
Let my life show forth Thy praise.

THE TUNE.

"St. Chad," a choral in D, with a four-bar unison, in the *Evangelical Hymnal*, is worthy of the hymn. Richard Redhead, the composer, organist of the Church of St. Mary Magdalene, Paddington, Eng., was born at Harrow, Middlesex, March 1, 1820, and educated at Magdalene College, Oxford. Graduated Bachelor of Music at Oxford, 1871. He published *Laudes Dominæ*, a Gregorian Psalter, 1843, a Book of Tunes for the *Christian Year*, and is the author of much ritual music.

"HOLY, HOLY, HOLY, LORD GOD ALMIGHTY."

There is nothing so majestic in Protestant hymnology as this Tersanctus of Bishop Heber.

The Rt. Rev. Reginald Heber, son of a clergyman of the same name, was born in Malpas, Cheshire, Eng., April 21st, 1783, and educated at Oxford. He served the church in Hodnet, Shropshire, for about twenty years, and was then appointed Bishop of Calcutta, E.I. His labors there were cut short in the prime of his life, his death occurring in 1826, at Trichinopoly on the 3d of April, his natal month.

His hymns, numbering fifty-seven, were collected by his widow, and published with his poetical works in 1842.

Holy! holy! holy! Lord God Almighty!
Early in the morning our song shall rise to Thee.
Holy! holy! holy! merciful and mighty,
God in Three Persons, blessed Trinity.
Holy! holy! holy! all the saints adore Thee,
Casting down their golden crowns around the glassy sea;
Cherubim and seraphim, falling down before Thee,
Which wert, and art, and evermore shall be.

THE TUNE.

Grand as the hymn is, it did not come to its full grandeur of sentiment and sound in song-worship till the remarkable music of Dr. John B. Dykes was joined to it. None was ever written that in performance illustrates more admirably the solemn beauty of congregational praise. The name "Nicæa" attached to the tune means nothing to the popular ear and mind, and it is known everywhere by the initial words of the first line.

Rev. John Bacchus Dykes, Doctor of Music, was born at Kingston-upon-Hull, in 1823; and graduated at Cambridge, in 1847. He became a master of tone and choral harmony, and did much to reform and elevate congregational psalmody in England. He was perhaps the first to demonstrate that hymn-tune making can be reduced to a science without impairing its spiritual purpose. Died Jan. 22, 1876.

"LORD OF ALL BEING, THRONED AFAR."

This noble hymn was composed by Dr. Oliver Wendell Holmes, born in Cambridge, Mass., 1809, and graduated at Harvard University. A physician by profession, he was known as a practitioner chiefly in literature, being a brilliant writer and long the leading poetical wit of America. He was, however, a man of deep religious feeling, and a devout attendant at King's Chapel, Unitarian, in Boston where he spent his life. He held the Harvard Professorship of Anatomy and Physiology more than fifty years, but his enduring work is in his poems, and his charming volume, *The Autocrat of the Breakfast Table*. Died Jan. 22, 1896.

THE TUNE.

Holmes' hymn is sung in some churches to "Louvan," V.C. Taylor's admirable praise tune. Other hymnals prefer with it the music of "Keble," one of Dr. Dykes' appropriate and finished melodies.

Virgil Corydon Taylor, an American vocal composer, was born in Barkhamstead, Conn., April 2, 1817, died 1891.

CHAPTER II.

SOME HYMNS OF GREAT WITNESSES.

JOHN OF DAMASCUS.

Ἔρχεσθε, ὦ πιστοί,
Ἀναστάσεως Ἡμέρα.

John of Damascus, called also St. John of Jerusalem, a theologian and poet, was the last but one of the Christian Fathers of the Greek Church. This eminent man was named by the Arabs "Ibn Mansur," Son (Servant?) of a Conqueror, either in honor of his father Sergius or because it was a Semitic translation of his family title. He was born in Damascus early in the 8th century, and seems to have been in favor with the Caliph, and served under him many years in some important civil capacity, until, retiring to Palestine, he entered the monastic order, and late in life was ordained a priest of the Jerusalem Church. He died in the Convent of St. Sabas near that city about A.D. 780.

His lifetime appears to have been passed in comparative peace. Mohammed having died before completing the conquest of Syria, the Moslem rule before whose advance Oriental Christianity was to lose its first field of triumph had not yet asserted its persecuting power in the north. This devout monk, in his meditations at St. Sabas, dwelt much upon the birth and the resurrection of Christ, and made hymns to celebrate them. It was probably four hundred years before Bonaventura (?) wrote the Christmas "Adeste Fideles" of the Latin West that John of Damascus composed his Greek "Adeste Fideles" for a Resurrection song in Jerusalem.

Come ye faithful, raise the strain
Of triumphant gladness,
* * * * * *

'Tis the spring of souls today
Christ hath burst His prison;
From the frost and gloom of death
Light and life have risen.

The nobler of the two hymns preserved to us, (or six stanzas of it) through eleven centuries is entitled "The Day of Resurrection."

The day of resurrection,
Earth, tell its joys abroad:
The Passover of gladness,
The Passover of God.
From death to life eternal,
From earth unto the sky,
Our Christ hath brought us over,
With hymns of victory.
Our hearts be pure from evil,
That we may see aright
The Lord in rays eternal
Of resurrection light;
And, listening to His accents,
May hear, so calm and plain,

21

His own, "All hail!" and hearing,
May raise the victor-strain.
Now let the heavens be joyful,
Let earth her song begin,
Let all the world keep triumph,
All that dwell therein.
In grateful exultation,
Their notes let all things blend,
For Christ the Lord is risen,
O joy that hath no end!
Both these hymns of John of Damascus were translated by John Mason Neale.

THE TUNE.

"The Day of Resurrection" is sung in the modern hymnals to the tune of "Rotterdam," composed by Berthold of Tours, born in that city of the Netherlands, Dec. 17, 1838. He was educated at the conservatory in Leipsic, and later made London his permanent residence, writing both vocal and instrumental music. Died 1897. "Rotterdam" is a stately, sonorous piece and conveys the flavor of the ancient hymn.

"Come ye faithful" has for its modern interpreter Sir Arthur Sullivan, the celebrated composer of both secular and sacred works, but best known in hymnody as author of the great Christian march, "Onward Christian Soldiers."

Hymns are known to have been written by the earlier Greek Fathers, Ephrem Syrus of Mesopotamia (A.D. 307–373), Basil the Great, Bishop of Cappadocia (A.D. 329–379) Gregory Nazianzen, Bishop of Constantinople (A.D. 335–390) and others, but their fragments of song which have come down to us scarcely rank them among the great witnesses—with the possible exception of the last name. An English scholar, Rev. Allen W. Chatfield, has translated the hymns extant of Gregory Nazianzen. The following stanzas give an idea of their quality. The lines are from an address to the Deity:

How, Unapproached! shall mind of man
Descry Thy dazzling throne,
And pierce and find Thee out, and scan
Where Thou dost dwell alone?
Unuttered Thou! all uttered things
Have had their birth from Thee;
The One Unknown, from Thee the spring
Of all we know and see.
And lo! all things abide in Thee
And through the complex whole,
Thou spreadst Thine own divinity,
Thyself of all the Goal.

This is reverent, but rather philosophical than evangelical, and reminds us of the Hymn of Aratus, more than two centuries before Christ was born.

ST. STEPHEN, THE SABAITE.

This pious Greek monk, (734–794,) nephew of St. John of Damascus, spent his life, from the age of ten, in the monastery of St. Sabas. His sweet hymn, known in Neale's translation,—

Art thou weary, art thou languid,
Art thou sore distrest?
Come to Me, saith One, and coming
Be at rest,

—is still in the hymnals, with the tunes of Dykes, and Sir Henry W. Baker (1821–1877), Vicar of Monkland, Herefordshire.

KING ROBERT II.

Veni, Sancte Spiritus.

Robert the Second, surnamed "Robert the Sage" and "Robert the Devout," succeeded Hugh Capet, his father, upon the throne of France, about the year 997. He has been called the gentlest monarch that ever sat upon a throne, and his amiability of character poorly prepared him to cope with his dangerous and wily adversaries. His last years were embittered by the opposition of his own sons, and the political agitations of the times. He died at Melun in 1031, and was buried at St. Denis.

Robert possessed a reflective mind, and was fond of learning and musical art. He was both a poet and a musician. He was deeply religious, and, from unselfish motives, was much devoted to the church.

Robert's hymn, "Veni, Sancte Spiritus," is given below. He himself was a chorister; and there was no kingly service that he seemed to love so well. We are told that it was his custom to go to the church of St. Denis, and in his royal robes, with his crown upon his head, to direct the choir at matins and vespers, and join in the singing. Few kings have left a better legacy to the Christian church than his own hymn, which, after nearly a thousand years, is still an influence in the world:

Come, Thou Holy Spirit, come,
And from Thine eternal home
Shed the ray of light divine;
Come, Thou Father of the poor,
Come, Thou Source of all our store,
Come, within our bosoms shine.
Thou of Comforters the best,
Thou the soul's most welcome Guest,
Sweet Refreshment here below!
In our labor Rest most sweet,
Grateful Shadow from the heat,
Solace in the midst of woe!
Oh, most blessed Light Divine,
Shine within these hearts of Thine,
And our inmost being fill;
If Thou take Thy grace away,
Nothing pure in man will stay,
All our good is turned to ill.
Heal our wounds; our strength renew
On our dryness pour Thy dew;
Wash the stains of guilt away!
Bend the stubborn heart and will,
Melt the frozen, warm the chill,
Guide the steps that go astray.

Neale's Translation.

THE TUNE.

The metre and six-line stanza, being uniform with those of "Rock of Ages," have tempted some to borrow "Toplady" for this ancient hymn, but Hastings' tune would refuse to sing other words; and, besides, the alternate rhymes would mar the euphony. Not unsuitable in spirit are several existing tunes of the right measure—like "Nassau" or "St. Athanasius"—but in truth the "Veni, Sancte Spiritus" in English waits for its perfect setting. Dr. Ray Palmer's paraphrase of it in sixes-and-fours, to fit "Olivet,"—

Come, Holy Ghost in love, etc.

—is objectionable both because the word Ghost is an archaism in Christian worship and more especially because Dr. Palmer's altered version usurps the place of his own hymn. "Olivet" with "My faith looks up to Thee" makes as inviolable a case of psalmodic monogamy as "Toplady" with "Rock of Ages."

ST. FULBERT.

"Chori Cantores Hierusalem Novae."

St. Fulbert's hymn is a worthy companion of Perronet's "Coronation"—if, indeed, it was not its original prompter—as KingRobert's great litany was the mother song of Watts' "Come, Holy Spirit, heavenly Dove;" and the countless other sacred lyrics beginning with similar words. As the translation stands in the Church of England, there are six stanzas now sung, though in America but four appear, and not in the same sequence. The first four of the six in their regular succession are as follows:

Ye choirs of New Jerusalem,
Your sweetest notes employ,
The Paschal victory to hymn
In strains of holy joy.
For Judah's Lion bursts His chains,
Crushing the serpent's head;
And cries aloud, through death's domains
To wake the imprisoned dead.
Devouring depths of hell their prey
At His command restore;
His ransomed hosts pursue their way

23

Where Jesus goes before.
Triumphant in His glory now,
To Him all power is given;
To Him in one communion bow
All saints in earth and heaven.

Bishop Fulbert, known in the Roman and in the Protestant ritualistic churches as St. Fulbert of Chartres, was a man of brilliant and versatile mind, and one of the most eminent prelates of his time. He was a contemporary of Robert II, and his intimate friend, continuing so after the Pope (Gregory V.) excommunicated the king for marrying a cousin, which was forbidden by the canons of the church.

Fulbert was for some time head of the Theological College at Chartres, a cathedral town of France, anciently the capital of Celtic Gaul, and afterwards he was consecrated as Bishop of that diocese. He died about 1029.

THE TUNE.

The modern tone-interpreter of Fulbert's hymn bears the name "La Spezia" in some collections, and was composed by James Taylor about the time the hymn was translated into English by Robert Campbell. Research might discover the ancient tune—for the hymn is said to have been sung in the English church during Fulbert's lifetime—but the older was little likely to be the better music. "La Spezia" is a choral of enlivening but easy chords, and a tread of triumph in its musical motion that suits the march of "Judah's Lion":

His ransomed hosts pursue their way
Where Jesus goes before.

James Taylor, born 1833, is a Doctor of Music, organist of the University of Oxford and Director of the Oxford Philharmonic Society.

Robert Campbell, the translator, was a Scotch lawyer, born in Edinburgh, who besides his work as an advocate wrote original hymns, and in other ways exercised a natural literary gift. He compiled the excellent Hymnal of the diocese of St. Andrews, and this was his best work. The date of his death is given as Dec. 29, 1868.

THOMAS OF CELANO.

Dies irae! dies illa,
Solvet saeclum in favilla,
Teste David cum Sybilla.
Day of wrath! that day of burning,
All the world to ashes turning,
Sung by prophets far discerning.

Latin ecclesiastical poetry reached its high water mark in that awful hymn. The solitaire of its sphere and time in the novelty of its rhythmic triplets, it stood a wonder to the church and hierarchy accustomed to the slow spondees of the ancient chant. There could be such a thing as a trochaic hymn!—and majestic, too!

It was a discovery that did not stale. The compelling grandeur of the poem placed it distinct and alone, and the very difficulty of staffing it for vocal and instrumental use gave it a zest, and helped to keep it unique through the ages.

Latin hymnody and hymnography, appealing to the popular ear and heart, had gradually substituted accent for quantity in verse; for the common people could never be moved by a Christian song in the prosody of the classics. The religion of the cross, with the song-preaching of its propagandists, created medieval Latin and made it a secondary classic—mother of four anthem languages of Western and Southern Europe. Its golden age was the 12th and 13th centuries. The new and more flexible school of speech and music in hymn and tune had perfected rhythmic beauty and brought in the winsome assonance of rhyme.

The "Dies Irae" was born, it is believed, about the year 1255. Its authorship has been debated, but competent testimony assures us that the original draft of the great poem was found in a box among the effects of Thomas di Celano after his death. Thomas—surnamed Thomas of Celano from his birthplace, the town of Celano in the province of Aquila, Southern Italy—was the pupil, friend and co-laborer of St. Francis of Assisi, and wrote his memoirs. He is supposed to have died near the end of the 13th century. That he wrote the sublime judgment song there is now practically no question.

The label on the discovered manuscript would suggest that the writer did not consider it either a hymn or a poem. Like the inspired prophets he had meditated—and while he was musing the fire burned. The only title he wrote over it was "*Prosa de mortuis,*" Prosa (or prosa oratio)— from *prorsus,* "straight forward"—appears here in the truly conventional sense it was beginning to bear, but not yet as the antipode of "poetry." The modest author, unconscious of the magnitude of his work, called it simply "Plain speech concerning the dead."[*]

24

* "Proses" were original passages introduced into ecclesiastical chants in the 10th century. During and after the 11th century they were called "Sequences" (i.e. *following* the "Gospel" in the liturgy), and were in metrical form, having a prayerful tone. "Sequentia pro defunctis" was the later title of the "Dies Irae."

The hymn is much too long to quote entire, but can be found in *Daniel's Thesaurus* in any large public library. As to the translations of it, they number hundreds—in English and German alone, and Italy, Spain and Portugal have their vernacular versions—not to mention the Greek and Russian and even the Hebrew. A few stanzas follow, with their renderings into English (always imperfect) selected almost at random:

> Quantus tremor est futurus
> Quando Judex est venturus,
> Cuncta stricte discussurus!
> Tuba mirum spargens sonum
> Per sepulcra regionum,
> Coget omnes ante thronum!
> O the dread, the contrite kneeling
> When the Lord, in Judgment dealing,
> Comes each hidden thing revealing!
> When the trumpet's awful tone
> Through the realms sepulchral blown,
> Summons all before the Throne!

The solemn strength and vibration of these tremendous trilineals suffers no general injury by the variant readings—and there are a good many. As a sample, the first stanza was changed by some canonical redactor to get rid of the heathen word Sybilla, and the second line was made the third:

> Dies Irae, dies illa
> Crucis expandens vexilla,
> Solvet saeclum in favilla.
> Day of wrath! that day foretold,
> With the cross-flag wide unrolled,
> Shall the world in fire enfold!

In some readings the original "in favilla" is changed to "*cum* favilla," "*with* ashes" instead of "in ashes"; and "Teste Petro" is substituted for "Teste David."

THE TUNE.

The varieties of music set to the "Hymn of Judgment" in the different sections and languages of Christendom during seven hundred years are probably as numerous as the pictures of the Holy Family in Christian art. It is enough to say that one of the best at hand, or, at least, accessible, is the solemn minor melody of Dr. Dykes in William Henry Monk's *Hymns Ancient and Modern*. It was composed about the middle of the last century. Both the *Evangelical* and *Methodist Hymnals* have Dean Stanley's translation of the hymn, the former with thirteen stanzas (six-line) to a D minor of John Stainer, and the latter to a C major of Timothy Matthews. The *Plymouth Hymnal* has seventeen of the trilineal stanzas, by an unknown translator, to Ferdinand Hiller's tune in F minor, besides one verse to another F minor—hymn and tune both nameless.

All the composers above named are musicians of fame. John Stainer, organist of St. Paul's Cathedral, was a Doctor of Music and Chevalier of the Legion of Honor, and celebrated for his works in sacred music, to which he mainly devoted his time. He was born June 6, 1840. He died March 31, 1901.

Rev. Timothy Richard Matthews, born at Colmworth, Eng., Nov. 20, 1826, is a clergyman of the Church of England, incumbent of a Lancaster charge to which he was appointed by Queen Alexandra.

Ferdinand Hiller, born 1811 at Frankfort-on-the-Main, of Hebrew parentage, was one of Germany's most eminent musicians. For many years he was Chapel Master at Cologne, and organized the Cologne Conservatory. His compositions are mostly for instrumental performance, but he wrote cantatas, motets, male choruses, and two oratorios, one on the "Destruction of Jerusalem." Died May 10, 1855.

The Very Rev. Arthur Penrhyn Stanley, Dean of Westminster, was an author and scholar whom all sects of Christians delighted to honor. His writings on the New Testament and his published researches in Palestine, made him an authority in Biblical study, and his contributions to sacred literature were looked for and welcomed as eagerly as a new hymn by Bonar or a new poem by Tennyson. Dean Stanley was born in 1815, and died July 18th, 1881.

THOMAS À KEMPIS.

Thomas à Kempis, sub-prior of the Convent of St. Agnes, was born at Hamerkin, Holland, about the year 1380, and died at Zwoll, 1471. This pious monk belonged to an order called the "Brethren of the Common Life" founded by Gerard de Groote, and his fame rests entirely upon his one book, the *Imitation of Christ*, which continues to be printed as a religious classic, and is unsurpassed as a manual of private devotion. His monastic life—as was true generally of the monastic life of the middle ages—was not one of useless idleness. The Brethren taught school and did mechanical work. Besides, before the invention of printing had been perfected and brought into common service, the multiplication of books was principally the work of monkish pens. Kempis spent his days copying the Bible and good books—as well as in exercises of devotion that promoted religious calm.

His idea of heaven, and the idea of his order, was expressed in that clause of John's description of the City of God, Rev. 22:3, *"and His servants shall serve Him."* Above all other heavenly joys that was his favorite thought. We can well understand that the pious quietude wrought in his mind and manners by his habit of life made him a saint in the eyes of the people. The frontispiece of one edition of his *Imitatio Christi* pictures him as being addressed before the door of a convent by a troubled pilgrim,—

"O where is peace?—for thou his paths hast trod,"

—and his answer completes the couplet,—

"In poverty, retirement, and with God."

Of all that is best in inward spiritual life, much can be learned from this inspired Dutchman. He wrote no hymns, but in his old age he composed a poem on "Heaven's Joys," which is sometimes called "Thomas à Kempis' Hymn":

High the angel choirs are raising
Heart and voice in harmony;
The Creator King still praising
Whom in beauty there they see.
Sweetest strains from soft harps stealing,
Trumpets' notes of triumph pealing,
Radiant wings and white stoles gleaming
Up the steps of glory streaming;
Where the heavenly bells are ringing;
"Holy! holy! holy!" singing
To the mighty Trinity!
"Holy! holy! holy!" crying,
For all earthly care and sighing
In that city cease to be!

These lines are not in the hymnals of today—and whether they ever found their way into choral use in ancient times we are not told. Worse poetry has been sung—and more un-hymnlike. Some future composer will make a tune to the words of a Christian who stood almost in sight of his hundredth year—and of the eternal home he writes about.

Dr. Martin
Luther

MARTIN LUTHER.

"Ein Feste Burg Ist Unser Gott."

Of Martin Luther Coleridge said, "He did as much for the Reformation by his hymns as he did by his translation of the Bible." The remark is so true that it has become a commonplace.

The above line—which may be seen inscribed on Luther's tomb atWittenberg—is the opening sentence and key-note of the Reformer's grandest hymn. The forty-sixth Psalm inspired it, and it is in harmony with sublime historical periods from its very nature, boldness, and sublimity. It was written, according to Welles, in the memorable year when the evangelical princes delivered their protest at the Diet of Spires, from which the word and the meaning of the word

"Protestant" is derived. "Luther used often to sing it in 1530, while the Diet of Augsburg was sitting. It soon became the favorite psalm with the people. It was one of the watchwords of the Reformation, cheering armies to conflict, and sustaining believers in the hours of fiery trial."

"After Luther's death, Melancthon, his affectionate coadjutor, being one day at Weimar with his banished friends, Jonas and Creuziger, heard a little maid singing this psalm in the street, and said, 'Sing on, my little girl, you little know whom you comfort:'"

A mighty fortress is our God,
A bulwark never failing;
Our helper He, amid the flood
Of mortal ills prevailing.
For still our ancient foe
Doth seek to work us woe;
His craft and power are great,
And, armed with cruel hate,
On earth is not his equal.

    *   *   *   *   *   *

The Prince of Darkness grim—
We tremble not for him:
His rage we can endure,
For lo! his doom is sure,
One little word shall fell him.
That word above all earthly powers—
No thanks to them—abideth;
The Spirit and the gifts are ours,
Through Him who with us sideth.
Let goods and kindred go,
This mortal life also;
The body they may kill,
God's truth abideth still,
His kingdom is for ever.

Martin Luther was born in Eisleben, in Saxony, Nov. 10, 1483. He was educated at the University of Erfurth, and became an Augustinian monk and Professor of Philosophy and Divinity in the University of Wittenberg. In 1517 he composed and placarded his ninety-five Theses condemning certain practices of the Romish Church and three years later the Pope published a bull excommunicating him, which he burnt openly before a sympathetic multitude in Wittenberg. His life was a stormy one, and he was more than once in mortal danger by reason of his antagonism to the papal authority, but he found powerful patrons, and lived to see the Reformation an organized fact. He died in his birthplace, Eisleben, Feb. 18th, 1546.

The translation of the "Ein feste burg," given above, in part, is by Rev. Frederick Henry Hedge, D.D., born in Cambridge, March 1805, a graduate of Harvard, and formerly minister of the Unitarian Church in Bangor, Me. Died, 1890.

Luther wrote thirty-six hymns, to some of which he fitted his own music, for he was a musician and singer as well as an eloquent preacher. The tune in which "Ein feste Burg" is sung in the hymnals, was composed by himself. The hymn has also a noble rendering in the music of Sebastian Bach, 8-4 time, found in *Hymns Ancient and Modern*.

BARTHOLOMEW RINGWALDT.
"Great God, What Do I See and Hear?"

The history of this hymn is somewhat indefinite, though common consent now attributes to Ringwaldt the stanza beginning with the above line. The imitation of the "Dies Irae" in German which was first in use was printed in Jacob Klug's "*Gesangbuch*" in 1535. Ringwaldt's hymn of the Last Day, also inspired from the ancient Latin original, appears in his *Handbuchlin* of 1586, but does not contain this stanza. The first line is, "The awful Day will surely come," (Es ist gewisslich an der Zeit). Nevertheless through the more than two hundred years that the hymn has been translated and re-translated, and gone through inevitable revisions, some vital identity in the spirit and tone of the one seven-line stanza has steadily connected it with Ringwaldt's name. Apparently it is the single survivor of a great lost hymn—edited and altered out of recognition. But its power evidently inspired the added verses, as we have them. Dr. Collyer found it, and, regretting that it was too short to sing in public service, composed stanzas 2d, 3d and 4th. It is likely that Collyer first met with it in *Psalms and Hymns for Public and Private Devotion*, Sheffield 1802, where it appeared anonymously. So far as known this was its first publication in English. Ringwaldt's stanza and two of Collyer's are here given:

Great God, what do I see and hear!

The end of things created!
The Judge of mankind doth appear
On clouds of glory seated.
The trumpet sounds, the graves restore
The dead which they contained before;
Prepare, my soul, to meet Him.
The dead in Christ shall first arise
At the last trumpet sounding,
Caught up to meet Him in the skies,
With joy their Lord surrounding.
No gloomy fears their souls dismay
His presence sheds eternal day
On those prepared to meet Him.
Far over space to distant spheres
The lightnings are prevailing
Th' ungodly rise, and all their tears
And sighs are unavailing.
The day of grace is past and gone;
They shake before the Judge's Throne
All unprepared to meet Him.

Bartholomew Ringwaldt, pastor of the Lutheran Church of Longfeld, Prussia, was born in 1531, and died in 1599. His hymns appear in a collection entitled *Hymns for the Sundays and Festivals of the Whole Year.*

Rev. William Bengo Collyer D.D., was born at Blackheath near London, April 14, 1782, educated at Homerton College and settled over a Congregational Church in Peckham. In 1812 he published a book of hymns, and in 1837 a *Service Book* to which he contributed eighty-nine hymns. He died Jan, 9, 1854.

THE TUNE.

Probably it was the customary singing of Ringwaldt's hymn (in Germany) to Luther's tune that gave it for some time the designation of "Luther's Hymn," the title by which the music is still known—an air either composed or adapted by Luther, and rendered perhaps unisonously or with extempore chords. It was not until early in the last century that Vincent Novello wrote to it the noble arrangement now in use. It is a strong, even-time harmony with lofty tenor range, and veryimpressive with full choir and organ or the vocal volume of a congregation. In *Cheetham's Psalmody* is it written with a trumpet obligato.

Vincent Novello, born in London, Sept. 6, 1781, the intimate friend of Lamb, Shelley, Keats, Hunt and Hazlitt, was a professor of music who attained great eminence as an organist and composer of hymn-tunes and sacred pieces. He was the founder of the publishing house of Novello and Ewer, and father of a famous musical family. Died at Nice, Aug. 9, 1861.

ST. FRANCIS XAVIER.
"O Deus, Ego Amo Te."

Francis Xavier, the celebrated Jesuit missionary, called "The Apostle of the Indies," was a Spaniard, born in 1506. While a student in Paris he met Ignatius Loyola, and joined him in the formation of the new "Society for the Propagation of the Faith." He was sent out on a mission to the East Indies and Japan, and gave himself to the work with a martyr's devotion. The stations he established in Japan were maintained more than a hundred years. He died in China, Dec. 1552.

His hymn, some time out of use, is being revived in later singing-books as expressive of the purest and highest Christian sentiment:

O Deus, ego amo Te.
Nec amo Te, ut salves me,
Aut quia non amantes Te
Æterno punis igne.
My God, I love Thee—not because
I hope for heaven thereby;
Nor yet because who love Thee not
Must burn eternally.

After recounting Christ's vicarious sufferings as the chief claim to His disciples' unselfish love, the hymn continues,—

Cur igitur non amem Te,
O Jesu amantissime!
Non, ut in cœlo salves me,
Aut in æternum damnes me.

Then why, O blessed Jesus Christ,
Should I not love Thee well?
Not for the sake of winning heaven,
Nor of escaping hell;
Not with the hope of gaining aught,
Nor seeking a reward,
But as Thyself hast lovéd me,
Oh, ever-loving Lord!
E'en so I love Thee, and will love,
And in Thy praise will sing;
Solely because Thou art my God
And my eternal King.

The translation is by Rev. Edward Caswall, 1814–1878, a priest in the Church of Rome. Besides his translations, he published the *Lyra Catholica*, the *Masque of Mary*, and several other poetical works. (Page 101.)

THE TUNE.

"St. Bernard"—apparently so named because originally composed to Caswall's translation of one of Bernard of Clairvaux's hymns—is by John Richardson, born in Preston, Eng., Dec. 4, 1817, and died there April 13, 1879. He was an organist in Liverpool, and noted as a composer of glees, but was the author of several sacred tunes.

SIR WALTER RALEIGH.

"Give Me My Scallop-Shell of Quiet."

Few of the hymns of the Elizabethan era survive, though the Ambrosian Midnight Hymn, "Hark, 'tis the Midnight Cry," and the hymns of St. Bernard and Bernard of Cluny, are still tones in the church, and the religious poetry of Sir Walter Raleigh comes down to us associated with the history of his brilliant, though tragic career. The following poem has some fine lines in the quaint English style of the period, and was composed by Sir Walter during his first imprisonment:

Give me my scallop-shell of quiet,
My staff of faith to walk upon,
My scrip of joy—immortal diet—
My bottle of salvation,
My gown of glory, hope's true gage—
And thus I take my pilgrimage.
Blood must be my body's balmer,
While my soul, like faithful palmer,
Travelleth toward the land of heaven;
Other balm will not be given.
Over the silver mountains
Where spring the nectar fountains,
There will I kiss the bowl of bliss,
And drink my everlasting fill,
Upon every milken hill;
My soul will be a-dry before,
But after that will thirst no more.

The musings of the unfortunate but high-souled nobleman in expectation of ignominious death are interesting and pathetic, but they have no claim to a tune, even if they were less rugged and unmetrical. But the poem stands notable among the pious witnesses.

MARY QUEEN OF SCOTS.

"O Domine Deus, Speravi in Te."

This last passionate prayer of the unhappy Mary Stuart just before her execution—in a language which perhaps flowed from her pen more easily than even her English or French—is another witness of supplicating faith that struggles out of darkness with a song. In her extremity the devoted Catholic forgets her petitions to the Virgin, and comes to Christ:

O Domine Deus, Speravi in Te;
O care mi Jesu, nunc libera me!
In dura catena, in misera poena
Desidero Te!
Languendo, gemendo, et genuflectendo
Adoro, imploro ut liberes me!
My Lord and my God! I have trusted in Thee;
O Jesus, my Saviour belov'd, set me free:

29

In rigorous chains, in piteous pains,
I am longing for Thee!
In weakness appealing, in agony kneeling,
I pray, I beseech Thee, O Lord, set me free!

One would, at first thought, judge this simple but eloquent cry worthy of an appropriate tone-expression—to be sung by prison evangelists like the Volunteers of America, to convicts in the jails and penitentiaries. But its special errand and burden are voiced so literally that hardened hearers would probably misapply it—however sincerely the petitioner herself meant to invoke spiritual rather than temporal deliverance. The hymn, if we may call it so, is *too* literal. Possibly at some time or other it may have been set to music but not for ordinary choir service.

SAMUEL RUTHERFORD.

The sands of time are sinking,

* * * * * *

But, glory, glory dwelleth
In Immanuel's Land.

This hymn is biographical, but not autobiographical. Like the discourses in Herodotus and Plutarch, it is the voice of the dead speaking through the sympathetic genius of the living after long generations. The strong, stern Calvinist of 1636 in Aberdeen was not a poet, but he bequeathed his spirit and life to the verse of a poet of 1845 in Melrose. Anne Ross Cousin read his two hundred and twenty letters written during a two years' captivity for his fidelity to the purer faith, and studied his whole history and experience till her soul took his soul's place and felt what he felt. Her poem of nineteen stanzas (152 lines) is the voice of Rutherford the Covenanter, with the prolixity of his manner and age sweetened by his triumphant piety, and that is why it belongs with the *Hymns of Great Witnesses*. The three or four stanzas still occasionally printed and sung are only recalled to memory by the above three lines.

Samuel Rutherford was born in Nisbet Parish, Scotland, in 1600. His settled ministry was at Anworth, in Galloway—1630–1651—with a break between 1636 and 1638, when Charles I. angered by his anti-prelatical writings, silenced and banished him. Shut up in Aberdeen, but allowed, like Paul in Rome, to live "in his own hired house" and write letters, he poured out his heart's love in Epistles to his Anworth flock and to the Non-conformists of Scotland. When his countrymen rose against the attempted imposition of a new holy Romish service-book on their churches, he escaped to his people, and soon after appeared in Edinburgh and signed the covenant with the assembled ministers. Thirteen years later, after Cromwell's death and the accession of Charles II. the wrath of the prelates fell on him at St. Andrews, where the Presbytery had made him rector of the college. The King's decree indicted him for treason, stripped him of all his offices, and would have forced him to the block had he not been stricken with his last sickness. When the officers came to take him he said, "I am summoned before a higher Judge and Judicatory, and I am behooved to attend them." He died soon after, in the year 1661.

The first, and a few other of the choicest stanzas of the hymn inspired by his life and death are here given:

The sands of time are sinking,
The dawn of heaven breaks,
The summer morn I've sighed for—
The fair, sweet morn—awakes.
Dark, dark hath been the midnight,
But dayspring is at hand;
And glory, glory dwelleth
In Immanuel's land.

* * * * * *

Oh! well it is for ever—
Oh! well for evermore:
My nest hung in no forest
Of all this death-doomed shore;
Yea, let this vain world vanish,
As from the ship the strand,
While glory, glory dwelleth
In Immanuel's land.

* * * * * *

The little birds of Anworth—
I used to count them blest;
Now beside happier altars
I go to build my nest;

O'er these there broods no silence
No graves around them stand;
For glory deathless dwelleth
In Immanuel's land.
I have borne scorn and hatred,
I have borne wrong and shame,
Earth's proud ones have reproached me
For Christ's thrice blesséd name.
Where God's seals set the fairest,
They've stamped their foulest brand;
But judgment shines like noonday
In Immanuel's land.
They've summoned me before them,
But there I may not come;
My Lord says, "Come up hither;"
My Lord says, "Welcome home;"
My King at His white throne
My presence doth command,
Where glory, glory dwelleth,
In Immanuel's land.

A reminiscence of St. Paul in his second Epistle to Timothy (chap. 4) comes with the last two stanzas.

THE TUNE.

The tender and appropriate choral in B flat, named "Rutherford" was composed by D'Urhan, a French musician, probably a hundred years ago. It was doubtless named by those who long afterwards fitted it to the words, and knew whose spiritual proxy the lady stood who indited the hymn. It is reprinted in Peloubet's *Select Songs*, and in the *Coronation Hymnal*. Naturally in the days of the hymn's more frequent use people became accustomed to calling "The sands of time are sinking," "Rutherford's Hymn." Rutherford's own words certainly furnished the memorable refrain with its immortal glow and gladness. One of his joyful exclamations as he lay dying of his lingering disease was, "Glory shineth in Immanuel's Land!"

Chretien (Christian) Urhan, or D'Urhan, was born at Montjoie, France, about 1788, and died, in Paris, 1845. He was a noted violin-player, and composer, also, of vocal and instrumental music.

Mrs. Anne Ross (Cundell) Cousin, daughter of David Ross Cundell, M.D., and widow of Rev. William Cousin of the Free church of Scotland, was born in Melrose (?), 1824. She wrote many poems, most of which are beautiful meditations rather than lyrics suitable for public song. Her "Rutherford Hymn" was first published in the *Christian Treasury*, 1857.

GUSTAVUS ADOLPHUS.

"Verzage Nicht Du Häuflein Klein."

The historian tells us that before the battle of Lutzen, during the Thirty Years' War (1618–1648), King Gustavus of Sweden, in the thick fog of an autumn morning, with the Bohemian and Austrian armies of Emperor Ferdinand in front of him, knelt before his troops, and his whole army knelt with him in prayer. Then ten thousand voices and the whole concert of regimental bands burst forth in this brave song:

Fear not, O little flock, the foe
Who madly seeks your overthrow,
Dread not his rage and power:
What though your courage sometimes faints,
His seeming triumph o'er God's saints
Lasts but a little hour.
Be of good cheer, your cause belongs
To Him who can avenge your wrongs;
Leave it to Him, our Lord:
Though hidden yet from all our eyes,
He sees the Gideon who shall rise
To save us and His word.
As true as God's own word is true,
Nor earth nor hell with all their crew,
Against us shall prevail:
A jest and by-word they are grown,
God is with us, we are His own,

31

Our victory cannot fail.
Amen, Lord Jesus, grant our prayer!
Great Captain, now Thine arm make bare,
Fight for us once again:
So shall Thy saints and martyrs raise
A mighty chorus to Thy praise,
World without end. Amen.

The army of Gustavus moved forward to victory as the fog lifted; but at the moment of triumph a riderless horse came galloping back to the camp. It was the horse of the martyred King.

The battle song just quoted—next to Luther's "Ein feste Burg" the most famous German hymn—has always since that day been called "Gustavus Adolphus' Hymn"; and the mingled sorrow and joy of the event at Lutzen named it also "King Gustavus' Swan Song." Gustavus Adolphus did not write hymns. He could sing them, and he could make them historic—and it was this connection that identified him with the famous battle song. Its author was the Rev. Johan Michael Altenburg, a Lutheran clergyman, who composed apparently both hymn and tune on receiving news of the king's victory at Leipsic a year before.

Gustavus Adolphus was born in 1594. His death on the battlefield occurred Nov. 5, 1632—when he was in the prime of his manhood. He was one of the greatest military commanders in history, besides being a great ruler and administrator, and a devout Christian. He was, during the Thirty Years' War (until his untimely death), the leading champion of Protestantism in Europe.

The English translator of the battle song was Miss Catherine Winkworth, born in London, Sept. 13, 1827. She was an industrious and successful translator of German hymns, contributing many results of her work to two English editions of the *Lyra Germania*, to the *Church Book of England*, and to *Christian Singers of Germany*. She died in 1878.

The tune of "Ravendale" by Walter Stokes (born 1847) is the best modern rendering of the celebrated hymn.

PAUL GERHARDT.

"Befiehl Du Deine Wege."

Paul Gerhardt was one of those minstrels of experience who are—
"Cradled into poetry by wrong,
And learn in suffering what they teach in song."
He was a graduate of that school when he wrote his "Hymn of Trust:"
Commit thou all thy griefs
And ways into His hands;
To His sure trust and tender care
Who earth and heaven commands.
Thou on the Lord rely,
So, safe, shalt thou go on;
Fix on His work thy steadfast eye,
So shall thy work be done.
* * * * * *

Give to the winds thy fears;
Hope, and be undismayed;
God hears thy sighs and counts thy tears,
He shall lift up thy head.
Through waves and clouds and storms
He gently clears thy way;
Wait thou His time, so shall this night
Soon end in joyous day.

Gerhardt was born at Grafenheinchen, Saxony, 1606. Through the first and best years of manhood's strength (during the Thirty Years' War), a wandering preacher tossed from place to place, he was without a parish and without a home.

After the peace of Westphalia he settled in the little village of Mittenwalde. He was then forty-four years old. Four years later he married and removed to a Berlin church. During his residence there he buried his wife, and four of his children, was deposed from the ministry because his Lutheran doctrines offended the Elector Frederick, and finally retired as a simple arch-deacon to a small parish in Lubben, where he preached, toiled, and suffered amid a rough and uncongenial people till he died, Jan. 16, 1676.

Few men have ever lived whose case more needed a "Hymn of Trust"—and fewer still could have written it themselves. Through all those trial years he was pouring forth his soul in devout verses, making in all no less than a hundred and twenty-five hymns—every one of them a comfort to others as well as to himself.

He became a favorite, and for a time *the* favorite, hymn-writer of all the German-speaking people. Among these tones of calm faith and joy we recognize today (in the English tongue),—

<blockquote>
Since Jesus is my Friend,
Thee, O Immanuel, we praise,
All my heart this night rejoices,
How shall I meet Thee,
</blockquote>

—and the English translation of his "O Haupt voll Blut und Wunden," turned into German by himself from St. Bernard Clairvaux's "Salve caput cruentatum," and made dear to us in Rev. James Alexander's beautiful lines—

<blockquote>
O sacred head now wounded,
With grief and shame weighed down,
Now scornfully surrounded
With thorns, Thine only crown.
</blockquote>

THE TUNE.

A plain-song by Alexander Reinagle is used by some congregations, but is not remarkably expressive. Reinagle, Alexander Robert, (1799–1877) of Kidlington, Eng., was organist to the church of St. Peter-in-the-East, Oxford.

The great "Hymn of Trust" could have found no more sympathetic interpreter than the musician of Gerhardt's own land and language, Schumann, the gentle genius of Zwickau. It bears the name "Schumann," appropriately enough, and its elocution makes a volume of each quatrain, notably the one—

<blockquote>
Who points the clouds their course,
Whom wind and seas obey;
He shall direct thy wandering feet,
He shall prepare thy way.
</blockquote>

Robert Schumann, Ph.D., was born in Zwickau, Saxony, June 8, 1810. He was a music director and conservatory teacher, and the master-mind of the pre-Wagnerian period. His compositions became popular, having a character of their own, combining the intellectual and beautiful in art. He published in Leipsic a journal promotive of his school of music, and founded a choral society in Dresden. Happy in the coöperation of his wife, herself a skilled musician, he extended his work to Vienna and the Netherlands; but his zeal wore him out, and he died at the age of forty-six, universally lamented as "the eminent man who had done so much for the happiness of others."

Gerhardt's Hymn (ten quatrains) is rarely printed entire, and where six are printed only four are usually sung. Different collections choose portions according to the compiler's taste, the stanza beginning—

<blockquote>
Give to the winds thy fears,
</blockquote>

—being with some a favorite first verse.

The translation of the hymn from the German is John Wesley's.

Purely legendary is the beautiful story of the composition of the hymn, "Commit thou all thy griefs"; how, after his exile from Berlin, traveling on foot with his weeping wife, Gerhardt stopped at a wayside inn and wrote the lines while he rested; and how a messenger from Duke Christian found him there, and offered him a home in Meresburg. But the most ordinary imagination can fill in the possible incidents in a life of vicissitudes such as Gerhardt's was.

LADY HUNTINGDON.

"When Thou My Righteous Judge Shalt Come."

Selina Shirley, Countess of Huntingdon, born 1707, died 1791, is familiarly known as the titled friend and patroness of Whitefield and his fellow-preachers. She early consecrated herself to God, and in the great spiritual awakening under Whitefield and the Wesleys she was a punctual and sympathetic helper. Uniting with the Calvinistic Methodists, she nevertheless stood aloof from none who preached a personal Christ, and whose watchwords were the salvation of souls and the purification of the Church. For more than fifty years she devoted her wealth to benevolence and spiritual ministries, and died at the age of eighty-four. "I have done my work," was her last testimony. "I have nothing to do but to go to my Father."

At various times Lady Huntingdon expressed her religious experience in verse, and the manful vigor of her school of faith recalls the unbending confidence of Job, for she was not a stranger to affliction.

> God's furnace doth in Zion stand,
> But Zion's God sits by,
> As the refiner views his gold,
> With an observant eye.
> His thoughts are high, His love is wise,
> His wounds a cure intend;
> And, though He does not always smile,
> He loves unto the end.

Her great hymn, that keeps her memory green, has the old-fashioned flavor. "Massa made God BIG!" was the comment on Dr. Bellany made by his old negro servant after that noted minister's death. In Puritan piety the sternest self-depreciation qualified every thought of the creature, while every allusion to the Creator was a magnificat. Lady Huntingdon's hymn has no flattering phrases for the human subject. "Worthless worm," and "vilest of them all" indicate the true Pauline or Oriental prostration of self before a superior being; but there is grandeur in the metre, the awful reverence, and the scene of judgment in the stanzas—always remembering the mighty choral that has so long given the lyric its voice in the church, and is ancillary to its fame:

> When Thou, my righteous Judge, shalt come
> To take Thy ransomed people home,
> Shall I among them stand?
> Shall such a worthless worm as I,
> Who sometimes am afraid to die,
> Be found at Thy right hand?
> I love to meet Thy people now,
> Before Thy feet with them to bow,
> Though vilest of them all;
> But can I bear the piercing thought,
> What if my name should be left out,
> When Thou for them shalt call?
> O Lord, prevent it by Thy grace:
> Be Thou my only hiding place,
> In this th' accepted day;
> Thy pardoning voice, oh let me hear,
> To still my unbelieving fear,
> Nor let me fall, I pray.
> Among Thy saints let me be found,
> Whene'er the archangel's trump shall sound,
> To see Thy smiling face;
> Then loudest of the throng I'll sing,
> While heaven's resounding arches ring
> With shouts of sovereign grace.

THE TUNE.

The tune of "Meribah," in which this hymn has been sung for the last sixty or more years, is one of Dr. Lowell Mason's masterpieces. An earlier German harmony attributed to Heinrich Isaac and named "Innsbruck" has in some few cases claimed association with the words, though composed two hundred years before Lady Huntingdon was born. It is strong and solemn, but its cold psalm-tune movement does not utter the deep emotion of the author's lines. "Meribah" was

34

inspired by the hymn itself, and there is nothing invidious in saying it illustrates the fact, memorable in all hymnology, of the natural obligation of a hymn to its tune.

Apropos of both, it is related that Mason was once presiding at choir service in a certain church where the minister gave out "When thou my righteous Judge shalt come" and by mistake directed the singers to "omit the second stanza." Mason sat at the organ, and while playing the last strain, "Be found at thy right hand," glanced ahead in the hymnbook and turned with a start just in time to command, "Sing the *next* verse!" The choir did so, and "O Lord, prevent it by Thy grace!" was saved from being a horrible prayer to be kept out of heaven.

ZINZENDORF.

"Jesus, Thy Blood and Righteousness."

Nicolaus Ludwig, Count Von Zinzendorf, was born at Dresden, May 26, 1700, and educated at Halle and Wittenberg. From his youth he evinced marked seriousness of mind, and deep religious sensibilities, and this character appeared in his sympathy with the persecuted Moravians, to whom he gave domicile and domain on his large estate. For eleven years he was Councillor to the Elector of Saxony, but subsequently, uniting with the Brethren's Church, he founded the settlement of Herrnhut, the first home and refuge of the reorganized sect, and became a Moravian minister and bishop.

Zinzendorf was a man of high culture, as well as profound and sincere piety and in his hymns (of which he wrote more than two thousand) he preached Christ as eloquently as with his voice. The real birth-moment of his religious life is said to have been simultaneous with his study of the "Ecce Homo" in the Dusseldorf Gallery, a wonderful painting of Jesus crowned with thorns. Visiting the gallery one day when a young man, he gazed on the sacred face and read the legend superscribed, "All this I have done for thee; What doest thou for me?" Ever afterwards his motto was "I have but one passion, and that is He, and only He"—a version of Paul's "For me to live is Christ."

Jesus, Thy blood and righteousness
My beauty are, my glorious dress:
'Midst flaming worlds, in these arrayed,
With joy shall I lift up my head.
Bold shall I stand in Thy great day,
For who aught to my charge shall lay?
Fully absolved through these I am—
From sin and fear, from guilt and shame.
Lord, I believe were sinners more
Than sands upon the ocean shore,
Thou hast for all a ransom paid,
For all a full atonement made.

Nearly all the hymns of the great Moravian are now out of general use, having accomplished their mission, like the forgotten ones of Gerhardt, and been superseded by others. More sung in Europe, probably, now than any of the survivors is, "Jesus, geh voran," ("Jesus, lead on,") which has been translated into English by Jane Borthwick'(1854). Two others, both translated by John Wesley, are with us, the one above quoted, and "Glory to God, whose witness train." "Jesus, Thy blood," which is the best known, frequently appears with the alteration—

Jesus, Thy *robe* of righteousness
My beauty *is*, my glorious dress.

* Born in Edinburgh 1813.

THE TUNE.

"Malvern," and "Uxbridge" a pure Gregorian, both by Lowell Mason, are common expressions of the hymn—the latter, perhaps, generally preferred, being less plaintive and speaking with a surer and more restful emphasis.

ROBERT SEAGRAVE.

"Rise, My Soul, and Stretch Thy Wings."

This hymn was written early in the 18th century, by the Rev. Robert Seagrave, born at Twyford, Leicestershire, Eng., Nov. 22, 1693. Educated at Cambridge, he took holy orders in the Established Church, but espoused the cause of the great evangelistic movement, and became a hearty co-worker with the Wesleys. Judging by the lyric fire he could evidently put into his verses, one involuntarily asks if he would not have written more, and been in fact the song-leader of the spiritual reformation if there had been no Charles Wesley. There is not a hymn of Wesley's in use on the same subject equal to the one immortal hymn of Seagrave, and the only other near its time that approaches it in vigor and appealing power is Doddridge's "Awake my soul, stretch every nerve."

But Providence gave Wesley the harp and appointed to the elder poet a branch of possibly equal usefulness, where he was kept too busy to enter the singers' ranks.

For eleven years he was the Sunday-evening lecturer at Lorimer's Hall, London, and often preached in Whitefield's Tabernacle. His hymn is one of the most soul-stirring in the English language:

Rise, my soul, and stretch thy wings;
Thy better portion trace;
Rise from transitory things
Toward Heaven, thy native place;
Sun and moon and stars decay,
Time shall soon this earth remove;
Rise, my soul and haste away
To seats prepared above.
Rivers to the ocean run,
Nor stay in all their course;
Fire ascending seeks the sun;
Both speed them to their source:
So a soul that's born of God
Pants to view His glorious face,
Upward tends to His abode
To rest in His embrace.

*   *   *   *   *   *

Cease, ye pilgrims, cease to mourn,
Press onward to the prize;
Soon your Saviour will return
Triumphant in the skies.
Yet a season, and you know
Happy entrance will be given;
All our sorrows left below,
And earth exchanged for heaven.

This hymn must have found its predestinated organ when it found—

THE TUNE.

"Amsterdam," the work of James Nares, had its birth and baptism soon after the work of Seagrave; and they have been breath and bugle to the church of God ever since they became one song. In *The Great Musicians*, edited by Francis Huffer, is found this account of James Nares:

"He was born at Hanwell, Middlesex, in 1715; was admitted chorister at the Chapel Royal, under Bernard Gates, and when he was able to play the organ was appointed deputy for Pigott, of St. George's Chapel, Windsor, and became organist at York Minster in 1734. He succeeded Greene as organist and composer to the Chapel Royal in 1756, and in the same year was made Doctor of Music at Cambridge. He was appointed master of the children of the Chapel Royal in 1757, on the death of Gates. This post he resigned in 1780, and he died in 1783, (February 10,) and was buried in St. Margaret's Church, Westminster.

"He had the reputation of being an excellent trainer of boy's voices, many of his anthems having been written to exhibit the accomplishments of his young pupils. The degree of excellence the boys attained was not won in those days without the infliction of much corporal punishment."

Judging from the high pulse and action in the music of "Amsterdam," one would guess the energy of the man who made boy choirs—and made good ones. In the old time the rule was, "Birds that can sing and won't sing, must be made to sing"; and the rule was sometimes enforced with the master's time-stick.

A tune entitled "Excelsius," written a hundred years later by John Henry Cornell, so nearly resembles "Amsterdam" as to suggest an intention to amend it. It changes the modal note from G to A, but while it marches at the same pace it lacks the jubilant modulations and the choral glory of the 18th-century piece.

SIR JOHN BOWRING.
"In the Cross of Christ I Glory."

In this hymn we see, sitting humbly at the feet of the great author of our religion, a man who impressed himself perhaps more than any other save Napoleon Bonaparte upon his own generation, and who was the wonder of Europe for his immense attainments and the versatility of his powers. Statesman, philanthropist, biographer, publicist, linguist, historian, financier, naturalist, poet, political economist—there is hardly a branch of knowledge or a field of research from which he did not enrich himself and others, or a human condition that he did not study and influence.

Sir John Bowring was born in 1792. When a youth he was Jeremy Bentham's political pupil, but gained his first fame by his vast knowledge of European literature, becoming acquainted with no less than thirteen* continental languages and dialects. He served in consular appointments at seven different capitals, carried important reform measures in Parliament, was Minister Plenipotentiary to China and Governor of Hong Kong, and concluded a commercial treaty with Siam, where every previous commissioner had failed. But in all his crowded years the pen of this tireless and successful man was busy. Besides his political, economic and religious essays, which made him a member of nearly every learned society in Europe, his translations were countless, and poems and hymns of his own composing found their way to the public, among them the tender spiritual song,—

How sweetly flowed the Gospel sound
From lips of gentleness and grace
When listening thousands gathered round,
And joy and gladness filled the place,

—and the more famous hymn indicated at the head of this sketch. Knowledge of all religions only qualified him to worship the Crucified with both faith and reason. Though nominally a Unitarian, to him, as to Channing and Martineau and Edmund Sears, Christ was "all we know of God."

* Exaggerated in some accounts to *forty*.

Bowring died Nov. 23, 1872. But his hymn to the Cross will never die:

In the cross of Christ I glory,
Towering o'er the wrecks of time;
All the light of sacred story
Gathers round its head sublime.
When the woes of life o'ertake me
Hopes deceive, and fears annoy,
Never shall the cross forsake me;
Lo! it glows with peace and joy.
When the sun of bliss is beaming
Light and love upon my way,
From the cross the radiance streaming
Adds new lustre to the day.
Bane and blessing, pain and pleasure
By the cross are sanctified,
Peace is there that knows no measure,
Joys that through all time abide.

THE TUNE.

Ithamar Conkey's "Rathbun" fits the adoring words as if they had waited for it. Its air, swelling through diatonic fourth and third to the supreme syllable, bears on its waves the homage of the lines from bar to bar till the four voices come home to rest full and satisfied in the final chord—

Gathers round its head sublime.

Ithamar Conkey, was born of Scotch ancestry, in Shutesbury, Mass., May 5th, 1815. He was a noted bass singer, and was for a long time connected with the choir of the Calvary church, New York City, and sang the oratorio solos. His tune of "Rathbun" was composed in 1847, and published in Greatorex's collection in 1851. He died in Elizabeth, N.J., April 30, 1867.

CHAPTER III.

HYMNS OF CHRISTIAN DEVOTION AND EXPERIENCE.

"JESU DULCIS MEMORIA."

"Jesus the Very Thought of Thee."

The original of this delightful hymn is one of the devout meditations of Bernard of Clairvaux, a Cistercian monk (1091–1153). He was born of a noble family in or near Dijon, Burgundy, and when only twenty-three years old established a monastery at Clairvaux, France, over which he presided as its first abbot. Educated in the University of Paris, and possessing great natural abilities, he soon made himself felt in both the religious and political affairs of Europe. For more than thirty years he was the personal power that directed belief, quieted turbulence, and arbitrated disputes, and kings and even popes sought his counsel. It was his eloquent preaching that inspired the second crusade.

His fine poem of feeling, in fifty Latin stanzas, has been a source of pious song in several languages:

Jesu, dulcis memoria
Dans vera cordi gaudia,
Sed super mel et omnium
Ejus dulcis presentia.
Literally—
Jesus! a sweet memory
Giving true joys to the heart,
But sweet above honey and all things
His *presence* [is].

The five stanzas (of Caswall's free translation) now in use are familiar and dear to all English-speaking believers:

Jesus, the very thought of Thee
With sweetness fills my breast,
But sweeter far Thy face to see,
And in Thy presence rest.

Nor voice can sing nor heart can frame
Nor can the memory find,
A sweeter sound than Thy blest name,
O Saviour of mankind.

The Rev. Edward Caswall was born in Hampshire, Eng., July 15, 1814, the son of a clergyman. He graduated with honors at Brazenose College, Oxford, and after ten years of service in the ministry of the Church of England joined Henry Newman's Oratory at Birmingham, was confirmed in the Church of Rome, and devoted the rest of his life to works of piety and charity. He died Jan. 2, 1878.

THE TUNE.

No single melody has attached itself to this hymn, the scope of selection being as large as the supply of appropriate common-metre tunes. Barnby's "Holy Trinity," Wade's "Holy Cross" and Griggs' tune (of his own name) are all good, but many, on the giving out of the hymn, would associate it at once with the more familiar "Heber" by George Kingsley and expect to hear it sung. It has the uplift and unction of John Newton's—

How sweet the name of Jesus sounds
In the believer's ear.

"GOD CALLING YET! SHALL I NOT HEAR?"

Gerhard Tersteegen, the original author of the hymn, and one of the most eminent religious poets of the Reformed German church in its early days, was born in 1697, in the town of Mors, in Westphalia. He was left an orphan in boyhood by the death of his father, and as his mother's means were limited, he was put to work as an apprentice when very young, at Muhlheim on the Ruhr, and became a ribbon weaver. Here, when about fifteen years of age, he became deeply concerned for his soul, and experienced a deep and abiding spiritual work. As a Christian, his religion partook of the ascetic type, but his mysticism did not make him useless to his fellow-men.

At the age of twenty-seven, he dedicated all his resources and energies to the cause of Christ, writing the dedication in his own blood. "God graciously called me," he says, "out of the world, and granted me the desire to belong to Him, and to be willing to follow Him." He gave up secular employments altogether, and devoted his whole time to religious instruction and to the poor. His house became famous as the "Pilgrims' Cottage," and was visited by people high and humble from all parts of Germany. In his lifetime he is said to have written one hundred and eleven hymns. Died April 3, 1769.

God calling yet! shall I not hear?
Earth's pleasures shall I still hold dear?
Shall life's swift-passing years all fly,
And still my soul in slumber lie?
*   *   *   *   *   *
God calling yet! I cannot stay;
My heart I yield without delay.
Vain world, farewell; from thee I part;
The voice of God hath reached my heart.

38

The hymn was translated from the German by Miss Jane Borthwick, born in Edinburgh, 1813. She and her younger sister, Mrs. Findlater, jointly translated and published, in 1854, *Hymns From the Land of Luther,* and contributed many poetical pieces to the *Family Treasury.* She died in 1897.

Another translation, imitating the German metre, is more euphonious, though less literal and less easily fitted to music not specially composed for it, on account of its "feminine" rhymes:

God calling yet! and shall I never hearken?
But still earth's witcheries my spirit darken;
This passing life, these passing joys all flying,
And still my soul in dreamy slumbers lying?

THE TUNE.

Dr. Dykes' "Rivaulx" is a sober choral that articulates the hymn-writer's sentiment with sincerity and with considerable earnestness, but breathes too faintly the interrogative and expostulary tone of the lines. To voice the devout solicitude and self-remonstrance of the hymn there is no tune superior to "Federal St."

The Hon. Henry Kemble Oliver, author of "Federal St.," was born in Salem, Mass., March, 1800, and was addicted to music from his childhood. His father compelled him to relinquish it as a profession, but it remained his favorite avocation, and after his graduation from Harvard the cares of none of the various public positions he held, from schoolmaster to treasurer of the state of Massachusetts, could ever wean him from the study of music and its practice. At the age of thirty-one, while sitting one day in his study, the last verse of Anne Steele's hymn—

So fades the lovely blooming flower,

—floated into his mind, and an unbidden melody came with it. As he hummed it to himself the words shaped the air, and the air shaped the words.

Then gentle patience smiles on pain,
Then dying hope revives again,

—became—

See gentle patience smile on pain;
See dying hope revive again;

—and with the change of a word and a tense the hymn created the melody, and soon afterward the complete tune was made. Two years later it was published by Lowell Mason, and Oliver gave it the name of the street in Salem on which his wife was born, wooed, won, and married. It adds a pathos to its history that "Federal St." was sung at her burial.

This first of Oliver's tunes was followed by "Harmony Grove," "Morning," "Walnut Grove," "Merton," "Hudson," "Bosworth," "Salisbury Plain," several anthems and motets, and a "Te Deum."

In his old age, at the great Peace Jubilee in Boston, 1872, the baton was put into his hands, and the gray-haired composer conducted the chorus of ten thousand voices as they sang the words and music of his noble harmony. The incident made "Federal St." more than ever a feature of New England history. Oliver died in 1885.

"MY GOD, HOW ENDLESS IS THY LOVE."

The spirited tune to this hymn of Watts, by Frederick Lampe, variously named "Kent" and "Devonshire," historically reaches back so near to the poet's time that it must have been one of the earliest expressions of his fervent words.

Johan Friedrich Lampe, born 1693, in Saxony, was educated in music at Helmstadt, and came to England in 1725 as a band musician and composer to Covent Garden Theater. His best-known secular piece is the music written to Henry Carey's burlesque, "The Dragon of Wantley."

Mrs. Rich, wife of the lessee of the theater, was converted under the preaching of the Methodists, and after her husband's death her house became the home of Lampe and his wife, where Charles Wesley often met him.

The influence of Wesley won him to more serious work, and he became one of the evangelist's helpers, supplying tunes to his singing campaigns. Wesley became attached to him, and after his death—in Edinburgh, 1752—commemorated the musician in a funeral hymn.

In popular favor Bradbury's tune of "Rolland" has now superseded the old music sung to Watts' lines—

My God, how endless is Thy love,
Thy gifts are every evening new,
And morning mercies from above
Gently distil like early dew.
*   *   *   *   *   *
I yield my powers to Thy command;
To Thee I consecrate my days;

Perpetual blessings from Thy hand
Demand perpetual songs of praise.

William Batchelder Bradbury, a pupil of Dr. Lowell Mason, and the pioneer in publishing Sunday-school music, was born 1816, in York, Me. His father, a veteran of the Revolution, was a choir leader, and William's love of music was inherited. He left his father's farm, and came to Boston, where he first heard a church-organ. Encouraged by Mason and others to follow music as a profession, he went abroad, studied at Leipsic, and soon after his return became known as a composer of sacred tunes. He died in Montclair, N.J., 1868.

"I'M NOT ASHAMED TO OWN MY LORD."

The favorite tune for this spiritual hymn, also by Watts, is old "Arlington," one of the most useful church melodies in the whole realm of English psalmody. Its name clings to a Boston street, and the beautiful chimes of Arlington St. church (Unitarian) annually ring its music on special occasions, as it has since the bells were tuned:

I'm not ashamed to own my Lord
Or to defend His cause,
Maintain the honor of His Word,
The glory of His cross.
Jesus, my God!—I know His Name;
His Name is all my trust,
Nor will He put my soul to shame
Nor let my hope be lost.

Dr. Thomas Augustine Arne, the creator of "Arlington," was born in London, 1710, the son of a King St. upholsterer. He studied at Eton, and though intended for the legal profession, gave his whole mind to music. At twenty-three he began writing operas for his sister, Susanna (a singer who afterwards became the famous tragic actress, Mrs. Cibber).

Arne's music to Milton's "Comus," and to "Rule Brittannia" established his reputation. He was engaged as composer to Drury Lane Theater, and in 1759 received from Oxford his degree of Music Doctor. Later in life he turned his attention to oratorios, and other forms of sacred music, and was the first to introduce female voices in choir singing. He died March 5, 1778, chanting hallelujahs, it is said, with his last breath.

"IS THIS THE KIND RETURN?"

Dr. Watts in this hymn gave experimental piety its hour and language of reflection and penitence:

Is this the kind return?
Are these the thanks we owe,
Thus to abuse Eternal Love
Whence all our blessings flow?
*   *   *   *   *   *
Let past ingratitude
Provoke our weeping eyes.

United in loving wedlock with these words in former years was "Golden Hill," a chime of sweet counterpoint too rare to bury its authorship under the vague phrase "A Western Melody." It was caught evidently from a forest bird' that flutes its clear solo in the sunsets of May and June. There can be no mistaking the imitation—the same compass, the same upward thrill, the same fall and warbled turn. Old-time folk used to call for it, "Sing, my Fairweather Bird." It lingers in a few of the twenty- or thirty-years-ago collections, but stronger voices have drowned it out of the new.

---

* The wood thrush.

"Thacher," (set to the same hymn,) faintly recalls its melody. Nevertheless "Thacher" is a good tune. Though commonly written in sharps, contrasting the B flat of its softer and more liquid rival of other days, it is one of Handel's strains, and lends the meaning and pathos of the lyric text to voice and instrument.

"WHEN I SURVEY THE WONDROUS CROSS."

This crown of all the sacred odes of Dr. Watts for the song-service of the church of God was called by Matthew Arnold the "greatest hymn in the English language." The day the eminent critic died he heard it sung in the Sefton Park Presbyterian Church, and repeated the opening lines softly to himself again and again after the services. The hymn is certainly *one* of the greatest in the language. It appeared as No. 7 in Watts' third edition (about 1710) containing five stanzas. The second line—

On which the Prince of Glory died,

40

—read originally—
Where the young Prince of Glory died.
Only four stanzas are now generally used. The omitted one—
His dying crimson like a robe
Spreads o'er His body on the tree;
Then am I dead to all the globe,
And all the globe is dead to me.
—is a flash of tragic imagination, showing the sanguine intensity of Christian vision in earlier time, when contemplating the Saviour's passion; but it is too realistic for the spirit and genius of song-worship. That the great hymn was designed by the writer for communion seasons, and was inspired by Gal. 6:14, explains the two last lines if not the whole of the highly colored verse.

THE TUNE.

One has a wide field of choice in seeking the best musical interpretation of this royal song of faith and self-effacement:
When I survey the wondrous Cross
On which the Prince of Glory died,
My richest gain I count but loss,
And pour contempt on all my pride.
Forbid it, Lord, that I should boast
Save in the death of Christ my God;
All the vain things that charm me most,
I sacrifice them to His blood.
See from His head, His hands, His feet,
Sorrow and love flow mingled down;
Did e'er such love and sorrow meet;
Or thorns compose so rich a crown?
Were the whole realm of Nature mine,
That were a present far too small;
Love so amazing, so divine,
Demands my soul, my life, my all.
To match the height and depth of these words with fitting glory of sound might well have been an ambition of devout composers. Rev. G.C. Wells' tune in the *Revivalist*, with its emotional chorus, I.B. Woodbury's "Eucharist" in the *Methodist Hymnal*, Henry Smart's effective choral in Barnby's *Hymnary* (No. 170), and a score of others, have woven the feeling lines into melody with varying success. Worshippers in spiritual sympathy with the words may question if, after all, old "Hamburg," the best of Mason's loved Gregorians, does not, alone, in tone and elocution, rise to the level of the hymn.

"LOVE DIVINE, ALL LOVES EXCELLING."

This evergreen song-wreath to the Crucified, was contributed by Charles Wesley, in 1746. It is found in his collection of 1756, *Hymns for Those That Seek and Those That Have Redemption in the Blood of Jesus Christ.*
Love Divine all loves excelling,
Joy of Heaven to earth come down,
Fix in us Thy humble dwelling,
All Thy faithful mercies crown.
*   *   *   *   *   *

Come Almighty to deliver,
Let us all Thy life receive,
Suddenly return, and never,
Nevermore Thy temples leave.
*   *   *   *   *   *

Finish then Thy new creation;
Pure and spotless let us be;
Let us see our whole salvation
Perfectly secured by Thee.
Changed from glory into glory
Till in Heaven we take our place,
Till we cast our crowns before Thee
Lost in wonder, love and praise!

41

The hymn has been set to H. Isaac's ancient tune (1490), to Wyeth's "Nettleton" (1810), to Thos. H. Bailey's (1777–1839) "Isle of Beauty, fare thee well" (named from Thomas Moore's song), to Edward Hopkins' "St. Joseph," and to a multitude of others more or less familiar.

Most familiar of all perhaps, (as in the instance of "Far from mortal cares retreating,") is its association with "Greenville," the production of that brilliant but erratic genius and freethinker, Jean Jacques Rousseau. It was originally a love serenade, ("Days of absence, sad and dreary") from the opera of *Le Devin du Village*, written about 1752. The song was commonly known years afterwards as "Rousseau's Dream." But the unbelieving philosopher, musician, and misguided moralist builded better than he knew, and probably better than he meant when he wrote his immortal choral. Whatever he heard in his "dream" (and one legend says it was a "song of angels") he created a harmony dear to the church he despised, and softened the hearts of the Christian world towards an evil teacher who was inspired, like Balaam, to utter one sacred strain.

Rousseau was born in Geneva, 1712, but he never knew his mother, and neither the affection or interest of his father or of his other relatives was of the quality to insure the best bringing up of a child.

He died July, 1778. But his song survives, while the world gladly forgets everything else he wrote. It is almost a pardonable exaggeration to say that every child in Christendom knows "Greenville."

"WHEN ALL THY MERCIES, O MY GOD."

This charming hymn was written by Addison, the celebrated English poet and essayist, about 1701, in grateful commemoration of his delivery from shipwreck in a storm off the coast of Genoa, Italy. It originally contained thirteen stanzas, but no more than four or six are commonly sung. It has put the language of devotional gratitude into the mouths of thousands of humble disciples who could but feebly frame their own:

When all Thy mercies, O my God
My rising soul surveys,
Transported with the view I'm lost
In wonder, love and praise.
Unnumbered comforts on my soul
Thy tender care bestowed
Before my infant heart conceived
From whom those comforts flowed.
When in the slippery paths of youth
With heedless steps I ran,
Thine arm unseen conveyed me safe,
And led me up to man.

Another hymn of Addison—

How are Thy servants bless'd, O Lord,

—was probably composed after the same return from a foreign voyage. It has been called his "Traveller's Hymn."

Joseph Addison, the best English writer of his time, was the son of Lancelot Addison, rector of Milston, Wiltshire, and afterwards Dean of Litchfield. The distinguished author was born in Milston Rectory, May 1, 1672, and was educated at Oxford. His excellence in poetry, both English and Latin, gave him early reputation, and a patriotic ode obtained for him the patronage of Lord Somers. A pension from King William III. assured him a comfortable income, which was increased by further honors, for in 1704 he was appointed Commissioner of Appeals, then secretary of the Lord Lieutenant of Ireland, and in 1717 Secretary of State. He died in Holland House, Kensington, near London, June 17, 1719.

His hymns are not numerous, (said to be only five), but they are remarkable for the simple beauty of their style, as well as for their Christian spirit. Of his fine metrical version of the 23rd Psalm,—

The Lord my pasture shall prepare,
And feed me with a shepherd's care,

—one of his earliest productions, the tradition is that he gathered its imagery when a boy living at Netheravon, near Salisbury Plain, during his lonely two-mile walks to school at Amesbury and back again. All his hymns appeared first in the *Spectator*, to which he was a prolific contributor.

THE TUNE.

The hymn "When all Thy mercies" still has "Geneva" for its vocal mate in some congregational manuals. The tune is one of the rare survivals of the old "canon" musical method, the parts coming in one after another with identical notes. It is always delightful as a performance with its glory of harmony and its sweet duet, and for generations it had no other words than Addison's hymn.

John Cole, author of "Geneva," was born in Tewksbury, Eng., 1774, and came to the United States in his boyhood (1785). Baltimore, Md. became his American home, and he was educated there. Early in life he became a musician and music publisher. At least twelve of his principal song collections from 1800 to 1832 are mentioned by Mr. Hubert P. Main, most of them sacred and containing many of his own tunes.

He continued to compose music till his death, Aug. 17, 1855. Mr. Cole was leader of the regimental band known as "The Independent Blues," which played in the war of 1812, and was present at the "North Point" fight, and other battles.

Besides "Geneva," for real feeling and harmonic beauty "Manoah," adapted from Haydn's Creation, deserves mention as admirably suited to "Addison's" hymn, and also "Belmont," by Samuel Webbe, which resembles it in style and sentiment.

Samuel Webbe, composer of "Belmont," was of English parentage but was born in Minorca, Balearic Islands, in 1740, where his father at that time held a government appointment; but his father, dying suddenly, left his family poor, and Samuel was apprenticed to a cabinet-maker. He served his apprenticeship, and immediately repaired to a London teacher and began the study of music and languages. Surmounting great difficulties, he became a competent musician, and made himself popular as a composer of glees. He was also the author of several masses, anthems, and hymn-tunes, the best of which are still in occasional use. Died in London, 1816.

"JESUS, I LOVE THY CHARMING NAME."

When Dr. Doddridge, the author of this hymn, during his useful ministry, had finished the preparation of a pulpit discourse that strongly impressed him, he was accustomed, while his heart was yet glowing with the sentiment that had inspired him, to put the principal thoughts into metre, and use the hymn thus written at the conclusion of the preaching of the sermon. This hymn of Christian ardor was written to be sung after a sermon from Romans 8:35, "Who shall separate us from the love of Christ?"

Jesus, I love Thy charming name,
'Tis music to mine ear:
Fain would I sound it out so loud
That earth and heaven should hear.
*   *   *   *   *   *

I'll speak the honors of Thy name
With my last laboring breath,
Then speechless, clasp Thee in my arms,
The conqueror of death.
Earlier copies have—
The *antidote* of death.

Philip Doddridge, D.D., was born in London, June 26, 1702. Educated at Kingston Grammar School and Kibworth Academy, he became a scholar of respectable attainments, and was ordained to the Non-conformist ministry. He was pastor of the Congregational church at Northampton, from 1729 until his death, acting meanwhile as principal of the Theological School in that place. In 1749 he ceased to preach and went to Lisbon for his health, but died there about two years later, of consumption, Oct. 26, 1752.

THE TUNE.

The hymn has been sometimes sung to "Pisgah," an old revival piece by J.C. Lowry (1820) once much heard in camp-meetings, but it is a pedestrian tune with too many quavers, and a headlong tempo.

Bradbury's "Jazer," in three-four time, is a melody with modulations, though more sympathetic, but it is hard to divorce the hymn from its long-time consort, old "Arlington." It has the accent of its sincerity, and the breath of its devotion.

"LO, ON A NARROW NECK OF LAND."

This hymn of Charles Wesley is always designated now by the above line, the first of the *second* stanza as originally written. It is said to have been composed at Land's End, in Cornwall, with the British Channel and the broad Atlantic in view and surging on both sides around a "narrow neck of land."

Lo! on a narrow neck of land,
Twixt two unbounded seas, I stand,
Secure, insensible:
A point of time, a moment's space,
Removes me to that heavenly place,

Or shuts me up in hell.
O God, mine inmost soul convert,
And deeply on my thoughtful heart
Eternal things impress:
Give me to feel their solemn weight,
And tremble on the brink of fate,
And wake to righteousness.

The preachers and poets of the great spiritual movement of the eighteenth century in England abated nothing in the candor of their words. The terrible earnestness of conviction tipped their tongues and pens with fire.

THE TUNE.

Lady Huntingdon would have lent "Meribah" gladly to this hymn, but Mason was not yet born. Many times it has been borrowed for Wesley's words since it came to its own, and the spirit of the pious Countess has doubtless approved the loan. It is rich enough to furnish forth her own lyric and more than one other of like matter and metre.

The muscular music of "Ganges" has sometimes carried the hymn, and there are those who think its thunder is not a whit more Hebraic than the words require.

"COME YE SINNERS POOR AND NEEDY."

Few hymns have been more frequently sung in prayer-meetings and religious assemblies during the last hundred and fifty years. Its author, Joseph Hart, spoke what he knew and testified what he felt. Born in London, 1712, and liberally educated, he was in his young manhood very religious, but he went so far astray as to indulge in evil practices, and even published writings, both original and translated, against Christianity and religion of any kind. But he could not drink at the Dead Sea and live. The apples of Sodom sickened him. Conscience asserted itself, and the pangs of remorse nearly drove him to despair till he turned back to the source he had forsaken. He alludes to this experience in the lines—

Let not conscience make you linger,
Nor of fitness fondly dream;
All the fitness He requireth
Is to feel your need of Him.

During Passion Week, 1767, he had an amazing view of the sufferings of Christ, under the stress of which his heart was changed. In the joy of this experience he wrote—

Come ye sinners poor and needy,

—and—

Come all ye chosen saints of God.
Probably no two hymn-lines have been oftener repeated than—

If you tarry till you're better
You will never come at all.

The complete form of the original stanzas is:

Come ye sinners poor and needy,
Weak and wounded, sick and sore;
Jesus ready stands to save you,
Full of pity, love and power.
He is able,
He is willing; doubt no more.

The whole hymn—ten stanzas—is not sung now as one, but two, the second division beginning with the line—

Come ye weary, heavy laden.

Rev. Joseph Hart became minister of Jewin St. Congregational Chapel, London, about 1760, where he labored till his death, May 24, 1768.

THE TUNE.

A revival song by Jeremiah Ingalls (1764–1828), written about 1804, with an easy, popular swing and a *sforzando* chorus—

Turn to the Lord and seek salvation,

—monopolized this hymn for a good many years. The tunes commonly assigned to it have since been "Greenville" and Von Weber's "Wilmot," in which last it is now more generally sung—dropping the echo lines at the end of each stanza.

Carl Maria Von Weber, son of a roving musician, was born in Eutin, Germany, 1786. He developed no remarkable genius till he was about twenty years old, though being a fine vocalist, his singing brought him popularity and gain; but in 1806 he nearly lost his voice by accidently drinking nitric acid. He was for several years private secretary to Duke Ludwig at Stuttgart, and in 1813 Chapel-Master at Prague, from which place he went to Dresden in 1817 as Musik-Director.

Von Weber's Korner songs won the hearts of all Germany; and his immortal "Der Freischutz" (the Free Archer), and numerous tender melodies like the airs to "John Anderson, my Jo" and "O Poortith Cauld" have gone to all civilized nations. No other composer had such feeling for beauty of sound.

This beloved musician was physically frail and delicate, and died of untimely decline, during a visit to London in 1826.

"O HAPPY SAINTS WHO DWELL IN LIGHT."

Sometimes printed "O happy *souls*." This poetical and flowing hymn seems to have been forgotten in the making up of most modern church hymnals. Hymns on heaven and heavenly joys abound in embarrassing numbers, but it is difficult to understand why this beautiful lyric should be *universally* neglected. It was written probably about 1760, by Rev. John Berridge, from the text, "Blessed are the dead who die in the Lord,"

The first line of the second stanza—

Released from sorrow, toil and strife,

—has been tinkered in some of the older hymn-books, where it is found to read—,

Released from sorrows toil and *grief*,

—not only committing a tautology, but destroying the perfect rhyme with "life" in the next line. The whole hymn, too, has been much altered by substituted words and shifted lines, though not generally to the serious detriment of its meaning and music.

The Rev. John Berridge—friend of the Wesleys, Whitefield, and Lady Huntingdon—was an eccentric but very worthy and spiritual minister, born the son of a farmer, in Kingston, Nottinghamshire, Eng., Mar. 1, 1716. He studied at Cambridge, and was ordained curate of Stapleford and subsequently located as vicar of Everton, 1775. He died Jan. 22, 1793. He loved to preach, and he was determined that his tombstone should preach after his voice was still. His epitaph, composed by himself, is both a testimony and a memoir:

"Here lie the earthly remains of John Berridge, late vicar of Everton, and an itinerant servant of Jesus Christ, who loved his Master and His work, and after running His errands many years, was called up to wait on Him above.

"Reader, art thou born again?

"No salvation without the new birth.

"I was born in sin, February, 1716.

"Remained ignorant of my fallen state till 1730.

"Lived proudly on faith and works for salvation till 1751.

"Admitted to Everton vicarage, 1755.

"Fled to Jesus alone for refuge, 1756.

"Fell asleep in Jesus Christ,—" (1793.)

THE TUNE.

The once popular score that easily made the hymn a favorite, was "Salem," in the old *Psalmodist*. It still appears in some note-books, though the name of its composer is uncertain. Its notes (in 6-8 time) succeed each other in syllabic modulations that give a soft dactylic accent to the measure and a wavy current to the lines:

O happy saints that dwell in light,
And walk with Jesus clothed in white,
Safe landed on that peaceful shore,
Where pilgrims meet to part no more:
Released from sorrow, toil and strife,
Death was the gate to endless life,
And now they range the heavenly plains
And sing His love in melting strains.
Another version reads:
——and welcome to an endless life,
Their souls have now begun to prove
The height and depth of Jesus' love.

"THOU DEAR REDEEMER, DYING LAMB."

The author, John Cennick, like Joseph Hart, was led to Christ after a reckless boyhood and youth, by the work of the Divine Spirit in his soul, independent of any direct outward influence. Sickened of his cards, novels, and playhouse pleasures, he had begun a sort of mechanical reform, when one day, walking in the streets of London, he suddenly seemed to hear the text spoken "I am thy salvation!" His consecration began at that moment.

He studied for the ministry, and became a preacher, first under direction of the Wesleys, then under Whitefield, but afterwards joined the Moravians, or "Brethren." He was born at Reading, Derbyshire, Eng., Dec. 12, 1718, and died in London, July 4, 1755.

45

THE TUNE.

The word "Rhine" (in some collections—in others "Emmons") names a revival tune once so linked with this hymn and so well known that few religious people now past middle life could enjoy singing it to any other. With a compass one note beyond an octave and a third, it utters every line with a clear, bold gladness sure to infect a meeting with its own spiritual fervor.

> Thou dear Redeemer, dying Lamb,
> I love to hear of Thee;
> No music like Thy charming name,
> Nor half so sweet can be.

The composer of the bright legato melody just described was Frederick Burgmüller, a young German musician, born in 1804. He was a remarkable genius, both in composition and execution, but his health was frail, and he did not live to fulfil the rich possibilities that lay within him. He died in 1824—only twenty years old. The tune "Rhine" ("Emmons") is from one of his marches.

"WHILE THEE I SEEK, PROTECTING POWER."

Helen Maria Williams wrote this sweet hymn, probably about the year 1800. She was a brilliant woman, better known in literary society for her political verses and essays than by her hymns; but the hymn here noted bears sufficient witness to her deep religious feeling:

> While Thee I seek, Protecting Power,
> Be my vain wishes stilled,
> And may this consecrated hour
> With better hopes be filled.
> Thy love the power of thought bestowed;
> To Thee my thoughts would soar,
> Thy mercy o'er my life has flowed,
> That mercy I adore.

Miss Williams was born in the north of England, Nov. 30, 1762, but spent much of her life in London, and in Paris, where she died, Dec. 14, 1827.

THE TUNE.

Wedded so many years to the gentle, flowing music of Pleyel's "Brattle Street," few lovers of the hymn recall its words without the melody of that emotional choral.

The plain psalm-tune, "Simpson," by Louis Spohr, divides the stanzas into quatrains.

"JESUS MY ALL TO HEAVEN IS GONE."

This hymn, by Cennick, was familiarized to the public more than two generations ago by its revival tune, sometimes called "Duane Street," long-metre double. It is staffed in various keys, but its movement is full of life and emphasis, and its melody is contagious. The piece was composed by Rev. George Coles, in 1835.

The fact that this hymn of Cennick with Coles's tune appears in the *New Methodist Hymnal* indicates the survival of both in modern favor.

> Jesus my all to heaven is gone,
> He whom I fixed my hopes upon;
> His track I see, and I'll pursue
> The narrow way till Him I view.
> The way the holy prophets went,
> The road that leads from banishment,
> The King's highway of holiness
> I'll go for all Thy paths are peace.

The memory has not passed away of the hearty unison with which prayer-meeting and camp-meeting assemblies used to "crescendo" the last stanza—

> Then will I tell to sinners round
> What a dear Saviour I have found;
> I'll point to His redeeming blood,
> And say "Behold the way to God."

The Rev. George Coles was born in Stewkley, Eng., Jan. 2, 1792, and died in New York City, May 1, 1858. He was editor of the *N.Y. Christian Advocate*, and *Sunday School Advocate*, for several years, and was a musician of some ability, besides being a good singer.

"SWEET THE MOMENTS, RICH IN BLESSING."

The Hon. and Rev. Walter Shirley, Rector of Loughgree, county of Galway, Ireland, revised this hymn under the chastening discipline of a most trying experience. His brother, the Earl of Ferrars, a licentious man, murdered an old and faithful servant in a fit of rage, and was executed at Tyburn for the crime. Sir Walter, after the disgrace and long distress of the imprisonment, trial, and final tragedy, returned to his little parish in Ireland, humbled but driven nearer to the Cross.

Sweet the moments, rich in blessing
Which before the Cross I spend;
Life and health and peace possessing
From the sinner's dying Friend.

All the emotion of one who buries a mortifying sorrow in the heart of Christ, and tries to forget, trembles in the lines of the above hymn as he changed and adapted it in his saddest but devoutest hours. Its original writer was the Rev. James Allen, nearly twenty years younger than himself, a man of culture and piety, but a Christian of shifting creeds. It is not impossible that he sent his hymn to Shirley to revise. At all events it owes its present form to Shirley's hand.

Truly blessèd is the station
Low before His cross to lie,
While I see Divine Compassion
Beaming in His gracious eye.'

* "Floating in His languid eye" seems to have been the earlier version.

The influence of Sir Walter's family misfortune is evident also in the mood out of which breathed his other trustful lines—

Peace, troubled soul, whose plaintive moan
Hath taught these rocks the notes of woe,

(changed now to "hath taught *these scenes*" etc).

Sir Walter Shirley, cousin of the Countess of Huntingdon, was born 1725, and died in 1786. Even in his last sickness he continued to preach to his people in his house, seated in his chair.

Rev. James Oswald Allen was born at Gayle, Yorkshire, Eng., June 24, 1743. He left the University of Cambridge after a year's study, and became an itinerant preacher, but seems to have been a man of unstable religious views. After roving from one Christian denomination to another several times, he built a Chapel, and for forty years ministered there to a small Independent congregation. He died in Gayle, Oct. 31, 1804.

The tune long and happily associated with "Sweet the Moments" is "Sicily," or the "Sicilian Hymn"—from an old Latin hymn-tune, "O Sanctissima."

"O FOR A CLOSER WALK WITH GOD."

The author, William Cowper, son of a clergyman, was born at Berkhampstead, Hertfordshire, Eng., Nov. 15, 1731, and died at Dereham, Norfolk, April 25, 1800. Through much of his adult life he was afflicted with a mental ailment inducing melancholia and at times partial insanity, during which he once attempted suicide. He sought literary occupation as an antidote to his disorder of mind, and besides a great number of lighter pieces which diverted him and his friends, composed "The Task," an able and delightful moral and domestic poetic treatise in blank verse, and in the same style of verse translated Homer's *Odyssey* and *Iliad*.

One of the most beloved of English poets, this suffering man was also a true Christian, and wrote some of our sweetest and most spiritual hymns. Most of these were composed at Olney, where he resided for a time with John Newton, his fellow hymnist, and jointly with him issued the volume known as the *Olney Hymns.*

THE TUNE.

Music more or less closely identified with this familiar hymn is Gardiner's "Dedham," and also "Mear," often attributed to Aaron Williams. Both, about equally with the hymn, are seasoned by time, but have not worn out their harmony—or their fitness to Cowper's prayer.

William Gardiner was born in Leicester, Eng., March 15, 1770, and died there Nov. 11, 1853. He was a vocal composer and a "musicographer" or writer on musical subjects.

One Aaron Williams, to whom "Mear" has by some been credited, was of Welsh descent, a composer of psalmody and clerk of the Scotch church in London. He was born in 1734, and died in 1776. Another account, and the more probable one, names a minister of Boston of still earlier date as the author of the noble old harmony. It is found in a small New England collection of 1726, but not in any English or Scotch collection. "Mear" is presumably an American tune.

"WHAT VARIOUS HINDRANCES WE MEET."

Another hymn of Cowper's; and no one ever suffered more deeply the plaintive regret in the opening lines, or better wrought into poetic expression an argument for prayer.

What various hindrances we meet
In coming to a mercy-seat!
Yet who that knows the worth of prayer
But wishes to be often there?

47

Prayer makes the darkest clouds withdraw,
Prayer climbs the ladder Jacob saw.

The whole hymn is (or once was) so thoroughly learned by heart as to be fixed in the church among its household words. Preachers to the diffident do not forget to quote—

Have you no words? ah, think again;
Words flow apace when you *complain.*

*   *   *   *   *   *

Were half the breath thus vainly spent
To Heaven in supplication sent,
Our cheerful song would oftener be,
"Hear what the Lord hath done for me!"

And there is all the lifetime of a proverb in the couplet—

Satan trembles when he sees
The weakest saint upon his knees.

Tune, Lowell Mason's "Rockingham."

"MY GRACIOUS REDEEMER I LOVE."

This is one of Benjamin Francis's lays of devotion. The Christian Welshman who bore that name was a Gospel minister full of Evangelical zeal, who preached in many places, though his pastoral home was with the Baptist church in Shortwood, Wales. Flattering calls to London could not tempt him away from his first and only parish, and he remained there till his triumphant death. He was born in 1734, and died in 1799.

My gracious Redeemer I love,
His praises aloud I'll proclaim,
And join with the armies above,
To shout His adorable name.
To gaze on His glories divine
Shall be my eternal employ;
To see them incessantly shine,
My boundless, ineffable joy.

Tune, "Birmingham"—an English melody. Anonymous.

"BLEST BE THE TIE THAT BINDS."

Perhaps the best hymn-expression of sacred brotherhood, at least it has had, and still has the indorsement of constant use. The author, John Fawcett, D.D., is always quoted as the example of his own words, since he sacrificed ambition and personal interest to Christian affection.

Born near Bradford, Yorkshire, Jan. 6, 1739, and converted under the preaching of Whitefield, he joined the Methodists, but afterwards became a member of the new Baptist church in Bradford. Seven years later he was ordained over the Baptist Society at Wainsgate. In 1772 he received a call to succeed the celebrated Dr. Gill, in London, and accepted. But at the last moment, when his goods were packed for removal, the clinging love of his people, weeping their farewells around him, melted his heart. Their passionate regrets were more than either he or his good wife could withstand.

"I will *stay*," he said; "you may unpack my goods, and we will live for the Lord lovingly together."

It was out of this heart experience that the tender hymn was born.

Our fears, our hopes, our aims are one,
Our comforts and our cares.

Dr. Fawcett died July 25, 1817.

Tune, "Boylston," L. Mason; or "Dennis," H.G. Nägeli.

"I LOVE THY KINGDOM, LORD."

"Dr. Dwight's Hymn," as this is known *par eminence* among many others from his pen, is one of the imperishable lyrics of the Christian Church. The real spirit of the hundred and twenty-second Psalm is in it, and it is worthy of Watts in his best moments.

Timothy Dwight was born at Northampton, Mass, May 14, 1752, and graduated at Yale College at the age of thirteen. He wrote several religious poems of considerable length. In 1795 he was elected President of Yale College, and in 1800 he revised Watts' Psalms, at the request of the General Association of Connecticut, adding a number of translations of his own.

I love Thy kingdom, Lord,
The house of Thine abode,
The Church our blest Redeemer saved
With His own precious blood.

48

I love Thy Church, O God;
Her walls before Thee stand,
Dear as the apple of Thine eye,
And graven on Thy hand.

Dr. Dwight died Jan. 11, 1817.

Tune, "St. Thomas," Aaron Williams, (1734–1776.)

Mr. Hubert P. Main, however, believes the author to be Handel. It appeared as the second movement of a four-movement tune in Williams's 1762 collection, which contained pieces by the great masters, with his own; but while not credited to Handel, Williams did not claim it himself.

"MID SCENES OF CONFUSION."

This hymn, common in chapel hymnbooks half a century and more ago, is said to have been written by the Rev. David Denham, about 1826.

THE TUNE.

"Home, Sweet Home" was composed, according to the old account, by John Howard Payne as one of the airs in his opera of "Clari, the Maid of Milan," which was brought out in London at Drury Lane in 1823. But Charles Mackay, the English poet, in the London Telegraph, asserts that Sir Henry Bishop, an eminent musician, in his vain search for a Sicilian national air, *invented* one, and that it was the melody of "Home, sweet Home," which he afterwards set to Howard Payne's words. Mr. Mackay had this story from Sir Henry himself.

Mid scenes of confusion and creature complaints
How sweet to my soul is communion with saints,
To find at the banquet of mercy there's room
And feel in the presence of Jesus at home.
Home, home, sweet, sweet home!
Prepare me, dear Savior for glory, my home.

John Howard Payne, author at least, of the original *words* of "Home, Sweet Home," was born in New York City June 9, 1791. He was a singer, and became an actor and theatrical writer. He composed the words of his immortal song in the year 1823, when he was himself homeless and hungry and sheltered temporarily in an attic in Paris.

His fortunes improved at last, and he was appointed to represent his native country as consul in Tunis, where he died, Apr. 9, 1852.

"O, COULD I SPEAK THE MATCHLESS WORTH."

The writer of this hymn of worshiping ardor and exalted Christian love was an English Baptist minister, the Rev. Samuel Medley. He was born at Cheshunt, Hertfordshire, June 23, 1738, and at eighteen years of age entered the Royal Navy, where, though he had been piously educated, he became dissipated and morally reckless. Wounded in a sea fight off Cape Lagos, and in dread of amputation he prayed penitently through nearly a whole night, and in the morning the surprised surgeon told him his limb could be saved.

The voice of his awakened conscience was not wholly disregarded, though it was not till some time after he left the navy that his vow to begin a religious life was sincerely kept. After teaching school for four years, he began to preach in 1766, Wartford in Hertfordshire being the first scene of his godly labors. He died in Liverpool July 17, 1799, at the end of a faithful ministry there of twenty-seven years. A small edition of his hymns was published during his lifetime, in 1789.

O could I speak the matchless worth,
O could I sound the glories forth
Which in my Saviour shine,
I'd soar and touch the heavenly strings
And vie with Gabriel while he sings,
In notes almost divine!

THE TUNE.

"Colebrook," a plain choral; but with a noble movement, by Henry Smart, is the English music to this fine lyric, but Dr. Mason's "Ariel" is the American favorite. It justifies its name, for it has wings—in both full harmony and duet—and its melody feels the glory of the hymn at every bar.

49

Augustus Montague
Toplady

"ROCK OF AGES CLEFT FOR ME."

Augustus Montagu Toplady, author of this almost universal hymn, was born at Farnham, Surrey, Eng., Nov. 4, 1740. Educated atWestminster School, and Trinity College, Dublin, he took orders in the Established Church. In his doctrinal debates with the Wesleys he was a harsh controversialist; but his piety was sincere, and marked late in life by exalted moods. Physically he was frail, and his fiery zeal wore out his body. Transferred from his vicarage at Broad Hembury, Devonshire, to Knightsbridge, London, at twenty-eight years of age, his health began to fail before he was thirty-five, and in one of his periods of illness he wrote—

When languor and disease invade
This trembling house of clay,
'Tis sweet to look beyond my pains
And long to fly away.

And the same homesickness for heaven appears under a different figure in another hymn—

At anchor laid remote from home,
Toiling I cry, "Sweet Spirit, come!
Celestial breeze, no longer stay,
But swell my sails, and speed my way!"

Possessed of an ardent religious nature, his spiritual frames exemplified in a notable degree the emotional side of Calvinistic piety. Edward Payson himself, was not more enraptured in immediate view of death than was this young London priest and poet. Unquestioning faith became perfect certainty. As in the bold metaphor of "Rock of Ages," the faith finds voice in—

A debtor to mercy alone,

—and other hymns in his collection of 1776, two years before the end came. Most of this devout writing was done in his last days, and he continued it as long as strength was left, until, on the 11th of August, 1778, he joyfully passed away.

Somehow there was always something peculiarly heartsome and "filling" to pious minds in the lines of Toplady in days when his minor hymns were more in vogue than now, and they were often quoted, without any idea whose making they were. "At anchor laid" was crooned by good old ladies at their spinning-wheels, and godly invalids found "When languor and disease invade" a comfort next to their Bibles.

"Rock of Ages" is said to have been written after the author, during a suburban walk, had been forced to shelter himself from a thundershower, under a cliff. This is, however, but one of several stories about the birth-occasion of the hymn.

It has been translated into many languages. One of the foreign dignitaries visiting Queen Victoria at her "Golden Jubilee" was a native of Madagascar, who surprised her by asking leave to sing, but delighted her, when leave was given, by singing "Rock of Ages." It was a favorite of hers—and of Prince Albert, who whispered it when he was dying. People who were school-children when Rev. Justus Vinton came home to Willington, Ct., with two Karen pupils, repeat to-day the "la-pa-ta, i-oo-i-oo" caught by sound from the brown-faced boys as they sang their native version of "Rock of Ages."

Gen. J.E.B. Stuart, the famous Confederate Cavalry leader, mortally wounded at Yellow Tavern, Va., and borne to a Richmond hospital, called for his minister and requested that "Rock of Ages" be sung to him.

The last sounds heard by the few saved from the wreck of the steamer "London" in the Bay of Biscay, 1866, were the voices of the helpless passengers singing "Rock of Ages" as the ship went down.

A company of Armenian Christians sang "Rock of Ages" in their native tongue while they were being massacred in Constantinople.

50

No history of this grand hymn of faith forgets the incident of Gladstone writing a Latin translation of it while sitting in the House of Commons. That remarkable man was as masterly in his scholarly recreations as in his statesmanship. The supreme Christian sentiment of the hymn had permeated his soul till it spoke to him in a dead language as eloquently as in the living one; and this is what he made of it:

TOPLADY.

Rock of ages, cleft for me,
Let me hide myself in Thee;
Let the water and the blood,
From Thy riven side which flowed,
Be of sin the double cure,
Cleanse me from its guilt and power.
Not the labor of my hands
Can fulfil Thy law's demands;
Could my zeal no respite know,
Could my tears for ever flow,
All for sin could not atone,
Thou must save, and Thou alone.
Nothing in my hand I bring,
Simply to Thy cross I cling;
Naked, come to Thee for dress,
Helpless, look to Thee for grace:
Foul, I to the fountain fly;
Wash, me, Saviour, or I die.
Whilst I draw this fleeting breath,
When my eyestrings break in death;
When I soar through tracts unknown,
See Thee on Thy judgment throne,
Rock of ages, cleft for me,
Let me hide myself in Thee.

GLADSTONE.

Jesus, pro me perforatus,
Condar intra tuum latus;
Tu per lympham profluentem,
Tu per sanguinem tepentem,
In peccata mi redunda,
Tolle culpam, sordes munda!
Coram Te nec justus forem
Quamvis tota vi laborem,
Nec si fide nunquam cesso,
Fletu stillans indefesso;
Tibi soli tantum munus—
Salva me, Salvator Unus!
Nil in manu mecum fero,
Sed me versus crucem gero:
Vestimenta nudus oro,
Opem debilis imploro,
Fontem Christi quæro immundus,
Nisi laves, moribundus.
Dum hos artus vita regit,
Quando nox sepulcro legit;
Mortuos quum stare jubes,
Sedens Judex inter nubes;—
Jesus, pro me perforatus,
Condar intra tuum latus!

The wonderful hymn has suffered the mutations common to time and taste.
When I soar thro' tracts unknown
—becomes—
When I soar to worlds unknown,
—getting rid of the unpoetic word, and bettering the elocution, but missing the writer's thought (of the unknown *path*,—instead of going to many "worlds"). The Unitarians have their version, with substitutes for the "atonement lines."

51

But the Christian lyric maintains its life and inspiration through the vicissitudes of age and use, as all intrinsically superior things can and will,—and as in the twentieth line,—

When my eyestrings break in death;
—modernized to—
When my eyelids close in death,

—the hymn will ever adapt itself to the new exigencies of common speech, without losing its vitality and power.

THE TUNE.

A happy inspiration of Dr. Thomas Hastings made the hymn and music inevitably one. Almost anywhere to call for the tune of "Toplady" (namesake of the pious poet) is as unintelligible to the multitude as "Key" would be to designate the "Star-spangled Banner." The common people—thanks to Dr. Hastings—have learned "Rock of Ages" by *sound*.

Thomas Hastings was born in Washington, Ct., 1784. For eight years he was editor of the *Western Recorder*, but he gave his life to church music, and besides being a talented tone-poet he wrote as many as six hundred hymns. In 1832, by invitation from twelve New York churches, he went to that city, and did the main work of his life there, dying, in 1872, at the good old age of eighty-nine. His musical collections number fifty-three. He wrote his famous tune in 1830.

Thomas
Hastings

"MY SOUL BE ON THY GUARD"

Strangely enough, this hymn, a trumpet note of Christian warning and resolution, was written by one who himself fell into unworthy ways.* But the one strong and spiritual watch-song by which he is remembered appeals for him, and lets us know possibly, something of his own conflicts. We can be thankful for the struggle he once made, and for the hymn it inspired. It is a voice of caution to others.

* I have been unable to verify this statement found in Mr. Butterworth's "Story of the Hymns."—T.B.

George Heath, the author, was an English minister, born in 1781; died 1822. For a time he was pastor of a Presbyterian Church at Honiton, Devonshire, and was evidently a prolific writer, having composed a hundred and forty-four hymns, an edition of which was printed.

THE TUNE.

No other has been so familiarly linked with the words as Lowell Mason's "Laban" (1830). It has dash and animation enough to reënforce the hymn, and give it popular life, even if the hymn had less earnestness and vigor of its own.

Ne'er think the vict'ry won
Nor lay thine armor down:
Thy arduous work will not be done
Till thou hast gained thy crown.
Fight on, my soul till death
Shall bring thee to thy God;
He'll take thee at thy parting breath
To His divine abode.

"PEOPLE OF THE LIVING GOD."

Montgomery *felt* every line of this hymn as he committed it to paper. He wrote it when, after years in the "swim" of social excitements and ambitions, where his young independence swept him on, he came back to the little church of his boyhood. His father and mother had gone to the West Indies as missionaries, and died there. He was forty-three years old when, led by divine light, he sought readmission to the Moravian "meeting" at Fulneck, and anchored happily in a haven of peace.

People of the living God

I have sought the world around,
Paths of sin and sorrow trod,
Peace and comfort nowhere found:
Now to you my spirit turns—
Turns a fugitive unblest;
Brethren, where your altar burns,
Oh, receive me into rest.

James Montgomery, son of Rev. John Montgomery, was born at Irvine, Ayeshire, Scotland, Nov. 4, 1771, and educated at the Moravian Seminary at Fulneck, Yorkshire, Eng. He became the editor of the *Sheffield Iris,* and his pen was busy in non-professional as well as professional work until old age. He died in Sheffield, April 30, 1854.

His literary career was singularly successful; and a glance through any complete edition of his poems will tell us why. His hymns were all published during his lifetime, and all, as well as his longer pieces, have the purity and polished beauty, if not the strength, of Addison's work. Like Addison, too, he could say that he had written no line which, dying, he would wish to blot.

The best of Montgomery was in his hymns. These were too many to enumerate here, and the more enduring ones too familiar to need enumeration. The church and the world will not soon forget "The Home in Heaven,"—

Forever with the Lord,
Amen, so let it be.
Life from the dead is in that word;
'Tis immortality.

Nor—

O where shall rest be found,

—with its impressive couplet—

'Tis not the whole of life to live
Nor all of death to die.

Nor the haunting sweetness of—

There is a calm for those who weep.

Nor, indeed, the hymn of Christian love just now before us.

THE TUNE.

The melody exactly suited to the gentle trochaic step of the home-song, "People of the living God," is "Whitman," composed for it by Lowell Mason. Few Christians, in America, we venture to say, could hear an instrument play "Whitman" without mentally repeating Montgomery's words.

"TO LEAVE MY DEAR FRIENDS."

This hymn, called "The Bower of Prayer," was dear to Christian hearts in many homes and especially in rural chapel worship half a century ago and earlier, and its sweet legato melody still lingers in the memories of aged men and women.

Elder John Osborne, a New Hampshire preacher of the "Christian" (*Christ-ian*) denomination, is said to have composed the tune (and possibly the words) about 1815—though apparently the music was arranged from a flute interlude in one of Haydn's themes. The warbling notes of the air are full of heart-feeling, and usually the best available treble voice sang it as a solo.

To leave my dear friends and from neighbors to part,
And go from my home, it affects not my heart
Like the thought of absenting myself for a day
From that blest retreat I have chosen to pray,
I have chosen to pray.
The early shrill notes of the loved nightingale
That dwelt in the bower, I observed as my bell:
It called me to duty, while birds in the air
Sang anthems of praises as I went to prayer,
As I went to prayer.*
How sweet were the zephyrs perfumed by the pine,
The ivy, the balsam, the wild eglantine,
But sweeter, O, sweeter superlative were
The joys that I tasted in answer to prayer,
In answer to prayer.

* The *American Vocalist* omits this stanza as too fanciful as well as too crude

"SAVIOUR, THY DYING LOVE."

This hymn of grateful piety was written in 1862, by Rev. S. Dryden Phelps, D.D., of New Haven, and first published in *Pure Gold*, 1871; afterwards in the (earlier) *Baptist Hymn and Tune Book.*

Saviour, Thy dying love
Thou gavest me,
Nor should I aught withhold
Dear Lord, from Thee.
   *   *   *   *   *   *
Give me a faithful heart,
Likeness to Thee,   ,
That each departing day
Henceforth may see
Some work of love begun,
Some deed of kindness done,
Some wand'rer sought and won,
Something for Thee.

The penultimate line, originally "Some sinful wanderer won," was altered by the author himself. The hymn is found in most Baptist hymnals, and was inserted by Mr. Sankey in *Gospel Hymns No. 1*. It has since won its way into several revival collections and undenominational manuals.

Rev. Sylvester Dryden Phelps, D.D., was born in Suffield, Ct., May 15, 1816, and studied at the Connecticut Literary Institution in that town. An early call to the ministry turned his talents to the service of the church, and his long settlement—comprising what might be called his principal life work—was in New Haven, where he was pastor of the First Baptist church twenty-nine years. He died there Nov. 23, 1895.

THE TUNE.

The Rev. Robert Lowry admired the hymn, and gave it a tune perfectly suited to its metre and spirit. It has never been sung in any other. The usual title of it is "Something for Jesus." The meaning and sentiment of both words and music are not unlike Miss Havergal's—
I gave my life for thee.

"IN SOME WAY OR OTHER."

This song of Christian confidence was written by Mrs. Martha A.W. Cook, wife of the Rev. Parsons Cook, editor of the *Puritan Recorder*, Boston.

It was published in the *American Messenger* in 1870, and is still in use here, as a German version of it is in Germany. The first stanza follows, in the two languages:

In some way or other the Lord will provide.
It may not be my way,
It may not be thy way,
And yet in His own way
The Lord will provide.
Sei's so oder anders, der Herr wird's versehn;
Mag's nicht sein, wie ich will,
Mag's nicht sein, wie du willst,
Doch wird's sein, wie Er will:
Der Herr wird's versehn.

In the English version the easy flow of the two last lines into one sentence is an example of rhythmic advantage over the foreign syntax.

Mrs. Cook was married to the well-known clergyman and editor, Parsons Cook, (1800–1865) in Bridgeport, Ct., and survived him at his death in Lynn, Mass. She was Miss Martha Ann Woodbridge, afterwards Mrs. Hawley, and a widow at the time of her re-marriage as Mr. Cook's second wife.

THE TUNE.

Professor Calvin S. Harrington, of Wesleyan University, Middletown, Ct., set music to the words as printed in *Winnowed Hymns* (1873) and arranged by Dr. Eben Tourjee, organizer of the great American Peace Jubilee in Boston. In the *Gospel Hymns* it is, however, superseded by the more popular composition of Philip Phillips.

Dr. Eben Tourjee, late Dean of the College of Music in Boston University, and founder and head of the New England Conservatory, was born in Warwick, R.I., June 1, 1834. With only an academy education he rose by native genius, from a hard-working boyhood to be a teacher of music and a master of its science. From a course of study in Europe he returned and soon made his reputation as an organizer of musical schools and sangerfests. The New England Conservatory of Music was first established by him in Providence, but removed in 1870 to

54

Boston, its permanent home. His doctorate of music was conferred upon him by Wesleyan University. Died in Boston, April 12, 1891.

Philip Phillips, known as "the singing Pilgrim," was born in Jamestown, Chautauqua, Co., N.Y., Aug. 13, 1834. He compiled twenty-nine collections of sacred music for Sunday schools, gospel meetings, etc.; also a *Methodist Hymn and Tune Book*, 1866. He composed a great number of tunes, but wrote no hymns. Some of his books were published in London, for he was a cosmopolitan singer, and traveled through Europe and Australia as well as America. Died in Delaware, O., June 25, 1875.

"NEARER, MY GOD, TO THEE."

Mr. William Stead, fond of noting what is often believed to be the "providential chain of causes" in everything that happens, recalls the fact that Benjamin Flower, editor of the *Cambridge Intelligencer*, while in jail (1798) at the instigation of Bp. Watson for an article defending the French Revolution, and criticising the Bishop's political course, was visited by several sympathizing ladies, one of whom was Miss Eliza Gould. The young lady's first acquaintance with him there in his cell led to an attachment which eventuated in marriage. Of that marriage Sarah Flower was born. By the theory of providential sequences Mr. Stead makes it appear that the forgotten vindictiveness of a British prelate "was the *causa causans* of one of the most spiritual and aspiring hymns in the Christian Hymnary."

"Nearer, My God, to Thee" was on the lips of President McKinley as he lay dying by a murderer's wicked shot. It is dear to President Roosevelt for its memories of the battle of Las Quasimas, where the Rough Riders sang it at the burial of their slain comrades. Bishop Marvin was saved by it from hopeless dejection, while practically an exile during the Civil War, by hearing it sung in the wilds of Arkansas, by an old woman in a log hut.

A letter from Pittsburg, Pa., to a leading Boston paper relates the name and experience of a forger who had left the latter city and wandered eight years a fugitive from justice. On the 5th of November, (Sunday,) 1905, he found himself in Pittsburg, and ventured into the Dixon Theatre, where a religious service was being held, to hear the music. The hymn "Nearer, My God, to Thee" so overcame him that he went out weeping bitterly. He walked the floor of his room all night, and in the morning telephoned for the police, confessed his name and crime, and surrendered himself to be taken back to the Boston authorities.

Mrs. Sarah Flower Adams, author of the noble hymn (supposed to have been written in 1840), was born at Harlow, Eng., Feb. 22, 1805, and died there in 1848. At her funeral another of her hymns was sung, ending—

When falls the shadow, cold in death
I yet will sing with fearless breath,
As comes to me in shade or sun,
"Father, Thy will, not mine, be done."

The attempts to *evangelize* "Nearer, My God, to Thee" by those who cannot forget that Mrs. Adams was a Unitarian, are to be deplored. Such zeal is as needless as trying to sectarianize an Old Testament Psalm. The poem is a perfect religious piece—to be sung as it stands, with thanks that it was ever created.

THE TUNE.

In English churches (since 1861) the hymn was and may still be sung to "Horbury," composed by Rev. John B. Dykes, and "St. Edmund," by Sir Arthur Sullivan. Both tunes are simple and appropriate, but such a hymn earns and inevitably acquires a single tune-voice, so that its music instantly names it by its words when played on instruments. Such a voice was given it by Lowell Mason's "Bethany," (1856). (Why not "Bethel," instead, every one who notes the imagery of the words must wonder.) "Bethany" appealed to the popular heart, and long ago (in America) hymn and tune became each other's property. It is even simpler than the English tunes, and a single hearing fixes it in memory.

"I NEED THEE EVERY HOUR."

Mrs. Annie Sherwood Hawks, who wrote this hymn in 1872, was born in Hoosick, N.Y., in 1835.

She sent the hymn (five stanzas) to Dr. Lowry, who composed its tune, adding a chorus, to make it more effective. It first appeared in a small collection of original songs prepared by Lowry and Doane for the National Baptist Sunday School Association, which met at Cincinnati, O., November, 1872, and was sung there.

I need Thee every hour,
Most gracious Lord,
No tender voice like Thine
Can peace afford.
CHORUS.

I need Thee, Oh, I need Thee,
Every hour I need Thee;
Oh, bless me now, my Saviour,
I come to Thee!

One instance, at least, of a hymn made doubly impressive by its chorus will be attested by all who have sung or heard the pleading words and music of Mrs. Hawks' and Dr. Lowry's "I need Thee, Oh, I need Thee."

"I GAVE MY LIFE FOR THEE."

This was written in her youth by Frances Ridley Havergal, and was suggested by the motto over the head of Christ in the great picture, "Ecce Homo," in the Art Gallery of Dusseldorf, Prussia, where she was at school. The sight—as was the case with young Count Zinzendorf—seems to have had much to do with the gifted girl's early religious experience, and indeed exerted its influence on her whole life. The motto read "I did this for thee; what doest thou for me?" and the generative effect of the solemn picture and its question soon appeared in the hymn that flowed from Miss Havergal's heart and pen.

I gave my life for thee,
My precious blood I shed,
That thou might'st ransomed be
And quickened from the dead.
I gave my life for thee:
What hast thou given for me?

Miss Frances Ridley Havergal, sometimes called "The Theodosia of the 19th century," was born at Astley, Worcestershire, Eng., Dec. 14, 1836. Her father, Rev. William Henry Havergal, a clergyman of the Church of England, was himself a poet and a skilled musician, and much of the daughter's ability came to her by natural bequest as well as by education. Born a poet, she became a fine instrumentalist, a composer and an accomplished linguist. Her health was frail, but her life was a devoted one, and full of good works. Her consecrated *words* were destined to outlast her by many generations.

"Writing is *praying* with me," she said. Death met her in 1879, when still in the prime of womanhood.

Frances Ridley
Havergal

THE TUNE.

The music that has made this hymn of Miss Havergal familiar in America is named from its first line, and was composed by the lamented Philip P. Bliss (christened Philipp Bliss*), a pupil of Dr. George F. Root.

* Mr. Bliss himself changed the spelling of his name, preferring to let the third P. do duty alone, as a middle initial.

He was born in Rome, Pa., Jan. 9, 1838, and less than thirty-nine years later suddenly ended his life, a victim of the awful railroad disaster at Ashtabula O., Dec. 29, 1876, while returning from a visit to his aged mother. His wife, Lucy Young Bliss, perished with him there, in the swift flames that enveloped the wreck of the train.

The name of Mr. Bliss had become almost a household word through his numerous popular Christian melodies, which were the American beginning of the series of *Gospel Hymns*. Many of these are still favorite prayer-meeting tunes throughout the country and are heard in song-service at Sunday-school and city mission meetings.

"JESUS KEEP ME NEAR THE CROSS."

This hymn, one of the best and probably most enduring of Fanny J. Crosby's sacred lyrics, was inspired by Col. 1:29.

Frances Jane Crosby (Mrs. Van Alstyne) the blind poet and hymnist, was born in Southeast, N.Y., March 24, 1820. She lost her eyesight at the age of six. Twelve years of her younger life were spent in the New York Institution for the Blind, where she became a teacher, and in 1858 was happily married to a fellow inmate, Mr. Alexander Van Alstyne, a musician.

George F. Root was for a time musical instructor at the Institution, and she began early to write words to his popular song-tunes. "Rosalie, the Prairie Flower," and the long favorite melody, "There's Music in the Air" are among the many to which she supplied the text and the song name.

She resides in Bridgeport, Ct., where she enjoys a serene and happy old age. She has written over six thousand hymns, and possibly will add other pearls to the cluster before she goes up to join the singing saints.

Jesus, keep me near the Cross,
There a precious Fountain
Free to all, a healing stream,
Flows from Calv'ry's mountain.
CHORUS.
In the Cross, in the Cross
Be my glory ever,
Till my raptured soul shall find
Rest beyond the river.

*   *   *   *   *   *

Near the Cross! O Lamb of God,
Bring its scenes before me;
Help me walk from day to day
With its shadows o'er me.
CHORUS.

William Howard Doane, writer of the music to this hymn, was born in Preston, Ct., Feb. 3, 1831. He studied at Woodstock Academy, and subsequently acquired a musical education which earned him the degree of Doctor of Music conferred upon him by Denison University in 1875. Having a mechanical as well as musical gift, he patented more than seventy inventions, and was for some years engaged with manufacturing concerns, both as employee and manager, but his interest in song-worship and in Sunday-school and church work never abated, and he is well known as a trainer of choirs and composer of some of the best modern devotional tunes. His home is in Cincinnati, O.

"I WOULD NOT LIVE ALWAY."

This threnody (we may almost call it) of W.A. Muhlenberg, illustrating one phase of Christian experience, was the outpouring of a poetic melancholy not uncommon to young and finely strung souls. He composed it in his twenties,—long before he became "Doctor" Muhlenberg,—and for years afterwards tried repeatedly to alter it to a more cheerful tone. But the poem had its mission, and it had fastened itself in the public imagination, either by its contagious sentiment or the felicity of its tune, and the author was obliged to accept the fame of it as it originally stood.

William Augustus Muhlenberg D.D. was born in Philadelphia, Sept. 16, 1796, the great-grandson of Dr. Henry M. Muhlenberg, founder of the Lutheran church in America. In 1817 he left his ancestral communion, and became an Episcopal priest.

As Rector of St. James church, Lancaster, Pa., he interested himself in the improvement of ecclesiastical hymnody, and did much good reforming work. After a noble and very active life as promoter of religious education and Christian union, and as a friend and benefactor of the poor, he died April, 8, 1877, in St. Luke's Hospital, N.Y.

THE TUNE.

This was composed by Mr. George Kingsley in 1833, and entitled "Frederick" (dedicated to the Rev. Frederick T. Gray). Issued first as sheet music, it became popular, and soon found a place in the hymnals. Dr. Louis Benson says of the conditions and the fancy of the time, "The standard of church music did not differ materially from that of parlor music.... Several editors have attempted to put a newer tune in the place of Mr. Kingsley's. It was in vain, simply because words and melody both appeal to the same taste."

"SUN OF MY SOUL, MY SAVIOUR DEAR."

This gem from Keble's *Christian Year* illustrates the life and character of its pious author, and, like all the hymns of that celebrated collection, is an incitive to spiritual thought for the thoughtless, as well as a language for those who stand in the Holy of Holies.

The Rev. John Keble was born in Caln, St. Aldwyn, April 25, 1792. He took his degree of A.M. and was ordained and settled at Fairford, where he began the parochial work that ceased only with his life. He died at Bournmouth, March 29, 1866.

His settlement at Fairford, in charge of three small curacies, satisfied his modest ambition, though altogether they brought him only about £100 per year. Here he preached, wrote his hymns and translations, performed his pastoral work, and was happy. Temptation to wider fields and larger salary never moved him.

THE TUNE.

The music to this hymn of almost unparalleled poetic and spiritual beauty was arranged from a German Choral of Peter Ritter (1760–1846) by William Henry Monk, Mus. Doc., born London, 1823. Dr. Monk was a lecturer, composer, editor, and professor of vocal music at King's College. This noble tune appears sometimes under the name "Hursley" and supersedes an earlier one ("Halle") by Thomas Hastings.

> Sun of my soul, my Saviour dear,
> It is not night if Thou be near.
> O may no earth-born cloud arise
> To hide Thee from Thy servants' eyes.
> *   *   *   *   *   *
> Abide with me from morn till eve,
> For without Thee I cannot live
> Abide with me when night is nigh,
> For without Thee I cannot die.

The tune "Hursley" is a choice example of polyphonal sweetness in uniform long notes of perfect chord.

The tune of "Canonbury," by Robert Schumann, set to Keble's hymn, "New every morning is the love," is deservedly a favorite for flowing long metres, but it could never replace "Hursley" with "Sun of my soul."

"DID CHRIST O'ER SINNERS WEEP?"

The Rev. Benjamin Beddome wrote this tender hymn-poem while pastor of the Baptist Congregation at Bourton-on-the-water, Gloucestershire, Eng. He was born at Henley, Chatwickshire, Jan. 23, 1717. Settled in 1743, he remained with the same church till his death, Sept. 3, 1795. His hymns were not collected and published till 1818.

THE TUNE.

"Dennis," a soft and smoothly modulated harmony, is oftenest sung to the words, and has no note out of sympathy with their deep feeling.

> Did Christ o'er sinners weep,
> And shall our cheeks be dry?
> Let floods of penitential grief
> Burst forth from every eye.
> The Son of God in tears
> Admiring angels see!
> Be thou astonished, O my soul;
> He shed those tears for thee.
> He wept that we might weep;
> Each sin demands a tear:
> In heaven alone no sin is found,
> And there's no weeping there.

The tune of "Dennis" was adapted by Lowell Mason from Johann Georg Nägeli, a Swiss music publisher, composer and poet. He was born in Zurich, 1768. It is told of him that his irrepressible genius once tempted him to violate the ethics of authorship. While publishing Beethoven's three great solo sonatas (Opus 31) he interpolated two bars of his own, an act much commented upon in musical circles, but which does not seem to have cost him Beethoven's friendship. Possibly, likeMurillo to the servant who meddled with his paintings, the great master forgave the liberty, because the work was so good.

Nägeli's compositions are mostly vocal, for school and church use, though some are of a gay and playful nature. The best remembered of his secular and sacred styles are his blithe aria to the song of Moore, "Life let us cherish, while yet the taper glows" and the sweet choral that voices Beddome's hymn.

"MY JESUS, I LOVE THEE."

The real originator of the *Coronation Hymnal*, a book into whose making went five years of prayer, was Dr. A.J. Gordon, late Pastor of the Clarendon St. Baptist church, Boston. While the volume was slowly taking form and plan he was wont to hum to himself, or cause to be played by

58

one of his family, snatches and suggestions of new airs that came to him in connection with his own hymns, and others which seemed to have no suitable music. The anonymous hymn, "My Jesus, I Love Thee," he found in a London hymn-book, and though the tune to which it had been sung in England was sent to him some time later, it did not sound sympathetic. Dissatisfied, and with the ideal in his mind of what the feeling should be in the melody to such a hymn, he meditated and prayed over the words till in a moment of inspiration the beautiful air sang itself to him* which with its simple concords has carried the hymn into the chapels of every denomination.

* The fact that this sweet melody recalls to some a similar tune sung sixty years ago reminds us again of the story of the tune "America." It is not impossible that an unconscious *memory* helped to shape the air that came to Dr. Gordon's mind; though unborrowed similarities have been inevitable in the whole history of music.

My Jesus, I love Thee, I know Thou art mine,
For Thee all the pleasures of sin I resign;
My gracious Redeemer, my Saviour art Thou,
If ever I loved Thee, my Jesus, 'tis now.
*　　*　　*　　*　　*　　*
I will love Thee in life, I will love Thee in death,
And praise Thee as long as Thou lendest me breath,
And say when the death-dew lies cold on my brow,
If ever I loved Thee, my Jesus, 'tis now.
In mansions of glory and endless delight
I'll ever adore Thee, unveiled to my sight,
And sing, with the glittering crown on my brow,
If ever I loved Thee, my Jesus, 'tis now.

The memory of the writer returns to a day in a railway-car en route to the great Columbian Fair in Chicago when the tired passengers were suddenly surprised and charmed by the music of this melody. A young Christian man and woman, husband and wife, had begun to sing "My Jesus, I love Thee." Their voices (a tenor and soprano) were clear and sweet, and every one of the company sat up to listen with a look of mingled admiration and relief. Here was something, after all, to make a long journey less tedious. They sang all the four verses and paused. There was no clapping of hands, for a reverential hush had been cast over the audience by the sacred music. Instead of the inevitable applause that follows mere entertainment, a gentle but eager request for more secured the repetition of the delightful duet. This occurred again and again, till every one in the car—and some had never heard the tune or words before—must have learned them by heart. Fatigue was forgotten, miles had been reduced to furlongs in a weary trip, and a company of strangers had been lifted to a holier plane of thought.

Besides this melody there are four tunes by Dr. Gordon in his collection, three of them with his own words. In all there are eleven of his hymns. Of these the "Good morning in Glory," set to his music, is an emotional lyric admirable in revival meetings, and the one beginning "O Holy Ghost, Arise" is still sung, and called for affectionately as "Gordon's Hymn."

Rev. Adoniram Judson Gordon D.D. was born in New Hampton, N.H., April 19, 1836, and died in Boston, Feb. 2d, 1895, after a life of unsurpassed usefulness to his fellowmen and devotion to his Divine Master. Like Phillips Brooks he went to his grave "in all his glorious prime," and his loss is equally lamented. He was a descendant of John Robinson of Leyden.

CHAPTER IV.

MISSIONARY HYMNS.

"JESUS SHALL REIGN WHERE'ER THE SUN."

One of Watts' sublimest hymns, this Hebrew ode to the final King and His endless dominion expands the majestic prophesy in the seventy-second Psalm:

Jesus shall reign where'er the sun
Does his successive journeys run,
His kingdom stretch from shore to shore
Till moons shall wax and wane no more.

The hymn itself could almost claim to be known "where'er the sun" etc., for Christian missionaries have sung it in every land, if not in every language.

One of the native kings in the South Sea Islands, who had been converted through the ministry of English missionaries, substituted a Christian for a pagan constitution in 1862. There were five thousand of his subjects gathered at the ceremonial, and they joined as with one voice in singing this hymn.

THE TUNE.

"Old Hundred" has often lent the notes of its great plain-song to the sonorous lines, and "Duke Street," with superior melody and scarcely inferior grandeur, has given them wings; but the choice of many for music that articulates the life of the hymn would be the tune of "Samson," from Handel's Oratorio so named. It appears as No. 469 in the *Evangelical Hymnal*.

Handel had no peer in the art or instinct of making a note speak a word.

"JOY TO THE WORLD! THE LORD IS COME!"

This hymn, also by Watts, is often sung as a Christmas song; but "The Saviour Reigns" and "He Rules the World" are bursts of prophetic triumph always apt and stimulating in missionary meetings.

Here, again, the great Handel lends appropriate aid, for "Antioch," the popular tone-consort of the hymn, is an adaptation from his "Messiah." The arrangement has been credited to Lowell Mason, but he seems to have taken it from an English collection by Clark of Canterbury.

"O'ER THE GLOOMY HILLS OF DARKNESS."

Dros y brinian tywyl niwliog.

This notable hymn was written, probably about 1750, by the Rev. William Williams, a Welsh Calvinistic Methodist, born at Cefnycoed, Jan. 7, 1717, near Llandovery. He began the study of medicine, but took deacon's orders, and was for a time an itinerant preacher, having left the established Church. Died at Pantycelyn, Jan. 1, 1781.

His hymn, like the two preceding, antedates the great Missionary Movement by many years.

O'er the gloomy hills of darkness
Look my soul! be still, and gaze!
See the promises advancing
To a glorious Day of grace!
Blessed Jubilee,
Let thy glorious morning dawn!
Let the dark, benighted pagan,
Let the rude barbarian see
That divine and glorious conquest
Once obtained on Calvary.
Let the Gospel
Loud resound from pole to pole.

This song of anticipation has dropped out of the modern hymnals, but the last stanza lingers in many memories.

Fly abroad, thou mighty Gospel!
Win and conquer, never cease;
May thy lasting wide dominion
Multiply and still increase.
Sway Thy scepter,
Saviour, all the world around!

THE TUNE.

Oftener than any other the music of "Zion" has been the expression of William Williams' Missionary Hymn. It was composed by Thomas Hastings, in Washington, Ct., 1830.

"HASTEN, LORD, THE GLORIOUS TIME."

Hasten, Lord, the glorious time
When beneath Messiah's sway
Every nation, every clime
Shall the Gospel call obey.
Mightiest kings its power shall own,
Heathen tribes His name adore,
Satan and his host o'erthrown
Bound in chains shall hurt no more.

Miss Harriet Auber, the author of this melodious hymn, was a daughter of James Auber of London, and was born in that city, Oct. 4, 1773. After leaving London she led a secluded life at Broxbourne and Hoddesdon, in Hertfordshire, writing devotional poetry and sacred songs and paraphrases.

60

Her *Spirit of the Psalms*, published in 1829, was a collection of lyrics founded on the Biblical Psalms. "Hasten Lord," etc., is from Ps. 72, known for centuries to Christendom as one of the Messianic Psalms. Her best-known hymns have the same inspiration, as—

Wide, ye heavenly gates, unfold.

Sweet is the work, O Lord.

With joy we hail the sacred day.

Miss Auber died in Hoddesdon, Jan. 20, 1862. She lived to witness and sympathise with the pioneer missionary enterprise of the 19th century, and, although she could not stand among the leaders of the battle-line in extending the conquest of the world for Christ, she was happy in having written a campaign hymn which they loved to sing. (It is curious that so pains-taking a work as Julian's *Dictionary of Hymns and Hymn-writers* credits "With joy we hail the sacred day" to both Miss Auber and Henry Francis Lyte. Coincidences are known where different hymns by different authors begin with the same line; and in this case one writer was dead before the other's works were published. Possibly the collector may have seen a forgotten hymn of Lyte's, with that first line.)

The tune that best interprets this hymn in spirit and in living *music* is Lowell Mason's "Eltham." Its harmony is like a chime of bells.

"LET PARTY NAMES NO MORE."

Let party names no more

The Christian world o'erspread;

Gentile and Jew, and bond and free,

Are one in Christ the Head.

This hymn of Rev. Benjamin Beddome sounds like a prelude to the grand rally of the Christian Churches a generation later for united advance into foreign fields. It was an after-sermon hymn—like so many of Watts and Doddridge—and spoke a good man's longing to see all sects stand shoulder to shoulder in a common crusade.

Tune—Boylston.

"WATCHMAN, TELL US OF THE NIGHT."

The tune written to this pealing hymn of Sir John Bowring by Lowell Mason has never been superseded. In animation and vocal splendor it catches the author's own clear call, echoing the shout of Zion's sentinels from city to city, and happily reproducing in movement and phrase the great song-dialogue. Words and music together, the piece ranks with the foremost missionary lyrics. Like the greater Mason-Heber world-song, it has acquired no arbitrary name, appearing in Mason's own tune-books under its first hymn-line and likewise in many others. A few hymnals have named it "Bowring," (and why not?) and some later ones simply "Watchman."

1.

Watchman, tell us of the night.

What its signs of promise are!

(Antistrophe)

Traveler, on yon mountain height.

See that glory-beaming star!

2

Watchman, does its beauteous ray

Aught of hope or joy foretell?

(Antistrophe)

Trav'ler, yes; it brings the day,

Promised day of Israel.

3

Watchman, tell us of the night;

Higher yet that star ascends.

(Antistrophe)

Trav'ler, blessedness and light

Peace and truth its course portends.

4

Watchman, will its beams alone

Gild the spot that gave them birth?

(Antistrophe)

Trav'ler, ages are its own.

See! it bursts o'er all the earth.

"YE CHRISTIAN HERALDS, GO PROCLAIM."

In some versions "Ye Christian *heroes*," etc.

Professor David R. Breed attributes this stirring hymn to Mrs. Vokes (or Voke) an English or Welsh lady, who is supposed to have written it somewhere near 1780, and supports the claim by its date of publication in *Missionary and Devotional Hymns* at Portsea, Wales, in 1797. In this Dr. Breed follows (he says) "the accepted tradition." On the other hand the *Coronation Hymnal* (1894) refers the authorship to a Baptist minister, the Rev. Bourne Hall Draper, of Southampton (Eng.), born 1775, and this choice has the approval of Dr. Charles Robinson. The question occurs whether, when the hymn was published in good faith as Mrs. Vokes', it was really the work of a then unknown youth of twenty-two.

The probability is that the hymn owns a mother instead of a father—and a grand hymn it is; one of the most stimulating in Missionary song-literature.

The stanza—

God shield you with a wall of fire!
With flaming zeal your breasts inspire;
Bid raging winds their fury cease,
And hush the tumult into peace,

—has been tampered with by editors, altering the last line to "Calm the troubled seas," etc., (for the sake of the longer vowel;) but the substitution, "*He'll* shield you," etc., in the first line, turns a prayer into a mere statement.

The hymn was—and should remain—a God-speed to men like William Carey, who had already begun to think and preach his immortal motto, "Attempt great things for God; expect great things of God."

THE TUNE

Is the "Missionary Chant," and no other. Its composer, Heinrich Christopher Zeuner, was born in Eisleben, Saxony, Sept. 20, 1795. He came to the United States in 1827, and was for many years organist at Park Street Church, Boston, and for the Handel and Haydn Society. In 1854 he removed to Philadelphia where he served three years as organist to St. Andrews Church, and Arch Street Presbyterian. He became insane in 1857, and in November of that year died by his own hand.

He published an oratorio "The Feast of Tabernacles," and two popular books, the *American Harp*, 1832, and *The Ancient Lyre*, 1833. His compositions are remarkably spirited and vigorous, and his work as a tune-maker was much in demand during his life, and is sure to continue, in its best examples, as long as good sacred music is appreciated.

To another beautiful missionary hymn of Mrs. Vokes, of quieter tone, but songful and sweet, Dr. Mason wrote the tune of "Migdol." It is its musical twin.

Soon may the last glad song arise
Through all the millions of the skies,
That song of triumph which records
That "all the earth is now the Lord's."

"ON THE MOUNTAIN TOP APPEARING."

This admired and always popular church hymn was written near the beginning of the last century by the Rev. Thomas Kelly, born in Dublin, 1760. He was the son of the Hon. Chief Baron Thomas Kelly of that city, a judge of the Irish Court of Common Pleas. His father designed him for the legal profession, but after his graduation at Trinity College he took holy orders in the Episcopal Church, and labored as a clergyman among the scenes of his youth for more than sixty years, becoming a Nonconformist in his later ministry. He was a sweet-souled man, who made troops of friends, and was honored as much for his piety as for his poetry, music, and oriental learning.

"I expect never to die," he said, when Lord Plunkett once told him he would reach a great age. He finished his earthly work on the 14th of May, 1855, when he was eighty-five years old. But he still lives. His zeal for the coming of the Kingdom of Christ prompted his best hymn.

On the mountain-top appearing,
Lo! the sacred herald stands,
Joyful news to Zion bearing,
Zion long in hostile lands;
Mourning captive,
God himself will loose thy bands.
Has the night been long and mournful?
Have thy friends unfaithful proved?
Have thy foes been proud and scornful,
By thy sighs and tears unmoved?
Cease thy mourning;
Zion still is well beloved.

62

To presume that Kelly made both words and music together is possible, for he was himself a composer, but no such original tune seems to survive. In modern use Dr. Hastings' "Zion" is most frequently attached to the hymn, and was probably written for it.

"YE CHRISTIAN HEROES, WAKE TO GLORY."

This rather crude parody on the "Marseillaise Hymn" (see Chap. 9) is printed in the *American Vocalist*, among numerous samples of early New England psalmody of untraced authorship. It might have been sung at primitive missionary meetings, to spur the zeal and faith of a Francis Mason or a Harriet Newell. It expresses, at least, the new-kindled evangelical spirit of the long-ago consecrations in American church life that first sent the Christian ambassadors to foreign lands, and followed them with benedictions.

Ye Christian heroes, wake to glory:
Hark, hark! what millions bid you rise!
See heathen nations bow before you,
Behold their tears, and hear their cries.
Shall pagan priest, their errors breeding,
With darkling hosts, and flags unfurled,
Spread their delusions o'er the world,
Though Jesus on the Cross hung bleeding?
To arms! To arms!
Christ's banner fling abroad!
March on! March on! all hearts resolved
To bring the world to God.

O, Truth of God! can man resign thee,
Once having felt thy glorious flame?
Can rolling oceans e'er prevent thee,
Or gold the Christian's spirit tame?
Too long we slight the world's undoing;
The word of God, salvation's plan,
Is yet almost unknown to man,
While millions throng the road to ruin.
To arms! to arms!
The Spirit's sword unsheath:
March on! March on! all hearts resolved,
To victory or death.

"HAIL TO THE LORD'S ANOINTED."

James Montgomery (says Dr. Breed) is "distinguished as the only layman besides Cowper among hymn-writers of the front rank in the English language." How many millions have recited and sung his fine and exhaustively descriptive poem,—

Prayer is the soul's sincere desire,

—selections from almost any part of which are perfect definitions, and have been standard hymns on prayer for three generations. English Hymnology would as unwillingly part with his missionary hymns,—

The king of glory we proclaim.
Hark, the song of jubilee!

—and, noblest of all, the lyric of prophecy and praise which heads this paragraph.

Hail to the Lord's anointed,
King David's greater Son!
Hail, in the time appointed
His reign on earth begun.
*   *   *   *   *   *

Arabia's desert ranger
To Him shall bow the knee,
The Ethiopian stranger
His glory come to see.
*   *   *   *   *   *

Kings shall fall down before Him
And gold and incense bring;
All nations shall adore Him,
His praise all people sing.

The hymn is really the seventy-second Psalm in metre, and as a version it suffers nothing by comparison with that of Watts. Montgomery wrote it as a Christmas ode. It was sung Dec. 25,

1821, at a Moravian Convocation, but in 1822 he recited it at a great missionary meeting in Liverpool, and Dr. Adam Clarke was so charmed with it that he inserted it in his famous *Commentary*. In no long time afterwards it found its way into general use.

The spirit of his missionary parents was Montgomery's Christian legacy, and in exalted poetical moments it stirred him as the divine afflatus kindled the old prophets.

THE TUNE.

The music editors in some hymnals have borrowed the favorite choral variously named "Webb" in honor of its author, and "The Morning Light is Breaking" from the first line of its hymn. Later hymnals have chosen Sebastian Wesley's "Aurelia" to fit the hymn, with a movement similar to that of "Webb"; also a German B flat melody "Ellacombe," undated, with livelier step and a ringing chime of parts. No one of these is inappropriate.

Samuel Sebastian Wesley, grandson of Charles Wesley the great hymnist, was born in London, 1810. Like his father, Samuel, he became a distinguished musician, and was organist at Exeter, Winchester and Gloucester Cathedrals. Oxford gave him the degree of Doctor of Music. He composed instrumental melodies besides many anthems, services, and other sacred pieces for choir and congregational singing. Died in Gloucester, April 19, 1876.

The Right Rev. Reginald
Heber, D.D.

"FROM GREENLAND'S ICY MOUNTAINS."

The familiar story of this hymn scarcely needs repeating; how one Saturday afternoon in the year 1819, young Reginald Heber, Rector of Hodnet, sitting with his father-in-law, Dean Shipley, and a few friends in the Wrexham Vicarage, was suddenly asked by the Dean to "write something to sing at the missionary meeting tomorrow," and retired to another part of the room while the rest went on talking; how, very soon after, he returned with three stanzas, which were hailed with delighted approval; how he then insisted upon adding another octrain to the hymn and came back with—

Waft, waft, ye winds, His story,
And you, ye waters, roll;

—and how the great lyric was sung in Wrexham Church on Sunday morning for the first time in its life. The story is old but always fresh. Nothing could better have emphasized the good Dean's sermon that day in aid of "The Society for the Propagation of the Gospel in Foreign Parts," than that unexpected and glorious lyric of his poet son-in-law.

By common consent Heber's "Missionary Hymn" is the silver trumpet among all the rallying bugles of the church.

THE TUNE.

The union of words and music in this instance is an example of spiritual affinity. "What God hath joined together let no man put asunder." The story of the tune is a record of providential birth quite as interesting as that of the hymn. In 1823, a lady in Savannah, Ga., having received and admired a copy of Heber's lyric from England, desired to sing it or hear it sung, but knew no music to fit the metre. She finally thought of a young clerk in a bank close by, Lowell Mason by name, who sometimes wrote music for recreation, and sent her son to ask him if he would make a tune that would sing the lines. The boy returned in half an hour with the composition that doubled Heber's fame and made his own.

In the words of Dr. Charles Robinson, "Like the hymn it voices, it was done at a stroke, and it will last through the ages."

"THE MORNING LIGHT IS BREAKING."

Not far behind Dr. Heber's *chef-d'œuvre* in lyric merit is the still more famous missionary hymn of Dr. S.F. Smith, author of "My Country, 'Tis of Thee." Another missionary hymn of his which is widely used is—

Yes, my native land, I love thee,
All thy scenes, I love them well.

Friends, connections, happy country,
Can I bid you all farewell?
Can I leave you
Far in heathen lands to dwell?

Drs. Nutter and Breed speak of "The Morning Light is Breaking," and its charm as a hymn of peace and promise, and intimate that it has "gone farther and been more frequently sung than any other missionary hymn." Besides the English, there are versions of it in four Latin nations, the Italian, Spanish, Portuguese and French, and oriental translations in Chinese and several East Indian tongues and dialects, as well as one in Swedish. It author had the rare felicity, while on a visit to his son, a missionary in Burmah, of hearing it sung by native Christians in their language, and of being welcomed with an ovation when they knew who he was.

The morning light is breaking!
The darkness disappears;
The sons of earth are waking
To penitential tears;
Each breeze that sweeps the ocean
Brings tidings from afar,
Of nations in commotion,
Prepared for Zion's war.
Rich dews of grace come o'er us
In many a gentle shower,
And brighter scenes before us
Are opening every hour.
Each cry to heaven going
Abundant answer brings,
And heavenly gales are blowing
With peace upon their wings.

*   *   *   *   *   *

Blest river of Salvation,
Pursue thy onward way;
Flow thou to every nation,
Nor in thy richness stay.
Stay not till all the lowly
Triumphant reach their home;
Stay not till all the holy
Proclaim, "The Lord is come!"

Samuel Francis Smith, D.D., was born in Boston in 1808, and educated in Harvard University (1825–1829). He prepared for the ministry, and was pastor of Baptist churches at Waterville, Me., and Newton, Mass., before entering the service of the American Baptist Missionary union as editor of its *Missionary Magazine*.

He was a scholarly and graceful writer, both in verse and prose, and besides his editorial work, he was frequently an invited participant or guest of honor on public occasions, owing to his fame as author of the national hymn. His pure and gentle character made him everywhere beloved and reverenced, and to know him intimately in his happy old age was a benediction. He died suddenly and painlessly in his seat on a railway train, November 16, 1895 in his eighty-eighth year.

Dr. Smith wrote twenty-six hymns now more or less in use in church worship, and eight for Sabbath school collections.

THE TUNE.

"Millennial Dawn" is the title given it by a Boston compiler, about 1844, but since the music and hymn became "one and indivisable" it has been named "Webb," and popularly *known* as "Morning Light" or oftener still by its first hymn-line, "The morning light is breaking."

George James Webb was born near Salisbury, Wiltshire, Eng., June 24, 1803. He studied music in Salisbury and for several years played the organ at Falmouth Church. When still a young man (1830), he came to the United States, and settled in Boston where he was long the leading organist and music teacher of the city. He was associate director of the Boston Academy of Music with Lowell Mason, and joint author and editor with him of several church-music collections. Died in Orange, N.J., Nov. 7, 1887.

65

James Webb

Dr. Webb's own account of the tune "Millennial Dawn" states that he wrote it at sea while on his way to America—and to secular words and that he had no idea who first adapted it to the hymn, nor when.

"IF I WERE A VOICE, A PERSUASIVE VOICE."

This animating lyric was written by Charles Mackay. Sung by a good vocalist, the fine solo air composed (with its organ chords) by I.B. Woodbury, is still a feature in some missionary meetings, especially the fourth stanza—

If I were a voice, an immortal voice,
I would fly the earth around:
And wherever man to his idols bowed,
I'd publish in notes both long and loud
The Gospel's joyful sound.
I would fly, I would fly, on the wings of day,
Proclaiming peace on my world-wide way,
Bidding the saddened earth rejoice—
If I were a voice, an immortal voice,
I would fly, I would fly,
I would fly on the wings of day.

Charles Mackay, the poet, was born in Perth, Scotland, 1814, and educated in London and Brussels; was engaged in editorial work on the *London Morning Chronicle* and *Glasgow Argus*, and during the Corn Law agitation wrote popular songs, notably "The Voice of the Crowd" and "There's a Good Time Coming," which (like the far inferior poetry of Ebenezer Elliot) won the lasting love of the masses for a superior man who could be "The People's Singer and Friend." He came to the United States in 1857 as a lecturer, and again in 1862, remaining three years as war correspondent of the *London Times*. Glasgow University made him LL.D. in 1847. His numerous songs and poems were collected in a London edition. Died Dec. 24, 1889.

Isaac Baker Woodbury was born in Beverly, Mass., 1819, and rose from the station of a blacksmith's apprentice to be a tone-teacher in the church. He educated himself in Europe, returned and sang his life songs, and died in 1858 at the age of thirty-nine.

A tune preferred by many as the finer music is the one written to the words by Mr. Sankey, *Sacred Songs*, No. 2.

"SPEED AWAY! SPEED AWAY!"

This inspiriting song of farewell to departing missionaries was written in 1890 to Woodbury's appropriate popular melody by Fanny J. Crosby, at the request of Ira D. Sankey. The key-word and refrain are adapted from the original song by Woodbury (1848), but in substance and language the three hymn-stanzas are the new and independent work of this later writer.

Speed away! speed away on your mission of light,
To the lands that are lying in darkness and night;
'Tis the Master's command; go ye forth in His name,
The wonderful gospel of Jesus proclaim;
Take your lives in your hand, to the work while 'tis day,
Speed away! speed away! speed away!
Speed away, speed away with the life-giving Word,
To the nations that know not the voice of the Lord;
Take the wings of the morning and fly o'er the wave,
In the strength of your Master the lost ones to save;
He is calling once more, not a moment's delay,
Speed away! speed away! speed away!
Speed away, speed away with the message of rest,

To the souls by the tempter in bondage oppressed;
For the Saviour has purchased their ransom from sin,
And the banquet is ready. O gather them in;
To the rescue make haste, there's no time for delay,
Speed away! speed away! speed away!

"ONWARD CHRISTIAN SOLDIERS!"

Rev. Sabine Baring-Gould, the author of this rousing hymn of Christian warfare, a rector of the Established Church of England and a writer of note, was born at Exeter, Eng., Jan. 28, 1834. Educated at Clare College, Cambridge, he entered the service of the church, and was appointed Rector of East Mersea, Essex, in 1871. He was the author of several hymns, original and translated, and introduced into England from Flanders, numbers of carols with charming old Christmas music. The "Christian Soldiers" hymn is one of his (original) processionals, and the most inspiring.

Onward, Christian soldiers,
Marching as to war,
With the cross of Jesus
Going on before.
Christ the Royal Master
Leads against the foe;
Forward into battle,
See, His banners go!
Onward, Christian soldiers, etc.
*   *   *   *   *

Like a mighty army
Moves the Church of God;
Brothers, we are treading
Where the saints have trod;
We are not divided,
All one body we,
One in hope, in doctrine,
One in charity.

THE TUNE.

Sir Arthur Seymour Sullivan, Doctor of Music, who wrote the melody for this hymn, was born in London, May 13, 1842. He gained the Mendelssohn Scholarship at the Royal Academy of Music, and also at the Conservatory of Leipsic. He was a fertile genius, and his compositions included operettas, symphonies, overtures, anthems, hymn-tunes, an oratorio ("The Prodigal Son"), and almost every variety of tone production, vocal and instrumental. Queen Victoria knighted him in 1883.

The grand rhythm of "Onward, Christian Soldiers"—hymn and tune—is irresistible whether in band march or congregational worship. Sir Arthur died in London, November 22, 1900.

"O CHURCH ARISE AND SING"

Designed originally for children's voices, the hymn of five stanzas beginning with this line was written by Hezekiah Butterworth, author of the *Story of the Hymns* (1875), *Story of the Tunes* (1890), and many popular books of historic interest for the young, the most widely read of which is *Zigzag Journeys in Many Lands*. He also composed and published many poems and hymns. He was born in Warren, R.I., Dec. 22, 1839, and for twenty-five years was connected with the *Youth's Companion* as regular contributor and member of its editorial staff. He died in Warren, R.I., Sept. 5, 1905.

The hymn "O Church, arise" was sung in Mason's tune of "Dort" until Prof. Case wrote a melody for it, when it took the name of the "Convention Hymn."

Professor Charles Clinton Case, music composer and teacher, was born in Linesville, Pa., June, 1843. Was a pupil of George F. Root and pursued musical study in Chicago, Ill., Ashland, O., and South Bend, Ind. He was associated with Root, McGranahan, and others in making secular and church music books, and later with D.L. Moody in evangelical work.

As author and compiler he has published numerous works, among them *Church Anthems*, the *Harvest Song* and *Case's Chorus Collection*.

O Church! arise and sing
The triumphs of your King,
Whose reign is love;
Sing your enlarged desires,
That conquering faith inspires,

Renew your signal fires,
And forward move!

*   *   *   *   *   *

Beneath the glowing arch
The ransomed armies march,
We follow on;
Lead on, O cross of Light,
From conquering height to height,
And add new victories bright
To triumphs won!

"THE BANNER OF IMMANUEL!"

This hymn, set to music and copyrighted in Buffalo as a floating waif of verse by an unknown author, and used in Sunday-school work, first appeared in Dr. F.N. Peloubet's *Select Songs* (Biglow and Main, 1884) with a tune by Rev. George Phipps.

The hymn was written by Rev. Theron Brown, a Baptist minister, who was pastor (1859–1870) of churches in South Framingham and Canton, Mass. He was born in Willimantic, Ct., April 29, 1832.

Retired from pastoral work, owing to vocal disability, he has held contributory and editorial relations with the *Youth's Companion* for more than forty years, for the last twenty years a member of the office staff.

Between 1880 and 1890 he contributed hymns more or less regularly to the quartet and antiphonal chorus service at the Ruggles St. Church, Boston, the "Banner of Immanuel" being one of the number. *The Blount Family, Nameless Women of the Bible, Life Songs* (a volume of poems), and several books for boys, are among his published works.

The banner of Immanuel! beneath its glorious folds
For life or death to serve and fight we pledge our loyal souls.
No other flag such honor boasts, or bears so proud a name,
And far its red-cross signal flies as flies the lightning's flame.

*   *   *   *   *   *

Salvation by the blood of Christ! the shouts of triumph ring;
No other watchword leads the host that serves so grand a King.
Then rally, soldiers of the Cross! Keep every fold unfurled,
And by Redemption's holy sign we'll conquer all the world.

The Rev. George Phipps, composer of the tune, "Immanuel's Banner," was born in Franklin, Mass., Dec. 11, 1838, was graduated at Amherst College, 1862, and at Andover Theological Seminary, 1865. Settled as pastor of the Congregational Church in Wellesley, Mass., ten years, and at Newton Highlands fifteen years.

He has written many Sunday-school melodies, notably the music to "My Saviour Keeps Me Company."

CHAPTER V.

HYMNS OF SUFFERING AND TRUST.

One inspiring chapter in the compensations of life is the record of immortal verses that were sorrow-born. It tells us in the most affecting way how affliction refines the spirit and "the agonizing throes of thought bring forth glory." Often a broken life has produced a single hymn. It took the long living under trial to shape the supreme experience.

—The anguish of the singer
Made the sweetness of the song.

Indeed, if there had been no sorrow there would have been no song.

"MY LORD, HOW FULL OF SWEET CONTENT."

Jeanne M.B. de la Mothe—known always as Madame Guyon—the lady who wrote these words in exile, probably sang more "songs in the night" than any hymn-writer outside of the Dark Ages. She was born at Montargis, France, in 1648, and died in her seventieth year, 1771, in the ancient city of Blois, on the Loire.

A convent-educated girl of high family, a wife at the age of fifteen, and a widow at twenty-eight, her early piety, ridiculed in the dazzling but corrupt society of Louis XIV's time, blossomed through a long life in religious ministries and flowers of sacred poetry.

She became a mystic, and her book *Spiritual Torrents* indicates the impetuous ardors of her soul. It was the way Divine Love came to her. She was the incarnation of the spiritualized Book of Canticles. An induction to these intense subjective visions and raptures had been the remark of a pious old Franciscan father, "Seek God in your heart, and you will find Him."

68

She began to teach as well as enjoy the new light so different from the glitter of the traditional worship. But her "aggressive holiness" was obnoxious to the established Church. "Quietism" was the brand set upon her written works and the offense that was punished in her person. Bossuet, the king of preachers, was her great adversary. The saintly Fenelon was her friend, but he could not shield her. She was shut up like a lunatic in prison after prison, till, after four years of dungeon life in the Bastile, expecting every hour to be executed for heresy, she was banished to a distant province to end her days.

Question as we may the usefulness of her pietistic books, the visions of her excessively exalted moods, and the passionate, almost erotic phraseology of her *Contemplations*, Madame Guyon has held the world's admiration for her martyr spirit, and even her love-flights of devotion in poetry and prose do not conceal the angel that walked in the flame.

Today, when religious persecution is unknown, we can but dimly understand the perfect triumph of her superior soul under suffering and the transports of her utter absorption in God that could make the stones of her dungeon "look like jewels." When we emulate a faith like hers—with all the weight of absolute certainty in it—we can sing her hymn:

My Lord, how full of sweet content
I pass my years of banishment.
Where'er I dwell, I dwell with Thee,
In heaven or earth, or on the sea.
To me remains nor place nor time:
My country is in every clime;
I can be calm and free from care
On any shore, since God is there.

And could a dearer *vade mecum* enrich a Christian's outfit than these lines treasured in memory?

While place we seek or place we shun,
The soul finds happiness in none;
But, with a God to guide our way,
'Tis equal joy to go or stay.

Cowper, and also Dr. Thomas Upham, translated (from the French) the religious poems of Madame Guyon. This hymn is Cowper's translation.

THE TUNE.

A gentle and sympathetic melody entitled "Alsace" well represents the temper of the words—and in name links the nationalities of writer and composer. It is a choral arranged from a sonata of the great Ludwig von Beethoven, born in Bonn, Germany, 1770, and died in Vienna, Mar. 1827. Like the author of the hymn he felt the hand of affliction, becoming totally deaf soon after his fortieth year. But, in spite of the privation, he kept on writing sublime and exquisite strains that only his soul could hear. His fame rests upon his oratorio, "The Mount of Olives," the opera of "Fidelio" and his nine wonderful "Symphonies."

"NO CHANGE IN TIME SHALL EVER SHOCK."

Altered to common metre from the awkward long metre of Tate and Brady, the three or four stanzas found in earlier hymnals are part of their version (probably Tate's) of the 31st Psalm—and it is worth calling to mind here that there is no hymn treasury so rich in tuneful faith and reliance upon God in trouble as the Book of Psalms. This feeling of the Hebrew poet was never better expressed (we might say, translated) in English than by the writer of this single verse—

No change of time shall ever shock
My trust, O Lord, in Thee,
For Thou hast always been my Rock,
A sure defense to me.

THE TUNE.

The sweet, tranquil choral long ago wedded to this hymn is lost from the church collections, and its very name forgotten. In fact the hymn itself is now seldom seen. If it ever comes back, old "Dundee" (Guillaume Franc 1500–1570) will sing for it, or some new composer may rise up to put the spirit of the psalm into inspired notes.

"WHY DO WE MOURN DEPARTED FRIENDS?"

This hymn of holy comfort, by Dr. Watts, was long associated with a remarkable tune in C minor, "a queer medley of melody" as Lowell Mason called it, still familiar to many old people as "China." It was composed by Timothy Swan when he was about twenty-six years of age (1784) and published in 1801 in the *New England Harmony*. It may have sounded consolatory to mature mourners, singers and hearers in the days when religious emotion habitually took a sad key, but its wild and thrilling chords made children weep. The tune is long out of use—though, strange to say, one of the most recent hymnals prints the hymn with a *new minor* tune.

> Why do we mourn departed friends,
> Or shake at death's alarms?
> 'Tis but the voice that Jesus sends
> To call them to His arms.
>
> Are we not tending upward too
> As fast as time can move?
> Nor should we wish the hours more slow
> To keep us from our Love.
>
> The graves of all His saints He blessed
> And softened every bed:
> Where should the dying members rest
> But with their dying Head?

Timothy Swan was born in Worcester, Mass., July 23, 1758, and died in Suffield, Ct., July 23, 1842. He was a self-taught musician, his only "course of study" lasting three weeks,—in a country singing school at Groton. When sixteen years old he went to Northfield, Mass., and learned the hatter's trade, and while at work began to practice making psalm-tunes. "Montague," in two parts, was his first achievement. From that time for thirty years, mostly spent in Suffield, Ct., he wrote and taught music while supporting himself by his trade. Many of his tunes were published by himself, and had a wide currency a century ago.

Swan was a genius in his way, and it was a true comment on his work that "his tunes were remarkable for their originality as well as singularity—unlike any other melodies." "China," his masterpiece, will be long kept track of as a curio, and preserved in replicates of old psalmody to illustrate self-culture in the art of song. But the major mode will replace the minor when tender voices on burial days sing—

> Why do we mourn departed friends?

Another hymn of Watts,—

> God is the refuge of His saints
> When storms of sharp distress invade,

—sung to Lowell Mason's liquid tune of "Ward," and the priceless stanza,—

> Jesus can make a dying bed
> Feel soft as downy pillows are,

doubly prove the claim of the Southampton bard to a foremost place with the song-preachers of Christian trust.

The psalm (Amsterdam version), "God is the refuge," etc., is said to have been sung by John Howland in the shallop of the Mayflower when an attempt was made to effect a landing in spite of tempestuous weather. A tradition of this had doubtless reached Mrs. Hemans when she wrote—

> Amid the storm they sang, etc.

"FATHER, WHATE'ER OF EARTHLY BLISS."

This hymn had originally ten stanzas, of which the three usually sung are the three last. The above line is the first of the eighth stanza, altered from—

> And O, whate'er of earthly bliss.

Probably for more than a century the familiar surname "Steele" attached to this and many other hymns in the hymn-books conveyed to the general public no hint of a mind and hand more feminine than Cowper's or Montgomery's. Even intelligent people, who had chanced upon sundry copies of *The Spectator*, somehow fell into the habit of putting "Steele" and "Addison" in the same category of hymn names, and Sir Richard Steele got a credit he never sought. But since stories of the hymns began to be published—and made the subject of evening talks in church conference rooms—many have learned what "Steele" in the hymn-book means. It introduces us now to a very retiring English lady, Miss Anna Steele, a Baptist minister's daughter. She was born in 1706, at Broughton, Hampshire, in her father's parsonage, and in her father's parsonage she spent her life, dying there Nov. 1778.

She was many years a severe sufferer from bodily illness, and a lasting grief of mind and heart was the loss of her intended husband, who was drowned the day before their appointed wedding. It is said that this hymn was written under the recent sorrow of that loss.

In 1760 and 1780 volumes of her works in verse and prose were published with her name, "Theodosia," and reprinted in 1863 as "*Hymns, Psalms, and Poems*, by Anna Steele." The hymn "Father, whate'er," etc., is estimated as her best, though some rank it only next to her—

> Dear Refuge of my weary soul.

Other more or less well-known hymns of this devout and loving writer are,—

Lord, how mysterious are Thy ways,
O Thou whose tender mercy hears,
Thou lovely Source of true delight,
Alas, what hourly dangers rise,
So fades the lovely blooming flower.

—to a stanza of which latter the world owes the tune of "Federal St."

THE TUNE.

The true musical mate of the sweet hymn-prayer came to it probably about the time of its hundredth birthday; but it came to stay. Lowell Mason's "Naomi" blends with it like a symphony of nature.

Father, whate'er of earthly bliss
Thy sovereign will denies,
Accepted at Thy throne of grace
Let this petition rise.
Give me a calm and thankful heart
From every murmer free.
The blessings of Thy grace impart,
And make me live to Thee.

"GUIDE ME, O THOU GREAT JEHOVAH."

This great hymn has a double claim on the name of Williams. We do not have it exactly in its original form as written by Rev. William Williams, "The Watts of Wales," familiarly known as "Williams of Pantycelyn." His fellow countryman and contemporary, Rev. Peter Williams, or "Williams of Carmarthen," who translated it from Welsh into English (1771) made alterations and substitutions in the hymn with the result that only the first stanza belongs indisputably to Williams of Pantycelyn, the others being Peter's own or the joint production of the two. As the former, however, is said to have approved and revised the English translation, we may suppose the hymn retained the name of its original author by mutual consent.

Guide me, O Thou Great Jehovah,
Pilgrim through this barren land.
I am weak, but Thou art mighty,
Hold me by Thy powerful hand;
Bread of heaven,
Feed me till I want no more.
Open Thou the crystal Fountain
Whence the healing streams do flow,
Let the fiery cloudy pillar
Lead me all my journey through.
Strong Deliverer,
Be Thou still my Strength and Shield!
When I tread the verge of Jordan
Bid my anxious fears subside;
Death of death, and hell's destruction,
Land me safe on Canaan's side.
Songs of praises
I will ever give to Thee.
Musing on my habitation,
Musing on my heavenly home,
Fills my heart with holy longing;
Come, Lord Jesus, quickly come.
Vanity is all I see,
Lord, I long to be with Thee.

The second and third stanzas have not escaped the touch of critical editors. The line,—

Whence the healing streams do flow

—becomes,—

Whence the healing waters flow,

—with which alteration there is no fault to find except that it is needless, and obliterates the ancient mark. But the third stanza, besides losing its second line for—

Bid the swelling stream divide,

' —is weakened by a more needless substitution. Its original third line—

Death of death, and hell's destruction,

—is exchanged for the commonplace—

Bear me through the swelling current.

71

That is modern taste; but when modern taste meddles with a stalwart old hymn it is sometimes more nice than wise.

It is probable that the famous hymn was sung in America before it obtained a European reputation. Its history is as follows: Lady Huntingdon having read one of Williams' books with much spiritual satisfaction, persuaded him to prepare a collection of hymns, to be called the *Gloria in Excelsis*, for special use in Mr. Whitefield's Orphans' House in America. In this collection appeared the original stanzas of "Guide me, O Thou Great Jehovah." In 1774, two years after its publication in the *Gloria in Excelsis*, it was republished in England in Mr. Whitefield's collections of hymns.

The Rev. Peter Williams was born in the parish of Llansadurnen, Carmarthenshire, Wales, Jan. 7, 1722, and was educated in Carmarthen College. He was ordained in the Established Church and appointed to a curacy, but in 1748 joined the Calvinistic Methodists. He was an Independent of the Independents however, and preached where ever he chose. Finally he built a chapel for himself on his paternal estate, where he ministered during the rest of his life. Died Aug. 8, 1796.

THE TUNE.

If "Sardius," the splendid old choral (triple time) everywhere identified with the hymn, be not its original music, its age at least entitles it to its high partnership. *The Sacred Lyre* (1858) ascribes it to Ludovic Nicholson, of Paisley, Scotland, violinist and amateur composer, born 1770; died 1852; but this is not beyond dispute. Of several names one more confidently referred to as its author is F.H. Barthelemon (1741–1808).

"PEACE, TROUBLED SOUL"

Is the brave faith-song of a Christian under deep but blameless humiliation—Sir Walter Shirley.*

* See page 127

THE TUNE.

Apparently the favorite in several (not recent) hymnals for the subdued but confident spirit of this hymn of Sir Walter Shirley is Mazzinghi's "Palestine," appearing with various tone-signatures in different books. The treble and alto lead in a sweet duet with slur-flights, like an obligato to the bass and tenor. The melody needs rich and cultured voices, and is unsuited for congregational singing. So, perhaps, is the hymn itself.

Peace, troubled soul, whose plaintive moan
Hath taught these rocks the notes of woe;
Cease thy complaint—suppress thy groan,
And let thy tears forget to flow;
Behold the precious balm is found,
To lull thy pain, to heal thy wound.

Come, freely come, by sin oppressed,
Unburden here thy weighty load;
Here find thy refuge and thy rest,
And trust the mercy of thy God.
Thy God's thy Saviour—glorious word!
For ever love and praise the Lord.

As now sung the word "scenes" is substituted for "rocks" in the second line, eliminating the poetry. Rocks give an *echo*; and the vivid thought in the author's mind is flattened to an unmeaning generality.

Count Joseph Mazzinghi, son of Tommasso Mazzinghi, a Corsican musician, was born in London, 1765. He was a boy of precocious talent. When only ten years of age he was appointed organist of the Portuguese Chapel, and when nineteen years old was made musical director and composer at the King's Theatre. For many years he held the honor of Music Master to the Princess of Wales, afterwards Queen Caroline, and his compositions were almost numberless. Some of his songs and glees that caught the popular fancy are still remembered in England, as "The Turnpike Gate," "The Exile," and the rustic duet, "When a Little Farm We Keep."

Of sacred music he composed only one mass and six hymn-tunes, of which latter "Palestine" is one. Mazzinghi died in 1844, in his eightieth year.

"BEGONE UNBELIEF, MY SAVIOUR IS NEAR."

The Rev. John Newton, author of this hymn, was born in London, July 24, 1725. The son of a sea-captain, he became a sailor, and for several years led a reckless life. Converted, he took holy orders and was settled as curate of Olney, Buckinghamshire, and afterwards Rector of St. Mary of Woolnoth, London, where he died, Dec. 21, 1807. It was while living at Olney that he and Cowper wrote and published the *Olney Hymns*. His defiance to doubt in these lines is the blunt utterance of a sailor rather than the song of a poet:

Begone, unbelief, my Saviour is near,
And for my relief will surely appear.
By prayer let me wrestle and He will perform;
With Christ in the vessel I smile at the storm.

THE TUNE

Old "Hanover," by William Croft (1677–1727), carries Newton's hymn successfully, but Joseph Haydn's choral of "Lyons" is more familiar—and better music.

"Hanover" often accompanies Charles Wesley's lyric,—

Ye servants of God, your Master proclaim.

"HOW FIRM A FOUNDATION."

The question of the author of this hymn is treated at length in Dr. Louis F. Benson's *Studies of Familiar Hymns.* The utmost that need to be said here is that two of the most thorough and indefatigable hymn-chasers, Dr. John Julian and Rev. H.L. Hastings, working independently of each other, found evidence fixing the authorship with strong probability upon Robert Keene, a precentor in Dr. John Rippon's church. Dr. Rippon was pastor of a Baptist Church in London from 1773 to 1836, and in 1787 he published a song-manual called *A Selection of Hymns from the Best Authors,* etc., in which "How Firm a Foundation" appears as a new piece, with the signature "K——."

The popularity of the hymn in America has been remarkable, and promises to continue. Indeed, there are few more reviving or more spiritually helpful. It is too familiar to need quotation. But one cannot suppress the last stanza, with its powerful and affecting emphasis on the Divine promise—

The soul that on Jesus has leaned for repose
I will not, I will not, desert to his foes;
That soul, though all hell should endeavor to shake,
I'll never, no never, no never forsake.

THE TUNE.

The grand harmony of "Portuguese Hymn" has always been identified with this song of trust.

One opinion of the date of the music writes it "about 1780." Since the habit of crediting it to John Reading (1677–1764) has been discontinued, it has been in several hymnals ascribed to Marco Portogallo (Mark, the Portuguese), a musician born in Lisbon, 1763, who became a composer of operas in Italy, but was made Chapel-Master to the Portuguese King. In 1807, when Napoleon invaded the Peninsula and dethroned the royal house of Braganza, Old King John VI. fled to Brazil and took Marco with him, where he lived till 1815, but returned and died in Italy, in 1830. Such is the story, and it is all true, only the man's name was Simao, instead of Marco. *Grove's Dictionary* appends to Simao's biography the single sentence, "His brother wrote for the church." That the Brazilian episode may have been connected with this brother's history by a confusion of names, is imaginable, but it is not known that the brother's name was Marco.

On the whole, this account of the authorship of the "Portuguese Hymn"—originally written for the old Christmas church song "Adeste Fideles"—is late and uncertain. Heard (perhaps for the first time) in the Portuguese Chapel, London, it was given the name which still clings to it. If proofs of its Portuguese origin exist, they may yet be found.

"How Firm a Foundation" was the favorite of Deborah Jackson, President Andrew Jackson's beloved wife, and on his death-bed the warrior and statesman called for it. It was the favorite of Gen. Robert E. Lee, and was sung at his funeral. The American love and familiar preference for the remarkable hymn was never more strikingly illustrated than when on Christmas Eve, 1898, a whole corps of the United States army Northern and Southern, encamped on the Quemados hills, near Havana, took up the sacred tune and words—

"Fear not, I am with thee, O be not dismayed."

Lieut. Col. Curtis Guild (since Governor Guild of Massachusetts) related the story in the Sunday School Times for Dec. 7, 1901, and Dr. Benson quotes it in his book.

"WHILE THEE I SEEK, PROTECTING POWER."

Miss Helen Maria Williams, who wrote this gentle hymn of confidence, in 1786, was born in the north of England in 1762. When but a girl she won reputation by her brilliant literary talents and a mental grasp and vigor that led her, like Gail Hamilton, "to discuss public affairs, besides clothing bright fancies and devout thoughts in graceful verse." Most of her life was spent in London, and in Paris, where she died, Dec. 14, 1827.

While Thee I seek, Protecting Power
Be my vain wishes stilled,

73

And may this consecrated hour
With better hopes be filled:

*   *   *   *   *   *

When gladness wings my favored hour,
Thy love my thoughts shall fill,
Resigned where storms of sorrow lower
My soul shall meet Thy will.
My lifted eye without a tear
The gathering storm shall see:
My steadfast heart shall know no fear:
My heart will rest on Thee.

THE TUNES.

Old "Norwich," from *Day's Psalter*, and "Simpson," adapted from Louis Spohr, are found with the hymn in several later manuals. In the memories of older worshipers "Brattle-Street," with its melodious choral and duet arranged from Pleyel by Lowell Mason, is inseparable from Miss Williams' words; but modern hymnals have dropped it, probably because too elaborate for average congregational use.

Ignaz Joseph Pleyel was born June 1, 1757, at Ruppersthal, Lower Austria. He was the *twenty-fourth* child of a village schoolmaster. His early taste and talent for music procured him friends who paid for his education. Haydn became his master, and long afterwards spoke of him as his best and dearest pupil. Pleyel's work—entirely instrumental—was much admired by Mozart.

During a few years spent in Italy, he composed the music of his best-known opera, "Iphigenia in Aulide," and, besides the thirty-four books of his symphonies and chamber-pieces, the results of his prolific genius make a list too long to enumerate. Most of his life was spent in Paris, where he founded the (present) house of Pleyel and Wolfe, piano makers and sellers. He died in that city, Nov. 14, 1831.

"COME UNTO ME."

Come unto Me, when shadows darkly gather,
When the sad heart is weary and distressed,
Seeking for comfort from your heavenly Father,
Come unto Me, and I will give you rest.

This sweet hymn, by Mrs. Catherine Esling, is well known to many thousands of mourners, as also is its equally sweet tune of "Henley," by Lowell Mason. Melody and words melt together like harp and flute.

Large are the mansions in thy Father's dwelling,
Glad are the homes that sorrows never dim,
Sweet are the harps in holy music swelling.
Soft are the tones that raise the heavenly hymn.

Mrs. Catherine Harbison Waterman Esling was born in Philadelphia, Apr. 12, 1812. A writer for many years under her maiden name, Waterman, she married, in 1840, Capt. George Esling, of the Merchant Marine, and lived in Rio Janeiro till her widowhood, in 1844.

John
Wesley

JOHN WESLEY'S HYMN.

How happy is the pilgrim's lot,
How free from every anxious thought.

These are the opening lines of "John Wesley's Hymn," so called because his other hymns are mostly translations, and because of all his own it is the one commonly quoted and sung.

John Wesley, the second son in the famous Epworth family of ministers, was a man who knew how to endure "hardness as a good soldier of Christ." He was born June 27, 1703, and studied at Charterhouse, London, and at Christ Church, Oxford, becoming a Fellow of Lincoln College. After taking holy orders he went as a missionary to Georgia, U.S., in 1735, and on his return began his remarkable work in England, preaching a more spiritual type of religion, and awakening the whole kingdom with his revival fervor and his brother's kindling songs. The following paragraph from his itinerant life, gathered probably from a page of his own journals, gives a glimpse of what the founder of the great Methodist denomination did and suffered while carrying his Evangelical message from place to place.

On February 17, 1746, when days were short and weather far from favorable, he set out on horseback from Bristol to Newcastle, a distance between three and four hundred miles. The journey occupied ten days. Brooks were swollen, and in some places the roads were impassable, obliging the itinerant to go round through the fields. At Aldrige Heath, in Staffordshire, the rain turned to snow, which the northerly wind drove against him, and by which he was soon crusted over from head to foot. At Leeds the mob followed him, and pelted him with whatever came to hand. He arrived at Newcastle, February 26, "free from every anxious thought," and "every worldly fear."

How lightly he regarded hardship and molestation appears from his verses—
Whatever molests or troubles life,
When past, as nothing we esteem,
And pain, like pleasure, is a dream.

And that he actually enjoys the heroic freedom of a rough-rider missionary life is hinted in his hymn—
Confined to neither court nor cell,
His soul disdains on earth to dwell,
He only sojourns here.

God evidently built John Wesley fire-proof and water-proof with a view to precisely what he was to undertake and accomplish. His frame was vigorous, and his spirit unconquerable. Besides all this he had the divine gift of a religious faith that could move mountains and a confidence in his mission that became a second nature. No wonder he could suffer, and *last*. The brave young man at thirty was the brave old man at nearly ninety. He died in London, March 2, 1791.

Blest with the scorn of finite good,
My soul is lightened of its load
And seeks the things above.
There is my house and portion fair;
My treasure and my heart are there,
And my abiding home.
For me my elder brethren stay,
And angels beckon me away.
And Jesus bids me come.

THE TUNE.

An air found in the *Revivalist* (1869), in sextuple time, that has the real camp-meeting swing, preserves the style of music in which the hymn was sung by the circuit-preachers and their congregations—ringing out the autobiographical verses with special unction. The favorite was—
No foot of land do I possess,
No cottage in this wilderness;
A poor wayfaring man,
I lodge awhile in tents below,
Or gladly wander to and fro
Till I my Canaan gain.

More modern voices sing the John Wesley hymn to the tune "Habakkuk," by Edward Hodges. It has a lively three-four step, and finer melody than the old.

Edward Hodges was born in Bristol, Eng., July 20, 1796, and died there Sept. 1876. Organist at Bristol in his youth, he was graduated at Cambridge and in 1825 received the doctorate of music from that University. In 1835 he went to Toronto, Canada, and two years later to New York city, where he was many years Director of Music at Trinity Church. Returned to Bristol in 1863.

"WHEN GATHERING CLOUDS AROUND I VIEW."

One of the restful strains breathed out of illness and affliction to relieve one soul and bless millions. It was written by Sir Robert Grant (1785–1838).

When gathering clouds around I view,
And days are dark, and friends are few,
On Him I lean who not in vain

75

Experienced every human pain.

The lines are no less admirable for their literary beauty than for their feeling and their faith. Unconsciously, it may be, to the writer, in this and the following stanza are woven an epitome of the Saviour's history. He—

Experienced every human pain,
—felt temptation's power,
—wept o'er Lazarus dead,
—and the crowning assurance of Jesus' human sympathy is expressed in the closing prayer,—

—when I have safely passed
Thro' every conflict but the last,
Still, still unchanging watch beside
My painful bed—for *Thou hast died.*

THE TUNE.

Of the few suitable six-line long metre part songs, the charming Russian tone-poem of "St. Petersburg" by Dimitri Bortniansky is borrowed for the hymn in some collections, and with excellent effect. It accords well with the mood and tenor of the words, and deserves to stay with it as long as the hymn holds its place.

Dimitri Bortniansky, called "The Russian Palestrina," was born in 1752 at Gloukoff, a village of the Ukraine. He studied music in Moscow, St. Petersburg, Vienna, Rome and Naples. Returning to his native land, he was made Director of Empress Catharine's church choir. He reformed and systematized Russian church music, and wrote original scores in the intervals of his teaching labors. His works are chiefly motets and concertos, which show his genius for rich harmony. Died 1825.

"JUST AS I AM, WITHOUT ONE PLEA."

Charlotte Elliott, of Brighton, Eng., would have been well-known through her admired and useful hymns,—

My God, my Father, while I stray,
My God, is any hour so sweet,
With tearful eyes I look around,

—and many others. But in "Just as I am" she made herself a voice in the soul of every hesitating penitent. The currency of the hymn has been too swift for its authorship and history to keep up with, but it is a blessed law of influence that good works out-run biographies. This master-piece of metrical gospel might be called Miss Elliott's spiritual-birth hymn, for a reply of Dr. Cæsar Malan of Geneva was its prompting cause. The young lady was a stranger to personal religion when, one day, the good man, while staying at her father's house, in his gentle way introduced the subject. She resented it, but afterwards, stricken in spirit by his words, came to him with apologies and an inquiry that confessed a new concern of mind. "You speak of coming to Jesus, but how? I'm not fit to come."

"Come just as you are," said Dr. Malan.

The hymn tells the result.

Like all the other hymns bound up in her *Invalid's Hymn-book*, it was poured from out the heart of one who, as the phrase is, "never knew a well day"—though she lived to see her eighty-second year.

Illustrative of the way it appeals to the afflicted, a little anecdote was told by the eloquent John B. Gough of his accidental seat-mate in a city church service. A man of strange appearance was led by the kind usher or sexton to the pew he occupied. Mr. Gough eyed him with strong aversion. The man's face was mottled, his limbs and mouth twitched, and he mumbled singular sounds. When the congregation sang he attempted to sing, but made fearful work of it. During the organ interlude he leaned toward Mr. Gough and asked how the next verse began. It was—

Just as I am, poor, wretched, blind.

"That's it," sobbed the strange man, "I'm blind—God help me!"—and the tears ran down his face—"and I'm wretched—and paralytic," and then he tried hard to sing the line with the rest.

"After that," said Mr. Gough, "the poor paralytic's singing was as sweet to me as a Beethoven symphony."

Charlotte Elliott was born March 18, 1789, and died in Brighton, Sept. 22, 1871. She stands in the front rank of female hymn-writers.

The tune of "Woodworth," by William B. Bradbury, has mostly superseded Mason's "Elliott," and is now the accepted music of this lyric of perfect faith and pious surrender.

Just as I am,—Thy love unknown
Hath broken every barrier down,
Now to be Thine, yea, Thine alone,

76

O Lamb of God, I come, I come.

"MY HOPE IS BUILT ON NOTHING LESS."

The Rev. Edward Mote was born in London, 1797. According to his own testimony his parents were not God-fearing people, and he "went to a school where no Bible was allowed;" but at the age of sixteen he received religious impressions from a sermon of John Hyatt in Tottenham Court Chapel, was converted two years later, studied for the ministry, and ultimately became a faithful preacher of the gospel. Settled as pastor of the Baptist Church in Horsham, Sussex, he remained there twenty-six years—until his death, Nov. 13, 1874. The refrain of his hymn came to him one Sabbath when on his way to Holborn to exchange pulpits:

On Christ the solid rock I stand,
All other ground is sinking sand.

There were originally six stanzas, the first beginning:

Nor earth, nor hell, my soul can move,
I rest upon unchanging love.

The refrain is a fine one, and really sums up the whole hymn, keeping constantly at the front the corner-stone of the poet's trust.

My hope is built on nothing less
Than Jesus' blood and righteousness.
I dare not trust the sweetest frame,
But only lean on Jesus' name.
On Christ the solid Rock I stand
All other ground is sinking sand.
When darkness veils His lovely face
I trust in His unchanging grace,
In every high and stormy gale
My anchor holds within the veil.
On Christ the solid Rock, etc.

Wm. B. Bradbury composed the tune (1863). It is usually named "The Solid Rock."

"ABIDE WITH ME! FAST FALLS THE EVENTIDE."

The Rev. Henry Francis Lyte, author of this melodious hymn-prayer, was born at Ednam, near Kelso, Scotland, June first, 1793. A scholar, graduated at Trinity College, Dublin; a poet and a musician, the hard-working curate was a man of frail physique, with a face of almost feminine beauty, and a spirit as pure and gentle as a little child's. The shadow of consumption was over him all his life. His memory is chiefly associated with the district church at Lower Brixham, Devonshire, where he became "perpetual curate" in 1823. He died at Nice, France, Nov. 20, 1847.

On the evening of his last Sunday preaching and communion service he handed to one of his family the manuscript of his hymn, "Abide with me," and the music he had composed for it. It was not till eight years later that Henry Ward Beecher introduced it, or a part of it, to American Congregationalists, and fourteen years after the author's death it began to be sung as we now have it, in this country and England.

Abide with me! Fast falls the eventide,
The darkness deepens,—Lord with me abide!
When other helpers fail, and comforts flee,
Help of the helpless, O abide with me!
*   *   *   *   *   *

Hold Thou Thy cross before my closing eyes;
Shine through the gloom, and point me to the skies;
Heaven's morning breaks, and earth's vain shadows flee;
In life, in death, O Lord, abide with me!

THE TUNE

There is a pathos in the neglect and oblivion of Lyte's own tune set by himself to his words, especially as it was in a sense the work of a dying man who had hoped that he might not be "wholly mute and useless" while lying in his grave, and who had prayed—

O Thou whose touch can lend
Life to the dead. Thy quickening grace supply,
And grant me swan-like my last breath to spend
In song that may not die!

His prayer was answered in God's own way. Another's melody hastened his hymn on its useful career, and revealed to the world its immortal value.

By the time it had won its slow recognition in England, it was probably tuneless, and the compilers of *Hymns Ancient and Modern*(1861) discovering the fact just as they were finishing their work, asked Dr. William Henry Monk, their music editor, to supply the want. "In ten minutes," it is said, "Dr. Monk composed the sweet, pleading chant that is wedded permanently to Lyte's swan song."

William Henry Monk, Doctor of Music, was born in London, 1823. His musical education was early and thorough, and at the age of twenty-six he was organist and choir director in King's College, London. Elected (1876) professor of the National Training School, he interested himself actively in popular musical education, delivering lectures at various institutions, and establishing choral services.

His hymn-tunes are found in many song-manuals of the English Church and in Scotland, and several have come to America.

Dr. Monk died in 1889.

"COME, YE DISCONSOLATE."

By Thomas Moore—about 1814. The poem in its original form differed somewhat from the hymn we sing. Thomas Hastings—whose religious experience, perhaps, made him better qualified than Thomas Moore for spiritual expression—changed the second line,—

Come, at God's altar fervently kneel,
—to—
Come to the mercy seat,
—and in the second stanza replaced—
Hope when all others die,
—with—
Hope of the penitent;
—and for practically the whole of the last stanza—
Go ask the infidel what boon he brings us,
What charm for aching hearts he can reveal.
Sweet as that heavenly promise hope sings us,
"Earth has no sorrow that heaven cannot heal,"
—Hastings substituted—
Here see the Bread of life, see waters flowing
Forth from the throne of God, pure from above!
Come to the feast Love, come ever knowing
Earth has no sorrow but heaven can remove.

Dr. Hastings was not much of a poet, but he could make a *singable* hymn, and he knew the rhythm and accent needed in a hymn-tune. The determination was to make an evangelical hymn of a poem "too good to lose," and in that view perhaps the editorial liberties taken with it were excusable. It was to Moore, however, that the real hymn-thought and key-note first came, and the title-line and the sweet refrain are his own—for which the Christian world has thanked him, lo these many years.

THE TUNE.

Those who question why Dr. Hastings' interest in Moore's poem did not cause him to make a tune for it, must conclude that it came to him with its permanent melody ready made, and that the tune satisfied him.

The "German Air" to which Moore tells us he wrote the words, probably took his fancy, if it did not induce his mood. Whether Samuel Webbe's tune now wedded to the hymn is an arrangement of the old air or wholly his own is immaterial. One can scarcely conceive a happier yoking of counterparts. Try singing "Come ye Disconsolate" to "Rescue the Perishing," for example, and we shall feel the impertinence of divorcing a hymn that has found its musical affinity.

"JESUS, I MY CROSS HAVE TAKEN."

This is another well-known and characteristic hymn of Henry Francis Lyte—originally six stanzas. We have been told that, besides his bodily affliction, the grief of an unhappy division or difference in his church weighed upon his spirit, and that it is alluded to in these lines—

Man may trouble and distress me,
'Twill but drive me to Thy breast,
Life with trials hard may press me,
Heaven will bring me sweeter rest.
O, 'tis not in grief to harm me
While Thy love is left to me,
O, 'tis not in joy to charm me
Were that joy unmixed with Thee.

Tunes, "Autumn," by F.H. Barthelemon, or "Ellesdie," (formerly called "Disciple") from Mozart—familiar in either.

78

"FROM EVERY STORMY WIND THAT BLOWS."

This is the much-sung and deeply-cherished hymn of Christian peace that a pious Manxman, Hugh Stowell, was inspired to write nearly a hundred years ago. Ever since it has carried consolation to souls in both ordinary and extraordinary trials.

It was sung by the eight American martyrs, Revs. Albert Johnson, John E. Freeman, David E. Campbell and their wives, and Mr. and Mrs. McMullen, when by order of the bloody Nana Sahib the captive missionaries were taken prisoners and put to death at Cawnpore in 1857. Two little children, Fannie and Willie Campbell, suffered with their parents.

From every stormy wind that blows,
From every swelling tide of woes
There is a calm, a sure retreat;
'Tis found beneath the Mercy Seat.
Ah, whither could we flee for aid
When tempted, desolate, dismayed,
Or how the hosts of hell defeat
Had suffering saints no Mercy Seat?
There, there on eagle wings we soar,
And sin and sense molest no more,
And heaven comes down our souls to greet
While glory crowns the Mercy Seat.

Rev. Hugh Stowell was born at Douglas on the Isle of Man, Dec. 3, 1799. He was educated at Oxford and ordained to the ministry 1823, receiving twelve years later the appointment of Canon to Chester Cathedral.

He was a popular and effective preacher and a graceful writer. Forty-seven hymns are credited to him, the above being the best known. To presume it is "his best," leaves a good margin of merit for the remainder.

"From every stormy wind that blows" has practically but one tune. It has been sung to Hastings "Retreat" ever since the music was made.

"CHILD OF SIN AND SORROW."

Child of sin and sorrow, filled with dismay,
Wait not for tomorrow, yield thee today.
Heaven bids thee come, while yet there's room,
Child of sin and sorrow, hear and obey.
Words and music by Thomas Hastings.

"LEAD, KINDLY LIGHT."

John Henry Newman, born in London, Feb. 21, 1801—known in religious history as Cardinal Newman—wrote this hymn when he was a young clergyman of the Church of England. "Born within the sound of Bow bells," says Dr. Benson, "he was an imaginative boy, and so superstitious, that he used constantly to cross himself when going into the dark." Intelligent students of the fine hymn will note this habit of its author's mind—and surmise its influence on his religious musings.

The agitations during the High Church movement, and the persuasions of Hurrell Froude, a Romanist friend, while he was a tutor at Oxford, gradually weakened his Protestant faith, and in his unrest he travelled to the Mediterranean coast, crossed to Sicily, where he fell violently ill, and after his recovery waited three weeks in Palermo for a return boat. On his trip to Marseilles he wrote the hymn—with no thought that it would ever be called a hymn.

When complimented on the beautiful production after it became famous he modestly said, "It was not the hymn but the *tune* that has gained the popularity. The tune is Dykes' and Dr. Dykes is a great master."

John
B. Dykes

Dr. Newman was created a Cardinal of the Church of Rome in the Catholic Cathedral of London, 1879. Died Aug. 11, 1890.

THE TUNE.

"Lux Benigna," by Dr. Dykes, was composed in Aug. 1865, and was the tune chosen for this hymn by a committee preparing the Appendix to *Hymns Ancient and Modern*. Dr. Dykes' statement that the tune came into his head while walking through the Strand in London "presents a striking contrast with the solitary origin of the hymn itself" (Benson).

Lead, kindly Light, amid th' encircling gloom,
Lead Thou me on.
The night is dark and I am far from home;
Lead Thou me on.
Keep Thou my feet; I do not ask to see
The distant scene,—one step enough for me.
*   *   *   *   *   *

So long Thy power hath bless'd me, sure it still
Will lead me on,
O'er moor and fen, o'er crag and torrent, till
The night is gone,
And with the morn those angel faces smile
Which I have loved long since, and lost awhile.

"I HEARD THE VOICE OF JESUS SAY."

Few if any Christian writers of his generation have possessed tuneful gifts in greater opulence or produced more vital and lasting treasures of spiritual verse than Horatius Bonar of Scotland. He inherited some of his poetic faculty from his grandfather, a clergyman who wrote several hymns, and it is told of Horatius that hymns used to "come to" him while riding on railroad trains. He was educated in the Edinburgh University and studied theology with Dr. Chalmers, and hislife was greatly influenced by Dr. Guthrie, whom he followed in the establishment of the Free Church of Scotland.

Born in 1808 in Edinburgh, he was about forty years old when he came back from a successful pastorate at Kelso to the city of his home and Alma Mater, and became virtually Chalmers' successor as minister of the Chalmers Memorial Church.

The peculiar richness of Bonar's sacred songs very early created for them a warm welcome in the religious world, and any devout lyric or poem with his name attached to it is sure to be read.

Dr. Bonar died in Edinburgh, July 31, 1889. Writing of the hymn, "I heard the voice," etc., Dr. David Breed calls it "one of the most ingenious hymns in the language," referring to the fact that the invitation and response exactly halve each stanza between them—song followed by countersong. "Ingenious" seems hardly the right word for a division so obviously natural and almost automatic. It is a simple art beauty that a poet of culture makes by instinct. Bowring's "Watchman, tell us of the night," is not the only other instance of similar countersong structure, and the regularity in Thomas Scott's little hymn, "Hasten, sinner, to be wise," is only a simpler case of the way a poem plans itself by the compulsion of its subject.

I heard the voice of Jesus say,
Come unto me and rest,
Lay down, thou weary one, lay down
Thy head upon My breast:
I came to Jesus as I was,
Weary and worn and sad,
I found in Him a resting-place,
And He has made me glad.

THE TUNE.

The old melody of "Evan," long a favorite; and since known everywhere through the currency given to it in the *Gospel Hymns*, has been in many collections connected with the words. It is good congregational psalmody, and not unsuited to the sentiment, taken line by line, but it divides the stanzas into quatrains, which breaks the happy continuity. "Evan" was made by Dr. Mason in 1850 from a song written four years earlier by Rev. William Henry Havergal, Canon of Worcester Cathedral, Eng. He was the father of Frances Ridley Havergal.

The more ancient "Athens," by Felice Giardini (1716–1796), author of the "Italian Hymn," has clung, and still clings lovingly to Bonar's hymn in many communities. Its simplicity, and the involuntary accent of its sextuple time, exactly reproducing the easy iambic of the verses, inevitably made it popular, and thousands of older singers today will have no other music with "I heard the voice of Jesus say."

"Vox Jesu," from the andante in one of the quartets of Louis Spohr (1784–1859), is a psalm-tune of good harmony, but too little feeling.

An excellent tune for all the shades of expression in the hymn, is the arrangement by Hubert P. Main from Franz Abt—in A flat, triple time. Gentle music through the first fifteen bars, in alternate duet and quartet, utters the Divine Voice with the true accent of the lines, and the second portion completes the harmony in glad, full chorus—the answer of the human heart.

"Vox Dilecti," by Dr. Dykes, goes farther and writes the Voice in B flat *minor*—which seems a needless substitution of divine sadness for divine sweetness. It is a tune of striking chords, but its shift of key to G natural (major) after the first four lines marks it rather for trained choir performance than for assembly song.

It is possible to make too much of a dramatic perfection or a supposed indication of structural design in a hymn. Textual equations, such as distinguish Dr. Bonar's beautiful stanzas, are not necessarily technical. To emphasize them as ingenious by an ingenious tune seems, somehow, a reflection on the spontaneity of the hymn.

Louis Spohr was Director of the Court Theatre Orchestra in Cassel, Prussia, in the first half of the last century. He was an eminent composer of both vocal and instrumental music, and one of the greatest violinists of Europe.

Hubert Platt Main was born in Ridgefield, Ct., Aug. 17, 1839. He read music at sight when only ten years old, and at sixteen commenced writing hymn-tunes. Was assistant compiler with both Bradbury and Woodbury in their various publications, and in 1868 became connected with the firm of Biglow and Main, and has been their book-maker until the present time. As music editor in the partnership he has superintended the publication of more than five hundred music-books, services, etc.

"I LOVE TO STEAL AWHILE AWAY."

The burdened wife and mother who wrote this hymn would, at the time, have rated her history with "the short and simple annals of the poor." But the poor who are "remembered for what they have done," may have a larger place in history than many rich who did nothing.

Phebe Hinsdale Brown, was born in Canaan, N.Y., in 1783. Her father, George Hinsdale, who died in her early childhood, must have been a man of good abilities and religious feeling, being the reputed composer of the psalm-tune, "Hinsdale," found in some long-ago collections.

Left an orphan at two years of age, Phebe "fell into the hands of a relative who kept the county jail," and her childhood knew little but the bitter fare and ceaseless drudgery of domestic slavery. She grew up with a crushed spirit, and was a timid, shrinking woman as long as she lived. She married Timothy H. Brown, a house-painter of Ellington, Ct., and passed her days there and in Monson, Mass., where she lived some twenty-five years.

In her humble home in the former town her children were born, and it was while caring for her own little family of four, and a sick sister, that the incident occurred (August 1818), which called forth her tender hymn. She was a devout Christian, and in pleasant weather, whenever she could find the leisure, she would "steal away" at sunset from her burdens a little while, to rest and commune with God. Her favorite place was a wealthy neighbor's large and beautiful flower garden. A servant reported her visits there to the mistress of the house, who called the "intruder" to account.

"If you want anything, why don't you come in?" was the rude question, followed by a plain hint that no stealthy person was welcome.

Wounded by the ill-natured rebuff, the sensitive woman sat down the next evening with her baby in her lap, and half-blinded by her tears, wrote "An Apology for my Twilight Rambles," in the verses that have made her celebrated.

She sent the manuscript (nine stanzas) to her captious neighbor—with what result has never been told.

Crude and simple as the little rhyme was, it contained a germ of lyric beauty and life. The Rev. Dr. Charles Hyde of Ellington, who was a neighbor of Mrs. Brown, procured a copy. He was assisting Dr. Nettleton to compile the *Village Hymns*, and the humble bit of devotional verse was at once judged worthy of a place in the new book. Dr. Hyde and his daughter Emeline giving it some kind touches of rhythmic amendment,

> I love to steal awhile away
> From little ones and care,

—became,—

> I love to steal awhile away
> From *every cumb'ring* care.

In the last line of this stanza—

> In gratitude and prayer

—was changed to—

81

In humble, grateful prayer,

—and the few other defects in syllabic smoothness or literary grace were affectionately repaired, but the slight furbishing it received did not alter the individuality of Mrs. Brown's work. It remained *hers*—and took its place among the immortals of its kind, another illustration of how little poetry it takes to make a good hymn. Only five stanzas were printed, the others being voted redundant by both author and editor. The second and third, as now sung, are—

I love in solitude to shed
The penitential tear,
And all His promises to plead
Where none but God can hear.
I love to think on mercies past
And future good implore,
And all my cares and sorrows cast
On Him whom I adore.

Phebe Brown died at Henry, Ill., in 1861; but she had made the church and the world her debtor not only for her little lyric of pious trust, but by rearing a son, the Rev. Samuel Brown, D.D., who became the pioneer American missionary to Japan—to which Christian calling two of her grandchildren also consecrated themselves.

THE TUNE.

Mrs. Brown's son Samuel, who, besides being a good minister, inherited his grandfather's musical gift, composed the tune of "Monson," (named in his mother's honor, after her late home), and it may have been the first music set to her hymn. It was the fate of his offering, however, to lose its filial place, and be succeeded by different melodies, though his own still survives in a few collections, sometimes with Collyer's "O Jesus in this solemn hour." It is good music for a hymn of *praise* rather than for meditative verse. Many years the hymn has been sung to "Woodstock," an appropriate and still familiar tune by Deodatus Dutton.

Dutton's "Woodstock" and Bradbury's "Brown," which often replaces it, are worthy rivals of each other, and both continue in favor as fit choral interpretations of the much-loved hymn.

Deodatus Dutton was born Dec. 22, 1808, and educated at Brown University and Washington College (now Trinity) Hartford Ct. While there he was a student of music and played the organ at Dr. Matthews' church. He studied theology in New York city, and had recently entered the ministry when he suddenly died, Dec. 16, 1832, a moment before rising to preach a sermon. During his brief life he had written several hymn-tunes, and published a book of psalmody. Mrs. Sigourney wrote a poem on his death.

"THERE'S A WIDENESS IN GOD'S MERCY."

Frederick William Faber, author of this favorite hymn-poem, had a peculiar genius for putting golden thoughts into common words, and making them sing. Probably no other sample of his work shows better than this his art of combining literary cleverness with the most reverent piety. Cant was a quality Faber never could put into his religious verse.

He was born in Yorkshire, Eng., June 28, 1814, and received his education at Oxford. Settled as Rector of Elton, in Huntingdonshire, in 1843, he came into sympathy with the "Oxford Movement," and followed Newman into the Romish Church. He continued his ministry as founder and priest for the London branch of the Catholic congregation of St. Philip Neri for fourteen years, dying Sept. 26, 1863, at the age of forty-nine.

His godly hymns betray no credal shibboleth or doctrinal bias, but are songs for the whole earthly church of God.

There's a wideness in God's mercy
Like the wideness of the sea;
There's a kindness in His justice
Which is more than liberty.
There is welcome for the sinner
And more graces for the good;
There is mercy with the Saviour,
There is healing in His blood.
There's no place where earthly sorrows
Are more felt than up in heaven;
There's no place where earthly failings
Have such kindly judgment given.
There is plentiful redemption
In the blood that has been shed,
There is joy for all the members
In the sorrows of the Head.

For the love of God is broader
Than the measure of man's mind,
And the heart of the Eternal
Is most wonderfully kind.
If our love were but more simple
We should take Him at His word,
And our lives would be all sunshine
In the sweetness of the Lord.

No tone of comfort has breathed itself more surely and tenderly into grieved hearts than these tuneful and singularly expressive sentences of Frederick Faber.

THE TUNE.

The music of S.J. Vail sung to Faber's hymn is one of that composer's best hymn-tunes, and its melody and natural movement impress the meaning as well as the simple beauty of the words.

Silas Jones Vail, an American music-writer, was born Oct., 1818, and died May 20, 1883. Another charming tune is "Wellesley," by Lizzie S. Tourjee, daughter of the late Dr. Eben Tourjee.

"HE LEADETH ME! OH, BLESSED THOUGHT."

Professor Gilmore, of Rochester University, N.Y., when a young Baptist minister (1861) supplying a pulpit in Philadelphia "jotted down this hymn in Deacon Watson's parlor" (as he says) and passed it to his wife, one evening after he had made "a conference-room talk" on the 23d Psalm.

Mrs. Gilmore, without his knowledge, sent it to the *Watchman and Reflector* (now the *Watchman*).

Years after its publication in that paper, when a candidate for the pastorate of the Second Baptist Church in Rochester, he was turning the leaves of the vestry hymnal in use there, and saw his hymn in it. Since that first publication in the *Devotional Hymn and Tune Book* (1865) it has been copied in the hymnals of various denominations, and steadily holds its place in public favor. The refrain added by the tunemaker emphasizes the sentiment of the lines, and undoubtedly enhances the effect of the hymn.

"He leadeth me" has the true hymn quality, combining all the simplicity of spontaneous thought and feeling with perfect accent and liquid rhythm.

He leadeth me! Oh, blessed thought,
Oh, words with heavenly comfort fraught;
Whate'er I do, where'er I be,
Still 'tis God's hand that leadeth me!
*   *   *   *   *   *

Lord, I would clasp Thy hand in mine,
Nor ever murmur nor repine—
Content, whatever lot I see,
Since 'tis my God that leadeth me.

Professor Joseph Henry Gilmore was born in Boston, April 29, 1834. He was graduated at Phillips Academy, Andover, at Brown University, and at the Newton Theological Institution, where he was afterwards Hebrew instructor.

After four years of pastoral service he was elected (1867) professor of the English Language and Literature in Rochester University. He has published *Familiar Chats on Books and Reading,* also several college text-books on rhetoric, logic and oratory.

THE TUNE.

The little hymn of four stanzas was peculiarly fortunate in meeting the eye of Mr. William B. Bradbury, (1863) and winning his musical sympathy and alliance. Few composers have so exactly caught the tone and spirit of their text as Bradbury did when he vocalized the gliding measures of "He leadeth me."

CHAPTER VI.

CHRISTIAN BALLADS.

Echoes of Hebrew thought, if not Hebrew psalmody, may have made their way into the more serious pagan literature. At least in the more enlightened pagans there has ever revealed itself more or less the instinct of the human soul that "feels after" God. St. Paul in his address to the Athenians made a tactful as well as scholarly point to preface a missionary sermon when he cited a line from a poem of Aratus (B.C. 272) familiar, doubtless, to the majority of his hearers.

Dr. Lyman Abbot has thus translated the passage in which the line occurs:

83

Let us begin from God. Let every mortal raise
The grateful voice to tune God's endless praise,
God fills the heaven, the earth, the sea, the air;
We feel His spirit moving everywhere,
And we His offspring are.* He, ever good,
Daily provides for man his daily food.
To Him, the First, the Last, all homage yield,—
Our Father wonderful, our help, our shield.

* Τοῦ γὰρ καὶ γένος ἐσμέν.

"RISE, CROWNED WITH LIGHT."

Alexander Pope, a Roman Catholic poet, born in London 1688, died at Twickenham 1744, was not a hymnist, but passages in his most serious and exalted flights deserve a tuneful accompaniment. His translations of Homer made him famous, but his ethical poems, especially his "Essay on Man," are inexhaustible mines of quotation, many of the lines and couplets being common as proverbs. His "Messiah," written about 1711, is a religious anthem in which the prophecies of Holy Writ kindle all the splendor of his verse.

THE TUNE.

The closing strain, indicated by the above line, has been divided into stanzas of four lines suitable to a church hymn-tune. The melody selected by the compilers of the *Plymouth Hymnal*, and of the *Unitarian Hymn and Tune Book* is "Savannah," an American sounding name for what is really one of Pleyel's chorals. The music is worthy of Pope's triumphal song.

The seas shall waste, the skies to smoke decay,
Rocks fall to dust, and mountains melt away,
But fixed His Word; His saving power remains:
Thy realm shall last; thy own Messiah reigns.

"OH, WHY SHOULD THE SPIRIT?"

This is a sombre poem, but its virile strength and its literary merit have given it currency, and commended it to the taste of many people, both weak and strong, who have the pensive temperament. Abraham Lincoln loved it and committed it to memory in his boyhood. Philip Phillips set it to music, and sang it—or a part of it—one day during the Civil war at the anniversary of the Christian Sanitary Commission, when President Lincoln, who was present, called for its repetition.* It was written by William Knox, born 1789, son of a Scottish farmer.

* This account so nearly resembles the story of Mrs. Gates' "Your Mission," sung to a similar audience, on a similar occasion, by the same man, that a possible confusion by the narrators of the incident has been suggested. But that Mr. Phillips sang twice before the President during the war does not appear to be contradicted. To what air he sang the above verses is uncertain.

The poem has fourteen stanzas, the following being the first and two last—

Oh, why should the spirit of mortal be proud?
Like a swift-fleeting meteor, a fast-flying cloud
A flash of the lightning, a break of the wave,
He passeth from life to rest in the grave.
*　　*　　*　　*　　*　　*

Yea, hope and despondency, pleasure and pain,
Are mingled together like sunshine and rain;
And the smile and the tear, the song and the dirge,
Still follow each other like surge upon surge.
'Tis the wink of an eye; 'tis the draft of a breath
From the blossom of health to the paleness of death,
From the gilded saloon to the bier and the shroud,
Oh, why should the spirit of mortal be proud?

Philip Phillips was born in Jamestown, Chautauqua Co., N.Y., Aug. 11, 1834, and died in Delaware, O., June 25, 1895. He wrote no hymns and was not an educated musician, but the airs of popular hymn-music came to him and were harmonized for him by others, most frequently by his friends, S.J. Vail and Hubert P. Main. He compiled and published thirty-one collections for Sunday-schools and gospel meetings, besides the *Methodist Hymn and Tune Book*, issued in 1866.

He was a pioneer gospel singer, and his tuneful journeys through America, England and Australia gave him the name of the "Singing Pilgrim," the title of his song collection (1867).

"WHEN ISRAEL OF THE LORD BELOVED."

The "Song of Rebecca the Jewess," in "Ivanhoe," was written by Sir Walter Scott, author of the Waverly Novels, "Marmion," etc., born in Edinburgh, 1771, and died at Abbotsford, 1832. The lines purport to be the Hebrew hymn with which Rebecca closed her daily devotions while in prison under sentence of death.

When Israel of the Lord beloved
Out of the land of bondage came
Her fathers' God before her moved,
An awful Guide in smoke and flame.
*   *   *   *   *   *

Then rose the choral hymn of praise,
And trump and timbrel answered keen,
And Zion's daughters poured their lays.
With priest's and warrior's voice between.
*   *   *   *   *   *

By day along th' astonished lands
The cloudy Pillar glided slow,
By night Arabia's crimson'd sands
Returned the fiery Column's glow.
*   *   *   *   *   *

And O, when gathers o'er our path
In shade and storm the frequent night
Be Thou, long suffering, slow to wrath,
A burning and a shining Light!

The "Hymn of Rebecca" has been set to music though never in common use as a hymn. Old "Truro", by Dr. Charles Burney (1726–1814) is a grand Scotch psalm harmony for the words, though one of the Unitarian hymnals borrows Zeuner's sonorous choral, the "Missionary Chant." Both sound the lyric of the Jewess in good Christian music.

"WE SAT DOWN AND WEPT BY THE WATERS."

The 137th Psalm has been for centuries a favorite with poets and poetical translators, and its pathos appealed to Lord Byron when engaged in writing his *Hebrew Melodies*.

Byron was born in London, 1788, and died at Missolonghi, Western Greece, 1824.

We sat down and wept by the waters
Of Babel, and thought of the day
When the foe, in the hue of his slaughters,
Made Salem's high places his prey,
And ye, Oh her desolate daughters,
Were scattered all weeping away.

—Written April, 1814. It was the fashion then for musical societies to call on the popular poets for contributions, and tunes were composed for them, though these have practically passed into oblivion.

Byron's ringing ballad (from II Kings 19:35)—

Th' Assyrian came down like a wolf on the fold
And his cohorts were gleaming in purple and gold,

—has been so much a favorite for recitation and declamation that the loss of its tune is never thought of.

Another poetic rendering of the "Captivity Psalm" is worthy of notice among the lay hymns not unworthy to supplement clerical sermons. It was written by the Hon. Joel Barlow in 1799, and published in a pioneer psalm-book at Northampton, Mass. It is neither a translation nor properly a hymn but a poem built upon the words of the Jewish lament, and really reproducing something of its plaintive beauty. Two stanzas of it are as follows:

Along the banks where Babel's current flows
Our captive bands in deep despondence strayed,
While Zion's fall in deep remembrance rose,
Her friends, her children mingled with the dead.
The tuneless harps that once with joy we strung
When praise employed, or mirth inspired the lay,
In mournful silence on the willows hung,
And growing grief prolonged the tedious day.

Like Pope, this American poet loved onomatope and imitative verse, and the last line is a word-picture of home-sick weariness. This "psalm" was the best piece of work in Mr. Barlow's series of attempted improvements upon Isaac Watts—which on the whole were not very successful. The sweet cantabile of Mason's "Melton" gave "Along the banks" quite an extended lease of life, though it has now ceased to be sung.

Joel Barlow was a versatile gentleman, serving his country and generation in almost every useful capacity, from chaplain in the continental army to foreign ambassador. He was born in Redding, Ct., 1755, and died near Cracow, Poland, Dec. 1812.

"AS DOWN IN THE SUNLESS."

Thomas Moore, the poet of glees and love-madrigals, had sober thoughts in the intervals of his gaiety, and employed his genius in writing religious and even devout poems, which have been spiritually helpful in many phases of Christian experience. Among them was this and the four following hymns, with thirty-four others, each of which he carefully labelled with the name of a music composer, though the particular tune is left indefinite. "The still prayer of devotion" here answers, in rhyme and reality, the simile of the sea-flower in the unseen deep, and the mariner's compass represents the constancy of a believer.

As, still to the star of its worship, though clouded,
The needle points faithfully o'er the dim sea,
So, dark as I roam in this wintry world shrouded,
The hope of my spirit turns trembling to Thee.

It is sung in *Plymouth Hymnal* to Barnby's "St. Botolph."

"THE TURF SHALL BE MY FRAGRANT SHRINE"

Is, in part, still preserved in hymn collections, and sung to the noble tune of "Louvan," Virgil Taylor's piece. The last stanza is especially reminiscent of the music.

There's nothing bright above, below,
From flowers that bloom to stars that glow;
But in its light my soul can see
Some feature of Thy deity.

"O THOU WHO DRY'ST THE MOURNER'S TEAR"

Is associated in the *Baptist Praise Book* with Woodbury's "Siloam."

"THE BIRD LET LOOSE IN EASTERN SKIES"

Has been sung in Mason's "Coventry," and the *Plymouth Hymnal* assigns it to "Spohr"—a namesake tune of Louis Spohr, while the *Unitarian Hymn and Tune Book* unites to it a beautiful triple-time melody from Mozart, and bearing his name.

"THOU ART, O GOD, THE LIFE AND LIGHT."

This is the best of the Irish poet's sacred songs—always excepting, "Come, Ye Disconsolate." It is said to have been originally set to a secular melody composed by the wife of Hon. Richard Brinsley Sheridan. It is joined to the tune of "Brighton" in the Unitarian books, and William Monk's "Matthias" voices the words for the *Plymouth Hymnal*. The verses have the true lyrical glow, and make a real song of praise as well a composition of more than ordinary literary beauty.

Thou art, O God, the life and light
Of all this wondrous world we see;
Its glow by day, its smile by night
Are but reflections caught from Thee.
Where'er we turn Thy glories shine,
And all things fair and bright are Thine.
*　　*　　*　　*　　*　　*
When night with wings of starry gloom
O'ershadows all the earth, and skies
Like some dark, beauteous bird, whose plume
Is sparkling with unnumbered eyes,
That sacred gloom, those fires divine,
So grand, so countless, Lord, are Thine.
When youthful spring around us breathes,
Thy Spirit warms her fragrant sigh,
And every flower the summer wreathes
Is born beneath that kindling eye.
Where'er we turn Thy glories shine,
And all things fair and bright are Thine.

"MOURNFULLY, TENDERLY, BEAR ON THE DEAD."

A tender funeral ballad by Henry S. Washburn, composed in 1846 and entitled "The Burial of Mrs. Judson." It is rare now in sheet-music form but the *American Vocalist*, to be found in the stores of most great music publishers and dealers, preserves the full poem and score.

Its occasion was the death at sea, off St. Helena, of the Baptist missionary, Mrs. Sarah Hall Boardman Judson, and the solemn committal of her remains to the dust on that historic island, Sept. 1, 1845. She was on her way to America from Burmah at the time of her death, and the ship proceeded on its homeward voyage immediately after her burial. The touching circumstances of the gifted lady's death, and the strange romance of her entombment where Napoleon's grave was made twenty-four years before, inspired Mr. Washburn, who was a prominent layman of the Baptist denomination, and interested in all its ecclesiastical and missionary activities, and he wrote this poetic memorial of the event:

Mournfully, tenderly, bear on the dead;
Where the warrior has lain, let the Christian be laid.
No place more befitting, O rock of the sea;
Never such treasure was hidden in thee.
Mournfully, tenderly, solemn and slow;
Tears are bedewing the path as ye go;
Kindred and strangers are mourners today;
Gently, so gently, O bear her away.
Mournfully, tenderly, gaze on that brow;
Beautiful is it in quietude now.
One look, and then settle the loved to her rest
The ocean beneath her, the turf on her breast.

Mrs. Sarah Judson was the second wife of the Rev. Adoniram Judson, D.D., the celebrated pioneer American Baptist missionary, and the mother by her first marriage, of the late Rev. George Dana Boardman, D.D., LL.D., of Philadelphia.

The Hon. Henry S. Washburn was born in Providence, R.I., 1813, and educated at Brown University. During most of his long life he resided in Massachusetts, and occupied there many positions of honor and trust, serving in the State Legislature both as Representative and Senator. He was the author of many poems and lyrics of high merit, some of which—notably "The Vacant Chair"—became popular in sheet-music and in books of religious and educational use. He died in 1903.

THE TUNE.

"The Burial of Mrs. Judson" became favorite parlor music when Lyman Heath composed the melody for it—of the same name. Its notes and movement were evidently inspired by the poem, for it reproduces the feeling of every line. The threnody was widely known and sung in the middle years of the last century, by people, too, who had scarcely heard of Mrs. Judson, and received in the music and words their first hint of her history. The poem prompted the tune, but the tune was the garland of the poem.

Lyman Heath of Bow, N.H., was born there Aug. 24, 1804. He studied music, and became a vocalist and vocal composer. Died July 30, 1870.

"TELL ME NOT IN MOURNFUL NUMBERS."

Longfellow's "Psalm of Life" was written when he was a young man, and for some years it carried the title he gave it, "What the Young Man's Heart Said to the Psalmist"—a caption altogether too long to bear currency.

The history of the beloved poet who wrote this optimistic ballad of hope and courage is too well known to need recounting here. He was born in Portland, Me., in 1807, graduated at Bowdoin College, and was for more than forty years professor of Belles Lettres in Harvard University. Died in Cambridge, March 4, 1882. Of his longer poems the most read and admired are his beautiful romance of "Evangeline," and his epic of "Hiawatha," but it is hardly too much to say that for the last sixty years, his "Psalm of Life" has been the common property of all American, if not English school-children, and a part of their education. When he was in London, Queen Victoria sent for him to come and see her at the palace. He went, and just as he was seating himself in the waiting coach after the interview, a man in working clothes appeared, hat in hand, at the coach window.

"Please sir, yer honor," said he, "an' are you Mr. Longfellow?"

"I am Mr. Longfellow," said the poet.

"An' did you write the Psalm of Life?" he asked.

"I wrote the Psalm of Life," replied the poet.

"An', yer honor, would you be willing to take a workingman by the hand?"

Mr. Longfellow gave the honest Englishman a hearty handshake, "And" (said he in telling the story) "I never in my life received a compliment that gave me more satisfaction."

The incident has a delightful democratic flavor—and it is perfectly characteristic of the amiable author of the most popular poem in the English language. The "Psalm of Life" is a wonderful example of the power of commonplaces put into tuneful and elegant verse.

The thought of setting the poem to music came to the compiler of one of the Unitarian church singing books. Some will question, however, whether the selection was the happiest that could have been made. The tune is "Rathbun," Ithamar Conkey's melody that always recalls Sir John Bowring's great hymn of praise.

"BUILD THEE MORE NOBLE MANSIONS."

This poem by Dr. Oliver Wendell Holmes, known among his works as "The Chambered Nautilus," was considered by himself as his worthiest achievement in verse, and his wish that it might live is likely to be fulfilled. It is stately, and in character and effect a rhythmic sermon from a text in "natural theology." The biography of one of the little molluscan sea-navigators that continually enlarges its shell to adapt it to its growth inspired the thoughtful lines. The third, fourth and fifth stanzas are as follows:

Year after year beheld the silent toil
That spread the lustrous coil;
Still, as the spiral grew,
He left the last year's dwelling for the new,
Stole with soft step the shining archway through,
Built up its idle door,
Stretched in his last-found home, and knew the old no more.
Thanks for the heavenly message brought by thee,
Child of the wand'ring sea,
Cast from her lap forlorn!
From thy dead lips a clearer note is born
Than ever Triton blew from wreathéd horn!
While on my ear it rings
Through the deep caves of thought I hear a voice that sings,
"Build thee more noble mansions, O my soul.
As the swift seasons roll:
Leave thy low-vaulted past!
Let each new temple, nobler than the last,
Shut thee from heaven with a dome more vast,
Till thou at length art free,
Leaving thy outgrown shell by life's unresting sea."

Dr. Frederic Hedge included the poem in his hymn-book but without any singing-supplement to the words.

WHITTIER'S SERVICE SONG.

It may not be our lot to wield
The sickle in the harvest field.

If this stanza and the four following do not reveal all the strength of John G. Whittier's spirit, they convey its serious sweetness. The verses were loved and prized by both President Garfield and President McKinley. On the Sunday before the latter went from his Canton, O., home to his inauguration in Washington the poem was sung as a hymn at his request in the services at the Methodist church where he had been a constant worshipper.

The second stanza is the one most generally recognized and oftenest quoted:

Yet where our duty's task is wrought
In unison with God's great thought,
The near and future blend in one,
And whatsoe'er is willed, is done.

John Greenleaf Whittier, the poet of the oppressed, was born in Haverhill, Mass., 1807, worked on a farm and on a shoe-bench, and studied at the local academy, until, becoming of age, he went to Hartford, Conn., and began a brief experience in editorial life. Soon after his return to Massachusetts he was elected to the Legislature, and after his duties ended there he left the state for Philadelphia to edit the *Pennsylvania Freeman*. A few years later he returned again, and established his home in Amesbury, the town with which his life and works are always associated.

He died in 1892 at Hampton Falls, N.H., where he had gone for his health.

THE TUNE.

"Abends," the smooth triple-time choral joined to Whittier's poem by the music editor of the new *Methodist Hymnal*, speaks its meaning so well that it is scarcely worth while to look for another. Sir Herbert Stanley Oakeley, the composer, was born at Ealing, Eng., July 22, 1830, and educated at Rugby and Oxford. He studied music in Germany, and became a superior organist, winning great applause by his recitals at Edinburgh University, where he was elected Musical Professor.

Archbishop Tait gave him the doctorate of music at Canterbury in 1871, and he was knighted by Queen Victoria in 1876.

Besides vocal duets, Scotch melodies and student songs, he composed many anthems and tunes for the church—notably "Edina" ("Saviour, blessed Saviour") and "Abends," originally written to Keble's "Sun of my Soul."

"THE BIRD WITH THE BROKEN PINION."

This lay of a lost gift, with its striking lesson, might have been copied from the wounded bird's own song, it is so natural and so clear-toned. The opportune thought and pen of Mr. Hezekiah Butterworth gave being to the little ballad the day he heard the late Dr. George Lorimer preach from a text in the story of Samson's fall (Judges 16:21) "The Philistines took him, and put out his eyes, and brought him down to Gaza ... and he did grind in the prison-house." A sentence in the course of the doctor's sermon, "The bird with a broken pinion never soars as high again," was caught up by the listening author, and became the refrain of his impressive song. Rev. Frank M. Lamb, the tuneful evangelist, found it in print, and wrote a tune to it, and in his voice and the voices of other singers the little monitor has since told its story in revival meetings, and mission and gospel services throughout the land.

I walked through the woodland meadows
Where sweet the thrushes sing,
And found on a bed of mosses
A bird with a broken wing.
I healed its wound, and each morning
It sang its old sweet strain,
But the bird with a broken pinion
Never soared as high again.
I found a young life broken
By sin's seductive art;
And, touched with a Christ-like pity,
I took him to my heart.
He lived—with a noble purpose,
And struggled not in vain;
But the life that sin had stricken
Never soared as high again.
But the bird with a broken pinion
Kept another from the snare,
And the life that sin had stricken
Saved another from despair.
Each loss has its compensation,
There is healing for every pain
But the bird with a broken pinion
Never soars as high again.

In the tune an extra stanza is added—as if something conventional were needed to make the poem a hymn. But the professional tone of the appended stanza, virtually all in its two lines—

Then come to the dear Redeemer,
He will cleanse you from every stain,

—is forced into its connection. The poem told the truth, and stopped there; and should be left to fasten its own impression. There never was a more solemn warning uttered than in this little apologue. It promises "compensation" and "healing," but not perfect rehabilitation. Sin will leave its scars. Even He who "became sin for us" bore them in His resurrection body.

Rev. Frank M. Lamb, composer and singer of the hymn-tune, was born in Poland, Me., 1860, and educated in the schools of Poland and Auburn. He was licensed to preach in 1888, and ordained the same year, and has since held pastorates in Maine, New York, and Massachusetts.

Besides his tune, very pleasing and appropriate music has been written to the little ballad of the broken wing by Geo. C. Stebbins.

UNDER THE PALMS.

In the cantata, "Under the Palms" ("Captive Judah in Babylon")—the joint production of George F. Root' and Hezekiah Butterworth, several of the latter's songs detached themselves, with their music, from the main work, and lingered in choral or solo service in places where the sacred operetta was presented, both in America and England. One of these is an effective solo in deep contralto, with a suggestion of recitative and chant—

By the dark Euphrates' stream,
By the Tigris, sad and lone

I wandered, a captive maid;
And the cruel Assyrian said,
"Awake your harp's sweet tone!"
I had heard of my fathers' glory from the lips of holy men,
And I thought of the land of my fathers; I thought of my fathers' land then.
Another is—
O church of Christ! our blest abode,
Celestial grace is thine.
Thou art the dwelling-place of God,
The gate of joy divine.
Whene'er I come to thee in joy,
Whene'er I come in tears,
Still at the Gate called Beautiful
My risen Lord appears.
—with the chorus—
Where'er for me the sun may set,
Wherever I may dwell,
My heart shall nevermore forget
Thy courts, Immanuel!

* See page 316.

Ellen
M.H. Gates

"IF YOU CANNOT ON THE OCEAN."

This popular Christian ballad, entitled "Your Mission," was written one stormy day in the winter of 1861–2 by Miss Ellen M. Huntington (Mrs. Isaac Gates), and made her reputation as one of the few didactic poets whose exquisite art wins a hearing for them everywhere. In a moment of revery, while looking through the window at the falling snow, the words came to her:

If you cannot on the ocean
Sail among the swiftest fleet.

She turned away and wrote the lines on her slate, following with verse after verse till she finished the whole poem. "It wrote itself," she says in her own account of it.

Reading afterwards what she had written, she was surprised at her work. The poem had a meaning and a "mission." So strong was the impression that the devout girl fell on her knees and consecrated it to a divine purpose. Free copies of it went to the Cooperstown, N.Y., local paper, and to the New York *Examiner*, and appeared in both. From that time the history and career of "Your Mission" presents a marked illustration of "catenal influence," or transmitted suggestion.

In the later days of the Civil War Philip Phillips, who had a wonderfully sweet tenor voice, was invited to sing at a great meeting of the United States Christian Commission in the Senate Chamber at Washington, February, 1865, President Lincoln and Secretary Seward (then president of the commission) were there, and the hall was crowded with leading statesmen, army generals, and friends of the Union. The song selected by Mr. Phillips was Mrs. Gates' "Your Mission":

If you cannot on the ocean
Sail among the swiftest fleet,
Rocking on the highest billows,
Laughing at the storms you meet,
You can stand among the sailors
Anchored yet within the bay;
You can lend a hand to help them
As they launch their boats away.

90

The hushed audience listened spell-bound as the sweet singer went on, their interest growing to feverish eagerness until the climax was reached in the fifth stanza:

If you cannot in the conflict
Prove yourself a soldier true,
If where fire and smoke are thickest
There's no work for you to do,
When the battlefield is silent
You can go with careful tread;
You can bear away the wounded,
You can cover up the dead.

In the storm of enthusiasm that followed, President Lincoln handed a hastily scribbled line on a bit of paper to Chairman Seward,

"Near the close let us have 'Your Mission' repeated."

Mr. Phillips' great success on this occasion brought him so many calls for his services that he gave up everything and devoted himself to his tuneful art. "Your Mission" so gladly welcomed at Washington made him the first gospel songster, chanting round the world the divine message of the hymns. It was the singing by Philip Phillips that first impressed Ira D. Sankey with the amazing power of evangelical solo song, and helped him years later to resign his lucrative business as a revenue officer and consecrate his own rare vocal gift to the Christian ministry of sacred music. Heaven alone can show the birth-records of souls won to God all along the journeys of the "Singing Pilgrims," and the rich succession of Mr. Sankey's melodies, that can be traced back by a chain of causes to the poem that "wrote itself" and became a hymn. And the chain may not yet be complete. In the words of that providential poem—

Though they may forget the singer
They will not forget the song.

Mrs. Ellen M.H. Gates, whose reputation as an author was made by this beautiful and always timely poem, was born in Torrington, Ct., and is the youngest sister of the late Collis P. Huntington. Her hymns—included in this volume and in other publications—are much admired and loved, both for their sweetness and elevated religious feeling, and for their poetic quality. Among her published books of verse are "Night," "At Noontide," and "Treasures of Kurium." Her address is New York City.

THE TUNE.

Sidney Martin Grannis, author of the tune, was born Sept. 23, 1827, in Geneseo, Livingston county, N.Y. Lived in Leroy, of the same state, from 1831 to 1884, when he removed to Los Angeles, Cal., where several of his admirers presented him a cottage and grounds, which at last accounts he still occupies. Mr. Grannis won his first reputation as a popular musician by his song "Do They Miss Me at Home," and his "Only Waiting," "Cling to the Union," and "People Will Talk You Know," had an equally wide currency. As a solo singer his voice was remarkable, covering a range of two octaves, and while travelling with members of the "Amphion Troupe," to which he belonged, he sang at more than five thousand concerts. His tune to "Your Mission" was composed in New Haven, Ct., in 1864.

"TOO LATE! TOO LATE! YE CANNOT ENTER NOW."

"Too Late" is a thrilling fragment or side-song of Alfred Tennyson's, representing the vain plea of the five Foolish Virgins. Its tune bears the name of a London lady, "Miss Lindsay" (afterwards Mrs. J. Worthington Bliss). The arrangement of air, duo and quartet is very impressive'.

Methodist Hymnal, No. 743.

"Late, late, so late! and dark the night and chill:
Late, late, so late! but we can enter still."
"Too late! too late! ye cannot enter now!"
"No light! so late! and dark and chill the night—
O let us in that we may find the light!"
"Too late! too late! ye cannot enter now!"
*   *   *   *   *   *
"Have we not heard the Bridegroom is so sweet?
O let us in that we may kiss his feet!"
"No, No—! too late! ye cannot enter now!"
The words are found in "Queen Guinevere," a canto of the "Idyls of the King."

"OH, GALILEE, SWEET GALILEE."

91

This is the chorus of a charming poem of three stanzas that shaped itself in the mind of Mr. Robert Morris while sitting over the ruins on the traditional site of Capernaum by the Lake of Genneseret.

Each cooing dove, each sighing bough,
That makes the eve so blest to me,
Has something far diviner now,
It bears me back to Galilee.
CHORUS
Oh, Galilee, sweet Galilee,
Where Jesus loved so much to be;
Oh, Galilee, blue Galilee,
Come sing thy song again to me.

Robert Morris, LL.D., born Aug. 31, 1818, was a scholar, and an expert in certain scientific subjects, and wrote works on numismatics and the "Poetry of Free Masonry." Commissioned to Palestine in 1868 on historic and archaeological service for the United Order, he explored the scenes of ancient Jewish and Christian life and event in the Holy Land, and being a religious man, followed the Saviour's earthly footsteps with a reverent zeal that left its inspiration with him while he lived. He died in the year 1888, but his Christian ballad secured him a lasting place in every devout memory.

THE TUNE.

The author wrote out his hymn in 1874 and sent it to his friend, the musician, Mr. Horatio R. Palmer,* and the latter learned it by heart, and carried it with him in his musings "till it floated out in the melody you know," (to use his own words.)

* See page 311.

CHAPTER VII.

OLD REVIVAL HYMNS.

The sober churches of the "Old Thirteen" states and of their successors far into the nineteenth century, sustained evening prayer-meetings more or less commonly, but necessity made them in most cases "cottage meetings" appointed on Sunday and here and there in the scattered homes of country parishes. Their intent was the same as that of "revival meetings," since so called, though the method—and the music—were different. The results in winning sinners, so far as they owed anything to the hymns and hymn-tunes, were apt to be a new generation of Christian recruits as sombre as the singing. "Lebanon" set forth the appalling shortness of human life; "Windham" gave its depressing story of the great majority of mankind on the "broad road," and other minor tunes proclaimed God's sovereignty and eternal decrees; or if a psalm had His love in it, it was likely to be sung in a similar melancholy key. Even in his gladness the good minister, Thomas Baldwin, of the Second Baptist Church, at Boston, North End, returning from Newport, N.H., where he had happily harmonized a discordant church, could not escape the strait-lace of a C minor for his thankful hymn—

From whence doth this union arise,
That hatred is conquered by love.

"The Puritans took their pleasures seriously," and this did not cease to be true till at least two hundred years after the Pilgrims landed or Boston was founded.

Time, that covered the ghastly faces on the old grave-stones with moss, gradually stole away the unction of minor-tune singing.

The songs of the great revival of 1740 swept the country with positive rather than negative music. Even Jonathan Edwards admitted the need of better psalm-books and better psalmody.

Edwards, during his life, spent some time among the Indians as a missionary teacher; but probably neither he nor David Brainerd ever saw a Christian hymn composed by an Indian. The following, from the early years of the last century, is apparently the first, certainly the only surviving, effort of a converted but half-educated red man to utter his thoughts in pious metre. Whoever trimmed the original words and measure into printable shape evidently took care to preserve the broken English of the simple convert. It is an interesting relic of the Christian thought and sentiment of a pagan just learning to prattle prayer and praise:

In de dark wood, no Indian nigh,
Den me look heaben, send up cry,
Upon my knees so low.
Dat God on high, in shinee place,
See me in night, with teary face,

De priest, he tell me so.
God send Him angel take me care;
Him come Heself and hear um prayer,
If Indian heart do pray.
God see me now, He know me here.
He say, poor Indian, neber fear,
Me wid you night and day.
So me lub God wid inside heart;
He fight for me, He take my part,
He save my life before.
God lub poor Indian in de wood;
So me lub God, and dat be good;
Me pray Him two times more.
When me be old, me head be gray,
Den He no lebe me, so He say:
Me wid you till you die.
Den take me up to shinee place,
See white man, red man, black man's face,
All happy 'like on high.
Few days, den God will come to me,
He knock off chains, He set me free,
Den take me up on high.
Den Indian sing His praises blest,
And lub and praise Him wid de rest,
And neber, neber cry.

The above hymn, which may be found in different forms in old New England tracts and hymn-books, and which used to be sung in Methodist conference and prayer-meetings in the same way that old slave-hymns and the "Jubilee Singers" refrains are sometimes sung now, was composed by William Apes, a converted Indian, who was born in Massachusetts, in 1798. His father was a white man, but married an Indian descended from the family of King Philip, the Indian warrior, and the last of the Indian chiefs. His grandmother was the king's granddaughter, as he claimed, and was famous for her personal beauty. He caused his autobiography and religious experience to be published. The original hymn is quite long, and contains some singular and characteristic expressions.

The authorship of the tune to which the words were sung has been claimed for Samuel Cowdell, a schoolmaster of Annapolis Valley, Nova Scotia, 1820, but the date of the lost tune was probably much earlier.

In the early days of New England, before the Indian missions had been brought to an end by the sweeping away of the tribes, several fine hymns were composed by educated Indians, and were used in the churches. The best known is that beginning—

When shall we all meet again?

It was composed by three Indians at the planting of a memorial pine on leaving Dartmouth College, where they had been studying. The lines indicate an expectation of missionary life and work.

When shall we all meet again?
When shall we all meet again?
Oft shall glowing hope expire,
Oft shall wearied love retire,
Oft shall death and sorrow reign
Ere we all shall meet again.
Though in distant lands we sigh,
Parched beneath a burning sky,
Though the deep between us rolls,
Friendship shall unite our souls;
And in fancy's wide domain,
There we all shall meet again.
When these burnished locks are gray,
Thinned by many a toil-spent day,
When around this youthful pine
Moss shall creep and ivy twine,
(Long may this loved bower remain!)
Here may we all meet again.

93

When the dreams of life are fled,
When its wasted lamps are dead,
When in cold oblivion's shade
Beauty, health, and strength are laid,
Where immortal spirits reign,
There we all shall meet again.

This parting piece was sung in religious meetings as a hymn, like the other once so common, but later,—

"When shall we meet again,
Meet ne'er to sever?"

—to a tune in B flat minor, excessively plaintive, and likely to sadden an emotional singer or hearer to tears. The full harmony is found in the *American Vocalist*, and the air is reprinted in the *Revivalist* (1868). The fact that minor music is the natural Indian tone in song makes it probable that the melody is as ancient as the hymn—though no date is given for either.

Tradition says that nearly fifty years later the same three Indians were providentially drawn to the spot where they parted, and met again, and while they were together composed and sang another ode. Truth to tell, however, it had only one note of gladness, and that was in the first stanza:

Parted many a toil-spent year,
Pledged in youth to memory dear,
Still to friendship's magnet true,
We our social joys renew;
Bound by love's unsevered chain,
Here on earth we meet again.

The remaining three stanzas dwell principally on the ravages time has made. The reunion ode of those stoical college classmates of a stoical race could have been sung in the same B flat minor.

"AWAKED BY SINAI'S AWFUL SOUND."

The name of the Indian, Samson Occum, who wrote this hymn (variously spelt Ockom, Ockum, Occam, Occom) is not borne by any public institution, but New England owes the foundation of Dartmouth College to his hard work. Dartmouth College was originally "Moore's Indian Charity School," organized (1750) in Lebanon, Ct., by Rev. Eleazer Wheelock and endowed (1755) by Joshua Moore (or More). Good men and women who had at heart the spiritual welfare of a fading race contributed to the school's support and young Indians resorted to it from both New England and the Middle States, but funds were insufficient, and it was foreseen that the charity must inevitably outgrow its missionary purpose and if continued at all must depend on a wider and more liberal patronage.

Samson Occum was born in Mohegan, New London Co., Ct., probably in the year 1722. Converted from paganism in 1740 (possibly under the preaching of Whitefield, who was in this country at that time) he desired to become a missionary to his people, and entered Eleazer Wheelock's school. After four years study, then a young man of twenty-two, he began to teach and preach among the Montauk Indians, and in 1759 the Presbytery of Suffolk Co., L.I., ordained him to the ministry. A benevolent society in Scotland, hearing of, his ability and zeal, gave him an appointment, under its auspices, among the Oneidas in 1761, where he labored four years. The interests of the school at Lebanon, where he had been educated, were dear to him, and he was tireless in its cause, procuring pupils for it, and working eloquently as its advocate with voice and pen. In 1765 he crossed the Atlantic to solicit funds for the Indian school, and remained four years in England and Scotland, lecturing in its behalf, and preaching nearly four hundred sermons. As a result he raised ten thousand pounds. The donation was put in charge of a Board of Trustees of which Lord Dartmouth was chairman. When it was decided to remove the school from Lebanon, Ct., the efforts of Governor Wentworth, of New Hampshire, secured its location at Hanover in that state. It was christened after Lord Dartmouth—and the names of Occum, Moore and Wheelock retired into the encyclopedias.

The Rev. Samson Occum died in 1779, while laboring among the Stockbridge (N.Y.) Indians. Several hymns were written by this remarkable man, and also "An Account of the Customs and Manners of the Montauks." The hymn, "Awaked by Sinai's Awful Sound," set to the stentorian tune of "Ganges," was a tremendous sermon in itself to old-time congregations, and is probably as indicative of the doctrines which converted its writer as of the contemporary belief prominent in choir and pulpit.

Awaked by Sinai's awful sound,
My soul in bonds of guilt I found,
And knew not where to go,

Eternal truth did loud proclaim
"The sinner must be born again.
Or sink in endless woe."
When to the law I trembling fled,
It poured its curses on my head:
I no relief could find.
This fearful truth increased my pain,
"The sinner must be born again,"
And whelmed my troubled mind.
＊　　＊　　＊　　＊　　＊　　＊

But while I thus in anguish lay,
Jesus of Nazareth passed that way;
I felt His pity move.
The sinner, once by justice slain,
Now by His grace is born again,
And sings eternal Love!

The rugged original has been so often and so variously altered and "toned down," that only a few unusually accurate aged memories can recall it. The hymn began going out of use fifty years ago, and is now seldom seen.

The name "S. Chandler," attached to "Ganges," leaves the identity of the composer in shadow. It is supposed he was born in 1760. The tune appeared about 1790.

"WHERE NOW ARE THE HEBREW CHILDREN?"

This quaint old unison, repeating the above three times, followed by the answer (thrice repeated) and climaxed with—
Safely in the Promised Land,
—was a favorite at ancient camp-meetings, and a good leader could keep it going in a congregation or a happy group of vocalists, improvising a new start-line after every stop until his memory or invention gave out.
They went up from the fiery furnace,
They went up from the fiery furnace,
They went up from the fiery furnace,
Safely to the Promised Land.
Sometimes it was—
Where now is the good Elijah?
—and,—
He went up in a chariot of fire;
—and again,—
Where now is the good old Daniel?
He went up from the den of lions;
—and so on, finally announcing—
By and by we'll go home for to meet him, [three times]
Safely in the Promised Land.
The enthusiasm excited by the swinging rhythm of the tune sometimes rose to a passionate pitch, and it was seldom used in the more controlled religious assemblies. If any attempt was ever made to print the song* the singers had little need to read the music. Like the ancient runes, it came into being by spontaneous generation, and lived in phonetic tradition.

* Mr. Hubert P. Main believes he once saw "The Hebrew Children" in print in one of Horace Waters' editions of the *Sabbath Bell.*

A strange, wild pæan of exultant song was one often heard from Peter Cartwright, the muscular circuit-preacher. A remembered fragment shows its quality:
Then my soul mounted higher
In a chariot of fire,
And the moon it was under my feet.
There is a tradition that he sang it over a stalwart blacksmith while chastising him for an ungodly defiance and assault in the course of one of his gospel journeys—and that the defeated blacksmith became his friend and follower.

Peter Cartwright was born in Amherst county, Va., Sept. 1, 1785, and died near Pleasant Plains, Sangamon county, Ill., Sept., 1872.

"THE EDEN OF LOVE."

This song, written early in the last century, by John J. Hicks, recalls the name of the eccentric traveling evangelist, Lorenzo Dow, born in Coventry, Ct., October 16, 1777; died in

Washington, D.C., Feb. 2, 1834. It was the favorite hymn of his wife, the beloved Peggy Dow, and has furnished the key-word of more than one devotional rhyme that has uplifted the toiling souls of rural evangelists and their greenwood congregations:

How sweet to reflect on the joys that await me
In yon blissful region, the haven of rest,
Where glorified spirits with welcome shall greet me,
And lead me to mansions prepared for the blest.
There, dwelling in light, and with glory enshrouded,
My happiness perfect, my mind's sky unclouded,
I'll bathe in the ocean of pleasure unbounded,
And range with delight through the Eden of love.

The words and tune were printed in *Leavitt's Christian Lyre*, 1830. The same strain in the same metre is continued in the hymn of Rev. Wm. Hunter, D.D., (1842) printed in his *Minstrel of Zion* (1845). J.W. Dadmun's *Melodian* (1860) copied it, retaining, apparently, the original music, with an added refrain of invitation, "Will you go? will you go?"

We are bound for the land of the pure and the holy,
The home of the happy, the kingdom of love;
Ye wand'rers from God on the broad road of folly,
O say, will you go to the Eden above?

The old hymn-tune has a brisk out-door delivery, and is full of revival fervor and the ozone of the pines.

"O CANA-AN, BRIGHT CANA-AN"

Was one of the stimulating melodies of the old-time awakenings, which were simply airs, and were sung unisonously. "O Cana-an" (pronounced in three syllables) was the chorus, the hymn-lines being either improvised or picked up miscellaneously from memory, the interline, "I am bound for the land of Cana-an," occurring between every two. John Wesley's "How happy is the pilgrim's lot" was one of the snatched stanzas swept into the current of the song. An example of the tune-leader's improvisations to keep the hymn going was—

If you get there before I do,—
I am bound for the land of Cana-an!
Look out for me, I'm coming too—
I am bound for the land of Cana-an!

And then hymn and tune took possession of the assembly and rolled on in a circle with—

O Cana-an, bright Cana-an!
I am bound for the land of Cana-an;
O Cana-an it is my hap-py home,
I am bound for the land of Cana-an

—till the voices came back to another starting-line and began again. There was always a movement to the front when that tune was sung, and—with all due abatement for superficial results in the sensation of the moment—it is undeniable that many souls were truly born into the kingdom of God under the sound of that rude woodland song.

Both its words and music are credited to Rev. John Maffit, who probably wrote the piece about 1829.

"A CHARGE TO KEEP I HAVE."

This hymn of Charles Wesley was often heard at the camp grounds, from the rows of tents in the morning while the good women prepared their pancakes and coffee, and

THE TUNE.

was invariably old "Kentucky," by Jeremiah Ingalls. Sung as a solo by a sweet and spirited voice, it slightly resembled "Golden Hill," but oftener its halting bars invited a more drawling style of execution unworthy of a hymn that merits a tune like "St. Thomas."

Old "Kentucky" was not field music.

"CHRISTIANS, IF YOUR HEARTS ARE WARM."

Elder John Leland, born in Grafton, Mass., 1754, was not only a strenuous personality in the Baptist denomination, but was well known everywhere in New England, and, in fact, his preaching trip to Washington (1801) with the "Cheshire Cheese" made his fame national. He is spoken of as "the minister who wrote his own hymns"—a peculiarity in which he imitated Watts and Doddridge. When some natural shrinking was manifest in converts of his winter revivals, under his rigid rule of immediate baptism, he wrote this hymn to fortify them:

Christians, if your hearts are warm,
Ice and cold can do no harm;
If by Jesus you are prized

Rise, believe and be baptized.

He found use for the hymn, too, in rallying church-members who staid away from his meetings in bad weather. The "poetry" expressed what he wanted to say—which, in his view, was sufficient apology for it. It was sung in revival meetings like others that he wrote, and a few hymnbooks now long obsolete contained it; but of Leland's hymns only one survives. Gray-headed men and women remember being sung to sleep by their mothers with that old-fashioned evening song to Amzi Chapin's* tune—

> The day is past and gone,
> The evening shades appear,
> O may we all remember well
> The night of death draws near;

—and with all its solemnity and other-worldness it is dear to recollection, and its five stanzas are lovingly hunted up in the few hymnals where it is found. Bradbury's "Braden," *(Baptist Praise Book,* 1873,) is one of its tunes.

* Amzi Chapin has left, apparently, nothing more than the record of his birth, March 2, 1768, and the memory of his tune. It appeared as early as 1805.

Elder Leland was a remarkable revival preacher, and his prayers—as was said of Elder Jabez Swan's fifty or sixty years later—"brought heaven and earth together." He traveled through the Eastern States as an evangelist, and spent a season in Virginia in the same work. In 1801 he revisited that region on a curious errand. The farmers of Cheshire, Mass., where Leland was then a settled pastor, conceived the plan of sending "the biggest cheese in America" to President Jefferson, and Leland (who was a good democrat) offered to go to Washington on an ox-team with it, and "preach all the way"—which he actually did.

The cheese weighed 1450 lbs.

Elder Leland died in North Adams, Mass., Jan. 14, 1844. Another of his hymns, which deserved to live with his "Evening Song," seemed to be answered in the brightness of his death-bed hope:

> O when shall I see Jesus
> And reign with Him above,
> And from that flowing fountain
> Drink everlasting love?

"AWAKE, MY SOUL, TO JOYFUL LAYS."

This glad hymn of Samuel Medley is his thanksgiving song, written soon after his conversion. In the places of rural worship no lay of Christian praise and gratitude was ever more heartily sung than this at the testimony meetings.

> Awake, my soul, to joyful lays,
> And sing thy great Redeemer's praise;
> He justly claims a song from me:
> His loving-kindness, oh, how free!
> Loving-kindness, loving-kindness,
> His loving-kindness, oh, how free!

THE TUNE,

With its queer curvet in every second line, had no other name than "Loving-Kindness," and was probably a camp-meeting melody in use for some time before its publication. It is found in *Leavitt's Christian Lyre* as early as 1830. The name "William Caldwell" is all that is known of its composer, though he is supposed to have lived in Tennessee.

"THE LORD INTO HIS GARDEN COMES."

Was a common old-time piece sure to be heard at every religious rally, and every one present, saint and sinner, had it by heart, or at least the chorus of it—

> Amen, amen, my soul replies,
> I'm bound to meet you in the skies,
> And claim my mansion there, etc.

The anonymous* "Garden Hymn, as old, at least, as 1800," has nearly passed out of reach, except by the long arm of the antiquary; but it served its generation.

* A "Rev." Mr. Campbell, author of "The Glorious Light of Zion," "There is a Holy City," and "There is a Land of Pleasure," has been sometimes credited with the origin of the Garden Hymn.

Its vigorous tune is credited to Jeremiah Ingalls (1764–1838).

> The Lord into His garden comes;
> The spices yield a rich perfume,

97

The lilies grow and thrive,
The lilies grow and thrive.
Refreshing showers of grace divine
From Jesus flow to every vine,
Which makes the dead revive,
Which makes the dead revive.

"THE CHARIOT! THE CHARIOT!"

Henry Hart Milman, generally known as Dean Milman, was born in 1791, and was educated at Oxford. In 1821 he was installed as university professor of poetry at Oxford, and it was while filling this position that he wrote this celebrated hymn, under the title of "The Last Day." It is not only a hymn, but a poem—a sublime ode that recalls, in a different movement, the tones of the "Dies Irae."

Dean Milman (of St Paul's), besides his many striking poems and learned historical works, wrote at least twelve hymns, among which are—

Ride on, ride on in majesty,
O help us Lord; each hour of need
Thy heavenly succor give,
When our heads are bowed with woe,

—which last may have been written soon after he laid three of his children in one grave, in the north aisle of Westminster Abbey. He lived a laborious and useful life of seventy-seven years, dying Sept. 24, 1868.

There were times in the old revivals when the silver clarion of the "Chariot Hymn" must needs replace the ruder blast of Occum in old "Ganges" and sinners unmoved by the invisible God of Horeb be made to behold Him—in a vision of the "Last Day."

The Chariot! the Chariot! its wheels roll in fire
When the Lord cometh down in the pomp of His ire,
Lo, self-moving, it drives on its pathway of cloud,
And the heavens with the burden of Godhead are bowed.
*   *   *   *   *   *
The Judgment! the Judgment! the thrones are all set,
Where the Lamb and the white-vested elders are met;
There all flesh is at once in the sight of the Lord,
And the doom of eternity hangs on His word.

The name "Williams" or "J. Williams" is attached to various editions of the trumpet-like tune, but so far no guide book gives us location, date or sketch of the composer.

"COME, MY BRETHREN."

Another of the "unstudied" revival hymns of invitation.

Come, my brethren, let us try
For a little season
Every burden to lay by,
Come and let us reason.
What is this that casts you down.
What is this that grieves you?
Speak and let your wants be known;
Speaking may relieve you.

This colloquial rhyme was apt to be started by some good brother or sister in one of the chilly pauses of a prayer-meeting. The air (there was never anything more to it) with a range of only a fifth, slurred the last syllable of every second line, giving the quaint effect of a bent note, and altogether the music was as homely as the verse. Both are anonymous. But the little chant sometimes served its purpose wonderfully well.

"BRETHREN, WHILE WE SOJOURN HERE."

This hymn was always welcome in the cottage meetings as well as in the larger greenwood assemblies. It was written by Rev. Joseph Swain, about 1783.

Brethren, while we sojourn here
Fight we must, but should not fear.
Foes we have, but we've a Friend,
One who loves us to the end;
Forward then with courage go;
Long we shall not dwell below,
Soon the joyful news will come,
"Child, your Father calls, 'Come home.'"

The tune was sometimes "Pleyel's Hymn," but oftener it was sung to a melody now generally forgotten of much the same movement but slurred in peculiarly sweet and tender turns. The cadence of the last tune gave the refrain line a melting effect:

Child, your Father calls, "Come home."

Some of the spirit of this old tune (in the few hymnals where the hymn is now printed) is preserved in Geo. Kingsley's "Messiah" which accompanies the words, but the modulations are wanting.

Joseph Swain was born in Birmingham, Eng. in 1761. Bred among mechanics, he was early apprenticed to the engraver's trade, but he was a boy of poetic temperament and fond of writing verses. After the spiritual change which brought a new purpose into his life, he was baptized by Dr. Rippon and studied for the ministry. At the age of about twenty-five, he was settled over the Baptist church in Walworth, where he remained till his death, April 16, 1796.

For more than a century his hymns have lived and been loved in all the English-speaking world. Among those still in use are—

How sweet, how heavenly is the sight,
Pilgrims we are to Canaan bound,
O Thou in whose presence my soul takes delight.

"HAPPY DAY."

O happy day that fixed my choice.
—*Doddridge.*
O how happy are they who the Saviour obey.
—*Charles Wesley.*

These were voices as sure to be heard in converts' meetings as the leader's prayer or text, the former sung inevitably to Rimbault's tune, "Happy Day," and the latter to a "Western Melody" quite as closely akin to Wesley's words.

Edward Francis Rimbault, born at Soho, Eng., June 13, 1816, was at sixteen years of age organist at the Soho Swiss Church, and became a skilled though not a prolific composer. He once received—and declined—the offer of an appointment as professor of music in Harvard College. Died of a lingering illness Sept, 26, 1876.

"COME, HOLY SPIRIT, HEAVENLY DOVE."

—*Watts.*

This was the immortal song-litany that fitted almost anywhere into every service. The Presbyterians and Congregationalists sang it in Tansur's "St. Martins," the Baptists in William Jones' "Stephens" and the Methodists in Maxim's "Turner" (which had the most music), but the hymn went about as well with one as with another.

The Rev. William Jones (1726–1800) an English rector, and Abraham Maxim of Buckfield, Me., (1773–1829) contributed quite a liberal share of the "continental" tunes popular in the latter part of the 18th century. Maxim was eccentric, but the tradition that an unfortunate affair of the heart once drove him into the woods to make away with himself, but a bird on the roof of a logger's hut, making plaintive sounds, interrupted him, and he sat down and wrote the tune "Hallowell," on a strip of white birch bark, is more likely legendary. The following words, said to have inspired his minor tune, are still set to it in the old collections:

As on some lonely building's top
The sparrow makes her moan,
Far from the tents of joy and hope
I sit and grieve alone.*

* Versified by Nahum Tate from Ps. 102:7.

Maxim was fond of the minor mode, but his minors, like "Hallowell," "New Durham," etc., are things of the past. His major chorals and fugues, such as "Portland," "Buckfield," and "Turner" had in them the spirit of healthier melody and longer life. He published at least two collections, *The Oriental Harmony,* in 1802, and *The Northern Harmony,* in 1805.

William Tansur (Tans-ur), author of "St. Martins" (1669–1783), was an organist, composer, compiler, and theoretical writer. He was born at Barnes, Surrey, Eng., (according to one account,) and died at St. Neot's.

"COME, THOU FOUNT OF EVERY BLESSING."

This hymn of Rev. Robert Robinson was almost always heard in the tune of "Nettleton," composed by John Wyeth, about 1812. The more wavy melody of "Sicily" (or "Sicilian Hymn") sometimes carried the verses, but never with the same sympathetic unction. The sing-song movement and accent of old "Nettleton" made it the country favorite.

Robert Robinson, born in Norfolk, Eng., Sept. 27, 1735, was a poor boy, left fatherless at eight years of age, and apprenticed to a barber, but was converted by the preaching of Whitefield and studied till he obtained a good education, and was ordained to the Methodist ministry. He is supposed to have written his well-known hymn in 1758. A certain unsteadiness of mind, however, caused him to revise his religious beliefs too often for his spiritual health or enjoyment, and after preaching as a Methodist, a Baptist, and an Independent, he finally became a Socinian. On a stage-coach journey, when a lady fellow-passenger began singing "Come, Thou Fount of Every Blessing," to relieve the monotony of the ride, he said to her, "Madam, I am the unhappy man who wrote that hymn many years ago; and I would give a thousand worlds, if I had them, if I could feel as I felt then."

Robinson died June 9, 1790.

John Wyeth was born in Cambridge, Mass., 1792, and died at Harrisburg, Pa., 1858. He was a musician and publisher, and issued a Music Book, *Wyeth's Repository of Sacred Music.*

"A POOR WAYFARING MAN OF GRIEF."

Written by James Montgomery, Dec., 1826, was a hymn of tide and headway in George Coles' tune of "Duane St.," with a step that made every heart beat time. The four picturesque eight-line stanzas made a practical sermon in verse and song from Matt. 25:35, telling how—

A poor wayfaring man of grief
Hath often crossed me on my way,
Who sued so humbly for relief
That I could never answer nay.
I had no power to ask his name,
Whither he went or whence he came,
Yet there was something in his eye
That won my love, I knew not why;

—and in the second and third stanzas the narrator relates how he entertained him, and this was the sequel—

Then in a moment to my view
The stranger started from disguise
The token in His hand I knew;
My Saviour stood before my eyes.

When once that song was started, every tongue took it up, (and it was strange if every foot did not count the measure,) and the coldest kindled with gospel warmth as the story swept on.*

* Montgomery's poem, "The Stranger," has seven stanzas. The full dramatic effect of their connection could only be produced by a set piece.

James
Montgomery

"WHEN FOR ETERNAL WORLDS I STEER."

It was no solitary experience for hearers in a house of prayer where the famous Elder Swan held the pulpit, to feel a climactic thrill at the sudden breaking out of the eccentric orator with this song in the very middle of his sermon—

When for eternal worlds I steer,
And seas are calm and skies are clear,
And faith in lively exercise,
And distant hills of Canaan rise,
My soul for joy then claps her wings,
And loud her lovely sonnet sings,
"Vain world, adieu!"
With cheerful hope her eyes explore
Each landmark on the distant shore,

100

The trees of life, the pastures green,
The golden streets, the crystal stream,
Again for joy, she claps her wings,
And loud her lovely sonnet sings,
"Vain world, adieu!"

Elder Jabez Swan was born in Stonington, Ct., Feb. 23, 1800, and died 1884. He was a tireless worker as a pastor (long in New London, Ct.,) and a still harder toiler in the field as an evangelist and as a helper eagerly called for in revivals; and, through all, he was as happy as a boy in vacation. He was unlearned in the technics of the schools, but always eloquent and armed with ready wit; unpolished, but poetical as a Hebrew prophet and as terrible in his treatment of sin. Scoffers and "hoodlums" who interrupted him in his meetings never interrupted him but once.

The more important and canonical hymnals and praise-books had no place for "Sonnet," as the bugle-like air to this hymn was called. Rev. Jonathan Aldrich, about 1860, harmonized it in his *Sacred Lyre*, but this, and the few other old vestry and field manuals that contain it, were compiled before it became the fashion to date and authenticate hymns and tunes. In this case both are anonymous. Another (and probably earlier) tune sung to the same words is credited to "S. Arnold," and appears to have been composed about 1790.

"I'M A PILGRIM, AND I'M A STRANGER."

This hymn still lives—and is likely to live, at least in collections that print revival music. Mrs. Mary Stanley (Bunce) Dana, born in Beaufort, S.C., Feb. 15, 1810, wrote it while living in a northern state, where her husband died. By the name Dana she is known in hymnology, though she afterwards became Mrs. Shindler. The tune identified with the hymn, "I'm a Pilgrim," is untraced, save that it is said to be an "Italian Air," and that its original title was "Buono Notte" (good night).

No other hymn better expresses the outreaching of ardent faith. Its very repetitions emphasize and sweeten the vision of longed-for fruition.

I can tarry, I can tarry but a night,
Do not detain me, for I am going.
*   *   *   *   *   *
There the sunbeams are ever shining,
O my longing heart, my longing heart is there.
*   *   *   *   *   *
Of that country to which I'm going,
My Redeemer, my Redeemer is the light.
There is no sorrow, nor any sighing,
Nor any sin there, nor any dying,
I'm a pilgrim, etc.

The same devout poetess also wrote (1840) the once popular consolatory hymn,—

O sing to me of heaven
When I'm about to die,

—sung to the familiar tune by Rev. E.W. Dunbar; also to a melody composed 1854 by Dr. William Miller.

The line was first written—

When I *am called* to die,

—in the author's copy. The hymn (occasioned by the death of a pious friend) was written Jan. 15, 1840.

Mrs. Dana (Shindler) died in Texas, Feb. 8, 1883.

"JOYFULLY, JOYFULLY ONWARD I MOVE."

The maker of this hymn has been confounded with the maker of its tune—partly, perhaps, from the fact that the real composer of the tune also wrote hymns. The author of the words was the Rev. William Hunter, D.D., an Irish-American, and a Methodist minister. He was born near Ballymoney, County Antrim, Ire., May, 1811, and was brought to America when a child six years old. He received his education in the common schools and at Madison College, Hamilton, N.Y., (now Madison University), and was successively a pastor, editor and Hebrew professor. Besides his work in these different callings, he wrote many helpful hymns—in all one hundred and twenty-five—of which "Joyfully, Joyfully," dated 1842, is the best. It began originally with the line—

Friends fondly cherished have passed on before,

—and the line,—

Home to the land of delight I will go.

—was written,—

Home to the land of bright spirits I'll go.

Dr. Hunter died in Ohio, 1877.

THE TUNE.

Rev. Abraham Dow Merrill, the author of the music to this triumphal death-song, was born in Salem, N.H., 1796, and died April 29, 1878. He also was a Methodist minister, and is still everywhere remembered by the denomination to which he belonged in New Hampshire and Vermont. He rode over these states mingling in revival scenes many years. His picture bears a close resemblance to that of Washington, and he was somewhat famous for this resemblance. His work was everywhere blessed, and he left an imperishable influence in New England. The tune, linked with Dr. Hunter's hymn, formed the favorite melody which has been the dying song of many who learned to sing it amid the old revival scenes:

Death, with thy weapons of war lay me low;
Strike, king of terrors; I fear not the blow.
Jesus has broken the bars of the tomb,
Joyfully, joyfully haste to thy home.

"'TIS THE OLD SHIP OF ZION, HALLELUJAH!"

This may be found, vocalized with full harmony, in the *American Vocalist*. With all the parts together (more or less) it must have made a vociferous song-service, but the hymn was oftener sung simply in soprano unison; and there was sound enough in the single melody to satisfy the most zealous.

All her passengers will land on the bright eternal shore,
O, glory hallelujah!
She has landed many thousands, and will land as many more,
O, glory hallelujah!

Both hymn and tune have lost their creators' names, and, like many another "voice crying in the wilderness," they have left no record of their beginning of days.

"MY BROTHER, I WISH YOU WELL."

My brother, I wish you well,
My brother, I wish you well;
When my Lord calls I trust you will
Be mentioned in the Promised Land.

Echoes that remain to us of those fervid and affectionate, as well as resolute and vehement, expressions of religious life as sung in the early revivals of New England, in parts of the South, and especially in the Middle West, are suggestive of spontaneous melody forest-born, and as unconscious of scale, clef or tempo as the song of a bird. The above "hand-shaking" ditty at the altar gatherings apparently took its tune self-made, inspired in its first singer's soul by the feeling of the moment—and the strain was so simple that the convert could join in at once and chant—

When my Lord comes I trust *I shall*

—through all the loving rotations of the crude hymn-tune. Such song-births of spiritual enthusiasm are beyond enumeration—and it is useless to hunt for author or composer. Under the momentum of a wrestling hour or a common rapture of experience, counterpoint was unthought of, and the same notes for every voice lifted pleading and praise in monophonic impromptu. The refrains—

O how I love Jesus,
O the Lamb, the Lamb, the loving Lamb,
I'm going home to die no more,
Pilgrims we are to Canaan's land,
O turn ye, O turn ye, for why will you die,
Come to Jesus, come to Jesus, just now,

—each at the sound of its first syllable brought its own music to every singer's tongue, and all—male and female—were sopranos together. This habit in singing those rude liturgies of faith and fellowship was recognized by the editors of the *Revivalist*, and to a multitude of them space was given only for the printed melody, and of this sometimes only the three or four initial bars. The tunes were the church's rural field-tones that everybody knew.

Culture smiles at this unclassic hymnody of long ago, but its history should disarm criticism. To wanderers its quaint music and "pedestrian" verse were threshold call and door-way welcome into the church of the living God. Even in the flaming days of the Second Advent following, in 1842–3, they awoke in many hardened hearts the spiritual glow that never dies. The delusion passed away, but the grace remained.

The church—and the world—owe a long debt to the old evangelistic refrains that rang through the sixty years before the Civil War, some of them flavored with tuneful piety of a remoter time. They preached righteousness, and won souls that sermons could not reach. They opened heaven to thousands who are now rejoicing there.

CHAPTER VIII.

SUNDAY-SCHOOL HYMNS.

SHEPHERD OF TENDER YOUTH.

Στόμιον πώλων ἀδάων

We are assured by repeated references in the patristic writings that the primitive years of the Christian Church were not only years of suffering but years of song. That the despised and often persecuted "Nazarenes," scattered in little colonies throughout the Roman Empire, did not forget to mingle tones of praise and rejoicing with their prayers could readily be believed from the much-quoted letter of a pagan lawyer, written about as long after Jesus' death, as from now back to the death of John Quincy Adams—the letter of Pliny the younger to the Emperor Trajan, in which he reports the Christians at their meetings singing "hymns to Christ as to a god."

Those disciples who spoke Greek seem to have been especially tuneful, and their land of poets was doubtless the cradle of Christian hymnody. Believers taught their songs to their children, and it is as certain that the oldest Sunday-school hymn was written somewhere in the classic East as that the Book of Revelation was written on the Isle of Patmos. The one above indicated was found in an appendix to the *Tutor*, a book composed by Titus Flavius Clemens of Alexandria, a Christian philosopher and instructor whose active life began late in the second century. It follows a treatise on Jesus as the Great Teacher, and, though his own words elsewhere imply a more ancient origin of the poem, it is always called "Clement's Hymn." The line quoted above is the first of an English version by the late Rev. Henry Martyn Dexter, D.D. It does not profess to be a translation, but aims to transfer to our common tongue the spirit and leading thoughts of the original.

Shepherd of tender youth,
Guiding in love and truth
Through devious ways;
Christ, our triumphant King,
We come Thy name to sing,
Hither our children bring
To shout Thy praise.

The last stanza of Dr. Dexter's version represents the sacred song spirit of both the earliest and the latest Christian centuries:

So now, and till we die
Sound we Thy praises high,
And joyful sing;
Infants, and the glad throng
Who to Thy church belong
Unite to swell the song
To Christ our King.

While they give us the sentiment and the religious tone of the old hymn, these verses, however, recognize the extreme difficulty of anything like verbal fidelity in translating a Greek hymn, and in this instance there are metaphors to avoid as being strange to modern taste. The first stanza, literally rendered and construed, is as follows:

Bridle of untaught foals,
Wing of unwandering birds,
Helm and Girdle of babes,
Shepherd of royal lambs!
Assemble Thy simple children
To praise holily,
To hymn guilelessly
With innocent mouths
Christ, the Guide of children.
Figures like—
Catching the chaste fishes,
Heavenly milk, etc.

—are necessarily avoided in making good English of the lines, and the profusion of adoring epithets in the ancient poem (no less than twenty-one different titles of Christ) would embarrass a modern song.

Dr. Dexter might have chosen an easier metre for his version, if (which is improbable) he intended it to be sung, since a tune written to sixes and fours takes naturally a more decided lyrical movement and emphasis than the hymn reveals in his stanzas, though the second and fifth possess much of the hymn quality and would sound well in Giardini's "Italian Hymn."

More nearly a translation, and more in the cantabile style, is the version of a Scotch Presbyterian minister, Rev. Hamilton M. Macgill, D.D., two of whose stanzas are these:

Thyself, Lord, be the Bridle
These wayward wills to stay;
Be Thine the Wing unwand'ring,
To speed their upward way.

*   *   *   *   *   *

Let them with songs adoring
Their artless homage bring
To Christ the Lord, and crown Him
The children's Guide and King.

The Dexter version is set to Monk's slow harmony of "St. Ambrose" in the *Plymouth Hymnal* (Ed. Dr. Lyman Abbott, 1894) without the writer's name—which is curious, inasmuch as the hymn was published in the *Congregationalist* in 1849, in *Hedge and Huntington's* (Unitarian) *Hymn-book* in 1853, in the *Hymnal of the Presbyterian Church* in 1866, and in Dr. Schaff's *Christ in Song* in 1869.

Clement died about A.D. 220.

Rev. Henry Martyn Dexter, D.D., for twenty-three years the editor of the *Congregationalist*, was born in Plymouth, Mass., Aug. 13, 1821. He was a graduate of Yale (1840) and Andover Divinity School (1844), a well-known antiquarian writer and church historian. Died Nov. 13, 1890.

"HOW HAPPY IS THE CHILD WHO HEARS."

This hymn was quite commonly heard in Sunday-schools during the eighteen-thirties and forties, and, though retained in few modern collections, its Sabbath echo lingers in the memory of the living generation. It was written by Michael Bruce, born at Kinneswood, Kinross-shire, Scotland, March 27, 1746. He was the son of a weaver, but obtained a good education, taught school, and studied for the ministry. He died, however, while in preparation for his expected work, July 5, 1767, at the age of twenty-one years, three months and eight days.

Young Bruce wrote hymns, and several poems, but another person wore the honors of his work. John Logan, who was his literary executor, appropriated the youthful poet's Mss. verses, and the hymn above indicated—as well as the beautiful poem, "To the Cuckoo,"—bore the name of Logan for more than a hundred years. In *Julian's Dictionary of Hymnology* is told at length the story of the inquiry and discussion which finally exposed the long fraud upon the fame of the rising genius who sank, like Henry Kirke White, in his morning of promise.

> *   Hail,   beauteous   stranger   of   the   wood,
> Attendant   on   the   Spring;
> Now   Heaven   repairs   thy   rural   seat,
> And woods thy welcome ring.

THE TUNE.

Old "Balerma" was so long the musical mouth-piece of the pious boy-schoolmaster's verses that the two became one expression, and one could not be named without suggesting the other.

"Balerma" (Palermo) was ages away in style and sound from the later type of Sunday-school tunes, resembling rather one of Palestrina's chorals than the tripping melodies that took its place; but in its day juvenile voices enjoyed it, and it suited very well the grave but winning words.

How happy is the child who hears
Instruction's warning voice,
And who celestial Wisdom makes
His early, only choice!
For she hath treasures greater far
Than East and West unfold,
And her rewards more precious are
Than all their stores of gold.
She guides the young with innocence
In pleasure's path to tread,
A crown of glory she bestows

Upon the hoary head.

Robert Simpson, author of the old tune,* was a Scottish composer of psalmody; born, about 1722, in Glasgow; and died, in Greenock, June, 1838.

* The tune was evidently reduced from the still older "Sardius" (or "Autumn")—*Hubert P. Main.*

"O DO NOT BE DISCOURAGED."

Written about 1803, by the Rev. John A. Grenade, born in 1770; died 1806.

O do not be discouraged,}
For Jesus is your Friend;} *bis*
He will give you grace to conquer,
And keep you to the end.
Fight on, ye little soldiers,}
The battle you shall win,} *bis*
For the Saviour is your Captain,
And He has vanquished sin.
And when the conflict's over,}
Before Him you shall stand,} *bis*
You shall sing His praise forever
In Canaan's happy land.

THE TUNE.

The hymn was made popular thirty or more years ago in a musical arrangement by Hubert P. Main, with a chorus,—

I'm glad I'm in this army,
And I'll battle for the school.

Children took to the little song with a keen relish, and put their whole souls—and bodies—into it.

"LITTLE TRAVELLERS ZIONWARD"

Belongs to a generation long past. Its writer was an architect by occupation, and a man whose piety equalled his industry. He was born in London 1791, and his name was James Edmeston. He loved to compose religious verses—so well, in fact, that he is said to have prepared a new piece every week for Sunday morning devotions in his family and in this way accumulated a collection which he published and called *Cottager's Hymns.* Besides these he is credited with a hundred Sunday-school hymns.

Little travellers Zionward,
Each one entering into rest
In the Kingdom of your Lord,
In the mansions of the blest,
There to welcome Jesus waits,
Gives the crown His followers win,
Lift your heads, ye golden gates,
Let the little travellers in.

The original tune is lost—and the hymn is vanishing with it; but the felicity of its rhyme and rhythm show how easily it adapted itself to music.

"I'M BUT A STRANGER HERE."

The simple beauty of this hymn, and the sympathetic sweetness of its tune made children love to sing it, and it found its way into a few Sunday-school collections, though not composed for such use.

A young Congregational minister. Rev. Thomas Rawson Taylor, wrote it on the approach of his early end. He was born at Osset, near Wakefield, Yorkshire, Eng., May 9, 1807, and studied in Bradford, where his father had taken charge of a large church, and at Manchester Academy and Airesdale College. Sensible of a growing ailment that might shorten his days, he hastened to the work on which his heart was set, preaching in surrounding towns and villages while a student, and finally quitting college to be ordained to his sacred profession. He was installed as pastor of Howard St. Chapel, Sheffield, July, 1830, whenonly twenty-three. But in less than three years his strength failed, and he went back to Bradford, where he occasionally preached for his father, when able to do so, during his last days. He died there March 15, 1835. Taylor was a brave and lovely Christian—and his hymn is as sweet as his life.

I'm but a stranger here,
Heaven is my home;
Earth is a desert drear,

Heaven is my home.
Dangers and sorrows stand
Round me on every hand;
Heaven is my Fatherland—
Heaven is my home.
What though the tempest rage,
Heaven is my home;
Short is my pilgrimage,
Heaven is my home.
And time's wild, wintry blast
Soon will be overpast;
I shall reach home at last—
Heaven is my home.

In his last attempt to preach, young Taylor uttered the words, "I want to die like a soldier, sword in hand." On the evening of the same Sabbath day he breathed his last. His words were memorable, and Montgomery, who loved and admired the man, made them the text of a poem, part of which is the familiar hymn "Servant of God, well done."*

* See page 498

THE TUNE.

Sir Arthur Sullivan put the words into classic expression, but, to American ears at least, the tune of "Oak," by Lowell Mason, is the hymn's true sister. It was composed in 1854.

"DEAR JESUS, EVER AT MY SIDE."

One of Frederick William Faber's sweet and simple lyrics. It voices that temper and spirit in the human heart which the Saviour first looks for and loves best. None better than Faber could feel and utter the real artlessness of Christian love and faith.

Dear Jesus, ever at my side,
How loving must Thou be
To leave Thy home in heaven to guard
A sinful child like me.
Thy beautiful and shining face
I see not, tho' so near;
The sweetness of Thy soft low voice
I am too deaf to hear.
I cannot feel Thee touch my hand
With pressure light and mild,
To check me as my mother did
When I was but a child;
But I have felt Thee in my thoughts
Fighting with sin for me,
And when my heart loves God I know
The sweetness is from Thee.

THE TUNE.

"Audientes" by Sir Arthur Sullivan is a gentle, emotional piece, rendering the first quatrain of each stanza in E flat unison, and the second in C harmony.

"TIS RELIGION THAT CAN GIVE."

This simple rhyme, which has been sung perhaps in every Sunday-school in England and the United States, is from a small English book by Mary Masters. In the preface to the work, we read, "The author of the following poems never read a treatise of rhetoric or an art of poetry, nor was ever taught her English grammar. Her education rose no higher than the spelling-book or her writing-master,"

'Tis religion that can give
Sweetest pleasure while we live;
'Tis religion can supply
Solid comfort when we die.
After death its joys shall be
Lasting as eternity.

Save the two sentences about herself, quoted above, there is no biography of the writer. That she was good is taken for granted.

The tune-sister of the little hymn is as scant of date or history as itself. No. 422 points it out in *The Revivalist*, where the name and initial seem to ascribe the authorship to Horace Waters.'

* From his *Sabbath Bell.* Horace Waters, a prominent Baptist layman, was born in Jefferson, Lincoln Co., Me., Nov. 1, 1812, and died in New York City, April 22, 1893. He was a piano-dealer and publisher.

"THERE IS A HAPPY LAND FAR, FAR AWAY"

This child's hymn was written by a lover of children, Mr. Andrew Young, head master of Niddrey St. School, Edinburgh, and subsequently English instructor at Madras College, E.I. He was born April 23, 1807, and died Nov. 30, 1899, and long before the end of the century which his life-time so nearly covered his little carol had become one of the universal hymns.

THE TUNE.

A Hindoo air or natural chanson, that may have been hummed in a pagan temple in the hearing of Mr. Young, was the basis of the little melody since made familiar to millions of prattling tongues.

Such running tone-rhythms create themselves in the instinct of the ruder nations and tribes, and even the South African savages have their incantations with the provincial "clicks" that mark the singers' time. With an ear for native chirrups and trills, the author of our pretty infant-school song succeeded in capturing one, and making a Christian tune of it.

The musician, Samuel Sebastian Wesley, sometime in the eighteen-forties, tried to substitute another melody for the lines, but "There is a happy land" needs its own birth-music.

"I HAVE A FATHER IN THE PROMISED LAND."

Another cazonet for the infant class. Instead of a hymn, however, it is only a refrain, and—like the ring-chant of the "Hebrew Children," and even more simple—owes its only variety to the change of one word. The third and fourth lines,—

My father calls me, I must go
To meet Him in the Promised Land,

—take their cue from the first, which may sing,—

I have a Saviour——
I have a mother——
I have a brother——

—and so on ad libitum. But the little ones love every sound and syllable of the lisping song, for it is plain and pleasing, and when a pinafore school grows restless nothing will sooner charm them into quiet than to chime its innocent unison.

Both words and tune are nameless and storyless.

"I THINK WHEN I READ THAT SWEET STORY"

While riding in a stage-coach, after a visit to a mission school for poor children, this hymn came to the mind of Mrs. Jemima Thompson Luke, of Islington, England. It speaks its own purpose plainly enough, to awaken religious feeling in young hearts, and guide and sanctify the natural childlike interest in the sweetest incident of the Saviour's life.

I think when I read that sweet story of old
When Jesus was here among men,
How He called little children as lambs to His fold,
I should like to have been with them then.
I wish that His hands had been laid on my head,
And I had been placed on His knee,
And that I might have seen His kind look when He said,
"Let the little ones come unto me."

This is not poetry, but it phrases a wish in a child's own way, to be melodized and fixed in a child's reverent and sensitive memory.

Mrs. Luke was born at Colebrook Terrace, near London, Aug. 19, 1813. She was an accomplished and benevolent lady who did much for the education and welfare of the poor. Her hymn—of five stanzas—was first sung in a village school at Poundford Park, and was not published until 1841.

THE TUNE.

It is interesting, not to say curious, testimony to the vital quality of this meek production that so many composers have set it to music, or that successive hymn-book editors have kept it, and printed it to so many different harmonies. All the chorals that carry it have substantially the same movement—for the spondaic accent of the long lines is compulsory—but their offerings sing "to one clear harp in divers tones."

The appearance of the words in one hymnal with Sir William Davenant's air (full scored) to Moore's love-song, "Believe me, if all those endearing young charms," now known as the tune of "Fair Harvard," is rather startling at first, but the adoption is quite in keeping with the policy of Luther and Wesley.

"St. Kevin" written to it forty years ago by John Henry Cornell, organist of St. Paul's, New York City, is sweet and sympathetic.

The newest church collection (1905) gives the beautiful air and harmony of "Athens" to the hymn, and notes the music as a "Greek Melody."

But the nameless English tune, of uncertain authorship* that accompanies the words in the smaller old manuals, and which delighted Sunday-schools for a generation, is still the favorite in the memory of thousands, and may be the very music first written.

* Harmonized by Hubert P. Main.

"WE SPEAK OF THE REALMS OF THE BLEST."

Mrs. Elizabeth Mills, wife of the Hon. Thomas Mills, M.P., was born at Stoke Newington, Eng., 1805. She was one of the brief voices that sing one song and die. This hymn was the only note of her minstrelsy, and it has outlived her by more than three-quarters of a century. She wrote it about three weeks before her decease in Finsbury Place, London, April 21, 1839, at the age of twenty-four.

We speak of the land of the blest,
A country so bright and so fair,
And oft are its glories confest,
But what must it be to be there!
*   *   *   *   *   *
We speak of its freedom from sin,
From sorrow, temptation and care,
From trials without and within,
But what must it be to be there!

THE TUNE.

The hymn, like several of the Gospel hymns besides, was carried into the Sunday-schools by its music. Mr. Stebbins' popular duet-and-chorus is fluent and easily learned and rendered by rote; and while it captures the ear and compels the voice of the youngest, it expresses both the pathos and the exaltation of the words.

George Coles Stebbins was born in East Carleton, Orleans Co., N.Y., Feb. 26, 1846. Educated at common school, and an academy in Albany, he turned his attention to music and studied in Rochester, Chicago, and Boston. It was in Chicago that his musical career began, while chorister at the First Baptist Church; and while holding the same position at Clarendon St. Church, Boston, (1874–6), he entered on a course of evangelistic work with D.L. Moody as gospel singer and composer. He was co-editor with Sankey and McGranahan of *Gospel Hymns.*

"ONLY REMEMBERED."

This hymn, beginning originally with the lines,—
Up and away like the dew of the morning,
Soaring from earth to its home in the sun,
—has been repeatedly altered since it left Dr. Bonar's hands. Besides the change of metaphors, the first personal pronoun singular is changed to the plural. There was strength, and a natural vivacity in—
So let *me* steal away gently and lovingly,
Only remembered for what *I* have done.
As at present sung the first stanza reads—,
Fading away like the stars of the morning
Losing their light in the glorious sun,
Thus would *we* pass from the earth and its toiling
Only remembered for what *we* have done.

The idea voiced in the refrain is true and beautiful, and the very euphony of its words helps to enforce its meaning and make the song pleasant and suggestive for young and old. It has passed into popular quotation, and become almost a proverb.

THE TUNE.

The tune (in *Gospel Hymns No. 6*) is Mr. Sankey's.

Ira David Sankey was born in Edinburgh, Lawrence Co., Pa., Aug. 28, 1840. He united with the Methodist Church at the age of fifteen, and became choir leader, Sunday-school superintendent and president of the Y.M.C.A., all in his native town. Hearing Philip Phillips sing impressed him deeply, when a young man, with the power of a gifted solo vocalist over assembled multitudes, but he did not fully realize his own capability till Dwight L. Moody heard his remarkable voice and convinced him of his divine mission to be a gospel singer.

The success of his revival tours with Mr. Moody in America and England is history.

Mr. Sankey has compiled at least five singing books, and has written the *Story of the Gospel Hymns*. Until overtaken by blindness, in his later years he frequently appeared as a lecturer on sacred music. The manuscript of his story of the *Gospel Hymns* was destroyed by accident, but, undismayed by the ruin of his work, and the loss of his eye-sight, like Sir Isaac Newton and Thomas Carlyle, he began his task again. With the help of an amanuensis the book was restored and, in 1905, given to the public. (See page 258.)

"SAVIOUR, LIKE A SHEPHERD LEAD US."

Mrs. Dorothy Ann Thrupp, of Paddington Green, London, the author of this hymn, was born June 20, 1799, and died, in London, Dec. 14, 1847. Her hymns first appeared in Mrs. Herbert Mayo's *Selection of Poetry and Hymns for the Use of Infant and Juvenile Schools*, (1838).

We are Thine, do Thou befriend us,
Be the Guardian of our way:
Keep Thy flock, from sin defend us,
Seek us when we go astray;
Blessed Jesus,
Hear, O hear us when we pray.

The tune everywhere accepted and loved is W.B. Bradbury's; written in 1856.

"YIELD NOT TO TEMPTATION"

A much used and valued hymn, with a captivating tune and chorus for young assemblies. Both words and music are by H.R. Palmer, composed in 1868.

Yield not to temptation,
For yielding is sin;
Each vict'ry will help you
Some other to win.
Fight manfully onward,
Dark passions subdue;
Look ever to Jesus,
He will carry you through.

Horatio Richmond Palmer was born in Sherburne, N.Y., April 26. 1834, of a musical family, and sang alto in his father's choir when only nine. He studied music unremittingly, and taught music at fifteen. Brought up in a Christian home, his religious life began in his youth, and he consecrated his art to the good of man and the glory of God.

He became well-known as a composer of sacred music, and as a publisher—the sales of his *Song Queen* amounting to 200,000 copies. As a leader of musical conventions and in the Church Choral Union, his influence in elevating the standard of song-worship has been widely felt.

"THERE ARE LONELY HEARTS TO CHERISH."

"While the days are going by" is the refrain of the song, and the line by which it is recognized. The hymn or poem was written by George Cooper. He was born in New York City, May 14, 1840—a writer of poems and magazine articles,—composed "While the days are going by" in 1870.

There are lonely hearts to cherish
While the days are going by.
There are weary souls who perish
While the days are going by.
Up! then, trusty hearts and true,
Though the day comes, night comes, too:
Oh, the good we all may do
While the days are going by!

There are few more practical and always-timely verses than this three-stanza poem.

THE TUNE.

A very musical tune, with spirited chorus, (in *Gospel Hymns*) bears the name of the refrain, and was composed by Mr. Sankey.

A sweet and quieter harmony (uncredited) is mated with the hymn in the old *Baptist Praise Book* (p. 507) and this was long the fixture to the words, in both Sunday-school and week-day school song-books.

Fanny J.
Crosby
(Mrs. Van Alstyne)

"JESUS THE WATER OF LIFE WILL GIVE."

This Sunday-school lyric is the work of Fanny J. Crosby (Mrs. Van Alstyne). Like her other and greater hymn, "Jesus keep me near the Cross," (noted on p. 156,) it reveals the habitual attitude of the pious author's mind, and the simple earnestness of her own faith as well as her desire to win others.

Jesus the water of life will give
Freely, freely, freely;
Jesus the water of life will give
Freely to those who love Him.
The Spirit and the Bride say "Come
Freely, freely, freely.
And he that is thirsty let him come
And drink the water of life."
Full chorus,—
The Fountain of life is flowing,
Flowing, freely flowing;
The Fountain of life is flowing,
Is flowing for you and for me.

THE TUNE.

The hymn must be sung as it was *made* to be sung, and the composer being many years *en rapport* with the writer, knew how to put all her metrical rhythms into sweet sound. The tune—in Mr. Bradbury's *Fresh Laurels* (1867)—is one of his sympathetic interpretations, and, with the duet sung by two of the best singers of the middle class Sunday-school girls, is a melodious and impressive piece.

"WHEN HE COMETH, WHEN HE COMETH."

The Rev. W.O. Cushing, with the beautiful thought in Malachi 3:17 singing in his soul, composed this favorite Sunday-school hymn, which has gone round the world.

When He cometh, when He cometh
To make up His jewels,
All the jewels, precious jewels,
His loved and His own.
Like the stars of the morning,
His bright brow adorning
They shall shine in their beauty
Bright gems for His crown.
He will gather, He will gather
The gems for His Kingdom,
All the pure ones, all the bright ones,
His loved and His own.
Like the stars, etc.
Little children, little children
Who love their Redeemer,
Are the jewels, precious jewels
His loved and His own,
Like the stars, etc.

Rev. William Orcutt Cushing of Hingham, Mass., born Dec. 31, 1823, wrote this little hymn when a young man (1856), probably with no idea of achieving a literary performance. But it rings; and even if it is a "ringing of changes" on pretty syllables, that is not all. There is a thought

110

in it that *sings*. Its glory came to it, however, when it got its tune—and he must have had a subconsciousness of the tune he wanted when he made the lines for his Sunday-school. He died Oct. 19, 1902.

THE TUNE.

The composer of the music for the "Jewel Hymn" was George F. Root, then living in Reading, Mass.

* Comparison of the "Jewel Hymn" tune with the old glee of "Johnny Schmoker" gives color to the assertion that Mr. Root caught up and adapted a popular ditty for his Christian melody—as was so often done in Wales, and in the Lutheran and Wesleyan reformations. He baptized the comic fugue, and promoted it from the vaudeville stage to the Sunday School.

A minister returning from Europe on an English steamer visited the steerage, and after some friendly talk proposed a singing service it something could be started that "everybody" knew—for there were hundreds of emigrants there from nearly every part of Europe.

"It will have to be an American tune, then," said the steerage-master; "try 'His jewels.'"

The minister struck out at once with the melody and words,—
> When He cometh, when He cometh,

—and scores of the poor half-fare multitude joined voices with him. Many probably recognized the music of the old glee, and some had heard the sweet air played in the church-steeples at home. Other voices chimed in, male and female, catching the air, and sometimes the words—they were so easy and so many times repeated—and the volume of song increased, till the singing minister stood in the midst of an international concert, the most novel that he ever led.

He tried other songs in similar visits during the rest of the voyage with some success, but the "Jewel Hymn" was the favorite; and by the time port was in sight the whole crowd of emigrants had it by heart.

The steamer landed at Quebec, and when the trains, filled with the new arrivals, rolled away, the song was swelling from nearly every car,—
> When He cometh, when He cometh,
> To make up His jewels.

The composer of the tune—with all the patriotic and sacred master-pieces standing to his credit—never reaped a richer triumph than he shared with his poet-partner that day, when "Precious Jewels" came back to them from over the sea. More than this, there was missionary joy for them both that their tuneful work had done something to hallow the homes of alien settlers with an American Christian psalm.

George Frederick Root, Doctor of Music, was born in Sheffield, Mass., 1820, eldest of a family of eight children, and spent his youth on a farm. His genius for music drew him to Boston, where he became a pupil of Lowell Mason, and soon advanced so far as to teach music himself and lead the choir in Park St. church. Afterwards he went to New York as director of music in Dr. Deems's Church of the Strangers. In 1852, after a year's absence and study in Europe, he returned to New York, and founded the Normal Musical Institute. In 1860, he removed to Chicago where he spent the remainder of his life writing and publishing music. He died Aug. 6, 1895, in Maine.

In the truly popular sense Dr. Root was the best-known American composer; not excepting Stephen C. Foster. Root's "Hazel Dell," "There's Music in the Air," and "Rosalie the Prairie Flower" were universal tunes—(words by Fanny Crosby,)—as also his music to Henry Washburn's "Vacant Chair." The songs in his cantata, "The Haymakers," were sung in the shops and factories everywhere, and his war-time music, in such melodies as "Shouting the Battle-cry of Freedom" and "Tramp, Tramp, Tramp, the Boys are Marching" took the country by storm.

"SCATTER SEEDS OF KINDNESS."

This amiable and tuneful poem, suggested by Rom. 12:10, is from the pen of Mary Louise Riley (Mrs. Albert Smith) of New York City. She was born in Brighton, Monroe Co., N.Y. May 27, 1843.
> Let us gather up the sunbeams
> Lying all along our path;
> Let us keep the wheat and roses
> Casting out the thorns and chaff.
> CHORUS.
> Then scatter seeds of kindness (*ter*)
> For our reaping by and by.

Silas Jones Vail, the tune-writer, for this hymn, was born Oct. 1818, and died May 20, 1883. For years he worked at the hatter's trade, with Beebe on Broadway, N.Y. and afterwards in an establishment of his own. His taste and talent led him into musical connections, and from time to time, after relinquishing his trade, he was with Horace Waters, Philip Phillips, W.B. Bradbury, and F.J. Smith, the piano dealer. He was a choir leader and a good composer.

"BY COOL SILOAM'S SHADY RILL."

This hymn of Bp. Heber inculcates the same lesson as that in the stanzas of Michael Bruce before noted, with added emphasis for the young on the briefness of time and opportunity even for them.

How fair the lily grows,
—is answered by—
The lily must decay,
—but, owing to the sweetness of the favorite melody, it was never a saddening hymn for children.

THE TUNE.

Though George Kingsley's "Heber" has in some books done service for the Bishop's lines, "Siloam," easy-flowing and finely harmonized, is knit to the words as no other tune can be. It was composed by Isaac Baker Woodbury on shipboard during a storm at sea. A stronger illustration of tranquil thought in terrible tumult was never drawn.

"O Galilee, Sweet Galilee," whose history has been given at the end of chapter six, was not only often sung in Sunday-schools, but chimed (in the cities) on steeple-bells—nor is it by any means forgotten today—on the Sabbath and in social singing assemblies. Like "Precious Jewels," it has been, in many places, taken up by street boys with a relish, and often displaced the play-house ditties in the lips of little newsboys and bootblacks during a leisure hour or a happy mood.

"I AM SO GLAD"

This lively little melody is still a welcome choice to many a lady teacher of fluttering five-year-olds, when both vocal indulgence and good gospel are needed for the prattlers in her class. It has been as widely sung in Scotland as in America. Mr. Philip P. Bliss, hearing one day the words of the familiar chorus—

O, how I love Jesus,
—suddenly thought to himself,—
"I have sung long enough of my poor love to Christ, and now I will sing of His love for me." Under the inspiration of this thought, he wrote—

I am so glad that our Father in heaven
Tells of His love in the book He has given
Wonderful things in the Bible I see,
This is the dearest—that Jesus loves me.
Both words and music are by Mr. Bliss.

The history of modern Sunday-school hymnody—or much of it—is so nearly identified with that of the *Gospel Hymns* that other selections like the last, which might be appropriate here, may be considered in a later chapter, where that eventful series of sacred songs receives special notice.

CHAPTER IX.

PATRIOTIC HYMNS.

The ethnic anthologies growing out of love of country are a mingled literature of filial and religious piety, ranging from war-like pæans to lyric prayers. They become the cherished inheritance of a nation, and, once fixed in the common memory and common heart, the people rarely let them die. The "Songs of the Fathers" have perennial breath, and in every generation—

The green woods of their native land
Shall whisper in the strain;
The voices of their household band
Shall sweetly speak again.
—*Felicia Hemans.*

ULTIMA THULE.

American pride has often gloried in Seneca's "Vision of the West," more than eighteen hundred years ago.

Venient annis
Sæcula seris, quibus Oceanus
Vincula rerum laxet, et ingens
Pateat tellus, Typhisque novos
Detegat orbes, nec sit terris
Ultima Thule.

A time will come in future ages far
When Ocean will his circling bounds unbar.
And, opening vaster to the Pilot's hand,
New worlds shall rise, where mightier kingdoms are,
Nor Thule longer be the utmost land.

This poetic forecast, of which Washington Irving wrote "the predictions of the ancient oracles were rarely so unequivocal," is part of the "chorus" at the end of the second act of Seneca's "Medea," written near the date of St. Paul's first Epistle to the Thessalonians.

Seneca, the celebrated Roman (Stoic) philosopher, was born at or very near the time of our Saviour's birth. There are legends of his acquaintance with Paul, at Rome, but though he wrote able and quotable treatises *On Consolation, On Providence, On Calmness of Soul,* and *On the Blessed Life,* there is no direct evidence that the savor of Christian faith ever qualified his works or his personal principles. He was a man of grand ideas and inspirations, but he was a time server and a flatterer of the Emperor Nero, who, nevertheless, caused his death when he had no further use for him.

His compulsory suicide occurred A.D. 65, the year in which St. Paul is supposed to have suffered martyrdom.

"THE BREAKING WAVES DASHED HIGH."

Sitting at the tea-table one evening, near a century ago, Mrs. Hemans read an old account of the "Landing of the Pilgrims," and was inspired to write this poem, which became a favorite in America—like herself, and all her other works.

The ballad is inaccurate in details, but presents the spirit of the scene with true poet insight. Mr. James T. Fields, the noted Boston publisher, visited the lady in her old age, and received an autograph copy of the poem, which is seen in Pilgrim Hall, Plymouth, Mass.

The breaking waves dashed high, on a stern and rock-bound coast,
And the woods against a stormy sky, their giant branches tossed,
And the heavy night hung dark, the hills and waters o'er,
When a band of exiles moored their bark on the wild New England shore.
Not as the conqueror comes, they, the true-hearted, came;
Not with the roll of stirring drums, and the trumpet that sings of fame;
Not as the flying come, in silence and in fear,—
They shook the depths of the desert's gloom with their hymns of lofty cheer.
Amidst the storm they sang, and the stars heard, and the sea!
And the sounding aisles of the dim woods rang to the anthem of the free!
The ocean eagle soared from his nest by the white waves' foam,
And the rocking pines of the forest roared,—this was their welcome home!
There were men with hoary hair amidst that pilgrim band,—
Why had *they* come to wither there, away from their childhood's land?
There was woman's fearless eye, lit by her deep love's truth;
There was manhood's brow, serenely high, and the fiery heart of youth.
What sought they thus afar? bright jewels of the mine?
The wealth of seas? the spoils of war?—They sought a faith's pure shrine!
Ay, call it holy ground, the soil where first they trod;
They left unstained what there they found,—freedom to worship God!

Felicia Dorothea Browne (Mrs. Hemans) was born in Liverpool, Eng., 1766, and died 1845.

THE TUNE.

The original tune is not now accessible. It was composed by Mrs. Mary E. (Browne) Arkwright, Mrs. Hemans' sister, and published in England about 1835. But the words have been sung in this country to "Silver St.," a choral not entirely forgotten, credited to an English composer, Isaac Smith, born, in London, about 1735, and died there in 1800.

"WESTWARD THE COURSE OF EMPIRE."

Usually misquoted "Westward the *Star* of Empire," etc. This poem of Bishop Berkeley possesses no lyrical quality but, like the ancient Roman's words, partakes of the prophetic spirit, and has always been dear to the American heart by reason of the above line. It seems to formulate the "manifest destiny" of a great colonizing race that has already absorbed a continent, and extended its sway across the Pacific ocean.

Not such as Europe breeds in her decay;
Such as she bred when fresh and young,
When heavenly flame did animate her clay,
By future poets shall be sung.
Westward the course of empire takes its way;

113

The four first acts already past,
The fifth shall close the drama of the day:
Time's noblest offspring is the last.

George Berkeley was born March 12, 1684, and educated at Trinity College, Dublin. A remarkable student, he became a remarkable man, as priest, prelate, and philosopher. High honors awaited him at home, but the missionary passion seized him. Inheriting a small fortune, he sailed to the West, intending to evangelize and educate the Indians of the "Summer Islands," but the ship lost her course, and landed him at Newport, R.I., instead of the Bermudas. Here he was warmly welcomed, but was disappointed in his plans and hopes of founding a native college by the failure of friends in England to forward funds, and after a residence of six years he returned home. He died at Cloyne, Ireland, 1753.

The house which Bishop Berkeley built is still shown (or was until very recently) at Newport after one hundred and seventy-eight years. He wrote the *Principles of Human Knowledge*, the *Minute Philosopher*, and many other works of celebrity in their time, and a scholarship in Yale bears his name; but he is best loved in this country for his *Ode to America*.

Pope in his list of great men ascribes—

To Berkeley every virtue under heaven.

"SOUND THE LOUD TIMBREL."

One would scarcely guess that this bravura hymn of victory and "Come, ye disconsolate," were written by the same person, but both are by Thomas Moore. The song has all the vigor and vivacity of his "Harp That Once Through Tara's Halls," without its pathos. The Irish poet chose the song of Miriam instead of the song of Deborah doubtless because the sentiment and strain of the first of these two great female patriots lent themselves more musically to his lyric verse—and his poem is certainly martial enough to convey the spirit of both.

Sound the loud timbrel o'er Egypt's dark sea!
Jehovah hath triumphed, His people are free!
Sing, for the pride of the tyrant is broken;
His chariots, his horsemen, all splendid and brave—
How vain was their boasting, the Lord hath but spoken,
And chariots and horsemen are sunk in the wave.

THE TUNE.

Of all the different composers to whose music Moore's "sacred songs" were sung—Beethoven, Mozart, Stevenson, and the rest—Avison seems to be the only one whose name and tune have clung to the poet's words; and we have the man and the melody sent to us, as it were, by the lyrist himself. The tune is now rarely sung except at church festivals and village entertainments, but the life and clamor of the scene at the Red Sea are in it, and it is something more than a mere musical curiosity. Its style, however, is antiquated—with its timbrel beat and its canorous harmony and "coda fortis"—and modern choirs have little use in religious service for the sonata written for viols and horns.

It was Moore's splendid hymn that gave it vogue in England and Ireland, and sent it across the sea to find itself in the house of its friends with the psalmody of Billings and Swan. Moore was the man of all men to take a fancy to it and make language to its string-and-trumpet concert. He was a musician himself, and equally able to adapt a tune and to create one. As a festival performance, replete with patriotic noise, let Avison's old "Sound the Timbrel" live.

Charles Avison was born at Newcastle-on-Tyne, 1710. He studied in Italy, wrote works on music, and composed sonatas and concertos for stringed orchestras. For many years he was organist of St. Nicholas' Kirk in his native town.

The tune to "Sound the Loud Timbrel" is a chorus from one of his longer compositions. He died in 1770.

"THE HARP THAT ONCE THROUGH TARA'S HALLS."

This is the only one of Moore's patriotic "Irish Melodies" that lives wherever sweet tones are loved and poetic feeling finds answering hearts. The exquisite sadness of its music and its text is strangely captivating, and its untold story beckons from its lines.

Tara was the ancient home of the Irish kings. King Dermid, who had apostatized from the faith of St. Patrick and his followers, in A.D., 554, violated the Christian right of sanctuary by taking an escaped prisoner from the altar of refuge in Temple Ruadan (Tipperary) and putting him to death. The patron priest and his clergy marched to Tara and solemnly pronounced a curse upon the King. Not long afterwards Dermid was assassinated, and superstition shunned the place "as a castle under ban." The last human resident of "Tara's Hall" was the King's bard, who lingered there, forsaken and ostracized, till he starved to death. Years later one daring visitor found his skeleton and his broken harp.

Moore utilized this story of tragic pathos as a figure in his song for "fallen Erin" lamenting her lost royalty—under a curse that had lasted thirteen hundred years.

The harp that once through Tara's halls
The soul of music shed,
Now hangs as mute on Tara's walls
As if that soul were fled.
So sleeps the pride of former days,
So glory's thrill is o'er,
And hearts that once beat high for praise
Now feel that pulse no more.

No one can read the words without "thinking" the tune. It is supposed that Moore composed them both.

THE MARSEILLAISE HYMN.

Ye sons of France, awake to glory!
Hark! hark! what millions bid you rise!

The "Marseillaise Hymn" so long supposed to be the musical as well as verbal composition of Roget de Lisle, an army engineer, was proved to be only his words set to an air in the "Credo" of a German mass, which was the work of one Holzman in 1726. De Lisle was known to be a poet and musician as well as a soldier, and, as he is said to have played or sung at times in the churches and convents, it is probable that he found and copied the manuscript of Holzman's melody. His haste to rush his fiery "Hymn" before the public in the fever of the Revolution allowed him no time to make his own music, and he adapted the German's notes to his words and launched the song in the streets of Strasburg. It was first sung in Paris by a band of chanters from Marseilles, and, like the trumpets blown around Jericho, it shattered the walls of the French monarchy to their foundations.

The "Marseillaise Hymn" is mentioned here for its patriotic birth and associations. An attempt to make a religious use of it is recorded in the Fourth Chapter.

ODE ON SCIENCE.

This is a "patriotic hymn," though a queer production with a queer name, considering its contents; and its author was no intimate of the Muses. Liberty is supposed to be somehow the corollary of learning, or vice versa—whichever the reader thinks.

The morning sun shines from the East
And spreads his glories to the West.
*   *   *   *   *   *
So Science spreads her lucid ray
O'er lands that long in darkness lay;
She visits fair Columbia,
And sets her sons among the stars.
Fair Freedom, her attendant, waits, etc.

THE TUNE

Was the really notable part of this old-time "Ode," the favorite of village assemblies, and the inevitable practice-piece for amateur violinists. The author of the crude symphony was Deacon Janaziah (or Jazariah) Summer, of Taunton, Mass., who prepared it—music and probably words—for the semi-centennial of Simeon Dagget's Academy in 1798. The "Ode" was subsequently published in Philadelphia, and also in Albany. It was a song of the people, and sang itself through the country for fifty or sixty years, always culminating in the swift crescendo chorus and repeat—

The British yoke and Gallic chain
Were urged upon our necks in vain;
All haughty tyrants we disdain,
And shout "Long live America!"

The average patriot did not mind it if "Columbi-*ay*" and "Ameri-*kay*" were not exactly classic orthoëpy.

"HAIL COLUMBIA."

This was written (1798) by Judge Joseph Hopkinson, born, in Philadelphia, 1770, and died there, 1843. He wrote it for a friend in that city who was a theatre singer, and wanted a song for Independence Day. The music (to which it is still sung) was "The President's March," by a composer named Fyles, near the end of the 18th century.

There is nothing hymn-like in the words, which are largely a glorification of Gen. Washington, but the tune, a concerted piece better for band than voices, has the drum-and-anvil

115

chorus quality suitable for vociferous mass singing—and a zealous Salvation Army corps on field nights could even fit a processional song to it with gospel words.

OLD "CHESTER."

Let tyrants shake their iron rod,
And slavery clank her galling chains:
We'll fear them not; we trust in God;
New England's God forever reigns.

Old "Chester," both words and tune the work of William Billings, is another of the provincial freedom songs of the Revolutionary period, and of the days when the Republic was young. Billings was a zealous patriot, and (says a writer in Moore's *Cyclopedia of Music*) "one secret, no doubt, of the vast popularity his works obtained was the patriotic ardor they breathed. The words above quoted are an example, and 'Chester,' it is said, was frequently heard from every fife in the New England ranks. The spirit of the Revolution was also manifest in his 'Lamentation over Boston,' his 'Retrospect,' his 'Independence,' his 'Columbia,' and many other pieces."

William Billings was born, in Boston, Oct. 7, 1746. He was a man of little education, but his genius for music spurred him to study the tuneful art, and enabled him to learn all that could be learned without a master. He began to make tunes and publish them, and his first book, the *New England Psalm-singer* was a curiosity of youthful crudity and confidence, but in considerable numbers it was sold, and sung—and laughed at. He went on studying and composing, and compiled another work, which was so much of an improvement that it got the name of *Billings' Best*. A third singing-book followed, and finally a fourth entitled the *Psalm Singer's Amusement*, both of which were popular in their day. His "Majesty" has tremendous capabilities of sound, and its movement is fully up to the requirements of Nahum Tate's verses,—

And on the wings of mighty winds
Came flying all abroad.

William Billings died in 1800, and his remains lie in an unmarked grave in the old "Granary" Burying Ground in the city of his birth.

National feeling has taken maturer speech and finer melody, but it was these ruder voices that set the pitch. They were sung with native pride and affection at fireside vespers and rural feasts with the adopted songs of Burns and Moore and Mrs. Hemans, and, like the lays of Scotland and Provence, they breathed the flavor of the country air and soil, and taught the generation of home-born minstrelsy that gave us the Hutchinson family, Ossian E. Dodge, Covert with his "Sword of Bunker Hill," and Philip Phillips, the "Singing Pilgrim."

THE STAR SPANGLED BANNER.

Near the close of the last war with England, Francis Scott Key, of Baltimore, the author of this splendid national hymn, was detained under guard on the British flag-ship at the mouth of the Petapsco, where he had gone under a flag of truce to procure the release of a captured friend, Dr. William Beanes of Upper Marlboro, Md.

The enemy's fleet was preparing to bombard Fort McHenry, and Mr. Key's return with his friend was forbidden lest their plans should be disclosed. Forced to stay and witness the attack on his country's flag, he walked the deck through the whole night of the bombardment until the break of day showed the brave standard still flying at full mast over the fort. Relieved of his patriotic anxiety, he pencilled the exultant lines and chorus of his song on the back of a letter, and, as soon as he was released, carried it to the city, where within twenty-four hours it was printed on flyers, circulated and sung in the streets to the air of "Anacreon in Heaven"—which has been the "Star Spangled Banner" tune ever since.

O say, can you see by the dawn's early light
What so proudly we hailed at the twilight's last gleaming?
Whose broad stripes and bright stars through the perilous fight
O'er the ramparts we watched, were so gallantly streaming,
And the rockets red glare, the bombs bursting in air
Gave proof through the night that the flag was still there:
O say, does the star-spangled banner yet wave,
O'er the land of the free and the home of the brave?

*   *   *   *   *   *

O thus be it ever when freemen shall stand,
Between their loved homes and the war's desolation;
Blessed with victory and peace, may the heaven-rescued land
Praise the Power that hath made and preserved us a nation.
Then conquer we must, when our cause it is just,
And this be our motto, "*In God is our trust.*"
And the star-spangled banner in triumph shall wave,

O'er the land of the free and the home of the brave.

The original star-spangled banner that waved over Fort McHenry in sight of the poet when he wrote the famous hymn was made and presented to the garrison by a girl of fifteen, afterwards Mrs. Sanderson, and is still preserved in the Sanderson family at Baltimore.

The additional stanza to the "Star-Spangled Banner"—

When our land is illumined with Liberty's smile, etc.,

—was composed by Dr. O.W. Holmes, in 1861.

The tune "Anacreon in Heaven" was an old English hunting air composed by John Stafford Smith, born at Gloucester, Eng. 1750. He was composer for Covent Garden Theater, and conductor of the Academy of Ancient Music. Died Sep. 20, 1836. The melody was first used in America to Robert Treat Paine's song, "Adams and Liberty." Paine, born 1778—died 1811, was the son of Robert Treat Paine, signer of the Declaration of Independence.

"STAND! THE GROUND'S YOUR OWN, MY BRAVES."

Sympathetic admiration for the air, "Scots wha hae wi' Wallace bled," (or "Bruce's address," as it was commonly called), with the syllables of Robert Burns' silvery verse, lingered long in the land after the wars were ended. It spoke in the poem of John Pierpont, who caught its pibroch thrill, and built the metre of "Warren's Address at the Battle of Bunker Hill" on the model of "Scots wha hae."

Stand! the ground's your own, my braves;
Will ye give it up to slaves?
Will ye look for greener graves?
*   *   *   *   *   *
In the God of battles trust:
Die we may, or die we must,
But O where can dust to dust
Be consigned so well,
As where Heaven its dews shall shed,
On the martyred patriot's bed,
And the rocks shall raise their head
Of his deeds to tell?

This poem, written about 1823, held a place many years in school-books, and was one of the favorite school-boy declamations. Whenever sung on patriotic occasions, the music was sure to be "Bruce's Address." That typical Scotch tune was played on the Highland bag-pipes long before Burns was born, and known as "Hey tuttie taite." "Heard on Fraser's hautboy, it used to fill my eyes with tears," Burns himself once wrote.

Rev. John Pierpont was born in Litchfield, Ct., April 6, 1785. He was graduated at Yale, 1804, taught school, studied law, engaged in trade, and finally took a course in theology and became a Unitarian minister, holding the pastorate of Hollis St. Church, Boston, thirty-six years. He travelled in the East, and wrote "Airs of Palestine." His poem, "The Yankee Boy," has been much quoted. Died in Medford, Mass., Aug. 26, 1866.

Samuel
F. Smith

"MY COUNTRY, 'TIS OF THEE."

This simple lyric, honored so long with the name "America," and the title "Our National Hymn," was written by Samuel Francis Smith, while a theological student at Andover, Feb. 2, 1832. He had before him several hymn and song tunes which Lowell Mason had received from Germany, and, knowing young Smith to be a good linguist, had sent to him for translation. One of the songs, of national character, struck Smith as adaptable to home use if turned into American words, and he wrote four stanzas of his own to fit the tune.

Mason printed them with the music, and under his magical management the hymn made its debut on a public occasion in Park St. Church, Boston, July 4, 1832. Its very simplicity, with its reverent spirit and easy-flowing language, was sure to catch the ear of the multitude and grow into familiar use with any suitable music, but it was the foreign tune that, under Mason's happy pilotage, winged it for the western world and launched it on its long flight.

My country, 'tis of thee,
Sweet land of liberty,
Of thee I sing;
Land where my fathers died,
Land of the pilgrims' pride,
From every mountain-side
Let freedom ring.

* * * * * *

Let music swell the breeze,
And ring from all the trees
Sweet Freedom's song;
Let mortal tongues awake,
Let all that breathe partake,
Let rocks their silence break,
The sound prolong.
Our fathers' God, to Thee,
Author of liberty,
To Thee we sing;
Long may our land be bright
With Freedom's holy light;
Protect us by Thy might,
Great God, our King.

THE TUNE.

Pages, and at least two volumes, have been written to prove the origin of that cosmopolitan, half-Gregorian descant known here as "America," and in England as "God Save the King." William C. Woodbridge of Boston brought it home with him from Germany. The Germans had been singing it for years (and are singing it now, more or less) to the words, "Heil Dir Im Siegel Kranz," and the Swiss to "Rufst Du mein Vaterland." It was sung in Sweden, also, and till 1833 it was in public use in Russia commonly enough to give it a national character. Von Weber introduced it in his "Jubel" overture, and Beethoven, in 1814, copied it in C Major and wrote piano variations on it. It has been ascribed to Henry Purcell (1696), to Lulli, a French composer (1670), to Dr. John Bull (1619), and to Thomas Ravenscroft and an old Scotch carol as old as 1609. One might fancy that the biography of the famous air resembled Melchizedek's.

The truth appears to be that certain bars of music which might easily happen to be similar, or even identical, when plain-song was the common style, were produced at different times and places, and one man finally harmonized the wandering strains into a complete tune. It is now generally conceded that the man was Henry Carey, a popular English composer and dramatist of the first half of the 18th century, who sang the melody as it now is, in 1740, at a public dinner given in honor of Admiral Vernon after his capture of Porto Bello (Brazil). This antedates any authenticated use of the tune *ipsissima forma* in England or continental Europe.

The American history of it simply is that Woodbridge gave it to Mason and Mason gave it to Smith—and Smith gave it "My Country 'Tis of Thee."

"BY THE RUDE BRIDGE."

This genuinely American poem, written by Ralph Waldo Emerson and called usually the "Concord Hymn," was prepared for the dedication of the Battle-monument in Concord, April 19, 1836, and sung there to the tune of "Old Hundred." Apparently no change has been made in the original except of a single word in the first line.

By the rude bridge that arched the flood,
Their flag to April's breeze unfurled,
Here once the embattled farmers stood,
And fired the shot heard round the world.
The foe long since in silence slept;
Alike the conqueror silent sleeps;
And Time the ruined bridge has swept
Down the dark stream which seaward creeps.
On this green bank, by this soft stream,
We set today a votive stone;
That memory may their deed redeem,
When, like our sires, our sons are gone.

Spirit, that made those heroes dare
To die, and leave their children free,
Bid Time and Nature gently spare
The shaft we raise to them and Thee.

This does not appear in the hymnals and owns no special tune. Its niche of honor is in the temple of anthology, but it will always be called the "Concord Hymn"—and the fourth line of its first stanza is a perennial quotation.

Ralph Waldo Emerson, LL.D., the renowned American essayist and poet, was born in Boston, 1803. He graduated at Harvard in 1821, and was ordained to the Unitarian ministry, but turned his attention to literature, writing and lecturing on ethical and philosophical themes, and winning universal fame by his original and suggestive prose and verse. He died April 27, 1882.

BATTLE HYMN OF THE REPUBLIC.

After a visit to the Federal camps on the Potomac in 1861, Mrs. Julia Ward Howe returned to her lodgings in Washington, fatigued, as she says, by her "long, cold drive," and slept soundly. Awakening at early daybreak, she began "to twine the long lines of a hymn which promised to suit the measure of the 'John Brown' melody."

This hymn was written out after a fashion in the dark, by Mrs. Howe, and she then went back to sleep.

Mine eyes have seen the glory of the coming of the Lord;
He is trampling out the vintage where the grapes of wrath are stored;
He hath loosed the fateful lightning of His terrible swift sword;
His truth is marching on.
I have seen Him in the watch-fires of a hundred circling camps,
They have builded Him an altar in the evening dews and damps;
I can read His righteous sentence by the dim and flaring lamps;
His day is marching on.
I have read a fiery gospel writ in burnished rows of steel;
"As ye deal with my contemners, so with you my grace shall deal;"
Let the Hero, born of woman, crush the serpent with His heel,
Since God is marching on.
He has sounded forth the trumpet that shall never call retreat;
He is sifting out the hearts of men before His judgment seat;
Oh, be swift, my soul, to answer Him! be jubilant my feet!
Our God is marching on.
In the beauty of the lilies Christ was born across the sea,
With a glory in His bosom that transfigures you and me;
As He died to make men holy, let us die to make men free.
While God is marching on.

THE TUNE.

The music of the old camp-meeting refrain,—
Say, brothers will you meet us?
—or,—
O brother, will you meet me,

(No. 173 in the *Revivalist*,) was written in 1855, by John William Steffe, of Richmond, Va., for a fire company, and was afterwards arranged by Franklin H. Lummis. The air of the "John Brown Song" was caught from this religious melody. The old hymn-tune had the "Glory, Hallelujah" coda, cadenced off with, "For ever, ever more."

In 1860–61 the garrison of soldiers at work on the half-dismantled defenses of Fort Warren in Boston Harbor, were fain to lighten labor and mock fatigue with any species of fun suggested by circumstances or accident, and, as for music, they sang everything they could remember or make up. John Brown's memory and fate were fresh in the Northern mind, and the jollity of the not very reverent army men did not exclude frequent allusions to the rash old Harper's Ferry hero.

A wag conjured his spirit into the camp with a witticism as to what he was doing, and a comrade retorted,
"Marchin' on, of course."
A third cried, "Pooh, John Brown's underground."
A serio-comic debate added more words, and in the midst of the banter, a musical fellow strung a rhythmic sentence and trolled it to the Methodist tune. "John Brown's body lies a mould'rin' in the ground" was taken up by others who knew the air, the following line was improvised almost instantly, and soon, to the accompaniment of pick, shovel and crowbar,—
His soul goes marching on,

119

—rounded the couplet with full lung power through all the repetitions, till the inevitable "glory, glory hallelujah" had the voice of every soldier in the fort. The song "took," and the marching chorus of the Federal armies of the Civil War was started on its way. Mrs. Howe gave it a poem that made its rusticity sublime, and the "Battle Hymn of the Republic" began a career that promises to run till battle hymns cease to be sung.

Julia Ward was born in New York city, May 27, 1819. In 1843 she became the wife of Samuel Gridley Howe, the far-famed philanthropist and champion of liberty, and with him edited an anti-slavery paper, the *Boston Commonwealth*, until the Civil War closed its mission. During the war she was active and influential—and has never ceased to be so—in the cause of peace and justice, and in every philanthropic movement. Her great hymn first brought her prominently before the public, but her many other writings would have made a literary reputation. Her four surviving children are all eminent in the scientific and literary world.

KELLER'S AMERICAN HYMN.

Naturally the title suggests the authorship of the ode, but fate made Keller a musician rather than a poet and hymnist, and the honors of the fine anthem are divided. At the grand performance which created its reputation, the hymn of Dr. O.W. Holmes was substituted for the composer's words. This is Keller's first stanza:

Speed our republic, O Father on high!
Lead us in pathways of justice and right,
Rulers, as well as the ruled, one and all,
Girdle with virtue the armor of might.
Hail! three times hail, to our country and flag!
Rulers, as well as the ruled, one and all,
Girdle with virtue the armor of might;
Hail! three times hail, to our country and flag!

"Flag" was the unhappy word at the end of every one of the four stanzas. To match a short vowel to an orotund concert note for two beats and a "hold" was impossible. When the great Peace Jubilee of 1872, in Boston, was projected, Dr. Holmes was applied to, and responded with a lyric that gave each stanza the rondeau effect designed by the composer, but replaced the flat final with a climax syllable of breadth and music:

Angel of Peace, thou hast wandered too long!
Spread thy white wings to the sunshine of love!
Come while our voices are blended in song,
Fly to our ark like the storm-beaten dove!
Fly to our ark on the wings of the dove,
Speed o'er the far-sounding billows of song,
Crown'd with thine olive-leaf garland of love,
Angel of Peace, thou hast waited too long!
*   *   *   *   *   *

Angels of Bethlehem, answer the strain!
Hark! a new birth-song is filling the sky!
Loud as the storm-wind that tumbles the main,
Bid the full breath of the organ reply,
Let the loud tempest of voices reply,
Roll its long surge like the earth-shaking main!
Swell the vast song till it mounts to the sky!
Angels of Bethlehem, echo the strain!

But the glory of the *tune* was Keller's own.

Soon after the close of the war a prize of $500 had been offered by a committee of American gentlemen for the best "national hymn" (meaning words and music). Mr. Keller, though a foreigner, was a naturalized citizen and patriot and entered the lists as a competitor with the zeal of a native and the ambition of an artist. Sometime in 1866 he finished and copyrighted the noble anthem that bears his name, and then began the struggle to get it before the public and test its merit. To enable him to bring it out before the New York Academy of Music, where (unfortunately) he determined to make his first trial, his brother kindly lent him four hundred dollars (which he had laid by to purchase a little home), and he borrowed two hundred more elsewhere.

The performance proved a failure, the total receipts being only forty-two dollars, Keller was $500 in debt, and his brother's house-money was gone. But he refused to accept his failure as final. Boston (where he should have begun) was introduced to his masterpiece at every opportunity, and gradually, with the help of the city bands and a few public concerts, a decided liking for it was worked up. It was entered on the program of the Peace Jubilee and sung by a chorus of ten thousand voices. The effect was magnificent. "Keller's American Hymn" became a recognized star number in the repertoire of "best" national tunes; and now few public occasions where patriotic music is demanded omit it in their menu of song.[*]

* In Butterworth's "*Story of the Tunes*," under the account of Keller's grand motet, the following sacred hymn is inserted as "often sung to it:"—

Father Almighty, we bow at thy feet;
Humbly thy grace and thy goodness we own.
Answer in love when thy children entreat,
Hear our thanksgiving ascend to thy throne.
Seeking thy blessing, in worship we meet,
Trusting our souls on thy mercy alone;
Father Almighty, we bow at thy feet.
Breathe, Holy Spirit, thy comfort divine,
Tune every voice to thy music of peace;
Hushed in our hearts, with one whisper of thine,
Pride and the tumult of passion will cease.
Joy of the watchful, who wait for thy sign,
Hope of the sinful, who long for release,
Breathe, Holy Spirit, thy comfort divine.
God of salvation, thy glory we sing,
Honors to thee in thy temple belong;
Welcome the tribute of gladness we bring,
Loud-pealing organ and chorus of song.
While our high praises, Redeemer and King,
Blend with the notes of the angelic throng,
God of salvation, thy glory we sing.

—Theron Brown.

It is pathetic to know that the composer's one great success brought him only a barren renown. The prize committee, on the ground that *none* of the competing pieces reached the high standard of excellence contemplated, withheld the $500, and Keller's work received merely the compliment of being judged worth presentation. The artist had his copyright, but he remained a poor man.

Matthias Keller was born at Ulm, Wurtemberg, March 20, 1813. In his youth he was both a musician and a painter. Coming to this country, he chose the calling that promised the better and quicker wages, playing in bands and theatre orchestras, but never accumulating money. He could make fine harmonies as well as play them, but English was not his mother-tongue, and though he wrote a hundred and fifty songs, only one made him well-known. When fame came to him it did not bring him wealth, and in his latter days, crippled by partial paralysis, he went back to his early art and earned a living by painting flowers and retouching portraits and landscapes. He died in 1875, only three years after his Coliseum triumph.

"GOD BLESS OUR NATIVE LAND."

This familiar patriotic hymn is notable—though not entirely singular—for having two authors. The older singing-books signed the name of J.S. Dwight to it, until inquiring correspondence brought out the testimony and the joint claim of Dwight and C.T. Brooks, and it appeared that both these scholars and writers translated it from the German. Later hymnals attach both their names to the hymn.[*]

* For a full account of this disputed hymn, and the curious trick of memory which confused *four* names in the question of its authorship, see Dr. Benson's *Studies of Familiar Hymns*, pp. 179–190

John Sullivan Dwight, born, in Boston, May 13, 1813, was a virtuoso in music, and an enthusiastic student of the art and science of tonal harmony. He joined a Harvard musical club known as "ThePierian Sodality" while a student at the University, and after his graduation became a prolific writer on musical subjects. Six years of his life were passed in the "Brook Farm Community." He was best known by his serial magazine, Dwight's *Journal of Music*, which was continued from 1852 to 1881. His death occurred in 1893.

Rev. Charles Timothy Brooks, the translator of Faust, was born, in Salem, Mass., June 20, 1813, being only about a month younger than his friend Dwight. Was a student at Harvard University and Divinity School 1829–1835, and was ordained to the Unitarian ministry and settled at Newport, R.I. He resigned his charge there (1871) on account of ill health, and occupied himself with literary work until his death, Jan. 14, 1883.

God bless our native land!
Firm may she ever stand
Through storm and night!
When the wild tempests rave.
Ruler of wind and wave,
Do Thou our country save
By Thy great might!
For her our prayer shall rise
To God above the skies;
On Him we wait.
Thou who art ever nigh,
Guarding with watchful eye;
To Thee aloud we cry,
God save the State!

The tune of "Dort," by Lowell Mason, has long been the popular melody for this hymn. Indeed the two were united by Mason himself. It is braver music than "America," and would have carried Dr. Smith's hymn nobly, but the borrowed tune, on the whole, better suits "My Country 'tis of thee,"—and besides, it has the advantage of a middle-register harmony easy for a multitude of voices.

"THOU, TOO, SAIL ON, O SHIP OF STATE."

The closing canto of Longfellow's "Launching of the Ship," almost deserves a patriotic hymn-tune, though its place and use are commonly with school recitations.

"GOD OF OUR FATHERS, KNOWN OF OLD."

Rudyard Kipling, in a moment of serious reflection on the flamboyant militarism of British sentiment during the South African War, wrote this remarkable "Recessional," so strikingly unlike his other war-time poems. It is to be hoped he did not suddenly repent his Christian impulse, but with the chauvinistic cry around him, "Our Country, right or wrong!" he seems to have felt the contrast of his prayer—and flung it into the waste-basket. His watchful wife rescued it (the story says) and bravely sent it to the London Times. The world owes her a debt. The hymn is not only an anthem for Peace Societies, but a tonic for true patriotism. When Freedom fights in self-defense, she need not force herself to "forget" the Lord of Hosts.

God of our fathers, known of old,
Lord of our far-flung battle-line,
Beneath whose awful hand we hold
Dominion over palm and pine;
Lord God of Hosts, be with us yet,
Lest we forget, lest we forget.
The tumult and the shouting dies,
The captains and the kings depart,
Still stands Thine ancient sacrifice,
An humble and a contrite heart.
Lord God of Hosts, be with us yet,
Lest we forget, lest we forget.
Far-called, our navies melt away,
On dune and headland sinks the fire;
Lo all our pomp of yesterday
Is one with Nineveh and Tyre.
Judge of the nations, spare us yet,
Lest we forget, lest we forget.
If, drunk with sight of power, we loose
Wild tongues that have not Thee in awe,
Such boasting as the Gentiles use
Or lesser breeds without the law,
Lord God of Hosts, be with us yet,
Lest we forget, lest we forget.
For heathen heart that puts her trust,
In recking tube and iron shard,
All valiant dust that builds on dust
And guarding, calls not Thee to guard,
For frantic boast and foolish word
Thy mercy on thy people, Lord!

122

Had Kipling cared more for his poem, and kept it longer in hand, he might have revised a line or two that would possibly seem commonplace to him—and corrected the grammar in the first line of the second stanza. But of so fine a composition there is no call for finical criticism. The "Recessional" is a product of the poet's holiest mood. "The Spirit of the Lord came upon him"—as the old Hebrew phrase is, and for the time he was a rapt prophet, with a backward and a forward vision. Providence saved the hymn, and it touched and sank into the better mind of the nation. It is already learned by heart—and sung—wherever English is the common speech, and will be heard in numerous translations, with the wish that there were more patriotic hymns of the same Christian temper and strength.

Rudyard Kipling was born in Hindostan in 1865. Even with his first youthful experiments in the field of literature he was hailed as the coming apostle of muscular poetry and prose. For a time he made America his home, and it was while here that he faced death through a fearful and protracted sickness that brought him very near to God. He has visited many countries and described them all, and, though sometimes his imagination drives a reckless pen, the Christian world hopes much from a man whose genius can make the dullest souls listen.

THE TUNE.

The music set to Kipling's hymn is Stainer's "Magdalen"—(not his "Magdalina," which is a common-metre tune)—and wonderfully fits the words and enhances their dignity. It is a grave and earnest melody in D flat, with two bars in unison at "Lord God of Hosts, be with us yet," making the utterance of the prayer a deep and powerful finale.

John Stainer, Doctor of Music, born June 6, 1840, was nine years the chorister of St. Paul's, London, and afterwards organist to the University of Oxford. He is a member of the various musical societies of the Kingdom, and a Chevalier of the Legion of Honor. His talent for sacred music is rare and versatile, and he seems to have consecrated himself as a musician and composer to the service of the church.

Every civilized nation has its patriotic hymns. In fact what makes a nation a nation is largely the unifying influences of its common song. Even the homeless Hebrew nation is kept together by its patriotic Psalms. The ethnic melodies would fill a volume with their story. The few presented in this chapter represent their range of quality and character—defiant as the Marseillaise, thrilling as "Scots' wha hae," joyful as "The Star-spangled Banner," breezy and bold as the "Ranz de Vaches," or sweet as the "Switzers' Song of Home."

CHAPTER X.

SAILORS' HYMNS.

The oldest sailors' hymn is found in the 107th Psalm, vss. 23–30:

They that go down to the sea in ships,
To do business in great waters,
These see the works of the Lord,
And His wonders in the deep, etc.

Montgomery has made this metrical rendering of these verses:

They that toil upon the deep,
And in vessels light and frail
O'er the mighty waters sweep
With the billows and the gale,
Mark what wonders God performs
When He speaks, and, unconfined,
Rush to battle all His storms
In the chariots of the wind.

The hymn is not in the collections, and has no tune. Addison paraphrased the succeeding verses of the Psalm in his hymn, "How are thy servants blessed O Lord," sung to Hugh Wilson's' tune of "Avon":

When by the dreadful tempest borne
High on the broken wave,
They know Thou art not slow to hear,
Nor impotent to save.
The storm is laid, the winds retire,
Obedient to Thy will;
The sea that roars at Thy command,
At Thy command is still.

* Hugh Wilson was a Scotch weaver of Kilmarnock, born 1764; died 1824.

123

"FIERCE WAS THE WILD BILLOW."

(Ζοφερᾶς τρικυμίας)

The ancient writer, Anatolius, who composed this hymn has for centuries been confounded with "St" Anatolius, patriarch of Constantinople, who died A.D. 458. The author of the hymn lived in the seventh century, and except that he wrote several hymns, and also poems in praise of the martyrs, nothing or next to nothing, is known of him. The "Wild Billow" song was the principle seaman's hymn of the early church. It is being introduced into modern psalmody, the translation in use ranking among the most successful of Dr. John Mason Neale's renderings from the Greek.

Fierce was the wild billow,
Dark was the night;
Oars labored heavily,
Foam glimmered white;
Trembled the mariners;
Peril was nigh;
Then said the God of God,
"Peace! It is I!"
Ridge of the mountain wave,
Lower thy crest!
Wall of Euroclydon,
Be thou at rest!
Sorrow can never be,
Darkness must fly,
When saith the Light of Light,
"Peace! It is I!"

THE TUNE.

The desire to represent the antiquity of the hymn and the musical style of Its age, and on the other hand the wish to utilize it in the tune-manuals for Manners' Homes and Seamen's Bethels, makes a difficulty for composers to study—and the task is still open to competition. Considering the peculiar tone that sailors' singing instinctively takes—and has taken doubtless from time immemorial perhaps the plaintive melody of "Neale," by J.H. Cornell, comes as near to a vocal success as could be hoped. The music is of middle register and less than octave range, natural scale, minor, and the triple time lightens a little the dirge-like harmony while the weird sea-song effect is kept. A chorus of singing tars must create uncommon emotion, chanting this coronach of the storm.

John Henry Cornell was born in New York city, May 8, 1838, and was for many years organist at St. Paul's Chapel, Trinity Church. He is the author of numerous educational works on the theory and practice of music. He composed the above tune in 1872. Died March 1, 1894.

"AVE, MARIS STELLA."

One of the titles which the Roman Catholic world applied to the Mother of Jesus, in the Middle Ages, was "Stella Maris," "Star of the Sea." Columbus, being a Catholic, sang this hymn, or caused it to be sung, every evening, it is said, during his perilous voyage to an unknown land. The marine epithet by which the Virgin Mary is addressed is admirable as a stroke of poetry, and the hymn—of six stanzas—is a prayer which, though offered to her as to a divine being, was no doubt sincere in the simple sailor hearts of 1492.

The two following quatrains finish the voyagers' petition, and point it with a doxology—

Vitam praesta puram,
Iter para tutum,
Ut videntes Jesum
Semper collaetemur.
Sit laus Deo Patri,
Summo Christo decus,
Spiritui Sancto,
Tribus honor unus!
A free translation is—
Guide us safe, unspotted
Through life's long endeavor
Till with Thee and Jesus
We rejoice forever.
Praise to God the Father,
Son and Spirit be;
One and equal honor

124

To the Holy Three.

Inasmuch as this ancient hymn did not attain the height of its popularity and appear in all the breviaries until the 10th century, its assumed age has been doubted, but its reputed author, Venantius Fortunatus, Bishop of Poitiers, was born about 531, at Treviso, Italy, and died about 609. Though a religious teacher, he was a man of romantic and convivial instincts—a strange compound of priest, poet and *beau chevalier*. Duffield calls him "the last of the classics and first of the troubadours," and states that he was the "first of the Christian poets to begin that worship of the Virgin Mary which rose to a passion and sank to an idolatry."

TUNES

To this ancient rogation poem have been composed by Aiblinger (Johann Caspar), Bavarian, (1779–1867,) by Proch (Heinrich), Austrian, (1809–1878,) by Tadolini (Giovanni), Italian, (1803–1872,) and by many others. The "Ave, Maris Stella" is in constant use in the Romish church, and its English translation by Caswall is a favorite hymn in the *Lyra Catholica*.

"AVE, SANCTISSIMA!"

This beautiful hymn is not introduced here in order of time, but because it seems akin to the foregoing, and born of its faith and traditions—though it sounds rather too fine for a sailor song, on ship or shore. Like the other, the tuneful prayer is the voice of ultramontane piety accustomed to deify Mary, and is entitled the "Evening Song to the Virgin."

Ave Sanctissima! we lift our souls to Thee
Ora pro nobis! 'tis nightfall on the sea.
Watch us while shadows lie
Far o'er the waters spread;
Hear the heart's lonely sigh;
Thine, too, hath bled.
Thou that hast looked on death,
Aid us when death is near;
Whisper of heaven to faith;
Sweet Mother, hear!
Ora pro nobis! the wave must rock our sleep;
Ora, Mater, ora! Star of the Deep!

This was first written in four separate quatrains, "'Tis nightfall on the sea" being part of the first instead of the second line, and "We lift our souls," etc., was "Our souls rise to Thee," while the apostrophe at the end read, "Thou Star of the Deep."

The fact of the modern origin of the hymn does not make it less probable that the earlier one of Fortunatus suggested it. It was written by Mrs. Hemans, and occurs between the forty-third and forty-fourth stanzas of her long poem, "The Forest Sanctuary."

A Spanish Christian who had embraced the Protestant faith fled to America (such is the story of the poem) to escape the cruelties of the Inquisition, and took with him his Catholic wife and his child. During the voyage the wife pined away and died, a martyr to her conjugal loyalty and love. The hymn to the Virgin purports to have been her daily evening song at sea, plaintively remembered by the broken-hearted husband and father in his forest retreat on the American shore with his motherless boy.

The music was composed by a sister of Mrs. Hemans, Mrs. Hughes, who probably arranged the lines as they now stand in the tune.

The song, though its words appear in the *Parochial Hymn-book*, seems to be in use rather as parlor music than as a part of the liturgy.

"JESUS, LOVER OF MY SOUL."

The golden quality of this best-known and loved of Charles Wesley's hymns is attested by two indorsements that cannot be impeached; its perennial life, and the blessings of millions who needed it.

Jesus, Lover of my soul
Let me to Thy bosom fly,
While the billows near me roll,
While the tempest still is high.
Hide me, O my Saviour, hide,
Till the storm of life is past,
Safe into the haven guide,
O receive my soul at last!

Wesley is believed to have written it when a young man, and story and legend have been busy with the circumstances of its birth. The most poetical account alleges that a dove chased by a hawk dashed through his open window into his bosom, and the inspiration to write the line—

Let me to Thy bosom fly,

125

—was the genesis of the poem. Another report has it that one day Mr. Wesley, being pursued by infuriated persecutors at Killalee, County Down, Ireland, took refuge in a milk-house on the homestead of the Island Band Farm. When the mob came up the farmer's wife, Mrs. Jane Lowrie Moore, offered them refreshments and secretly let out the fugitive through a window to the back garden, where he concealed himself under a hedge till his enemies went away. When they had gone he had the hymn in his mind and partly jotted down. This tale is circumstantial, and came through Mrs. Mary E. Hoover, Jane Moore's granddaughter, who told it many years ago to her pastor, Dr. William Laurie of Bellefonte, Pa. So careful a narrative deserves all the respect due to a family tradition. Whether this or still another theory of the incidental cause of the wonderful hymn shall have the last word may never be decided nor is it important.

There is "antecedent probability," at least, in the statement that Wesley wrote the first two stanzas soon after his perilous experience in a storm at sea during his return voyage from America to England in 1736. In a letter dated Oct. 28 of that year, he describes the storm that washed away a large part of the ship's cargo, strained her seams so that the hardest pumping could not keep pace with the inrushing water, and finally forced the captain to cut the mizzen-mast away. Young Wesley was ill and sorely alarmed, but knew, he says, that he "abode under the shadow of the Almighty," and finally, "in this dreadful moment," he was able to encourage his fellow-passengers who were "in an agony of fear," and to pray with and for them.

It was his awful hazard and bare escape in that tempest that prompted the following stanzas—

O Thou who didst prepare
The ocean's caverned cell,
And teach the gathering waters there
To meet and dwell;
Toss'd in our reeling bark
Upon this briny sea,
Thy wondrous ways, O Lord, we mark,
And sing to Thee.
*   *   *   *   *   *

Borne on the dark'ning wave,
In measured sweep we go,
Nor dread th' unfathomable grave,
Which yawns below;
For He is nigh who trod
Amid the foaming spray,
Whose billows own'd th' Incarnate God,
And died away.

And naturally the memory of his almost shipwreck on the wild Atlantic colored more or less the visions of his muse, and influenced the metaphors of his verse for years.

The popularity of "Jesus, Lover of my Soul" not only procured it, at home, the name of "England's song of the sea," but carried it with "the course of Empire" to the West, where it has reigned with "Rock of Ages," for more than a hundred and fifty years, joint primate of inspired human songs.

Compiled incidents of its heavenly service would fill a chapter. A venerable minister tells of the supernal comfort that lightened his after years of sorrow from the dying bed of his wife who whispered with her last breath, "Hide me, O my Saviour, hide."

A childless and widowed father in Washington remembers with a more than earthly peace, the wife and mother's last request for Wesley's hymn, and her departure to the sound of its music to join the spirit of her babe.

A summer visitor in Philadelphia, waiting on a hot street-corner for a car to Fairmount Park, overheard a quavering voice singing the same hymn and saw an emaciated hand caressing a little plant in an open window—and carried away the picture of a fading life, and the words—

Other refuge have I none,
Hangs my helpless soul on Thee.

On one of the fields of the Civil War, just after a bloody battle, the Rev. James Rankin of the United Presbyterian Church bent over a dying soldier. Asked if he had any special request to make, the brave fellow replied, "Yes, sing 'Jesus, Lover of my Soul.'"

The clergyman belonged to a church that sang only Psalms. But what a tribute to that ubiquitous hymn that such a man knew it by heart! A moment's hesitation and he recalled the words, and, for the first time in his life, sang a sacred song that was not a Psalm. When he reached the lines,—

Safe into the haven guide,

O receive my soul at last,

—his hand was in the frozen grip of a dead man, whose face wore "the light that never was on sea or land." The minister went away saying to himself, "If this hymn is good to die by, it is good to live by."

William B.
Bradbury

THE TUNE.

Of all the tone-masters who have studied and felt this matchless hymn, and given it vocal wings—Marsh, Zundel, Bradbury, Dykes, Mason—none has so exquisitely uttered its melting prayer, syllable by syllable, as Joseph P. Holbrook in his "Refuge." Unfortunately for congregational use, it is a duo and quartet score for select voices; but the four-voice portion can be a chorus, and is often so sung. Its form excludes it from some hymnals or places it as an optional beside a congregational tune. But when rendered by the choir on special occasions its success in conveying the feeling and soul of the words is complete. There is a prayer in the swell of every semitone and the touch of every accidental, and the sweet concord of the duet— soprano with tenor or bass—pleads on to the end of the fourth line, where the full harmony reinforces it like an organ with every stop in play. The tune is a rill of melody ending in a river of song.

* Holbrook has also an arrangement of Franz Abt's, "When the Swallows Homeward Fly" written to "Jesus, Lover of my Soul," but with Wesley's words it is far less effective than his original work. "Refuge" is not a manufacture but an inspiration.

For general congregational use, Mason's "Whitman" has wedded itself to the hymn perhaps closer than any other. It has revival associations reaching back more than sixty years.

"WHEN MARSHALLED ON THE NIGHTLY PLAIN."

Perhaps no line in all familiar hymnology more readily suggests the name of its author than this. In the galaxy of poets Henry Kirke White was a brief luminary whose brilliancy and whose early end have appealed to the hearts of three generations. He was born at Nottingham, Eng., in the year 1795. His father was a butcher, but the son, disliking the trade, was apprenticed to a weaver at the age of fourteen. Two years later he entered an attorney's office as copyist and student.

The boy imbibed sceptical notions from some source, and might have continued to scoff at religion to the last but for the experience of his intimate friend, a youth named Almond, whose life was changed by witnessing one day the happy death of a Christian believer. Decided to be a Christian himself, it was some time before he mustered courage to face White's ridicule and resentment. He simply drew away from him. When White demanded the reason he was obliged to tell him that they two must henceforth walk different paths.

"Good God!" exclaimed White, "you surely think worse of me than I deserve!"

The separation was a severe shock to Henry, and the real grief of it sobered his anger to reflection and remorse. The light of a better life came to him when his heart melted—and from that time he and Almond were fellows in faith as well as friendship.

In his hymn the young poet tells the stormy experience of his soul, and the vision that guided him to peace.

When, marshalled on the nightly plain,
The glittering host bestud the sky,
One star alone of all the train
Can fix the sinner's wandering eye.
Hark, hark! to God the chorus breaks,
From every host, from every gem,
But one alone the Saviour speaks;
It is the Star of Bethlehem.

127

Once on the raging seas I rode:
The storm was loud, the night was dark;
The ocean yawned, and rudely blowed
The wind that tossed my foundering bark.
Deep horror then my vitals froze,
Death-struck, I ceased the tide to stem,
When suddenly a star arose;
It was the Star of Bethlehem.
It was my guide, my light, my all,
It bade my dark forebodings cease;
And through the storm and danger's thrall,
It led me to the port of peace.
Now, safely moored, my perils o'er,
I'll sing, first in night's diadem,
For ever and for evermore,
The Star, the Star of Bethlehem!

Besides this delightful hymn, with its graphic sea-faring metaphors, two others, at least, of the same boy-poet hold their place in many of the church and chapel collections:

The Lord our God is clothed with might,
The winds obey His will;
He speaks, and in his heavenly height
The rolling sun stands still.

And—

Oft in danger, oft in woe,
Onward, Christians, onward go.

Henry Kirke White died in the autumn of 1806, when he was scarcely twenty years old. His "Ode to Disappointment," and the miscellaneous flowers and fragments of his genius, make up a touching volume. The fire of a pure, strong spirit burning through a consumptive frame is in them all.

THE TUNE.

"When, marshalled on the mighty plain" has a choral set to it in the *Methodist Hymnal*—credited to Thos. Harris, and entitled "Crimea"—which divides the three stanzas into six, and breaks the continuity of the hymn. Better sing it in its original form—long metre double—to the dear old melody of "Bonny Doon." The voices of Scotland, England and America are blended in it.

The origin of this Caledonian air, though sometimes fancifully traced to an Irish harper and sometimes to a wandering piper of the Isle of Man, is probably lost in antiquity. Burns, however, whose name is linked with it, tells this whimsical story of it, though giving no date save "a good many years ago,"—(apparently about 1753). A virtuoso, Mr. James Millar, he writes, wishing he were able to compose a Scottish tune, was told by a musical friend to sit down to his harpsichord and make a rhythm of some kind *solely on the black keys*, and he would surely turn out a Scotch tune. The musical friend, pleased at the result of his jest, caught the string of plaintive sounds made by Millar, and fashioned it into "Bonny Doon."

"LAND AHEAD!"

The burden of this hymn was suggested by the dying words of John Adams, one of the crew of the English ship Bounty who in 1789 mutinied, set the captain and officers adrift, and ran the vessel to a tropical island, where they burned her. In a few years vice and violence had decimated the wicked crew, who had exempted themselves from all divine and human restraint, until the last man alive was left with only native women and half-breed children for company. His true name was Alexander Smith, but he had changed it to John Adams.

The situation forced the lonely Englishman to a sense of solemn responsibility, and in bitter remorse, he sought to retrieve his wasted life, and spend the rest of his exile in repentance and repentant works. He found a Bible in one of the dead seamen's chests, studied it, and organized a community on the Christian plan. A new generation grew up around him, reverencing him as governor, teacher, preacher and judge, and speaking his language—and he was wise enough to exercise his authority for the common good, and never abuse it. Pitcairn's Island became "the Paradise of the Pacific." It has not yet belied its name. Besides its opulence of rural beauty and natural products, its inhabitants, now the third generation from the "mutineer missionary," are a civilized community without the vices of civilization. There is no licentiousness, no profanity, no Sabbath-breaking, no rum or tobacco—and *no sickness*.

John Adams died in 1829—after an island residence of forty years. In his extreme age, while he lay waiting for the end, he was asked how he felt in view of the final voyage.

128

"Land ahead!" murmured the old sailor—and his last words were, "Rounding the Cape—into the harbor."

That the veteran's death-song should be perpetuated in sacred music is not strange.

Land ahead! its fruits are waving
O'er the hills of fadeless green;
And the living waters laving
Shores where heavenly forms are seen.
CHORUS.
Rocks and storms I'll fear no more,
When on that eternal shore;
Drop the anchor! furl the sail!
I am safe within the veil.
Onward, bark! the cape I'm rounding;
See, the blessed wave their hands;
Hear the harps of God resounding
From the bright immortal bands.

The authorship of the hymn is credited to Rev. E. Adams—whether or not a descendant of the Island Patriarch we have no information. It was written about 1869.

The ringing melody that bears the words was composed by John Miller Evans, born Nov. 30, 1825; died Jan. 1, 1892. The original air—with a simple accompaniment—was harmonized by Hubert P. Main, and published in *Winnowed Hymns* in 1873.

"ETERNAL FATHER, STRONG TO SAVE."

This is sung almost universally on English ships. It is said to have been one of Sir Evelyn Wood's favorites. The late William Whiting wrote it in 1860, and it was incorporated with some alterations in the standard English Church collection entitled *Hymns Ancient and Modern*. It is a translation from a Latin hymn, a triune litany addressing a stanza each to Father, Son and Holy Spirit. The whole four stanzas have the same refrain, and the appeal to the Father, who bids—

—the mighty ocean deep
Its own appointed limits keep,
—varies in the appeal to Christ, who—
—*walked* upon the foaming deep.

The third and fourth stanzas are the following:

O Holy Spirit, Who didst brood
Upon the waters dark and rude,
And bid their angry tumult cease,
And give, for wild confusion, peace;
Oh, hear us when we cry to Thee
For those in peril on the sea.
O Trinity of love and power,
Our brethren shield in danger's hour;
From rock and tempest, fire and foe,
Protect them wheresoe'er they go:
Thus evermore shall rise to Thee
Glad hymns of praise from land to sea.

William Whiting was born at Kensington, London, Nov. 1, 1825. He was Master of Winchester College Chorister's School Died in 1878.

THE TUNE.

The choral named "Melita" (in memory of St. Paul's shipwreck) was composed by Dr. Dykes in 1861, and its strong and easy chords and moderate note range are nobly suited to the devout hymn.

"THE OCEAN HATH NO DANGER."

This charming sailors' lyric is the work of the Rev. Godfrey Thring. Its probable date is 1862, and it appeared in Morell and Howe's collection and in *Hymns Congregational and Others*, published in 1866, which contained a number from his pen. Rector Thring was born at Alford, Somersetshire, Eng., March 25, 1823, and educated at Shrewsbury School and Baliol College, Oxford. In 1858 he succeeded his father as Rector of Alford.

He compiled *A Church of England Hymnbook* in 1880.

The ocean hath no danger
For those whose prayers are made
To Him who in a manger
A helpless Babe was laid,
Who, born to tribulation

And every human ill,
The Lord of His creation,
The wildest waves can still.

*   *   *   *   *   *

Though life itself be waning
And waves shall o'er us sweep,
The wild winds sad complaining
Shall lull us still to sleep,
For as a gentle slumber
E'en death itself shall prove
To those whom Christ doth number
As worthy of His love.

The tune "Morlaix," given to the hymn by Dr. Dykes, is simple, but a very sweet and appropriate harmony.

"FIERCE RAGED THE TEMPEST ON THE DEEP."

This fine lyric, based on the incident in the storm on the Sea of Galilee, is the work of the same writer and owes its tune "St. Aelred" to the same composer.

The melody has an impressive rallentando of dotted semibreves to the refrain, "Peace, be still," after the more rapid notes of the three-line stanzas.

The wild winds hushed, the angry deep
Sank like a little child to sleep,
The sullen waters ceased to leap.

*   *   *   *   *   *

So when our life is clouded o'er
And storm-winds drift us from the shore
Say, lest we sink to rise no more,
"Peace! be still."

"PULL FOR THE SHORE."

When a shipwrecked crew off a rocky coast were hurrying to the long-boat, a sailor begged leave to run back to the ship's forecastle and save some of his belongings.

"No sir," shouted the Captain, "she's sinking! There's nothing to do but to pull for the shore." Philip P. Bliss caught up the words, and wrought them into a hymn and tune.

Light in the darkness, sailor, day is at hand!
See o'er the foaming billows fair Haven's land;
Drear was the voyage, sailor, now almost o'er;
Safe in the life-boat, sailor, pull for the shore!
CHORUS.
Pull for the shore, sailor, pull for the shore!
Heed not the rolling waves, but bend to the oar;
Safe in the life-boat, sailor, cling to self no more;
Leave the poor old stranded wreck and pull for the shore!

The hymn-tune is a buoyant allegro—solo and chorus—full of hope and courage, and both imagery and harmony appeal to the hearts of seamen. It is popular, and has long been one of the song numbers in demand at religious services both on sea and land.

"JESUS, SAVIOUR, PILOT ME."

The Rev. Edward Hopper, D.D. wrote this hymn while pastor of Mariner's Church at New York harbor, "The Church of the Sea and Land." He was born in 1818, and graduated at Union Theological Seminary in 1843.

Jesus, Saviour, pilot me
Over life's tempestuous sea,
Unknown waves before me roll,
Hiding rock and treacherous shoal;
Chart and compass come from Thee,
Jesus, Saviour, pilot me!

Only three stanzas of this rather lengthy hymn are in common use.

THE TUNE.

Without title except "Savior, pilot me." A simple and pleasing melody composed by John Edgar Gould, late of the firm of Gould and Fischer, piano dealers, Phila., Pa. He was born in Bangor, Me., April 9, 1822. Conductor of music and composer of psalm and hymn tunes and glees, he also compiled and published no less than eight books of church, Sunday-school, and secular songs. Died in Algiers, Africa, Feb. 13, 1875.

This is one of the popular refrains that need but a single hearing to fix themselves in common memory and insure their own currency and *eclat*.

The Rev. E.S. Ufford, well-known as a Baptist preacher, lecturer, and evangelist, was witnessing a drill at the life-saving station on Point Allerton, Nantasket Beach, when the order to "throw out the life-line" and the sight of the apparatus in action, combined with the story of a shipwreck on the spot, left an echo in his mind till it took the form of a song-sermon. Returning home, he pencilled the words of this rousing hymn, and, being himself a singer and player, sat down to his instrument to match the lines with a suitable air. It came to him almost as spontaneously as the music of "The Ninety and Nine" came to Mr. Sankey. In fifteen minutes the hymn-tune was made—so far as the melody went. It was published in sheet form in 1888, and afterwards purchased by Mr. Sankey, harmonized by Mr. Stebbins, and published in *Winnowed Songs*, 1890. Included in *Gospel Hymns*, Nov. 6, 1891.

Ever since it has been a favorite with singing seamen, and has done active service as one of our most stirring field-songs in revival work.

Throw out the Life-line across the dark wave,
There is a brother whom some one should save;
Somebody's brother! oh, who, then, will dare
To throw out the Life-line, his peril to share?
Throw out the Life-line with hand quick and strong!
Why do you tarry, why linger so long?
See! he is sinking; oh, hasten today—
And out with the Life-boat! away, then away!
CHORUS.
Throw out the Life-line!
Throw out the Life-line!
Some one is drifting away;
Throw out the Life-line!
Throw out the Life-line!
Some one is sinking today.

One evening, in the midst of their hilarity at their card-tables, a convivial club in one of the large Pennsylvania cities heard a sweet, clear female voice singing this solo hymn, followed by a chime of mingled voices in the chorus. A room in the building had been hired for religious meetings, and tonight was the first of the series. A strange coolness dampened the merriment in the club-room, as the singing went on, and the gradual silence became a hush, till finally one member threw down his cards and declared, "If what they're saying is right, then we're wrong."

Others followed his example, then another, and another.

There is a brother whom some one should save.

Quietly the revellers left their cards, cigars and half-emptied glasses and went home.

Said the ex-member who told the story years after to Mr. Ufford, "'Throw Out the Life-line' broke up that club."

He is today one of the responsible editors of a great city daily—and his old club-mates are all holding positions of trust.

A Christian man, a prosperous manufacturer in a city of Eastern Massachusetts, dates his first religious impressions from hearing this hymn when sung in public for the first time, twenty years ago.

Visiting California recently, Mr. Ufford sang his hymn at a watch-meeting and told the story of the loss of the Elsie Smith on Cape Cod in 1902, exhibiting also the very life-line that had saved sixteen lives from the wreck. By chance one of those sixteen was in the audience.

An English clergyman who was on duty at Gibraltar when an emigrant ship went on the rocks in a storm, tells with what pathetic power and effect "Throw out the Life-line" was sung at a special Sunday service for the survivors.

At one of Evan Roberts' meetings in Laughor, Wales, one speaker related the story of a "vision," when in his room alone, and a Voice that bade him pray, and when he knelt but could not pray, commanded him to "Throw out the Life-line." He had scarcely uttered these words in his story when the whole great congregation sprang to its feet and shouted the hymn together like the sound of many waters.

"There is more electricity in that song than in any other I ever heard," Dr. Cuyler said to Mr. Sankey when he heard him sing it. Its electricity has carried it nearly round the world.

The Rev. Edward Smith Ufford was born in Newark, N.J., in 1851, and educated at Stratford Academy (Ct.) and Bates Theological Seminary, Me. He held several pastorates in Maine and Massachusetts, but a preference for evangelistic work led him to employ his talent for object-teaching in illustrated religious lectures through his own and foreign lands, singing his hymn and enforcing it with realistic representation. He is the author and compiler of several Sunday-school and chapel song-manuals, as *Converts' Praise, Life-long Songs, Wonderful Love* and *Gathered Gems*.

CHAPTER XI.

HYMNS OF WALES.

In writing this chapter the task of identifying the *tune*, and its author, in the case of every hymn, would have required more time and labor than, perhaps, the importance of the facts would justify.

Peculiar interest, however, attaches to Welsh hymns, even apart from the airs which accompany them, and a general idea of Welsh music may be gathered from the tone and metre of the lyrics introduced. More particular information would necessitate printing the music itself.

From the days of the Druids, Wales has been a land of song. From the later but yet ancient time when the people learned the Christian faith, it has had its Christian psalms. The "March of the White Monks of Bangor" (7th century) is an epic of bravery and death celebrating the advance of Christian martyrs to their bloody fate at the hands of the Saxon savages. "Its very rhythm pictures the long procession of white-cowled patriots bearing peaceful banners and in faith taking their way to Chester to stimulate the valor of their countrymen." And ever since the "Battle of the Hallelujahs"—near Chirk on the border, nine miles from Wrexham—when the invading Danes were driven from the field in fright by the rush of the Cymric army shouting that mighty cry, every Christian poet in Wales has had a hallelujah in his verse.

Through the centuries, while chased and hunted by their conquerors among the Cambrian hills, but clinging to their independent faith, or even when paralyzed into spiritual apathy under tribute to a foreign church, the heavenly song still murmured in a few true hearts amidst the vain and vicious lays of carnal mirth. It survived even when people and priest alike seemed utterly degenerate and godless. The voice of Walter Bute (1372) rang true for the religion of Jesus in its purity. Brave John Oldcastle, the martyr, (1417) clung to the gospel he learned at the foot of the cross. William Wroth, *clergyman*, saved from fiddling at a drunken dance by a disaster that turned a house of revelry into a house of death, confessed his sins to God and became the "Apostle of South Wales." The young vicar, Rhys Pritchard (1579) rose from the sunken level of his profession, rescued through an incident less tragic. Accustomed to drink himself to inebriety at a public-house—a socially winked-at indulgence then—he one day took his pet goat with him, and poured liquor down the creature's throat. The refusal of the poor goat to go there again forced the reckless priest to reflect on his own ways. He forsook the ale-house and became a changed man.

Among his writings—later than this—is found the following plain, blunt statement of what continued long to be true of Welsh society, as represented in the common use of Sunday time.

> Of all the days throughout the rolling year
> There's not a day we pass so much amiss,
> There's not a day wherein we all appear
> So irreligious, so profaned as this.
> A day for drunkenness, a day for sport,
> A day to dance, a day to lounge away,
> A day for riot and excess, too short
> Amongst the Welshmen is the Sabbath day.
> A day to sit, a day to chat and spend,
> A day when fighting 'mongst us most prevails,
> A day to do the errands of the Fiend—
> Such is the Sabbath in most parts of Wales.

Meantime some who could read the language—and the better educated (like the author of the above rhymes) knew English as well as Welsh—had seen a rescued copy of *Wycliffs New Testament*, a precious publication seized and burnt (like the bones of its translator) by hostile ecclesiastics, and suppressed for nearly two hundred years. Walter Bute, like Obadiah who hid the hundred prophets, may well be credited with such secret salvage out of the general destruction. And there were doubtless others equally alert for the same quiet service. We can imagine how far the stealthy taste of that priceless book would help to strengthen a better religion than the one doled out professionally to the multitude by a Civil church; and how it kept the hallelujah alive in silent but constant souls; and in how many cases it awoke a conscience long hypnotized under corrupt custom, and showed a renegade Christian how morally untuned he was.

132

Daylight came slowly after the morning star, but when the dawn reddened it was in welcome to Pritchard's and Penry's gospel song; and sunrise hastened at the call of Caradoc, and Powell, and Erbury, and Maurice, the holy men who followed them, some with the trumpet of Sinai and some with the harp of Calvary.

Cambria was being prepared for its first great revival of religion.

There was no rich portfolio of Christian hymns such as exists to-day, but surely there were not wanting pious words to the old chants of Bangor and the airs of "Wild Wales." When time brought Howell Harris and Daniel Rowland, and the great "Reformation" of the eighteenth century, the renowned William Williams, "the Watts of Wales," appeared, and began his tuneful work. The province soon became a land of hymns. The candles lit and left burning here and there by Penry, Maurice, and the Owens, blazed up to beacon-fires through all the twelve counties when Harris, at the head of the mighty movement, carried with him the sacred songs of Williams, kindling more lights everywhere between the Dee and the British Channel.

William Williams of Pantycelyn was born in 1717, at Cefncoed Farm, near Llandovery. Three years younger than Harris, (an Oxford graduate,) and educated only at a village school and an academy at Llwynllwyd, he was the song protagonist of the holy campaign as the other was its champion preacher. From first to last Williams wrote nine hundred and sixteen hymns, some of which are still heard throughout the church militant, and others survive in local use and affection. He died Jan. 11, 1791, at Pantycelyn, where he had made his home after his marriage. One of the hymns in his *Gloria*, his second publication, may well have been his last. It was dear to him above others, and has been dear to devout souls in many lands.

My God, my portion and my love;
My all on earth, my all above,
My all within the tomb;
The treasures of this world below
Are but a vain, delusive show,
Thy bosom is my home.

It was fitting that Williams should name the first collection of his hymns (all in his native Welsh) *The Hallelujah*. Its lyrics are full of adoration for the Redeemer, and thanksgivings for His work.

"ONWARD RIDE IN TRIUMPH, JESUS,"
Marchog, Jesu, yn llwyddiannus,
Has been sung in Wales for a century and a half, and is still a favorite.
Onward ride in triumph, Jesus,
Gird thy sword upon thy thigh;
Neither earth nor Hell's own vastness
Can Thy mighty power defy.
In Thy Name such glory dwelleth
Every foe withdraws in fear,
All the wide creation trembleth
Whensoever Thou art near.*

* The following shows the style of Rev. Elvet Lewis' translation:
Blessed Jesus, march victorious
With Thy sword fixed at Thy side;
Neither death nor hell can hinder
The God-Warrior in His ride.

The unusual militant strain in this pæan of conquest soon disappears, and the gentler aspects of Christ's atoning sacrifice occupy the writer's mind and pen.

"IN EDEN—O THE MEMORY!"
Yn Eden cofiaf hyny byth!
The text, "He was wounded for our transgressions," is amplified in this hymn, and the Saviour is shown bruising Himself while bruising the serpent.
The first stanza gives the key-note,—
In Eden—O the memory!
What countless gifts were lost to me!
My crown, my glory fell;
But Calvary's great victory
Restored that vanished crown to me;
On this my songs shall dwell;

133

—and the multitude of Williams' succeeding "songs" that chant the same theme shows how well he kept his promise. The following hymn in Welsh (*Cymmer, Jesu fi fel'r ydwyf*) antedates the advice of Dr. Malan to Charlotte Elliott, "Come just as you are"—

Take me as I am, O Saviour,
Better I can never be;
Thou alone canst bring me nearer,
Self but draws me far from Thee.
I can never
But within Thy wounds be saved;

—and another (*Mi dafla maich oddi ar fy ngway*) reminds us of Bunyan's Pilgrim in sight of the Cross:

I'll cast my heavy burden down,
Remembering Jesus' pains;
Guilt high as towering mountain tops
Here turns to joyful strains.
*   *   *   *   *
He stretched His pure white hands abroad,
A crown of thorns He wore,
That so the vilest sinner might
Be cleansed forevermore;

Williams was called "The Sweet Singer of Wales" and "The Watts of Wales" because he was the chief poet and hymn-writer of his time, but the lady he married, Miss Mary Francis, was *literally* a singer, with a voice so full and melodious that the people to whom he preached during his itineraries, which she sometimes shared with him, were often more moved by her sweet hymnody than by his exhortations. On one occasion the good man, accompanied by his wife, put up at Bridgend Tavern in Llangefin, Anglesea, and a mischievous crowd, wishing to plague the "Methodists," planned to make night hideous in the house with a boisterous merry-making. The fiddler, followed by a gang of roughs, pushed his way to the parlor, and mockingly asked the two guests if they would "have a tune."

"Yes," replied Williams, falling in with his banter, "anything you like, my lad; 'Nancy Jig' or anything else."

And at a sign from her husband, as soon as the fellow began the jig, Mrs. Williams struck in with one of the poet-minister's well-known Welsh hymns in the same metre,—

Gwaed Dy groes sy'n c' odi fyny
Calvary's blood the weak exalteth
More than conquerors to be,'

—and followed the player note for note, singing the sacred words in her sweet, clear voice, till he stopped ashamed, and took himself off with all his gang.

* A less literal but more hymn-like translation is:
Jesu's blood can raise the feeble
As a conqueror to stand;
Jesu's blood is all-prevailing
O'er the mighty of the land:
Let the breezes
Blow from Calvary on me.
Says the author of *Sweet Singers of Wales*, "This refrain has been the password of many powerful revivals."
Another hymn—
O' Llefara! addfwyn Jesu,
Speak, O speak, thou gentle Jesus,
—recalls the well-known verse of Newton, "How sweet the name of Jesus sounds." Like many of Williams' hymns, it was prompted by occasion. Some converts suffered for lack of a "clear experience" and complained to him. They were like the disciples in the ship, "It was dark, and Jesus had not yet come unto them." The poet-preacher immediately made this hymn-prayer for all souls similarly tried. Edward Griffiths translates it thus:
Speak, I pray Thee, gentle Jesus,
O how passing sweet Thy words,
Breathing o'er my troubled spirit,
Peace which never earth affords,
All the world's distracting voices,
All th' enticing tones of ill,

At Thy accents, mild, melodious
Are subdued, and all is still.
Tell me Thou art mine, O Saviour
Grant me an assurance clear,
Banish all my dark misgivings,
Still my doubting, calm my fear.

Besides his Welsh hymns, published in the first and in the second and larger editions of his *Hallelujah*, and in two or three other collections, William Williams wrote and published two books of English hymns,* the *Hosanna* (1759) and the *Gloria* (1772). He fills so large a space in the hymnology and religious history of Wales that he will necessarily reappear in other pages of this chapter.

From the days of the early religious awakenings under the 16th century preachers, and after the ecclesiastical dynasty of Rome had been replaced by that of the Church of England, there were periods when the independent conscience of a few pious Welshmen rose against religious formalism, and the credal constraints of "established" teaching—and suffered for it. Burning heretics at the stake had ceased to be a church practice before the 1740's, but Howell Harris, Daniel Rowlands, and the rest of the "Methodist Fathers," with their followers, were not only ostracised by society and haled before magistrates to be fined for preaching, and sometimes imprisoned, but they were chased and beaten by mobs, ducked in ponds and rivers, and pelted with mud and garbage when they tried to speak or sing. But they kept on talking and singing. Harris (who had joined the army in 1760) owned a commission, and once he saved himself from the fury of a mob while preaching—with cloak over his ordinary dress—by lifting his cape and showing the star on his breast. No one dared molest an officer of His Britannic Majesty. But all were not able to use St. Paul's expedient in critical moments.*

William Williams often found immunity in his hymns, for like Luther—and like Charles Wesley among the Cornwall sea-robbers—he caught up the popular glees and ballad-refrains of the street and market and his wife sang their music to his words. It is true many of these old Welsh airs were minors, like "Elvy" and "Babel" (a significant name in English) and would not be classed as "glees" in any other country—always excepting Scotland—but they had the *swing*, and their mode and style were catchy to a Welsh multitude. In fact many of these uncopyrighted bits of musical vernacular were appropriated by the hymnbook makers, and christened with such titles as "Pembroke," "Arabia," "Brymgfryd," "Cwyfan," "Thydian," and the two mentioned above.

It was the time when Whitefield and the Wesleys were sweeping the kingdom with their conquering eloquence, and Howell Harris (their fellow-student at Oxford) had sided with the conservative wing of the Gospel Reformation workers, and become a "Whitfield Methodist." The Welsh Methodists, *ad exemplum*, marched with this Calvinistic branch—as they do today. Each division had its Christian bard. Charles Wesley could put regenerating power into sweet, poetic hymns, and William Williams' lyrical preaching made the Bible a travelling pulpit. The great "Beibl Peter Williams" with its commentaries in Welsh, since so long reverenced and cherished in provincial families, was not published till 1770, and for many the printed Word was far to seek. But the gospel minstrels carried the Word with them. Some of the long hymns contained nearly a whole body of divinity.

The Welsh learn their hymns by heart, as they do the Bible—a habit inherited from those old days of scarcity, when memory served pious people instead of print—so that a Welsh prayer-meeting is never embarrassed by a lack of books. An anecdote illustrates this characteristic readiness. In February, 1797, when Napoleon's name was a terror to England, the French landed some troops near Fishguard, Pembrokeshire. Mounted heralds spread the news through Wales, and in the village of Rhydybont, Cardiganshire, the fright nearly broke up a religious meeting; but one brave woman, Nancy Jones, stopped a panic by singing this stanza of one of Thomas Williams' hymns,—

Diuw os wyt am ddylenu'r bya

If Thou wouldst end the world, O Lord,
Accomplish first Thy promised Word,
And gather home with one accord
From every part Thine own,
Send out Thy Word from pole to pole,
And with Thy blood make thousands whole,
And, *after that come down.*

Nancy Jones would have been a useful member of the "Singing Sisters" band, so efficient a century or more afterwards.

The *tunes* of the Reformation under the "Methodist Fathers" continued far down the century to be the country airs of the nation, and reverberations of the great spiritual movement were heard in their rude music in the mountain-born revival led by Jack Edward Watkin in 1779 and in the local awakenings of 1791 and 1817. Later in the 19th century new hymns, and many of the old, found new tunes, made for their sake or imported from England and America.

The sanctified gift of song helped to make 1829 a year of jubilee in South Wales, nor was the same aid wanting during the plague in 1831, when the famous Presbyterian preacher, John Elias,* won nearly a whole county to Christ.

* Those who read his biography will call him the "Seraphic John Elias."

His name was John Jones when he was admitted a member of the presbytery. What followed is a commentary on the embarrassing frequency of a common name, nowhere realized so universally as it is in Wales.

"What is his father's name?" asked the moderator when John Jones was announced.

"Elias Jones," was the answer.

"Then call the young man John Elias," said the speaker, "otherwise we shall by and by have nobody but John Joneses."

And "John Elias" it remained.

An accession of temperance hymns in Wales followed the spread of the "Washingtonian" movement on the other side of the Atlantic in 1840, and began a moral reformation in the county of Merioneth that resulted in a spiritual one, and added to the churches several thousand converts, scarcely any of whom fell away.

The revival of 1851–2 was a local one, but was believed by many to have been inspired by a celestial antiphony. The remarkable sounds were either a miracle or a psychic wonder born of the intense imagination of a sensitive race. A few pious people in a small village of Montgomeryshire had been making special prayer for an outpouring of the spirit, but after a week of meetings with no sign of the result hoped for, they were returning to their homes, discouraged, when they heard strains of sweet music in the sky. They stopped in amazement, but the beautiful singing went on—voices as of a choir invisible, indistinct but melodious, in the air far above the roof of the chapel they had just left. Next day, when the astonished worshippers told the story, numbers in the district said they had heard the same sounds. Some had gone out at eleven o'clock to listen, and thought that angels must be singing. Whatever the music meant, the good brethren's and sisters' little meetings became crowded very soon after, and the longed-for out-pouring came mightily upon the neighborhood. Hundreds from all parts flocked to the churches, all ages joining in the prayers and hymns and testimonies, and a harvest of glad believers followed a series of meetings "led by the Holy Ghost."

The sounds in the sky were never explained; but the belief that God sent His angels to sing an answer to the anxious prayers of those pious brethren and sisters did no one any harm.

Whether this event in Montgomeryshire was a preparation for what took place six or seven years later is a suggestive question only, but when the wave of spiritual power from the great American revival of 1857–8 reached England, its first messenger to Wales, Rev. H.R. Jones, a Wesleyan, had only to drop the spark that "lit a prairie fire." The reformation, chiefly under the leadership of Mr. Jones and Rev. David Morgan, a Presbyterian, with their singing bands, was general and lasting, hundreds of still robust and active Christians today dating their new birth from the Pentecost of 1859 and its ingathering of eighty thousand souls.

A favorite hymn of that revival was the penitential cry,—

O'th flaem, O Dduw! 'r wy'n dyfod,

—in the seven-six metre so much loved in Wales.

Unto Thy presence coming,
O God, far off I stand:
"A sinner" is my title,
No other I demand.
For mercy I am seeking

For mercy still shall cry;
Deny me not Thy mercy;
O grant it or I die!
*　　*　　*　　*　　*　　*
I heard of old that Jesus,
Who still abides the same,
To publicans gave welcome,
And sinners deep in shame.
Oh God! receive me with them,
Me also welcome in,
And pardon my transgression,
Forgetting all my sin.

The author of the hymn was Thomas Williams of Glamorganshire, born 1761; died 1844. He published a volume of hymns, *Waters of Bethesda* in 1823.

The Welsh minor tune of "Clwyd" may appropriately have been the music to express the contrite prayer of the words. The living composer, John Jones, has several tunes in the Welsh revival manual of melodies, *Ail Attodiad.*

The unparalleled religious movement of 1904–5 was a praying and singing revival. The apostle and spiritual prompter of that unbroken campaign of Christian victories—so far as any single human agency counted—was Evan Roberts, of Laughor, a humble young worker in the mines, who had prayed thirteen years for a mighty descent of the heavenly blessing on his country and for a clear indication of his own mission. His convictions naturally led him to the ministry, and he went to Newcastle Emlyn to study. Evangelical work had been done by two societies, made up of earnest Christians, and known as the "Forward Movement" and the "Simultaneous Mission." Beginnings of a special season of interest as a result of their efforts, appeared in the young people's prayer meetings in February, 1904, at New Quay, Cardiganshire. The interest increased, and when branch-work was organized a young praying and singing band visited Newcastle Emlyn in the course of one of their tours, and held a rally meeting. Evan Roberts went to the meeting and found his own mission. He left his studies and consecrated himself, soul and body, to revival work. In every spiritual and mental quality he was surpassingly well-equipped. To the quick sensibility of his poetic nature he added the inspiration of a seer and the zeal of a devotee. Like Moses, Elijah, and Paul in Arabian solitudes, and John in the Dead Sea wilds, he had prepared himself in silence and alone with God; and though, on occasion, he could use effectively his gift of words, he stood distinct in a land of matchless pulpit orators as "the silent leader." Without preaching he dominated the mood of his meetings, and without dictating he could change the trend of a service and shape the next song or prayer on the intuition of a moment. In fact, judged by its results, it was God Himself who directed the revival, only He endowed His minister with the power of divination to watch its progress and take the stumbling-blocks out of the way. By a kind of hallowed psychomancy, that humble man would detect a discordant presence, and hush the voices of a congregation till the stubborn soul felt God in the stillness, and penitently surrendered.

Many tones of the great awakening of 1859 heard again in 1904-5,—the harvest season without a precedent, when men, women and children numbering ten per cent of the whole population of a province were gathered into the membership of the church of Christ. But there were tones a century older heard in the devotions of that harvest-home in Wales. A New England Christian would have felt at home, with the tuneful assemblies at Laughor, Trencynon, Bangor, Bethesda, Wrexham, Cardiff, or Liverpool, singing Lowell Mason's "Meribah" or the clarion melody of Edson's "Lenox" to Wesley's—

Blow ye the trumpet, blow,
The gladly solemn sound;
—or to his other well-known—
Arise my soul, arise,
Shake off thy guilty fears,
The bleeding Sacrifice
In thy behalf appear.

In short, the flood tide of 1904 and 1905 brought in very little new music and very few new hymns. "Aberystwyth" and "Tanymarian," the minor harmonies of Joseph Parry and Stephens; E.M. Price's "St. Garmon;" R.M. Pritchard's, "Hyfrydol," and a few others, were choral favorites, but their composers were all dead, and the congregations loved the still older singers who had found familiar welcome at their altars and firesides. The most cherished and oftenest chosen hymns were those of William Williams and Ann Griffiths, of Charles Wesley, of Isaac Watts—indeed the very tongues of fire that appeared at Jerusalem took on the Cymric speech, and sang the burning lyrics of the poet-saints. And in their revival joy Calvinistic Wales sang the New Testament with more of its Johannic than of its Pauline texts. The covenant of peace—Christ and His Cross—is the theme of all their hymns.

Isaac
Watts, D.D.

"HERE BEHOLD THE TENT OF MEETING."
Dyma Babell y cyfarfod.

This hymn, written by Ann Griffiths, is entitled "Love Eternal," and praises the Divine plan to satisfy the Law and at the same time save the sinner. The first stanza gives an idea of the thought:

Here behold the tent of meeting,
In the blood a peace with heaven,
Refuge from the blood-avengers,
For the sick a Healer given.
Here the sinner nestles safely
At the very Throne divine,
And Heaven's righteous law, all holy.
Still on him shall smile and shine.

"HOW SWEET THE COVENANT TO REMEMBER."
Bydd melus gofio y cyfammod.

This, entitled "Mysteries of Grace," is also from the pen of Ann Griffiths. It has the literalness noticeable in much of the Welsh religious poetry, and there is a note of pietism in it. The two last stanzas are these:

He is the great Propitiation
Who with the thieves that anguish bare;
He nerved the arms of His tormentors
To drive the nails that fixed Him there.
While He discharged the sinner's ransom,
And made the Law in honor be,
Righteousness shone undimmed, resplendent,
And me the Covenant set free.
My soul, behold Him laid so lowly,
Of peace the Fount, of Kings the Head,
The vast creation in Him moving
And He low-lying with the dead!
The Life and portion of lost sinners,
The marvel of heaven's seraphim,
To sea and land the God Incarnate
The choir of heaven cries, "Unto Him!"

Ann Griffiths' earliest hymn will be called her sweetest. Fortunately, too, it is more poetically translated. It was before the vivid consciousness and intensity of her religious experience had given her spiritual writings a more involved and mystical expression.

My soul, behold the fitness
Of this great Son of God,
Trust Him for life eternal
And cast on Him thy load,
A man—touched with the pity
Of every human woe,
A God—to claim the kingdom
And vanquish every foe.

138

This stanza, the last of her little poem on the "Eternal Fitness of Jesus," came to her when, returning from an exciting service, filled with thoughts of her unworthiness and of the glorious beauty of her Saviour, she had turned down a sheltered lane to pray alone. There on her knees in communion with God her soul felt the spirit of the sacred song. By the time she reached home she had formed it into words.

The first and second stanzas, written later, are these:

Great Author of salvation
And providence for man,
Thou rulest earth and heaven
With Thy far-reaching plan.
Today or on the morrow,
Whatever woe betide,
Grant us Thy strong assistance,
Within Thy hand to hide.
What though the winds be angry,
What though the waves be high
While wisdom is the Ruler,
The Lord of earth and sky?
What though the flood of evil
Rise stormily and dark?
No soul can sink within it;
God is Himself the ark.

Mrs. Ann Griffiths, of Dolwar Fechan, Montgomeryshire, was born in 1776, and died in 1805. "She remains," says Dr. Parry, her fellow-countryman, "a romantic figure in the religious history of Wales. Her hymns leave upon the reader an undefinable impression both of sublimity and mysticism. Her brief life-history is most worthy of study both from a literary and a religious point of view."

A suggestive chapter of her short earthly career is compressed in a sentence by the author of "Sweet Singers of Wales:"

"She had a Christian life of eight years and a married life of ten months."

She died at the age of twenty-nine. In 1904, near the centennial of her death, amid the echoes of her own hymns, and the rising waves of the great Refreshing over her native land, the people of Dolwar Fechan dedicated the new "Ann Griffiths Memorial Chapel" to her name and to the glory of God.

Although the Welsh were not slow to adopt the revival tones of other lands, it was the native, and what might be called the national, lyrics of that emotional race that were sung with the richest unction and *hwyl* (as the Cymric word is) during the recent reformation, and that evinced the strongest hold on the common heart. Needless to say that with them was the world-famous song of William Williams,—

Guide me, O Thou Great Jehovah;
Arghwydd ar wain trwy'r anialoch;
—and that of Dr. Heber Evans,—
Keep me very near to Jesus,
Though beneath His Cross it be,
In this world of evil-doing
'Tis the Cross that cleanseth me;
—and also that native hymn of expectation, high and sweet, whose writer we have been unable to identify—
The glory is coming! God said it on high,
When light in the evening will break from the sky;
The North and South and the East and the West,
With joy of salvation and peace will be bless'd.
*   *   *   *   *   *
O summer of holiness, hasten along!
The purpose of glory is constant and strong;
The winter will vanish, the clouds pass away;
O South wind of Heaven, breath softly today!

Of the almost countless hymns that voiced the spirit of the great revival, the nine following are selected because they are representative, and all favorites—and because there is no room for a larger number. The first line of each is given in the original Welsh:

"DWY ADEN COLOMEN PE CAWN."

O had I the wings of a dove

How soon would I wander away
To gaze from Mount Nebo I'd love
On realms that are fairer than day.
My vision, not clouded nor dim,
Beyond the dark river should run;
I'd sing, with my thoughts upon Him,
The sinless, the crucified one.

This is another of Thomas Williams' hymns. One of the tunes suitable to its feeling and its measure was "Edom," by Thomas Evans. It was much sung in 1859, as well as in 1904.

"CAELBOD YN FORSEC DAN YR IAN."

Early to bear the yoke excels
By far the joy in sin that dwells;
The paths of wisdom still are found
In peace and solace to abound.
The young who serve Him here below
The wrath to come shall never know;
Of such in heaven are pearls that shine
Unnumbered in the crown divine.

Written for children and youth by Rev. Thomas Jones, of Denbigh, born 1756; died 1820,—a Calvinistic Methodist preacher, author of a biography of Thomas Charles of Bala, and various theological works.

"DYMA GARIAD FEL Y MOROEDD, TOSTURIASTHAN FEL Y LLI."

Love unfathomed as the ocean
Mercies boundless as the wave!
Lo the King of Life, the guiltless,
Dies my guilty soul to save;
Who can choose but think upon it,
Who can choose but praise and sing?
Here is love, while heaven endureth,
Nought can to oblivion bring.

This is called "The great Welsh love-song." It was written by Rev. William Rees, D.D., eminent as a preacher, poet, politician and essayist. One of the greatest names of nineteenth century Wales. He died in 1883.

The tune, "Cwynfan Prydian," sung to this hymn is one of the old Welsh minors that would sound almost weird to our ears, but Welsh voices can sing with strange sweetness the Saviour's passion on which Christian hearts of that nation love so well to dwell, and the shadow of it, with His love shining through, creates the paradox of a joyful lament in many of their chorals. We cannot imitate it.

"RHYFEDDODAU DYDD YR ADGYFODIDD."

Unnumbered are the marvels
The Last Great Day shall see,
With earth's poor storm-tossed children
From tribulation free,
All in their shining raiment
Transfigured, bright and brave,
Like to their Lord ascending
In triumph from the grave.

The author of this Easter hymn is unknown.

The *most* popular Welsh hymns would be named variously by different witnesses according to the breadth and length of their observation. Two of them, as a Wrexham music publisher testifies, are certainly the following; "Heaven and Home," and "Lo, a Saviour for the Fallen." The first of these was sung in the late revival with "stormy rapture."

"O FRYNAU CAERSALEM CEIR GIVELED."

The heights of fair Salem ascended,
Each wilderness path we shall see;
Now thoughts of each difficult journey
A sweet meditation shall be.
On death, on the grave and its terrors
And storms we shall gaze from above
And freed from all cares we shall revel (?)
In transports of heavenly love.

140

According to the mood of the meeting this was pitched in three sharps to Evelyn Evans' tune of "Eirinwg" or with equal Welsh enthusiasm in the C minor of old "Darby."

The author of the hymn was the Rev. David Charles, of Carmarthen, born 1762; died 1834. He was a heavenly-minded man who loved to dwell on the divine and eternal wonders of redemption. A volume of his sermons was spoken of as "Apples of gold in pictures of silver," and the beautiful piety of all his writings made them strings of pearls. He understood English as well as Welsh, and enjoyed the hymns not only of William and Thomas Williams but of Watts, Wesley, Cowper, and Newton.*

> * The following verses were written by him in English:
> Spirit of grace and love divine,
> Help me to sing that Christ is mine;
> And while the theme my tongue employs
> Fill Thou my soul with living joys.
> Jesus is mine—surpassing thought!
> Well may I set the world at nought;
> Jesus is mine, O can it be
> That Jesus lived and died for me?

"DYMA GEIDWAD I R COLLEDIG."

Lo! a Saviour for the fallen,
Healer of the sick and sore,
One whose love the vilest sinners
Seeks to pardon and restore.
Praise Him, praise Him
Who has loved us evermore!

The little now known of the Rev. Morgan Rhys, author of this hymn, is that he was a schoolmaster and preacher, and that he was a contemporary and friend of William Williams. Several of his hymns remain in use of which the oftenest sung is one cited above, and "O agor fy llygaid i weled:"

I open my eyes to this vision,
The deeps of Thy purpose and word;
The law of Thy lips is to thousands
Of gold and of silver preferred;
When earth is consumed, and its treasure,
God's words will unchanging remain,
And to know the God-man is my Saviour
Is life everlasting to gain.

"Lo! a Saviour for the Fallen" finds an appropriate voice in W.M. Robert's tune of "Nesta," and also, like many others of the same measure, in the much-used minors "Llanietyn," "Catharine," and "Bryn Calfaria."

"O SANCTEIDDIA F'ENAID ARGLWYDD."

Sanctify, O Lord, my spirit,
Every power and passion sway,
Bid Thy holy law within me
Dwell, my wearied soul to stay;
Let me never
Rove beyond Thy narrow way.

This one more hymn of William Williams is from his "Song of a Cleansed Heart" and is amply provided with tunes, popular ones like "Tyddyn Llwyn," "Y Delyn Aur," or "Capel-Y-Ddol" lending their deep minors to its lines with a thrilling effect realized, perhaps, only in the land of Taliessin and the Druids.

The singular history and inspiring cause of one old Welsh hymn which after various mutilations and vicissitudes survives as the key-note of a valued song of trust, seems to illustrate the Providence that will never let a good thing be lost. It is related of the Rev. David Williams, of Llandilo, an obscure but not entirely forgotten preacher, that he had a termagant wife, and one stormy night, when her bickerings became intolerable, he went out in the rain and standing by the river composed in his mind these lines of tender faith:

In the waves and mighty waters
No one will support my head
But my Saviour, my Beloved,
Who was stricken in my stead.
In the cold and mortal river

He would hold my head above;
I shall through the waves go singing
For one look of Him I love.

Apparently the sentiment and substantially the expression of this humble hymn became
the burden of more than one Christian lay. Altered and blended with a modern gospel hymn, it
was sung at the crowded meetings of 1904 to Robert Lowry's air of "Jesus Only," and often
rendered very impressively as a solo by a sweet female voice.

In the deep and mighty waters
There is none to hold my head
But my loving Bridegroom, Jesus,
Who upon the cross hath bled.
If I've Jesus, Jesus only
Then my sky will have a gem
He's the Sun of brightest splendor,
He's the Star of Bethlehem.
He's the Friend in Death's dark river,
He will lift me o'er the waves,
I will sing in the deep waters
If I only see His face.
If I've Jesus, Jesus only, etc.

A few of the revival tunes have living authors and are of recent date; and the minor
harmony of "Ebenezer" (marked "Ton Y Botel"), which was copied in this country by the New
York *Examiner,* with its hymn, is apparently a contemporary piece. It was first sung at Bethany
Chapel, Cardiff, Jan, 8, 1905, the hymn bearing the name of Rev. W.E. Winks.

Send Thy Spirit, I beseech Thee,
Gracious Lord, send while I pray;
Send the Comforter to teach me,
Guide me, help me in Thy way.
Sinful, wretched, I have wandered
Far from Thee in darkest night,
Precious time and talents squandered,
Lead, O lead me into light.
Thou hast heard me; light is breaking—
Light I never saw before.
Now, my soul with joy awaking,
Gropes in fearful gloom no more:
O the bliss! my soul, declare it;
Say what God hath done for thee;
Tell it out, let others share it—
Christ's salvation, full and free.

One cannot help noticing the fondness of the Welsh for the 7-6, 8-7, and 8-7-4 metres.
These are favorites since they lend themselves so naturally to the rhythms of their national
music—though their newest hymnals by no means exclude exotic lyrics and melodies. Even "O
mother dear, Jerusalem," one of the echoes of Bernard of Cluny's great hymn, is cherished in
their tongue (*O, Frynian Caerselem*) among the favorites of song. Old "Truro" by Dr. Burney
appears among their tunes, Mason's "Ernan," "Lowell" and "Shawmut," I.B. Woodbury's
"Nearer Home" (to Phebe Cary's hymn), and even George Hews' gently-flowing "Holley." Most
of these tunes retain their own hymns, but in Welsh translation. To find our Daniel Read's old
"Windham" there is no surprise. The minor mode—a song-instinct of the Welsh, if not of the
whole Celtic family of nations, is their rural inheritance. It is in the wind of their mountains and
the semitones of their streams; and their nature can make it a gladness as the Anglo-Saxon
cannot. So far from being a gloomy people, their capacity for joy in spiritual life is phenomenal.
In psalmody their emotions mount on wings, and they find ecstasy in solemn sounds.

"A temporary excitement" is the verdict of skepticism on the Reformation wave that for a
twelvemonth swept over Wales with its ringing symphonies of hymn and tune. But such
excitements are the May-blossom seasons of God's eternal husbandry. They pass because human
vigor cannot last at flood-tide, but in spiritual economy they will always have their place, "If the
blossoms had not come and gone there would be no fruit."

CHAPTER XII.

FIELD HYMNS.

Hymns of the hortatory and persuasive tone are sufficiently numerous to make an "embarrassment of riches" in a compiler's hands. Not a few songs of invitation and awakening are either quoted or mentioned in the chapter on "Old Revival Hymns," and many appear among those in the last chapter, (on the *Hymns of Wales*,) but the *working* songs of Christian hymnology deserve a special space *as* such.

"COME HITHER ALL YE WEARY SOULS,"

Sung to "Federal St.," is one of the older soul-winning calls from the great hymn-treasury of Dr. Watts; and another note of the same sacred bard,—

Life is the time to serve the Lord,

—is always coupled with the venerable tune of "Wells."* Aged Christians are still remembered who were wont to repeat or sing with quavering voices the second stanza,—

The living know that they must die,
But all the dead forgotten lie;
Their memory and their sense are gone,
Alike unknowing and unknown.

And likewise from the fourth stanza,—

There are no acts of pardon passed
In the cold grave to which we haste.

* One of Israel Holroyd's tunes. He was born in England, about 1690, and was both a composer and publisher of psalmody. His chief collection is dated 1746.

"AND WILL THE JUDGE DESCEND?"

Is one of Doddridge's monitory hymns, once sung to J.C. Woodman's tune of "State St." with the voice of both the Old and New Testaments in the last verse:

Ye sinners, seek His grace
Whose wrath ye cannot bear;
Fly to the shelter of His Cross,
And find Salvation there.

Jonathan Call Woodman was born in Newburyport, Mass., July 12, 1813, and was a teacher, composer, and compiler. Was organist of St. George's Chapel, in Flushing, L.I., and in 1858 published *The Musical Casket*. Died January, 1894. He wrote "State St." for William B. Bradbury, in August, 1844.

"HASTEN SINNER, TO BE WISE"

Is one of the few unforgotten hymns of Thomas Scott, every second line repeating the solemn caution,—

Stay not for tomorrow's sun,

—and every line enforcing its exhortation with a new word, "To be wise," "to implore," "to return," and "to be blest" were natural cumulatives that summoned and wooed the sinner careless and astray. It is a finished piece of work, but it owes its longevity less to its structural form than to its spirit. For generations it has been sung to "Pleyel's Hymn."

The Rev. Thomas Scott (not Rev. Thomas Scott the Commentator) was born in Norwich, Eng., in 1705, and died at Hupton, in Norfolk, 1776. He was a Dissenting minister, pastor for twenty-one years—until disabled by feeble health—at Lowestoft in Suffolk. He was the author of—

Angels roll the rock away.

"MUST JESUS BEAR THE CROSS ALONE?"

This emotional and appealing hymn still holds its own in the hearts of millions, though probably two hundred years old. It was written by a clergyman of the Church of England, the Rev. Thomas Shepherd, Vicar of Tilbrook, born in 1665. Joining the Nonconformists in 1694, he settled first in Castle Hill, Nottingham, and afterward in Bocking, Essex, where he remained until his death, January, 1739. He published a selection of his sermons, and *Penitential Cries*, a book of sacred lyrics, some of which still appear in collections.

The startling question in the above line is answered with emphasis in the third of the stanza,—

No! There's a cross for every one,
And there's a cross for *me*,

—and this is followed by the song of resolve and triumph,—

The consecrated cross I'll bear,
Till death shall set me free.
And then go home my crown to wear,
For there's a crown for me.

143

*   *   *   *   *   *

O precious cross! O glorious crown!
O Resurrection Day!
Ye angels from the stars flash down
And bear my soul away!

The hymn is a personal New Testament. No one who analyzes it and feels its Christian vitality will wonder why it has lived so long.

THE TUNE.

For half a century George N. Allen, composer of "Maitland," the music inseparable from the hymn, was credited with the authorship of the words also, but his vocal aid to the heart-stirring poem earned him sufficient praise. The tune did not meet the hymn till the latter was so old that the real author was mostly forgotten, for Allen wrote the music in 1849; but if the fine stanzas needed any renewing it was his tune that made them new. Since it was published nobody has wanted another.

George Nelson Allen was born in Mansfield, Mass., Sept. 7, 1812, and lived at Oberlin, O. It was there that he composed "Maitland," and compiled the *Social and Sabbath Hymn-book*— besides songs for the *Western Bell*, published by Oliver Ditson and Co. He died in Cincinnati, Dec. 9, 1877.

"AWAKE MY SOUL, STRETCH EVERY NERVE!"

This most popular of Dr. Doddridge's hymns is also the richest one of all in lyrical and spiritual life. It is a stadium song that sounds the starting-note for every young Christian at the outset of his career, and the slogan for every faint Christian on the way.

A *heavenly* race demands thy zeal,
And an immortal crown.

Like the "Coronation" hymn, it transports the devout singer till he feels only the momentum of the words and forgets whether it is common or hallelujah metre that carries him along.

A cloud of witnesses around
Hold thee in full survey;
Forget the steps already trod,
And onward urge thy way!
'Tis God's all-animating voice
That calls thee from on high,
'Tis His own hand presents the prize
To thine aspiring eye.

In all persuasive hymnology there is no more kindling lyric that this. As a field-hymn it is indispensable.

THE TUNE.

Whenever and by whomsoever the brave processional known as "Christmas" was picked from among the great Handel's Songs and mated with Doddridge's lines, the act gave both hymn and tune new reason to endure, and all posterity rejoices in the blend. Old "Christmas" was originally one of the melodies in the great Composer's Opera of "Circe" (Cyrus) 1738. It was written to Latin words (*Non vi piacque*) and afterwards adapted to an English versification of Job 29:15, "I was eyes to the blind."

Handel, himself became blind at the age of sixty eight (1753).

George Frederick
Handel

"THERE IS A GREEN HILL FAR AWAY."

Written in 1848 by Miss Cecil Frances Humphreys, an Irish lady, daughter of Major John Humphreys of Dublin. She was born in that city in 1823. Her best known name is Mrs. Cecil Frances Alexander, her husband being the Rt. Rev. William Alexander, Bishop of Derry. Among

144

her works are *Hymns for Little Children, Narrative Hymns, Hymns Descriptive and Devotional,* and *Moral Songs.* Died 1895.

"There is a *green* hill" is poetic license, but the hymn is sweet and sympathetic, and almost childlike in its simplicity.

There is a green hill far away
Without the city wall,
Where our dear Lord was crucified
Who died to save us all.
We may not know, we cannot tell
What pains He had to bear;
But we believe it was for us
He hung and suffered there.

THE TUNES.

There is no room here to describe them all. Airs and chorals by Berthold Tours, Pinsuti, John Henry Cornell, Richard Storrs Willis, George C. Stebbins and Hubert P. Main have been adapted to the words—one or two evidently composed for them. It is a hymn that attracts tune-makers—literally so commonplace and yet so quiet and tender, with such a theme and such natural melody of line—but most of the scores indicated are choir music rather than congregational. Mr. Stebbins' composition comes nearest to being the favorite, if one judges by the extent and frequency of its use. It can be either partly or wholly choral; and the third stanza makes the refrain—

O dearly, dearly has He loved
And we must love Him too,
And trust in His redeeming blood,
And try His works to do.

"REJOICE AND BE GLAD!"

This musical shout of joy, written by Dr. Horatius Bonar, scarcely needs a new song helper, as did Bishop Heber's famous hymn—not because it is better than Heber's but because It was wedded at once to a tune worthy of it.

Rejoice and be glad! for our King is on high;
He pleadeth for us on His throne in the sky.
Rejoice and be glad! for He cometh again;
He cometh in glory, the Lamb that was slain
Hallelujah! Amen.

The hymn was composed in 1874.

THE TUNE.

The author of the "English Melody" (as ascribed in *Gospel Hymns*) is said to have been John Jenkins Husband, born in Plymouth, Eng., about 1760. He was clerk at Surrey Chapel and composed several anthems. Came to the United States In 1809. Settled in Philadelphia, where he taught music and was clerk of St. Paul's P.E. Church. Died there in 1825.

His tune, exactly suited to the hymn, is a true Christian pæan. It has few equals as a rouser to a sluggish prayer-meeting—whether sung to Bonar's words or those of Rev. William Paton Mackay (1866)—

We praise Thee, O God, for the Son of Thy love,

—with the refrain of similar spirit in both hymns—

Hallelujah! Thine the glory, Hallelujah! Amen,
Hallelujah! Thine the glory; revive us again;

—or,—

Sound His praises! tell the story of Him who was slain!
Sound His praises! tell with gladness, "He liveth again."

Husband's tune is supposed to have been written very early in the last century. Another tune composed by him near the same date to the words—

"We are on our journey home
To the New Jerusalem,"

—is equally musical and animating, and with a vocal range that brings out the full strength of choir and congregation.

"COME, SINNER, COME."

A singular case of the same tune originating in the brain of both author and composer is presented in the history of this hymn of Rev. William Ellsworth Witter, D.D., born in La Grange, N.Y., Dec. 9, 1854. He wrote the hymn in the autumn of 1878, while teaching a district school near his home. The first line—

While Jesus whispers to you,

—came to him during a brief turn of outdoor work by the roadside and presently grew to twenty-four lines. Soon after, Prof. Horatio Palmer, knowing Witter to be a verse writer, invited him to contribute a hymn to a book he had in preparation, and this hymn was sent. Dr. Palmer set it to music, it soon entered into several collections, and Mr. Sankey sang it in England at the Moody meetings.

Dr. Witter gives this curious testimony,

"While I cannot sing myself, though very fond of music, the hymn sang itself to me by the roadside *in almost the exact tune given to it by Professor Palmer.*" Which proves that Professor Palmer had the feeling of the hymn—and that the maker of a true hymn has at least a sub-consciousness of its right tune, though he may be neither a musician nor a poet.

While Jesus whispers to you,
Come, sinner, come!
While we are praying for you,
Come, sinner, come!
Now is the time to own Him,
Come, sinner, come!
Now is the time to know Him,
Come, sinner, come!

"ONE MORE DAY'S WORK FOR JESUS."

The writer of this hymn was Miss Anna Warner, one of the well-known "Wetherell Sisters," joint authors of *The Wide World, Queechy,* and a numerous succession of healthful romances very popular in the middle and later years of the last century. Her own pen name is "Amy Lothrop," under which she has published many religious poems, hymns and other varieties of literary work. She was born in 1820, at Martlaer, West Point, N.Y., where she still resides.

One more day's work for Jesus,
One less of life for me:
But heaven is nearer,
And Christ is dearer
Than yesterday to me.
His love and light
Fill all my soul tonight.
REFRAIN:—
One more day's work for Jesus, *(ter)*
One less of life for me.

The hymn has five stanzas all expressing the gentle fervor of an active piety loving service:

THE TUNE

was composed by the Rev. Robert Lowry, and first published in *Bright Jewels.*

THE GOSPEL HYMNS.

These popular religious songs have been criticised as "degenerate psalmody" but those who so style them do not seem to consider the need that made them.

The great majority of mankind can only be reached by missionary methods, and in these art and culture do not play a conspicuous part. The multitude could be supplied with technical preaching and technical music for their religious wants, but they would not rise to the bait, whereas nothing so soon kindles their better emotions or so surely appeals to their better nature as even the humblest sympathetic hymn sung to a simple and stirring tune. If the music is unclassical and the hymn crude there is no critical audience to be offended.

The artless, almost colloquial, words "of a happily rhymed camp-meeting lyric and the wood-notes wild" of a new melody meet a situation. Moral and spiritual lapse makes it necessary at times for religion to put on again her primitive raiment, and be "a voice crying in the wilderness."

Between the slums and the boulevards live the masses that shape the generations, and make the state. They are wage-earners who never hear the great composers nor have time to form fine musical and literary tastes. The spiritual influences that really reach them are of a very direct and simple kind; and for the good of the church—and the nation—it is important that at least this elementary education in the school of Christ should be supplied them.

It is the popular hymn tunes that speed a reformation. So say history and experience. Once in two hundred years a great revival movement may produce a Charles Wesley, but the humbler singers carry the divine fire that quickens religious life in the years between.

All this is not saying that the gospel hymns, as a whole, are or ever professed to be suitable for the stated service of the sanctuary. Their very style and movement show exactly what they were made for—to win the hearing of the multitude, and put the music of God's praise and Jesus' love into the mouths and hearts of thousands who had been strangers to both. They are the modern lay songs that go with the modern lay sermons. They give voice to the spirit and sentiment of the conference, prayer and inquiry meetings, the Epworth League and Christian Endeavor meetings, the temperance and other reform meetings, and of the mass-meetings in the cities or the seaside camps.

During their evangelistic mission in England and Scotland in 1873, Dwight L. Moody and Ira D. Sankey used the hymnbook of Philip Phillips, a compilation entitled *Hallowed Songs*, some of them his own. To these Mr. Sankey added others of his own composing from time to time which were so enthusiastically received that he published them in a pamphlet. This, with the simultaneous publication in America of the revival melodies of Philip P. Bliss, was the beginning of that series of popular hymn-and-tune books, which finally numbered six volumes. Sankey's *Sacred Songs and Solos* combined with Bliss's *Gospel Songs* were the foundation of the *Gospel Hymns*.

Subjectively their utterances are indicative of ardent piety and unquestioning faith, and on the other hand their direct and intimate appeal and dramatic address are calculated to affect a throng as if each individual in it was the person meant by the words. The refrain or chorus feature is notable in nearly all.

A selection of between thirty and forty of the most characteristic is here given.

"HALLELUJAH! 'TIS DONE."

This is named from its chorus. The song is one of the spontaneous thanksgivings in revival meetings that break out at the announcement of a new conversion.

'Tis the promise of God full salvation to give
Unto him who on Jesus His Son will believe,
Hallelujah! 'tis done; I believe on the Son;
I am saved by the blood of the crucified One.
Though the pathway be lonely and dangerous too,
Surely Jesus is able to carry me through—
Hallelujah! etc.

The words and music are both by P.P. Bliss.

THE NINETY AND NINE.

The hymn was written by Mrs. Elizabeth Cecilia Clephane at Melrose, Scotland, early in 1868. She was born in Edinburgh, June 10, 1830, and died of consumption, Feb. 19, 1869. The little poem was seen by Mr. Sankey in the *Christian Age*, and thinking it might be useful, he cut it out. At an impressive moment in one of the great meetings in Edinburgh, Mr. Moody said to him in a quiet aside, "Sing something." Precisely what was wanted for the hour and theme, and for the thought in the general mind, was in Mr. Sankey's vest pocket. But how could it be sung without a tune? With a silent prayer for help, the musician took out the slip containing Mrs. Clephane's poem, laid it on the little reed-organ and began playing, and singing. He had to read the unfamiliar words and at the same time make up the music. The tune came—and grew as he went along till he finished the first verse. He remembered it well enough to repeat it with the second, and after that it was easy to finish the hymn. A new melody was born—in the presence of more than a thousand pairs of eyes and ears. It was a feat of invention, of memory, of concentration— and such was the elocution of the trained soloist that not a word was lost. He had a tearful audience at the close to reward him; but we can easily credit his testimony,

"It was the most intense moment of my life."

In a touching interview afterwards, a sister of Mrs. Clephane told Mr. Sankey the authoress had not lived to see her hymn in print and to know of its blessed mission.

The first six lines give the situation of the lost sheep in the parable of that name—

There were ninety and nine that safely lay
In the shelter of the fold;
But one was out on the hills away,
Far off from the gates of gold.
Away on the mountains wild and bare,
Away from the tender Shepherd's care.

And, after describing the Shepherd's arduous search, the joy at his return is sketched and spiritualized in the concluding stanza—

But all through the mountains, thunder-riven,
And up from the rocky steeps
There arose a cry to the gate of heaven,
"Rejoice! I have found my sheep."
And the angels echoed around the Throne,
"Rejoice! for the Lord brings back His own."

"HOLD THE FORT!"

This is named also from its chorus. The historic foundation of the hymn was the flag-signal waved to Gen. G.M. Corse by Gen. Sherman's order from Kenesaw Mountain to Altoona during the "March through Georgia," in October, 1863. The flag is still in the possession of A.D. Frankenberry, one of the Federal Signal-Corps whose message to the besieged General said, "Hold the fort! We are coming!" A visit to the scene of the incident inspired P.P. Bliss to write both the words and the music.

Ho! my comrades, see the signal
Waving in the sky!
Reinforcements now appearing,
Victory is nigh.
"Hold the fort, for I am coming!"
Jesus signals still;
Wave the answer back to heaven,
"By Thy grace we will!"

The popularity of the song (it has been translated into several languages), made it the author's chief memento in many localities. On his monument in Rome, Pennsylvania, is inscribed "P.P. Bliss—author of 'Hold the Fort.'"

"RESCUE THE PERISHING."

Few hymns, ancient or modern, have been more useful, or more variously used, than this little sermon in song from Luke 14:23, by the blind poet, Fanny J. Crosby, (Mrs. Van Alstyne). It is sung not only in the church prayer-meetings with its spiritual meaning and application, but in Salvation Army camps and marches, in mission-school devotions, in social settlement services, in King's Daughters and Sons of Temperance Meetings, and in the rallies of every reform organization that seeks the lost and fallen.

Rescue the perishing, care for the dying,
Snatch them in pity from sin and the grave;
Weep o'er the erring ones, lift up the fallen,
Tell them of Jesus, the Mighty to Save.
* * * * * *
Down in the human heart crushed by the Tempter,
Feelings lie buried that grace can restore.
Touched by a loving heart, wakened by kindness,
Chords that were broken will vibrate once more.

The tune is by W.H. Doane, Mus. D., composed in 1870.

"WHAT A FRIEND WE HAVE IN JESUS."

The author was a pious gentleman of Dublin, Ireland, who came to Canada when he was twenty-five. His name was Joseph Scriven, born in Dublin, 1820, and graduated at Trinity College. The accidental death by drowning of his intended bride on the eve of their wedding day, led him to consecrate his life and fortune to the service of Christ. He died in Canada, Oct. 10, 1886, (Sankey's *Story of the Gospel Hymns*, pp. 245–6.)

THE TUNE.

The music was composed by Charles Crozat Converse, LL.D., musician, lawyer, and writer. He was born in Warren, Mass., 1832; a descendant of Edward Converse, the friend of Gov. Winthrop and founder of Woburn, Mass. He pursued musical and other studies in Leipsic and Berlin. His compositions are numerous including concert overtures, symphonies and many sacred and secular pieces. Residence at Highwood, Bergen Co., N.J.

The hymn is one of the most helpful of the Gospel Collections, and the words and music have strengthened many a weak and failing soul to "try again."

Have we trials and temptations?
Is there trouble anywhere?
We should never be discouraged:
Take it to the Lord in prayer.

"I HEAR THE SAVIOUR SAY."

This is classed with the *Gospel Hymns*, but it was a much-used and much-loved revival hymn—especially in the Methodist churches—several years before Mr. Moody's great evangelical movement. It was written by Mrs. Elvina M. Hall (since Mrs. Myers) who was born in Alexandria, Va., in 1818. She composed it in the spring of 1865, while sitting in the choir of the M.E. Church, Baltimore, and the first draft was pencilled on a fly-leaf of a singing book, *The New Lute of Zion.*

I hear the Saviour say,
Thy strength indeed is small;

Child of weakness, watch and pray,
Find in me thine all in all.

The music of the chorus helped to fix its words in the common mind, and some idea of the Atonement acceptable, apparently, to both Arminians and Calvinists; for Sunday-school children in the families of both, hummed the tune or sang the refrain when alone—

Jesus paid it all,
All to Him I owe,
Sin had left a crimson stain;
He washed it white as snow.

THE TUNE.

John Thomas Grape, who wrote the music, was born in Baltimore, Md., May 6, 1833. His modest estimate of his work appears in his remark that he "dabbled" in music for his own amusement. Few composers have amused themselves with better results.

"TELL ME THE OLD, OLD STORY."

Miss Kate Hankey, born about 1846, the daughter of an English banker, is the author of this very devout and tender Christian poem, written apparently in the eighteen-sixties. At least it is said that her little volume, *Heart to Heart*, was published in 1865 or 1866, and this volume contains "Tell me the Old, Old Story," and its answer.

We have been told that Miss Hankey was recovering from a serious illness, and employed her days of convalescence in composing this song of devotion, beginning it in January and finishing it in the following November.

The poem is very long—a thesaurus of evangelical thoughts, attitudes, and moods of faith—and also a magazine of hymns. Four quatrains of it, or two eight-line stanzas, are the usual length of a hymnal selection, and editors can pick and choose anywhere among its expressive verses.

Tell me the old, old story
Of unseen things above,
Of Jesus and His glory,
Of Jesus and His love.
Tell me the story simply
As to a little child,
For I am weak and weary,
And helpless and defiled.
* * * * * *

Tell me the story simply
That I may take it in—
That wonderful Redemption,
God's remedy for sin.

THE TUNE.

Dr. W.H. Doane was present at the International Conference of the Y.M.C.A. at Montreal in 1867, and heard the poem read—with tears and in a broken voice—by the veteran Major-General Russell. It impressed him so much that he borrowed and copied it, and subsequently set it to music during a vacation in the White Mountains.

The poem of fifty stanzas was entitled "The Story Wanted;" the sequel or answer to it, by Miss Hankey, was named "The Story Told." This second hymn, of the same metre but different accent, was supplied with a tune by William Gustavus Fischer.

I love to tell the story
Of unseen things above,
Of Jesus and His glory,
Of Jesus and His love.
* * * * * *

I love to tell the story
Because I know its true;
It satisfies my longings
As nothing else can do.
CHORUS.
I love to tell the story;
'Twill be my theme in glory;
To tell the old, old story
Of Jesus and his love.

William Gustavus Fischer was born in Baltimore, Md., Oct. 14, 1835. He was a piano-dealer in the firm (formerly) of Gould and Fischer. His melody to the above hymn was written in 1869, and was harmonized the next year by Hubert P. Main.

THE PRODIGAL CHILD.

This is not only an impressive hymn as sung in sympathetic music, but a touching poem.

Come home! come home!
You are weary at heart,
For the way has been dark
And so lonely and wild—
O prodigal child,
Come home!
Come home! Come home!
For we watch and we wait,
And we stand at the gate
While the shadows are piled;
O prodigal child,
Come home!

The author is Mrs. Ellen M.H. Gates, known to the English speaking world by her famous poem, "Your Mission."

THE TUNE

To "The Prodigal Child" was composed by Dr. Doane in 1869 and no hymn ever had a fitter singing ally. All a mother's yearning is in the refrain and cadence.

Come home! Oh, come home!

"LET THE LOWER LIGHTS BE BURNING!"

An illustration, recited in Mr. Moody's graphic fashion in one of his discourses, suggested this hymn to P.P. Bliss.

"A stormy night on Lake Erie, and the sky pitch dark."
'Pilot, are you sure this is Cleveland? There's only one light.'
'Quite sure, Cap'n.'
'Where are the lower lights?'
'Gone out, sir.'
'Can you run in?'
'*We've got to,* Cap'n—or die.'
"The brave old pilot did his best, but, alas, he missed the channel. The boat was wrecked, with a loss of many lives. The lower lights had gone out.

"Brethren, the Master will take care of the great Lighthouse. It is our work to keep the lower lights burning!"

Brightly beams our Father's mercy
From His lighthouse evermore;
But to us He gives the keeping
Of the lights along the shore.
CHORUS.
Let the lower lights be burning!
Send a gleam across the wave;
Some poor fainting, struggling seaman
You may rescue, you may save.

Both words and music—composed in 1871—are by Mr. Bliss. There are wakening chords in the tune—and especially the chorus—when the counterpoint is well vocalized; and the effect is more pronounced the greater the symphony of voices. Congregations find a zest in every note. "Hold the Fort" can be sung in the street. "Let the Lower Lights be Burning" is at home between echoing walls.

The use of the song in "Bethel" meetings classes it with sailors' hymns.

"SWEET HOUR OF PRAYER."

Included with the *Gospel Hymns,* but of older date. Rev. William W. Walford, a blind English minister, was the author, and it was probably written about the year 1842. It was recited to Rev. Thomas Salmon, Congregational pastor at Coleshill, Eng., who took it down and brought it to New York, where it was published in the New York *Observer.*

Little is known of Mr. Walford save that in his blindness, besides preaching occasionally, he employed his mechanical skill in making small useful articles of bone and ivory.

The tune was composed by W.B. Bradbury in 1859, and first appeared with the hymn in *Cottage Melodies.*

Sweet hour of prayer, sweet hour of prayer
That calls me from a world of care,
And bids me at my Father's throne
Make all my wants and wishes known.
In seasons of distress and grief
My soul has often found relief,
And oft escaped the tempter's snare
By thy return, sweet hour of prayer.

"O BLISS OF THE PURIFIED! BLISS OF THE FREE!"

Rev. Francis Bottome, D.D., born in Belper, Derbyshire, Eng., May 26, 1823, removed to the United States in 1850, and entered the Methodist ministry. A man of sterling character and exemplary piety. He received the degree of Doctor of Divinity at Dickinson College, Carlisle, Pa. Was assistant compiler of several singing books, and wrote original hymns. The above, entitled "O sing of His mighty love" was composed by him in 1869. The last stanza reads,—

O Jesus the Crucified! Thee will I sing,
My blessed Redeemer, my God and my King!
My soul, filled with rapture shall shout o'er the grave
And triumph in death in the Mighty to save.
CHORUS.
O sing of His mighty love (*ter*)
Mighty to save!

Dr. Bottome returned to England, and died at Tavistock June 29, 1894.

THE TUNE.

Bradbury's "Songs of the Beautiful" (in *Fresh Laurels*). The hymn was set to this chorus in 1871.

"WHAT SHALL THE HARVEST BE?"

Very popular in England. Mr. Sankey in his *Story of the Gospel Hymns* relates at length the experience of Rev. W.O. Lattimore, pastor of a large church in Evanston, Ill., who was saved to Christian manhood and usefulness by this hymn. It has suffered some alterations, but its original composition was Mrs. Emily Oakey's work. The Parables of the Sower and of the Tares may have been in her mind when she wrote the lines in 1850, but more probably it was the text in Gal. 6:7—

Sowing the seed by the daylight fair,
Sowing the seed by the noonday glare,
Sowing the seed by the fading light,
Sowing the seed in the solemn night.
O, what shall the harvest be?

Lattimore, the man whose history was so strangely linked with this hymn, entered the army in 1861, a youth of eighteen with no vices, but when promoted to first lieutenant he learned to drink in the officers' mess. The habit so contracted grew upon him till when the war was over, though he married and tried to lead a sober life, he fell a victim to his appetite, and became a physical wreck. One day in the winter of 1876 he found himself in a half-drunken condition, in the gallery of Moody's Tabernacle, Chicago. Discovering presently that he had made a mistake, he rose to go out, but Mr. Sankey's voice chained him. He sat down and heard the whole of the thrilling hymn from beginning to end. Then he stumbled out with the words ringing in his ears.

Sowing the seed of a lingering pain,
Sowing the seed of a maddened brain,
Sowing the seed of a tarnished name,
Sowing the seed of Eternal shame.
O, what shall the harvest be?

In the saloon, where he went to drown the awakenings of remorse, those words stood in blazing letters on every bottle and glass. The voice of God in that terrible song of conviction forced him back to the Tabernacle, with his drink untasted. He went into the inquiry meeting where he found friends, and was led to Christ. His wife and child, from whom he had long been exiled, were sent for and work was found for him to do. A natural eloquence made him an attractive and efficient helper in the meetings, and he was finally persuaded to study for the ministry. His faithful pastorate of twenty years in Evanston ended with his death in 1899.

Mrs. Emily Sullivan Oakey was an author and linguist by profession, and though in her life of nearly fifty-four years she "never enjoyed a day of good health," she earned a grateful memory. Born in Albany, N.Y., Oct. 8, 1829, she was educated at the Albany Female Academy, and fitted herself for the position of teacher of languages and English literature in the same school, which she honored by her service while she lived. Her contributions to the daily press and to magazine literature were numerous, but she is best known by her remarkable hymn. Her death occurred on the 11th of May, 1883.

THE TUNE,

By P.P. Bliss, is one of that composer's tonal successes. The march of the verses with their recurrent words is so automatic that it would inevitably suggest to him the solo and its organ-chords; and the chorus with its sustained soprano note dominating the running concert adds the last emphasis to the solemn repetition. The song with its warning cry owes no little of its power to this choral appendix—

Gathered in time or eternity,
Sure, ah sure will the harvest be.

"O THINK OF THE HOME OVER THERE."

A hymn of Rev. D.W.C. Huntington, suggested by Ps. 55:6. It was a favorite from the first.

Rev. DeWitt Clinton Huntington was born at Townshend, Vt., Apr.27, 1830. He graduated at the Syracuse University, and received the degrees of D.D. and LL.D. from Genesee College. Preacher, instructor and author—Removed to Lincoln, Nebraska.

O think of the home over there,
By the side of the river of light,
Where the saints all immortal and fair
Are robed in their garments of white.
Over there, (rep)
O think of the friends over there,
Who before us the journey have trod,
Of the songs that they breathe on the air,
In their home in the palace of God.
Over there. (rep)

THE TUNE.

The melody was composed by Tullius Clinton O'Kane, born in Delaware, O., March 10, 1830, a hymnist and musician. It is a flowing tune, with sweet chords, and something of the fugue feature in the chorus as an accessory. The voices of a multitude in full concord make a building tremble with it.

"WHEN JESUS COMES."

Down life's dark vale we wander
Till Jesus comes;
We watch and wait and wonder
Till Jesus comes.

Both words and music are by Mr. Bliss. A relative of his family, J.S. Ellsworth, says the song was written in Peoria, Illinois, in 1872, and was suggested by a conversation on the second coming of Christ, a subject very near his heart. The thought lingered in his mind, and as he came down from his room, soon after, the verses and notes came to him simultaneously on the stairs. Singing them over, he seized pencil and paper, and in a few minutes fixed hymn and tune in the familiar harmony so well known.

No more heart-pangs nor sadness
When Jesus comes;
All peace and joy and gladness
When Jesus comes.

The choral abounds in repetition, and is half refrain, but among all Gospel Hymns remarkable for their tone-delivery this is unsurpassed in the swing of its rhythm.

All joy his loved ones bringing
When Jesus comes.
All praise thro' heaven ringing
When Jesus comes.
All beauty bright and vernal
When Jesus comes.
All glory grand, eternal
When Jesus comes.

"TO THE WORK, TO THE WORK."

One of Fanny Crosby's most animating hymns—with Dr. W.H. Doane's full part harmony to re-enforce its musical accent. Mr. Sankey says, "I sang it for the first time in the home of Mr. and Mrs. J.B. Cornell at Long Branch. The servants gathered from all parts of the house while I was singing, and looked into the parlor where I was seated. When I was through one of them said, 'That is the finest hymn I have heard for a long time,' I felt that this was a test case, and if the hymn had such power over those servants it would be useful in reaching other people as well; so I published it in the *Gospel Hymns* in 1875, where it became one of the best work-songs for our meetings that we had." (*Story of the Gospel Hymns.*)

The hymn, written in 1870, was first published in 1871 in "*Pure Gold*"—a book that had a sale of one million two hundred thousand copies.

To the work! to the work! there is labor for all,
For the Kingdom of darkness and error shall fall,
And the name of Jehovah exalted shall be,
In the loud-swelling chorus, "Salvation is free!"
CHORUS.
Toiling on, toiling on, toiling on, toiling on! (*rep*)
Let us hope and trust, let us watch and pray,
And labor till the Master comes.

"O WHERE ARE THE REAPERS?"

Matt. 13:30 is the text of this lyric from the pen of Eben E. Rexford.
Go out in the by-ways, and search them all,
The wheat may be there though the weeds are tall;
Then search in the highway, and pass none by,
But gather them all for the home on high.
CHORUS.
Where are the reapers? O who will come,
And share in the glory of the harvest home?
O who will help us to garner in
The sheaves of good from the fields of sin?

THE TUNE.

Hymn and tune are alike. The melody and harmony by Dr. George F. Root have all the eager trip and tread of so many of the gospel hymns, and of so much of his music, and the lines respond at every step. Any other composer could not have escaped the compulsion of the final spondees, and much less the author of "Tramp, Tramp, Tramp," and all the best martial song-tunes of the great war. In this case neither words nor notes can say to the other, "We have piped unto you and ye have not danced," but a little caution will guard too enthusiastic singing against falling into the drum-rhythm, and travestying a sacred piece.

Eben Eugene Rexford was born in Johnsburg, N.Y., July 16, 1841, and has been a writer since he was fourteen years old. He is the author of several popular songs, as "Silver Threads Among the Gold," "Only a Pansy Blossom" etc., and many essays and treatises on flowers, of which he is passionately fond.

"IT IS WELL WITH MY SOUL."

Horatio Gates Spafford, the writer of this hymn, was a lawyer, a native of New York state, born Oct. 30, 1828. While connected with an institution in Chicago, as professor of medical jurisprudence, he lost a great part of his fortune by the great fire in that city. This disaster was followed by the loss of his children on the steamer, Ville de Havre, Nov. 22, 1873. He seems to have been a devout Christian, for he wrote his hymn of submissive faith towards the end of the same year—

When peace like a river attendeth my way,
When sorrows like sea-billows roll—
Whatever my lot, Thou hast taught me to say,
"It is well, it is well with my soul."

A friend of Spafford who knew his history read this hymn while repining under an inferior affliction of his own. "If he can feel like that after suffering what he has suffered," he said, "I will cease my complaints."

It may not have been the weight of Mr. Spafford's sorrows wearing him down, but one would infer some mental disturbance in the man seven or eight years later. "In 1881" [writes Mr. Hubert P. Main] "he went to Jerusalem under the hallucination that he was a second Messiah—and died there on the seventh anniversary of his landing in Palestine, Sept. 5, 1888." The aberrations of an over-wrought mind are beckonings to God's compassion. When reason wanders He takes the soul of His helpless child into his own keeping—and "it is well."

The tune to Spafford's hymn is by P.P. Bliss; a gentle, gliding melody that suits the mood of the words.

"WAITING AND WATCHING FOR ME."

153

Written by Mrs. Marianne Farningham Hearn, born in Kent, Eng., Dec. 17, 1834. The hymn was first published in the fall of 1864 in the *London Church World*. Its unrhythmical first line—

When mysterious whispers are floating about,

—was replaced by the one now familiar—

When my final farewell to the world I have said,
And gladly lain down to my rest,
When softly the watchers shall say, "He is dead,"
And fold my pale hands on my breast,
And when with my glorified vision at last
The walls of that City I see,
Will any one there at the Beautiful Gate
Be waiting and watching for me?

Mrs. Hearn—a member of the Baptist denomination—has long been the editor of the (English) *Sunday School Times*, but her literary work has been more largely in connection with the *Christian World* newspaper of which she has been a staff-member since its foundation.

THE TUNE.

The long lines, not easily manageable for congregational singing, are wisely set by Mr. Bliss to duet music. There is a weighty thought in the hymn for every Christian, and experience has shown that a pair of good singers can make it very affecting, but the only use of the repeat, by way of a chorus, seems to be to give the miscellaneous voices a brief chance to sing.

"HE WILL HIDE ME."
(Isa. 49:2.)

Miss Mary Elizabeth Servoss, the author of this trustful hymn, was born in Schenectady, N.Y., Aug. 22, 1849. When a very young girl heradmiration of Fanny Crosby's writings, and the great and good service they were doing in the world, inspired her with a longing to resemble her. Though her burden was as real, it was not like the other's, and her opportunities for religious meditation and literary work were fewer than those of the elder lady, but the limited number of hymns she has written have much of the spirit and beauty of their model.

Providence decreed for her a life of domestic care and patient waiting. For eighteen years she was the constant attendant of a disabled grandmother, and long afterwards love and duty made her the home nurse during her mother's protracted illness and the last sickness of her father, until both parents passed away.

From her present home in Edeson, Ill., some utterances of her chastened spirit have found their way to the public, and been a gospel of blessing. Besides "He Will Hide Me" other hymns of Miss Servoss are "Portals of Light," "He Careth," "Patiently Enduring," and "Gates of Praise," the last being the best known.

When the storms of life are raging,
Tempests wild on sea and land,
I will seek a place of refuge
In the shadow of God's hand.
CHORUS.
He will hide me, He will hide me,
Where no harm can e'er betide me,
He will hide me, safely hide me
In the shadow of His hand.
*　　*　　*　　*　　*　　*

So while here the cross I'm bearing,
Meeting storms and billows wild,
Jesus for my soul is caring,
Naught can harm His Father's child.
He will hide me, etc.

THE TUNE.

An animating choral in nine-eight tempo, with a swinging movement and fugue chorus, is rather florid for the hymn, but undeniably musical. Mr. James McGranahan was the composer. He was born in Adamsville, Pa., July 4, 1840. His education was acquired mostly at the public schools, and both in general knowledge and in musical accomplishments it may be said of him that he is "self-made."

Music was born in him, and at the age of nineteen, with some valuable help from men like Bassini, Webb, Root and Zerrahn, he had studied to so good purpose that he taught music classes himself. This talent, joined to the gift of a very sweet tenor voice, made him the natural successor of the lamented Bliss, and, with Major D.W. Whittle, he entered on a career of gospel work, making between 1881 and 1885 two successful tours of England, Scotland and Ireland, and through the chief American cities.

Among his publications are the *Male Chorus Book, Songs of the Gospel* and the *Gospel Male Choir*.

Resides at Kinsman, O.

"REVIVE THY WORK, O LORD."
(Heb. 3:2.)

The supposed date of the hymn is 1860; the author, Albert Midlane. He was born at Newport on the Isle of Wight, Jan. 23, 1825 a business man, but, being a Sunday-school teacher, he was prompted to write verses for children. The habit grew upon him till he became a frequent and acceptable hymn-writer, both for juvenile and for general use. English collections have at least three hundred credited to him.

Revive Thy work, O Lord,
Thy mighty arm make bare,
Speak with the voice that wakes the dead,
And make Thy people hear.

THE TUNE.

Music and words together make a song-litany alive with all the old psalm-tune unction and the new vigor; and both were upon Mr. McGranahan when he wrote the choral. It is one of his successes.

Revive thy work, O Lord,
Exalt Thy precious name,
And by the Holy Ghost our love
For Thee and Thine inflame.
REFRAIN.
Revive Thy work, O Lord,
And give refreshing showers;
The glory shall be all Thine own,
The blessing shall be ours.

"WHERE IS MY WANDERING BOY TO-NIGHT?"

This remarkable composition—words and music by Rev. Robert Lowry—has a record among sacred songs like that of "The Prodigal Son" among parables.

A widowed lady of culture, about forty years of age, who was an accomplished vocalist, had ceased to sing, though her sweet voice was still in its prime. The cause was her sorrow for her runaway boy. She had not heard from him for five years. While spending a week with friends in a city distant from home, her hidden talent was betrayed by the friends to the pastor of their church, where a revival was in progress, and persuasion that seemed to put a duty upon her finally procured her consent to sing a solo.

The church was crowded. With a force and feeling that can easily be guessed she sang "Where Is My Boy Tonight?" and finished the first stanza. She began the second,—

Once he was pure as morning dew,
As he knelt at his mother's knee,
No face was so bright, no heart more true,
And none were so sweet as he;

—and as the congregation caught up the refrain,—

O where is my boy tonight?
O where is my boy tonight?
My heart overflows, for I love him he knows,
O where is my boy tonight?

—a young man who had been sitting in a back seat made his way up the aisle and sobbed, "Mother, I'm here!" The embrace of that mother and her long-lost boy turned the service into a general hallelujah. At the inquiry meeting that night there were many souls at the Mercy Seat who never knelt there before—and the young wanderer was one.

Mr. Sankey, when in California with Mr. Moody, sang this hymn in one of the meetings and told the story of a mother in the far east who had commissioned him to search for her missing son. By a happy providence the son was in the house—and the story and the song sent him home repentant.

At another time Mr. Sankey sang the same hymn from the steps of a snow-bound train, and a man between whose father and himself had been trouble and a separation, was touched, and returned to be reconciled after an absence of twenty years.

At one evening service in Stanberry, Mo., the singing of the hymn by the leader of the choir led to the conversion of one boy who was present, and whose parents were that night praying for him in an eastern state, and inspired such earnest prayer in the hearts of two other runaway boys' parents that the same answer followed.

There would not be room in a dozen pages to record all the similar saving incidents connected with the singing of "Where Is My Wandering Boy?" The rhetoric of love is strong in every note and syllable of the solo, and the tender chorus of voices swells the song to heaven like an antiphonal prayer.

Strange to say, Dr. Lowry set lightly by his hymns and tunes, and deprecated much mention of them though he could not deny their success. An active Christian since seventeen years of age, through his early pulpit service, his six years' professorship, and the long pastorate in Plainfield, N.J., closed by his death, he considered preaching to be his supreme function as it certainly was his first love. Music was to him "a side-issue," an "efflorescence," and writing a hymn ranked far below making and delivering a sermon. "I felt a sort of meanness when I began to be known as a composer," he said. And yet he was the author of a hymn and tune which "has done more to bring back wandering boys than any other" ever written.[*]

* "Where Is My Boy Tonight" was composed for a book of temperance hymns, *The Fountain of Song*, 1877.

"ETERNITY."

This is the title and refrain of both Mrs. Ellen M.H. Gates' impressive poem and its tune.

O the clanging bells of Time!
Night and day they never cease;
We are weaned with their chime,
For they do not bring us peace.
And we hush our hearts to hear,
And we strain our eyes to see
If thy shores are drawing near
Eternity! Eternity!

Skill was needed to vocalize this great word, but the ear of Mr. Bliss for musical prosody did not fail to make it effective. After the beautiful harmony through the seven lines, the choral reverently softens under the rallentando of the closing bars, and dwelling on the awe-inspiring syllables, solemnly dies away.

TRIUMPH BY AND BY.

This rally-song of the Christian arena is wonderfully stirring, especially in great meetings, for it sings best in full choral volume.

The prize is set before us,
To win His words implore us,
The eye of God is o'er us
From on high.
His loving tones are falling
While sin is dark, appalling,
'Tis Jesus gently calling;
He is nigh!
CHORUS.
By and by we shall meet Him,
By and by we shall greet Him,
And with Jesus reign in glory,
By and by!
We'll follow where He leadeth,
We'll pasture where He feedeth,
We'll yield to Him who pleadeth
From on high.
Then nought from Him shall sever,
Our hope shall brighten ever
And faith shall fail us never;
He is nigh.
CHORUS— By and by, etc.

Dr. Christopher Ruby Blackall, the author of the hymn, was born in Albany, N.Y., Sept. 18, 1830. He was a surgeon in the Civil War, and in medical practice fifteen years, but afterwards became connected with the American Baptist Publication Society as manager of one of its branches. He has written several Sunday-school songs set to music by W.H. Doane.

THE TUNE,

156

By Horatio R. Palmer is exactly what the hymn demands. The range scarcely exceeds an octave, but with the words "From on high," the stroke of the soprano on upper D carries the feeling to unseen summits, and verifies the title of the song. From that note, through melody and chorus the "Triumph by and by" rings clear.

"NOT HALF HAS EVER BEEN TOLD"

This is emotional, but every word and note is uplifting, and creates the mood for religious impressions. The writer, Rev. John Bush Atchison, was born at Wilson, N.Y., Feb. 18, 1840, and died July 15, 1882.

> I have read of a beautiful city
> Far away in the kingdom of God,
> I have read how its walls are of jasper,
> How its streets are all golden and broad;
> In the midst of the street is Life's River
> Clear as crystal and pure to behold,
> But not half of that city's bright glory
> To mortals has ever been told.

The chorus (twice sung)—

> Not half has been told,

—concludes with repeat of the two last lines of this first stanza.

Mr. Atchison was a Methodist clergyman who composed several good hymns. "Behold the Stone is Rolled Away," "O Crown of Rejoicing," and "Fully Persuaded," indicate samples of his work more or less well-known. "Not Half Has Ever Been Told" was written in 1875.

THE TUNE.

Dr. Otis F. Presbry, the composer, was a young farmer of York, Livingston Co., N.Y., born there the 20th of December, 1820. Choice of a professional life led him to Berkshire Medical College, where he graduated in 1847. In after years his natural love of musical studies induced him to give his time to compiling and publishing religious tunes, with hymns more especially for Sunday-schools.

He became a composer and wrote the melody to Atchison's words in 1877, which was arranged by a blind musician of Washington, D.C., J.W. Bischoff by name, with whom he had formed a partnership. The solo is long—would better, perhaps, have been four-line instead of eight—but well sung, it is a flight of melody that holds an assembly, and touches hearts.

Dr. Presbry's best known book was *Gospel Bells* (1883), the joint production of himself, Bischoff, and Rev. J.E. Rankin. He died Aug. 20, 1901.

"COME."

One of the most characteristic (both words and music) of the *Gospel Hymns*—"Mrs. James Gibson Johnson" is the name attached to it as its author, though we have been unable to trace and verify her claim.

> O, word of words the sweetest,
> O, words in which there lie
> All promise, all fulfillment,
> And end of mystery;
> Lamenting or rejoicing,
> With doubt or terror nigh,
> I hear the "Come" of Jesus,
> And to His cross I fly.

CHORUS.

> Come, come—
> Weary, heavy-laden, come, O come to me.

THE TUNE,

Composed by James McGranahan, delivers the whole stanza in soprano or tenor solo, when the alto, joining the treble, leads off the refrain in duet, the male voices striking alternate notes until the full harmony in the last three bars. The style and movement of the chorus are somewhat suggestive of a popular glee, but the music of the duet is flexible and sweet, and the bass and tenor progress with it not in the ride-and-tie-fashion but marking time with the title-syllable.

The contrast between the spiritual and the intellectual effect of the hymn and its wakeful tune is illustrated by a case in Baltimore. While Moody and Sankey were doing their gospel work in that city, a man, who, it seems, had brought a copy of the *Gospel Hymns*, walked out of one of the meetings after hearing this hymn-tune, and on reaching home, tore out the leaves that contained the song and threw them into the fire, saying he had "never heard such twaddle" in all his life.

157

The sequel showed that he had been too hasty. The hymn would not leave him. After hearing it night and day in his mind till he began to realize what it meant, he went to Mr. Moody and told him he was "a vile sinner" and wanted to know how he could "come" to Christ. The divine invitation was explained, and the convicted man underwent a vital change. His converted opinion of the hymn was quite as remarkably different. He declared it was "the sweetest one in the book." (*Story of the Gospel Hymns*.)

"ALMOST PERSUADED."

The Rev. Mr. Brundage tells the origin of this hymn. In a sermon preached by him many years ago, the closing words were:

"He who is almost persuaded is almost saved, but to be almost saved is to be entirely lost." Mr. Bliss, being in the audience, was impressed with the thought, and immediately set about the composition of what proved one of his most popular songs, deriving his inspiration from the sermon of his friend, Mr. Brundage. *Memoir of Bliss.*

Almost persuaded now to believe,
Almost persuaded Christ to receive;
Seems now some soul to say
"Go Spirit, go thy way,
Some more convenient day
On Thee I'll call."

* * * * * *

Almost persuaded—the harvest is past!

Both hymn and tune are by Mr. Bliss—and the omission of a chorus is in proper taste. This revival piece brings the eloquence of sense and sound to bear upon the conscience in one monitory pleading. Incidents in this country and in England related in Mr. Sankey's book, illustrate its power. It has a convicting and converting history.

"MY AIN COUNTREE."

This hymn was written by Miss Mary Augusta Lee one Sabbath day in 1860 at Bowmount, Croton Falls, N.Y., and first published in the *New York Observer*, Dec, 1861. The authoress had been reading the story of John Macduff who, with his wife, left Scotland for the United States, and accumulated property by toil and thrift in the great West. In her leisure after the necessity for hard work was past, the Scotch woman grew homesick and pined for her "ain countree." Her husband, at her request, came east and settled with her in sight of the Atlantic where she could see the waters that washed the Scotland shore. But she still pined, and finally to save her life, John Macduff took her back to the heather hills of the mother-land, where she soon recovered her health and spirits.

I am far from my hame an' I'm weary aften whiles
For the langed-for hame-bringing an' my Father's welcome smiles.
I'll ne'er be fu' content until mine eyes do see
The shinin' gates o' heaven an' mine ain countree.
The airt' is flecked wi' flowers mony-tinted, frish an' gay,
The birdies warble blithely, for my Father made them sae,
But these sights an' these soun's will naething be to me
When I hear the angels singin' in my ain countree.

Miss Lee was born in Croton Falls in 1838, and was of Scotch descent, and cared for by her grandfather and a Scotch nurse, her mother dying in her infancy. In 1870 she became the wife of a Mr. Demarest, and her married life was spent in Passaic, N.J., until their removal to Pasadena, Cal., in hope of restoring her failing health. She died at Los Angeles, Jan. 8, 1888.

THE TUNE

Is an air written in 1864 in the Scottish style by Mrs. Ione T. Hanna, wife of a banker in Denver, Colo., and harmonized for choral use by Hubert P. Main in 1873. Its plaintive sweetness suits the words which probably inspired it. The tone and metre of the hymn were natural to the young author's inheritance; a memory of her grandfather's home-land melodies, with which he once crooned "little Mary" to sleep.

Sung as a closing hymn, "My ain countree" sends the worshipper away with a tender, unworldly thought that lingers.

Mrs. Demarest wrote an additional stanza in 1881 at the request of Mr. Main.

Some really good gospel hymns and tunes among those omitted in this chapter will cry out against the choice that passed them by. Others are of the more ephemeral sort, the phenomena (and the demand) of a generation. Carols of pious joy with inordinate repetition, choruses that surprise old lyrics with modern thrills, ballads of ringing sound and slender verse, are the spray of tuneful emotion that sparkles on every revival high-tide, but rarely leaves floodmarks that time will not erase. Religious songs of the demonstrative, not to say sensational, kind spring impromptu from the conditions of their time—and give place to others equally spontaneous when the next spiritual wave sweeps by. Their value lingers in the impulse their novelty gave to the life of sanctuary worship, and in the Christian characters their emotional power helped into being.

CHAPTER XIII.

HYMNS, FESTIVAL AND OCCASIONAL.

CHRISTMAS.

"ADESTE FIDELES."

This hymn is of doubtful authorship, by some assigned to as late a date as 1680, and by others to the 13th century as one of the Latin poems of St. Bonaventura, Bishop of Albano, who was born at Bagnarea in Tuscany, A.D. 1221. He was a learned man, a Franciscan friar, one of the greatest teachers and writers of his church, and finally a cardinal. Certainly Roman Catholic in its origin, whoever was its author, it is a Christian hymn qualified in every way to be sung by the universal church.

Adeste, fideles
Laeti triumphantes,
Venite, venite in Bethlehem;
Natum videte Regem angelorum.
CHORUS.
Venite, adoremus,
Venite, adoremus!
Venite, adoremus Dominum.

This has been translated by Rev. Frederick Oakeley (1808–1880) and by Rev. Edward Caswall (1814–1878) the version of the former being the one in more general use. The ancient hymn is much abridged in the hymnals, and even the translations have been altered and modernized in the three or four stanzas commonly sung. Caswall's version renders the first line "Come hither, ye faithful," literally construing the Latin words.

The following is substantially Oakeley's English of the "Adeste, fideles."

O come all ye faithful
Joyful and triumphant,
To Bethlehem hasten now with glad accord;
Come and behold Him,
Born the King of Angels.
CHORUS.
O come, let us adore Him,
O come, let us adore Him,
O come, let us adore Him,
Christ, the Lord.
Sing choirs of angels,
Sing in exultation
Through Heaven's high arches be your praises poured;
Now to our God be
Glory in the highest!
O come, let us adore Him!
Yea, Lord, we bless Thee,
Born for our salvation
Jesus, forever be Thy name adored!
Word of the Father
Now in flesh appearing;
O come, let us adore Him!

The hymn with its primitive music as chanted in the ancient churches, was known as "The Midnight Mass," and was the processional song of the religious orders on their way to the sanctuaries where they gathered in preparation for the Christmas morning service. The modern tune—or rather the tune in modern use—is the one everywhere familiar as the "Portuguese Hymn." (See page 205.)

MILTON'S HYMN TO THE NATIVITY.

It was the winter wild
While the Heavenly Child
All meanly wrapped in the rude manger lies.

159

Nature in awe of Him
Had doffed her gaudy trim
With her great Master so to sympathize.
* * * * * *
No war nor battle sound
Was heard the world around.
The idle spear and shield were high uphung.
The hooked chariot stood
Unstained with hostile blood,
The trumpets spake not to the armed throng,
And Kings sat still with awful eye
As if they knew their Sovereign Lord was by.

This exalted song—the work of a boy of scarcely twenty-one—is a Greek ode in form, of two hundred and sixteen lines in twenty-seven strophes. Some of its figures and fancies are more to the taste of the seventeenth century than to ours, but it is full of poetic and Christian sublimities, and its high periods will be heard in the Christmas hymnody of coming centuries, though it is not the fashion to sing it now.

John Milton, son and grandson of John Miltons, was born in Breadstreet, London, Dec. 9, 1608, fitted for the University in St. Paul's school, and studied seven years at Cambridge. His parents intended him for the church, but he chose literature as a profession, travelled and made distinguished friendships in Italy, Switzerland and France, and when little past his majority was before the public as a poet, author of the Ode to the Nativity, of a Masque, and of many songs and elegies. In later years he entered political life under the stress of his Puritan sympathies, and served under Cromwell and his successor as Latin Secretary of State through the time of the Commonwealth. While in public duty he became blind, but in his retirement composed "Paradise Lost and Paradise Regained." Died in 1676.

THE TUNE.

In the old "Carmina Sacra" a noble choral (without name except "No war nor battle sound") well interprets portions of the 4th and 5th stanzas of the great hymn, but replaces the line—

"The idle spear and shield were high uphung."

—with the more modern and less figurative—

"No hostile chiefs to furious combat ran."

Three stanzas are also added, by the Rev. H.O. Dwight, missionary to Constantinople. The substituted line, which is also, perhaps, the composition of Mr. Dwight, rhymes with—

"His reign of peace upon the earth began,"

—and as it is not un-Miltonic, few singers have ever known that it was not Milton's own.

Dr. John Knowles Paine, Professor of Music at Harvard University, and author of the Oratorio of "St. Peter," composed a cantata to the great Christmas Ode of Milton, probably about 1868.

Professor Paine died Apr. 25, 1906.

It is worth noting that John Milton senior, the great poet's father, was a skilled musician and a composer of psalmody. The old tunes "York" and "Norwich," in Ravenscroft's collection and copied from it in many early New England singing-books, are supposed to be his.

The Miltons were an old Oxfordshire Catholic family, and John, the poet's father, was disinherited for turning Protestant, but he prospered in business, and earned the comfort of a country gentleman. He died, very aged, in May, 1646, and his son addressed a Latin poem ("Ad Patrem") to his memory.

"HARK! THE HERALD ANGELS SING."

This hymn of Charles Wesley, dating about 1730, was evidently written with the "Adeste Fideles" in mind, some of the stanzas, in fact, being almost like translations of it. The form of the two first lines was originally—

Hark! how all the welkin rings,
"Glory to the King of Kings!"

—but was altered thirty years later by Rev. Martin Madan (1726–1790) to—

Hark! the herald angels sing
Glory to the new-born King!

Other changes by the same hand modified the three following stanzas, and a fifth stanza was added by John Wesley—

Hail the heavenly Prince of Peace!
Hail the Sun of Righteousness!
Light and life to all He brings,

Ris'n with healing in His wings.

THE TUNE.

"Mendelssohn" is the favorite musical interpreter of the hymn. It is a noble and spirited choral from Felix Mendelssohn Bartholdy's cantata, "Gott ist Licht."

"JOY TO THE WORLD, THE LORD IS COME!"

This inspirational lyric of Dr. Watts never grows old. It was written in 1719.

Joy to the world! the Saviour reigns!
Let men their songs employ
While fields and floods, rocks, hills and plains
Repeat the sounding joy.

Dr. Edward Hodges (1796–1867) wrote an excellent psalm-tune to it which is still in occasional use, but the music united to the hymn in the popular heart is "Antioch," an adaptation from Handel's Messiah. This companionship holds unbroken from hymnal to hymnal and has done so for sixty or seventy years; and, in spite of its fugue, the tune—apparently by some magic of its own—contrives to enlist the entire voice of a congregation, the bass falling in on the third beat as if by intuition. The truth is, the tune has become the habit of the hymn, and to the thousands who have it by heart, as they do in every village where there is a singing school, "Antioch" is "Joy to the World," and "Joy to the World" is "Antioch."

"HARK! WHAT MEAN THOSE HOLY VOICES?"

This fine hymn, so many years appearing with the simple sign "Cawood" or "J. Cawood" printed under it, still holds its place by universal welcome.

Hark! what mean those holy voices
Sweetly sounding through the skies?
Lo th' angelic host rejoices;
Heavenly hallelujahs rise.
Hear them tell the wondrous story,
Hear them chant in hymns of joy,
Glory in the highest, glory,
Glory be to God on high!

The Rev. John Cawood, a farmer's son, was born at Matlock, Derbyshire, Eng., March 18, 1775, graduated at Oxford, 1801, and was appointed perpetual curate of St. Anne's in Bendly, Worcestershire. Died Nov. 7, 1852. He is said to have written seventeen hymns, but was too modest to publish any.

THE TUNE.

Dr. Dykes' "Oswald," and Henry Smart's "Bethany" are worthy expressions of the feeling in Cawood's hymn. In America, Mason's "Amaland," with fugue in the second and third lines, has long been a favorite.

"WHILE SHEPHERDS WATCHED THEIR FLOCKS."

This was written by Nahum Tate (1652–1715), and after two hundred years the church remembers and sings the song. Six generations have grown up with their childhood memory of its pictorial verses illustrating St. Luke's Christmas story.

While shepherds watched their flocks by night,
All seated on the ground,
The angel of the Lord came down
And glory shone around.
"Fear not" said he, for mighty dread
Had seized their troubled mind,
"Glad tidings of great joy I bring
To you and all mankind."

THE TUNE.

Modern hymnals have substituted "Christmas" and other more or less spirited tunes for Read's "Sherburne," which was the first musical translation of the hymn to American ears. But, to show the traditional hold that the New England fugue melody maintains on the people, many collections print it as alternate tune. Some modifications have been made in it, but its survival is a tribute to its real merit.

Daniel Read, the creator of "Sherburne," "Windham," "Russia," "Stafford," "Lisbon," and many other tunes characteristic of a bygone school of psalmody, was born in Rehoboth, Mass., Nov. 2, 1757. He published *The American Singing Book*, 1785, *Columbian Harmony*, 1793, and several other collections. Died in New Haven, Ct., 1836.

"IT CAME UPON THE MIDNIGHT CLEAR."

161

Rev. Edmund Hamilton Sears, author of this beautiful hymn-poem, was born at Sandisfield, Berkshire Co., Mass., April 6, 1810, and educated at Union College and Harvard University. He became pastor of the Unitarian Church in Wayland, Mass., 1838. Died in the adjoining town of Weston, Jan. 14, 1876. The hymn first appeared in the *Christian Register* in 1857.

It came upon the midnight clear,
That glorious song of old,
From angels bending near the earth
To touch their harps of gold.
"Peace to the earth, good will to men
From Heaven's all-gracious King."
The world in solemn stillness lay,
To hear the angels sing.
Still through the cloven skies they come
With peaceful wings unfurled
And still their heavenly music floats
O'er all the weary world.
Above its sad and lonely plains
They bend on hovering wing,
And ever o'er its Babel sounds
The blessed angels sing.

THE TUNE.

No more sympathetic music has been written to these lines than "Carol," the tune composed by Richard Storrs Willis, a brother of Nathaniel Parker Willis the poet, and son of Deacon Nathaniel Willis, the founder of the *Youth's Companion.* He was born Feb, 10, 1819, graduated at Yale in 1841, and followed literature as a profession. He was also a musician and composer. For many years he edited the *N.Y. Musical World,* and, besides contributing frequently to current literature, published *Church Chorals and Choir Studies, Our Church Music* and several other volumes on musical subjects. Died in Detroit, May 7, 1900.

The much-loved and constantly used advent psalm of Mr. Sears,—

Calm on the listening ear of night
Come heaven's melodious strains
Where wild Judea stretches far
Her silver-mantled plains,

—was set to music by John Edgar Gould, and the smooth choral with its sweet chords is a remarkable example of blended voice and verse.

"O LITTLE TOWN OF BETHLEHEM!"

Phillips Brooks, the eloquent bishop of Massachusetts, loved to write simple and tender poems for the children of his church and diocese. They all reveal his loving heart and the beauty of his consecrated imagination. This one, the best of his *Christmas Songs,* was slow in coming to public notice, but finally found its place in hymn-tune collections.

O little town of Bethlehem,
How still we see thee lie!
Above thy deep and dreamless sleep
The silent stars go by;
Yet in thy dark streets shineth
The everlasting light;
The hopes and fears of all the years
Are met in thee tonight.
For Christ is born of Mary,
And gathered all above,
While mortals sleep, the angels keep
Their watch of wondering love.
O morning stars, together
Proclaim the holy birth!
And praises sing to God the King
And peace to men on earth.
How silently, how silently,
The wondrous gift is given!
So God imparts to human hearts
The blessings of His heaven.
No ear may hear His coming,
But in this world of sin,

162

Where meek souls will receive Him still
The dear Christ enters in.

Phillips Brooks, late bishop of the diocese of Massachusetts, was born in Boston, Dec. 13, 1835; died Jan. 23, 1893. He was graduated at Harvard in 1855, and at the Episcopal Divinity School of Alexandria, Va., 1859. The first ten years of his ministry were spent in Pennsylvania, after which he became rector of Trinity Church, Boston, and was elected bishop in 1891. He was an inspiring teacher and preacher, an eloquent pulpit orator, and a man of deep and rich religious life.

The hymn was written in 1868, and it was, no doubt, the ripened thought of his never-forgotten visit to the "little town of Bethlehem" two years before.

THE TUNE.

"Bethlehem" is the appropriate name of a tune written by J. Barnby, and adapted to the words, but it is the hymn's first melody (named "St. Louis" by the compiler who first printed it in the *Church Porch* from original leaflets) that has the credit of carrying it to popularity.

The composer was Mr. Redner, organist of the Church of the Holy Trinity, Philadelphia, of which Rector Brooks was then in charge. Lewis Henry Redner, born 1831, was not only near the age of his friend and pastor but as much devoted to the interests of the Sunday-school, for whose use the hymn was written, and he had promised to write a score to which it could be sung on the coming Sabbath. Waking in the middle of the night, after a busy Saturday that sent him to bed with his brain "in a whirl," he heard "an angel strain," and immediately rose and pricked the notes of the melody. The tune had come to him just in time to be sung. A much admired tune has also been written to this hymn by Hubert P. Main.

PALM SUNDAY.

FAURE'S "PALM BRANCHES."

Sur nos chemins les rameaux et les fleurs
Sont repandos—

O'er all the way green palms and blossoms gay
Are strewn to-day in festive preparation,
Where Jesus comes to wipe our tears away.
E'en now the throng to welcome Him prepare;
Join all and sing.—

Jean Baptiste Faure, author of the words and music, was born at Moulins, France, Jan. 15, 1830. As a boy he was gifted with a beautiful voice, and crowds used to gather wherever he sang in the streets of Paris. Little is known of his parentage, and apparently the sweet voice of the wandering lad was his only fortune. He found wealthy friends who sent him to the *Conservatoire*, but when his voice matured it ceased to serve him as a singer. He went on with his study of instrumental music, but mourned for his lost vocal triumphs, and his longing became a subject of prayer. He promised God that if his power to sing were given back to him he would use it for charity and the good of mankind. By degrees he recovered his voice, and became known as a great baritone. As professional singer and composer at the Paris*Grand Opera*, he had been employed largely in dramatic work, but his "Ode to Charity" is one of his enduring and celebrated pieces, and his songs written for benevolent and religious services have found their way into all Christian lands.

His "Palm-Branches" has come to be a *sine qua non* on its calendar Sunday wherever church worship is planned with any regard to the Feasts of the Christian year.

EASTER.

Perhaps the most notable feature in the early hymnology of the Oriental Church was its Resurrection songs. Being hymns of joy, they called forth all the ceremony and spectacle of ecclesiastical pomp. Among them—and the most ancient one of those preserved—is the hymn of John of Damascus, quoted in the second chapter (p. 54). This was the proclamation-song in the watch-assemblies, when exactly on the midnight moment at the shout of "Christos egerthe!" (Χριστὸς ἠγέρθη.) "Christ is risen!" thousands of torches were lit, bells and trumpets pealed, and (in the later centuries) salvos of cannon shook the air.

Another favorite hymn of the Eastern Church was the "*Salve, Beate Mane,*" "Welcome, Happy Morning," of Fortunatus. (Chap. 10,p. 357.) This poem furnished cantos for Easter hymns of the Middle Ages. Jerome of Prague sang stanzas of it on his way to the stake.

163

An anonymous hymn, *"Poneluctum, Magdelena,"* in medieval Latin rhyme, is addressed to Mary Magdelene weeping at the empty sepulchre. The following are the 3d and 4th stanzas, with a translation by Prof. C.S. Harrington of Wesleyan University:

Gaude, plaude, Magdalena!
Tumba Christus exiit!
Tristis est peracta scena,
Victor mortis rediit;
Quem deflebas morientem,
Nunc arride resurgentem!
Alleluia!
Tolle vultum, Magdalena!
Redivivum aspice;
Vide frons quam sit amœna,
Quinque plagas inspice;
Fulgent, sic ut margaritæ,
Ornamenta novæ vitæ.
Alleluia!
*   *   *   *   *   *

Magdalena, shout for gladness!
Christ has left the gloomy grave;
Finished is the scene of sadness;
Death destroyed, He comes to save;
Whom with grief thou sawest dying,
Greet with smiles, the tomb defying.
Hallelujah!
Lift thine eyes, O Magdalena!
Lo! thy Lord before thee stands;
See! how fair the thorn-crowned forehead;
Mark His feet, His side, His hands;
Glow His wounds with pearly whiteness!
Hallowing life with heavenly brightness!
Hallelujah!

The hymnaries of the Christian Church for seventeen hundred years are so rich in Easter hallelujahs and hosannas that to introduce them all would swell a chapter to the size of an encyclopedia—and even to make a selection is a responsible task.

Simple mention must suffice of Luther's—
In the bonds of death He lay;
—of Watts'—
He dies, the Friend of sinners dies;
—of John Wesley's—
Our Lord has gone up on high;
—of C.F. Gellert's—
Christ is risen! Christ is risen!
He hath burst His bonds in twain;
—omitting hundreds which have been helpful in psalmody, and are, perhaps, still in choir or congregational use.

"CHRIST THE LORD IS RISEN TODAY"

Begins a hymn of Charles Wesley's and is also the first line of a hymn prepared for Sunday-school use by Mrs. Storrs, wife of the late Dr. Richard Salter Storrs of Brooklyn, N.Y.

Wesley's hymn is sung—with or without the hallelujah interludes—to "Telemann's Chant," (Zeuner), to an air of Mendelssohn, and to JohnStainer's "Paschale Gaudium." Like the old New England "Easter Anthem" it appears to have been suggested by an anonymous translation of some more ancient (Latin) antiphony.

Jesus Christ is risen to day,
Hallelujah!
Our triumphant holy day,
Hallelujah!
*   *   *   *   *   *

Who endured the cross and grave.
Hallelujah!
Sinners to redeem and save,
Hallelujah!

AN ANTHEM FOR EASTER.

This work of an amateur genius, with its rustic harmonies, suited the taste of colonial times, and no doubt the devout church-goers of that day found sincere worship and thanksgiving in its flamboyant music. "An Anthem for Easter," in A major by William Billings (1785) occupied several pages in the early collections of psalmody and "the sounding joy" was in it. Organs were scarce, but beyond the viols of the village choirs it needed no instrumental accessories. The language is borrowed from the New Testament and *Young's Night Thoughts*.

The Lord is risen indeed!
Hallelujah!
The Lord is risen indeed!
Hallelujah!

Following this triumphant overture, a recitative bass solo repeats I Cor. 15:20, and the chorus takes it up with crowning hallelujahs. Different parts, *per fugam*, inquire from clef to clef—

And did He rise?
And did He rise?—
Hear [the answer], O ye nations!
Hear it, O ye dead!

Then duet, trio and chorus sing it, successively—

He rose! He rose! He rose!
He burst the bars of death,
And triumphed o'er the grave!

The succeeding thirty-four bars—duet and chorus—take home the sacred gladness to the heart of humanity—

Then, then *I* rose,
*   *   *   *   *   *
And seized eternal youth,
Man all immortal, hail!
Heaven's all the glory, man's the boundless bliss.

Philip
Doddridge, D.D.

"YES, THE REDEEMER ROSE."

In the six-eight syllable verse once known as "hallelujah metre"—written by Dr. Doddridge to be sung after a sermon on the text in 1st Corinthians noted in the above anthem—

Yes, the Redeemer rose,
The Saviour left the dead,
And o'er our hellish foes
High raised His conquering head.
In wild dismay the guards around
Fall to the ground and sink away.

Lewis Edson's "Lenox" (1782) is an old favorite among its musical interpreters.

"O SHORT WAS HIS SLUMBER."

This hymn for the song-service of the Ruggles St. Church, Boston, was written by Rev. Theron Brown.

O short was His slumber; He woke from the dust;
The Saviour death's chain could not hold;
And short, since He rose, is the sleep of the just;
They shall wake, and His glory behold.
*   *   *   *   *   *
Dear grave in the garden; hope smiled at its door
Where love's brightest triumph was told;
Christ lives! and His life will His people restore!

They shall wake, and His glory behold.
The music is Bliss' tune to Spafford's "When Peace Like a River."
Another by the same writer, sung by the same church chorus, is—

He rose! O morn of wonder!
They saw His light go down
Whose hate had crushed Him under,
A King without a crown.
No plume, no garland wore He,
Despised death's Victor lay,
And wrapped in night His glory,
That claimed a grander day.

*   *   *   *   *   *

He rose! He burst immortal
From death's dark realm alone,
And left its heavenward portal
Swung wide for all his own.
Nor need one terror seize us
To face earth's final pain,
For they who follow Jesus,
But die to live again.

The composer's name is lost, the tune being left nameless when printed. The impression is that it was a secular melody. A very suitable tune for the hymn is Geo. J. Webb's "Millennial Dawn" ("the Morning Light is breaking.")

THANKSGIVING.

"DIE FELDER WIR PFLÜGEN UND STREUEN."

We plow the fields and scatter
The good seed on the land,
But it is fed and watered
By God's Almighty hand,
He sends the snow in winter,
The warmth to swell the grain,
The breezes, and the sunshine
And soft, refreshing rain,
All, all good gifts around us
Are sent from heaven above
Then thank the Lord, O thank the Lord
For all His love!

Matthias Claudius, who wrote the German original of this little poem, was a native of Reinfeld, Holstein, born 1770 and died 1815. He wrote lyrics, humorous, pathetic and religious, some of which are still current in Germany.

The translator of the verses is Miss Jane Montgomery Campbell, whose identity has not been traced. Hers is evidently one of the retiring names brought to light by one unpretending achievement. English readers owe to her the above modest and devout hymn, which was first published here in Rev. C.S. Bere's *Garland of Songs with Tunes*, 1861.

Little is known of Arthur Cottman, composer to Miss Campbell's words. He was born in 1842, and died in 1879.

"WITH SONGS AND HONORS SOUNDING LOUD."

Stanzas of this enduring hymn of Watts' have been as often recited as sung.

He sends His showers of blessing down
To cheer the plains below;
He makes the grass the mountains crown,
And corn in valleys grow.

THE TUNE,

One of the chorals—if not the best—to claim partnership with this sacred classic, is John Cole's "Geneva," distinguished among the few fugue tunes which the singing world refuses to dismiss. There is a growing grandeur in the opening solo and its following duet as they climb the first tetra-chord, when the full harmony suddenly reveals the majesty of the music. The little parenthetic duo at the eighth bar breaks the roll of the song for one breath, and the concord of voices closes in again like a diapason. One thinks of a bird-note making a waterfall listen.

"HARVEST HOME."

Let us sing of the sheaves, when the summer is done,
And the garners are stored with the gifts of the sun.
Shouting home from the fields like the voice of the sea,
Let us join with the reapers in glad jubilee,—
REFRAIN.
Harvest home! (*double rep.*)
Let us chant His praise who has crowned our days
With bounty of the harvest home.
Who hath ripened the fruits into golden and red?
Who hath grown in the valleys our treasures of bread,
That the owner might heap, and the stranger might glean
For the days when the cold of the winter is keen?
Harvest home!
Let us chant, etc.
For the smile of the sunshine, again and again,
For the dew on the garden, the showers on the plain,
For the year, with its hope and its promise that end,
Crowned with plenty and peace, let thanksgiving ascend,
Harvest home!
Let us chant, etc.
We shall gather a harvest of glory, we know,
From the furrows of life where in patience we sow.
Buried love in the field of the heart never dies,
And its seed scattered here will be sheaves in the skies,
Harvest home!
Let us chant, etc.
Thanksgiving Hymn. Boston, 1890. Theron Brown.
Tune "To the Work, To the Work." W.H. Doane.

"THE GOD OF HARVEST PRAISE."

Written by James Montgomery in 1840, and published in the *Evangelical Magazine* as the Harvest Hymn for that year.

The God of harvest praise;
In loud thanksgiving raise
Heart, hand and voice.
The valleys smile and sing,
Forests and mountains sing,
The plains their tribute bring,
The streams rejoice.
 *   *   *   *   *   *

The God of harvest praise;
Hearts, hands and voices raise
With sweet accord;
From field to garner throng,
Bearing your sheaves along,
And in your harvest song
Bless ye the Lord.
Tune, "Dort"—Lowell Mason.

Lowell
Mason

167

"STILL, STILL WITH THEE."

These stanzas of Mrs. Harriet Beecher Stowe, with their poetic beauty and grateful religious spirit, have furnished an orison worthy of a place in all the hymn books. In feeling and in faith the hymn is a matin song for the world, supplying words and thoughts to any and every heart that worships.

Still, still with Thee, when purple morning breaketh,
When the bird waketh and the shadows flee;
Fairer than morning, lovelier than daylight,
Dawns the sweet consciousness, I am with Thee.
Alone with Thee, amid the mystic shadows
The solemn hush of nature newly born;
Alone with Thee, in breathless adoration,
In the calm dew and freshness of the morn.

*   *   *   *   *   *

When sinks the soul, subdued by toil, to slumber,
Its closing eyes look up to Thee in prayer,
Sweet the repose beneath Thy wings o'ershadowing,
But sweeter still to wake and find Thee there.

THE TUNES.

Barnby's "Windsor," and "Stowe" by Charles H. Morse (1893)—both written to the words.

Mendelssohn's "Consolation" is a classic interpretation of the hymn, and finely impressive when skillfully sung, but simpler—and sweeter to the popular ear—is Mason's "Henley," written to Mrs. Eslings'—

"Come unto me when shadows darkly gather."

EVENING HYMNS.

John Keble's beautiful meditation—
Sun of my soul, Thou Saviour dear;
John Leland's—
The day is past and gone;
and Phebe Brown's—
I love to steal awhile away;
—have already been noticed. Bishop Doane's gentle and spiritual lines express nearly everything that a worshipping soul would include in a moment of evening thought. The first and last stanzas are the ones most commonly sung.

Softly now the light of day
Fades upon my sight away:
Free from care, from labor free,
Lord I would commune with Thee.

*   *   *   *   *   *

Soon for me the light of day
Shall forever pass away;
Then, from sin and sorrow free,
Take me, Lord, to dwell with Thee.

THE TUNE.

Both Kozeluck and J.E. Gould, besides Louis M. Gottschalk and Dr. Henry John Gauntlett, have tried their skill in fitting music to this hymn, but only Gottschalk and Kozeluck approach the mood into which its quiet words charm a pious and reflective mind. Possibly its frequent association with "Holley," composed by George Hews, may influence a hearer's judgement of other melodies but there is something in that tune that makes it cling to the hymn as if by instinctive kinship.

Others may have as much or more artistic music but "Holley" in its soft modulations seems to breathe the spirit of every word.

It was this tune to which a stranger recently heard a group of mill-girls singing Bishop Doane's verses. The lady, a well-known Christian worker, visited a certain factory, and the superintendent, after showing her through the building, opened a door into a long work-room, where the singing of the girls delighted and surprised her. It was sunset, and their hymn was—

Softly now the light of day.

Several of the girls were Sunday-school teachers, who had encouraged others to sing at that hour, and it had become a habit.

"Has it made a difference?" the lady inquired.

"There is seldom any quarrelling or coarse joking among them now," said the superintendent with a smile.

Dr. S.F. Smith's hymn of much the same tone and tenor—

Softly fades the twilight ray
Of the holy Sabbath day,

—is commonly sung to the tune of "Holley."

George Hews, an American composer and piano-maker, was born in Massachusetts 1800, and died July 6, 1873. No intelligence of him or his work or former locality is at hand, beyond this brief note in Baptie, "He is believed to have followed his trade in Boston, and written music for some of Mason's earlier books."

DEDICATION.

"CHRIST IS OUR CORNER-STONE."

This reproduces in Chandler's translation a song-service in an ancient Latin liturgy (*angulare fundamentum*).

Christ is our Corner-Stone;
On Him alone we build,
With His true saints alone
The courts of heaven are filled,
On His great love
Our hopes we place
Of present grace
And joys above.
O then with hymns of praise
These hallowed courts shall ring;
Our voices we will raise
The Three-in-One to sing.
And thus proclaim
In joyful song
But loud and long
That glorious Name.

The Rev. John Chandler was born at Witley, Surrey, Eng. June 16, 1806. He took his A.M. degree at Oxford, and entered the ministry of the Church of England, was Vicar of Witley many years, and became well-known for his translations of hymns of the primitive church. Died at Putney, July 1, 1876.

THE TUNE.

Sebastian Wesley's "Harewood" is plainer and of less compass, but Zundel's "Brooklyn" is more than its rival, both in melody and vivacity.

"OH LORD OF HOSTS WHOSE GLORY FILLS THE BOUNDS OF THE ETERNAL HILLS."

A hymn of Dr. John Mason Neale—

Endue the creatures with Thy grace
That shall adorn Thy dwelling-place
The beauty of the oak and pine,
The gold and silver, make them Thine.
The heads that guide endue with skill,
The hands that work preserve from ill,
That we who these foundations lay
May raise the top-stone in its day.

THE TUNE.

"Welton," by Rev. Caesar Malan—author of "Hendon," once familiar to American singers.

Henri Abraham Cæsar Malan was born at Geneva, Switzerland, 1787, and educated at Geneva College. Ordained to the ministry of the State church, (Reformed,) he was dismissed for preaching against its formalism and spiritual apathy; but he built a chapel of his own, and became a leader with D'Aubigne, Monod, and others in reviving the purity of the Evangelical faith and laboring for the conversion of souls.

169

Malan wrote many hymns, and published a large collection, the "*Chants de Sion*," for the Evangelical Society and the French Reformed Church. He composed the music of his own hymns. Died at Vandosurre, 1864.

"DAUGHTER OF ZION, FROM THE DUST."

Cases may occur where an *exhortation* hymn earns a place with dedication hymns.

The charred fragment of a hymn-book leaf hangs in a frame on the auditorium wall of the "New England Church," Chicago. The former edifice of that church, all the homes of its resident members, and all their business offices except one, were destroyed in the great fire. In the ruins of their sanctuary the only scrap of paper found on which there was a legible word was this bit of a hymn-book leaf with the two first stanzas of Montgomery's hymn,

Daughter of Zion, from the dust,
Exalt thy fallen head;
Again in thy Redeemer trust,
He calls thee from the dead.
Awake, awake! put on thy strength,
Thy beautiful array;
The day of freedom dawns at length,
The Lord's appointed day.

The third verse was not long in coming to every mind—

Rebuild thy walls! thy bounds enlarge!

—and even without that added word the impoverished congregation evidently enough had received a message from heaven. They took heart of grace, overcame all difficulties, and in good time replaced their ruined Sabbath-home with the noble house in which they worship today.*

* The story is told by Rev. William E. Barton D.D. of Oak Park, Ill.

If the "New England Church" of Chicago did not sing this hymn at the dedication of their new temple it was for some other reason than lack of gratitude—not to say reverence.

THE SABBATH.

The very essence of all song-worship pitched on this key-note is the ringing hymn of Watts—

Sweet is the day of sacred rest,
No mortal cares disturb my breast, etc.

—but it has vanished from the hymnals with its tune. Is it because profane people or thoughtless youth made a travesty of the two next lines—

O may my heart in tune be found
Like David's harp of solemn sound?

THE TUNE.

Old "Portland" by Abraham Maxim, a fugue tune in F major of the canon style, expressed all the joy that a choir could put into music, though with more sound than skill. The choral is a relic among relics now, but it is a favorite one.

"Sweet is the Light of Sabbath Eve" by Edmeston; Stennett's "Another Six Days' Work is Done," sung to "Spohr," the joint tune of Louis Spohr and J.E. Gould; and Doddridge's "Thine Earthly Sabbath, Lord, We Love" retain a feeble hold among some congregations. And Hayward's "Welcome Delightful Morn," to the impossible tune of "Lischer," survived unaccountably long in spite of its handicap. But special Sabbath hymns are out of fashion, those classed under that title taking an incidental place under the general head of "Worship."

COMMUNION.

"BREAD OF HEAVEN, ON THEE WE FEED."

This hymn of Josiah Conder, copying the physical metaphors of the 6th of John, is still occasionally used at the Lord's Supper.

Vine of Heaven, Thy blood supplies
This blest cup of sacrifice,
Lord, Thy wounds our healing give,
To Thy Cross we look and live.

The hymn is notable for the felicity with which it combines imagery and reality. Figure and fact are always in sight of each other.

Josiah Conder was born in London, September 17, 1789. He edited the *Eclectic Review*, and was the author of numerous prose works on historic and religious subjects. Rev. Garrett Horder says that more of his hymns are in common use now than those of any other except Watts and Doddridge. More *in proportion to the relative number* may be nearer the truth. In his lifetime Conder wrote about sixty hymns. He died Dec. 27, 1855.

THE TUNE.

The tune "Corsica" sometimes sung to the words, though written by the famous Von Gluck, shows no sign of the genius of its author. Born at Weissenwang, near New Markt, Prussia, July 2, 1714, he spent his life in the service of operatic art, and is called "the father of the lyric drama," but he paid little attention to sacred music. Queen Marie Antoinette was for a while his pupil. Died Nov. 25, 1787.

"Wilmot," (from Von Weber) one of Mason's popular hymn-tune arrangements, is a melody with which the hymn is well acquainted. It has a fireside rhythm which old and young of the same circles take up naturally in song.

Carl von
Weber

"HERE, O MY LORD, I SEE THEE FACE TO FACE."

Written in October, 1855, by Dr. Horatius Bonar. James Bonar, brother of the poet-preacher, just after the communion for that month, asked him to furnish a hymn for the communion record. It was the church custom to print a memorandum of each service at the Lord's table, with an appropriate hymn attached, and an original one would be thrice welcome. Horatius in a day or two sent this hymn:

Here, O my Lord, I see Thee face to face,
Here would I touch and handle things unseen
Here grasp with firmer hand th' eternal grace
And all my weariness upon Thee lean.
*   *   *   *   *   *
Too soon we rise; the symbols disappear;
The feast, though not the love, is past and gone;
The bread and wine remove, but Thou art here
Nearer than ever—still my Shield and Sun.

THE TUNE.

"Morecambe" is an anonymous composition printed with the words by the *Plymouth Hymnal* editors. "Berlin" by Mendelssohn is better. The metre of Bonar's hymn is unusual, and melodies to fit it are not numerous, but for a meditative service it is worth a tune of its own.

"O THOU MY SOUL, FORGET NO MORE."

The author of this hymn found in the Baptist hymnals, and often sung at the sacramental seasons of that denomination, was the first Hindoo convert to Christianity.

Krishna Pal, a native carpenter, in consequence of an accident, came under the care of Mr. Thomas, a missionary who had been a surgeon in the East Indies and was now an associate worker with William Carey. Mr. Thomas set the man's broken arm, and talked of Jesus to him and the surrounding crowd with so much tact and loving kindness that Krishna Pal was touched. He became a pupil of the missionaries; embraced Christ, and influenced his wife and daughter and his brother to accept his new faith.

He alone, however, dared the bitter persecution of his caste, and presented himself for church-membership. He and Carey's son were baptized in the Ganges by Dr. Carey, Dec. 28, 1800, in the presence of the English Governor and an immense concourse of people representing four or five different religions.

Krishna Pal wrote several hymns. The one here noted was translated from the Bengalee by Dr. Marshman.

O thou, my soul, forget no more
The Friend who all thy sorrows bore;
Let every idol be forgot;

But, O my soul, forget him not.
Renounce thy works and ways, with grief,
And fly to this divine relief;
Nor Him forget, who left His throne,
And for thy life gave up His own.
Eternal truth and mercy shine
In Him, and He Himself is thine:
And canst thou then, with sin beset,
Such charms, such matchless charms forget?
Oh, no; till life itself depart,
His name shall cheer and warm my heart;
And lisping this, from earth I'll rise,
And join the chorus of the skies.

THE TUNE.

There is no scarcity of good long-metre tunes to suit the sentiment of this hymn. More commonly in the Baptist manuals its vocal mate is Bradbury's "Rolland" or the sweet and serious Scotch melody of "Ward," arranged by Mason. Best of all is "Hursley," the beautiful Ritter-Monk choral set to "Sun of My Soul."

NEW YEAR.

Two representative hymns of this class are John Newton's—
While with ceaseless course the sun,
—and Charles Wesley's—
Come let us anew our journey pursue;
the one a voice at the next year's threshold, the other a song at the open door.
While with ceaseless course the sun
Hasted thro' the former year
Many souls their race have run
Nevermore to meet us here.
*   *   *   *   *   *

As the winged arrow flies
Speedily the mark to find,
As the lightening from the skies
Darts and leaves no trace behind,
Swiftly thus our fleeting days
Bear we down life's rapid stream,
Upward, Lord, our spirits raise;
All below is but a dream.

A grave occasion, whether unexpected or periodical, will force reflection, and so will a grave truth; and when both present themselves at once, the truth needs only commonplace statement. If the statement is in rhyme and measure more attention is secured. Add a *tune* to it, and the most frivolous will take notice. Newton's hymn sung on the last evening of the year has its opportunity—and never fails to produce a solemn effect; but it is to the immortal music given to it in Samuel Webbe's "Benevento" that it owes its unique and permanent place. Dykes' "St. Edmund" may be sung in England, but in America it will never replace Webbe's simple and wonderfully impressive choral.

Charles Wesley's hymn is the antipode of Newton's in metre and movement.
Come, let us anew our journey pursue,
Roll round with the year
And never stand still till the Master appear.
His adorable will let us gladly fulfil
And our talents improve
By the patience of hope and the labor of love.
Our life is a dream, our time as a stream
Glides swiftly away,
And the fugitive moment refuses to stay.
The arrow is flown, the moment is gone,
The millennial year,
Rushes on to our view, and eternity's near.

One could scarcely imagine a greater contrast than between this hymn and Newton's. In spite of its eccentric metre one cannot dismiss it as rhythmical jingle, for it is really a sermon shaped into a popular canticle, and the surmise is not a difficult one that he had in mind a secular air that was familiar to the crowd. But the hymn is not one of Wesley's *poems*. Compilers who object to its lilting measure omit it from their books, but it holds its place in public use, for it carries weighty thoughts in swift sentences.

O that each in the Day of His coming may say,
"I have fought my way through,
I have finished the work Thou didst give me to do."
O that each from the Lord may receive the glad word,
"Well and faithfully done,
Enter into my joy, and sit down on my throne."

For a hundred and fifty years this has been sung in the Methodist watch-meetings, and it will be long before it ceases to be sung—and reprinted in Methodist, and some Baptist hymnals.

The tune of "Lucas," named after James Lucas, its composer, is the favorite vehicle of song for the "Watch-hymn." Like the tune to "O How Happy Are They," it has the movement of the words and the emphasis of their meaning.

No knowledge of James Lucas is at hand except that he lived in England, where one brief reference gives his birth-date as 1762 and "about 1805" as the birth-date of the tune.

"GREAT GOD, WE SING THAT MIGHTY HAND."

The admirable hymn of Dr. Doddridge may be noted in this division with its equally admirable tune of "Melancthon," one of the old Lutheran chorals of Germany.

Great God, we sing that mighty hand
By which supported still we stand.
The opening year Thy mercy shows;
Thy mercy crown it till its close!
By day, by night, at home, abroad,
Still we are guarded by our God.

As this last couplet stood—and ought now to stand—pious parents teaching the hymn to their children heard them repeat—

By day, by night, at home, abroad,
We are surrounded still with God.

Many are now living whose first impressive sense of the Divine Omnipresence came with that line.

PARTING.

"GOD BE WITH YOU TILL WE MEET AGAIN."

A lyric of benediction, born, apparently, at the divine moment for the need of the great "Society of Christian Endeavor," and now adopted into the Christian song-service of all lands. The author, Rev. Jeremiah Eames Rankin, D.D., LL.D., was born in Thornton, N.H., Jan. 2, 1828. He was graduated at Middlebury College, Vt., in 1848, and labored as a Congregational pastor more than thirty years. For thirteen years he was President of Howard University, Washington, D.C. Besides the "Parting Hymn" he wrote *The Auld Scotch Mither,Ingleside Rhymes, Hymns pro Patria*, and various practical works and religious essays. Died 1904.

THE TUNE.

As in a thousand other partnerships of hymnist and musician, Dr. Rankin was fortunate in his composer. The tune is a symphony of hearts—subdued at first, but breaking into a chorus strong with the uplift of hope. It is a farewell with a spiritual thrill in it.

Its author, William Gould Tomer, was born in Finesville, Warren Co., N.J., October 5, 1832; died in Phillipsburg, N.J., Sept. 26, 1896. He was a soldier in the Civil War and a writer of good ability as well as a composer. For some time he was editor of the *High Bridge Gazette*, and music with him was an avocation rather than a profession. He wrote the melody to Dr. Rankin's hymn in 1880, Prof. J.W. Bischoff supplying the harmony, and the tune was first published in *Gospel Bells*the same year.

FUNERALS.

The style of singing at funerals, as well as the character of the hymns, has greatly changed—if, indeed, music continues to be a part of the service, as frequently, in ordinary cases, it is not. "China" with its comforting words—and terrifying chords—is forever obsolete, and not only that, but Dr. Muhlenberg's, "I Would Not Live Alway," with its sadly sentimental tune of "Frederick," has passed out of common use. Anna Steele's "So Fades the Lovely, Blooming Flower," on the death of a child, is occasionally heard, and now and then Dr. S.F. Smith's,

"Sister, Thou Wast Mild and Lovely," (with its gentle air of "Mt. Vernon,") on the death of a young lady. Standard hymns like Watts', "Unveil Thy Bosom, Faithful Tomb," to the slow, tender melody of the "Dead March," (from Handel's oratorio of "Saul") and Montgomery's "Servant of God, Well Done," to "Olmutz," or Woodbury's "Forever with the Lord," still retain their prestige, the music of the former being played on steeple-chimes on some burial occasions in cities, during the procession—

Nor pain nor grief nor anxious fear
Invade thy bounds; no mortal woes
Can reach the peaceful sleeper here
While angels watch the soft repose.

The latter hymn (Montgomery's) is biographical—as described onpage 301—

Servant of God, well done;
Rest from thy loved employ;
The battle fought, the victory won,
Enter thy Master's joy.

Only five stanzas of this long poem are now in use.

The exquisite elegy of Montgomery, entitled "The Grave,"—

There is a calm for those who weep,
A rest for weary mortals found
They softly lie and sweetly sleep
Low in the ground.

—is by no means discontinued on funeral occasions, nor Margaret Mackay's beloved hymn,—

Asleep in Jesus, blessed sleep,

—melodized in Bradbury's "Rest."

Mrs. Margaret Mackay was born in 1801, the daughter of Capt. Robert Mackay of Hedgefield, Inverness, and wife of a major of the same name. She was the author of several prose works and *Lays of Leisure Hours*, containing seventy-two original hymns and poems, of which "Asleep in Jesus" is one. She died in 1887.

"MY JESUS, AS THOU WILT."
(Mein Jesu, wie du willst.)

This sweet hymn for mourners, known to us here in Jane Borthwick's translation, was written by Benjamin Schmolke (or Schmolk) late in the 17th century. He was born at Brauchitzchdorf, in Silesia, Dec. 21, 1672, and received his education at the Labau Gymnasium and Leipsic University. A sermon preached while a youth, for his father, a Lutheran pastor, showed such remarkable promise that a wealthy man paid the expenses of his education for the ministry. He was ordained and settled as pastor of the Free Church at Schweidnitz, Silesia, in which charge he continued from 1701 till his death.

Schmolke was the most popular hymn-writer of his time, author of some nine hundred church pieces, besides many for special occasions. Withal he was a man of exalted piety and a pastor of rare wisdom and influence.

His death, of paralysis, occurred on the anniversary of his wedding, Feb. 12, 1737.

My Jesus, as Thou wilt,
Oh may Thy will be mine!
Into Thy hand of love
I would my all resign.
Thro' sorrow or thro' joy
Conduct me as Thine own,
And help me still to say,
My Lord, Thy will be done.

The last line is the refrain of the hymn of four eight-line stanzas.

THE TUNE.

"Sussex," by Joseph Barnby, a plain-song with a fine harmony, is good congregational music for the hymn.

But "Jewett," one of Carl Maria Von Weber's exquisite flights of song, is like no other in its intimate interpretation of the prayerful words. We hear Luther's "bird in the heart" singing softly in every inflection of the tender melody as it glides on. The tune, arranged by Joseph Holbrook, is from an opera—the overture to Weber's DerFreischutz—but one feels that the gentle musician when he wrote it must have caught an inspiration of divine trust and peace. The wish among the last words he uttered when dying in London of slow disease was, "Let me go back to my own (home), and then God's will be done." That wish and the sentiment of Schmolke's hymn belong to each other, for they end in the same way.

My Jesus, as Thou wilt:
All shall be well for me;
Each changing future scene
I gladly trust with Thee.
Straight to my home above
I travel calmly on,
And sing in life or death
My Lord, Thy will be done.

"I CANNOT ALWAYS TRACE THE WAY."

In later years, when funeral music is desired, the employment of a male quartette has become a favorite custom. Of the selections sung in this manner few are more suitable or more generally welcomed than the tender and trustful hymn of Sir John Bowring, rendered sometimes in Dr. Dykes' "Almsgiving," but better in the less-known but more flexible tune composed by Howard M. Dow—

I cannot always trace the way
Where Thou, Almighty One, dost move,
But I can always, always say
That God is love.
When fear her chilling mantle flings
O'er earth, my soul to heaven above
As to her native home upsprings,
For God is love.
When mystery clouds my darkened path,
I'll check my dread, my doubts reprove;
In this my soul sweet comfort hath
That God is love.
Yes, God is love. A thought like this
Can every gloomy thought remove,
And turn all tears, all woes to bliss
For God is love.

The first line of the hymn was originally, "'Tis seldom I can trace the way."

Howard M. Dow has been many years a resident of Boston, and organist of the Grand Lodge of Freemasons at the Tremont St. (Masonic) Temple.

WEDDING.

Time was when hymns were sung at weddings, though in America the practice was never universal. Marriage, among Protestants, is not one of the sacraments, and no masses are chanted for it by ecclesiastical ordinance. The question of music at private marriages depends on convenience, vocal or instrumental equipment, and the general drift of the occasion. At public weddings the organ's duty is the "Wedding March."

To revive a fashion of singing at home marriages would be considered an oddity—and, where civil marriages are legal, a superfluity—but in the religious ceremony, just after the prayer that follows the completion of the nuptial formula, it will occur to some that a hymn would "tide over" a proverbially awkward moment. Even good, quaint old John Berridge's lines would happily relieve the embarrassment—besides reminding the more thoughtless that a wedding is not a mere piece of social fun—

Since Jesus truly did appear
To grace a marriage feast
O Lord, we ask Thy presence here
To make a wedding guest.
Upon the bridal pair look down
Who now have plighted hands;
Their union with Thy favor crown
And bless the nuptial bands
*   *   *   *   *   *
In purest love these souls unite
That they with Christian care
May make domestic burdens light
By taking each a share.
Tune, "Lanesboro," Mason.

175

A wedding hymn of more poetic beauty is the one written by Miss Dorothy Bloomfield (now Mrs. Gurney), born 1858, for her sister's marriage in 1883.

O perfect Love, all human thought transcending,
Lowly we kneel in prayer before Thy throne
That their's may be a love which knows no ending
Whom Thou forevermore dost join in one.
O perfect Life, be Thou their first assurance
Of tender charity and steadfast faith,
Of patient hope and quiet, brave endurance,
With childlike trust that fears nor pain nor death.
Grant them the joy which brightens earthly sorrow,
Grant them the peace which calms all earthly strife,
And to their day the glorious unknown morrow
That dawns upon eternal love and life.
Tune by Joseph Barnby, "O Perfect Love."

FRUITION DAY.

"LO! HE COMES WITH CLOUDS DESCENDING."

Thomas Olivers begins one of his hymns with this line. The hymn is a Judgment-day lyric of rude strength and once in current use, but now rarely printed. The "Lo He Comes," here specially noted, is the production of John Cennick, the Moravian.

Lo! He comes with clouds descending
Once for favored sinners slain,
Thousand thousand saints attending
Swell the triumph of His train.
Hallelujah!
God appears on earth to reign.
*   *   *   *   *   *
Yea, amen; let all adore Thee
High on Thy eternal throne.
Saviour, take the power and glory,
Claim the kingdom for thine own;
O come quickly;
Hallelujah! Come, Lord, come.

THE TUNES.

Various composers have written music to this universal hymn, but none has given it a choral that it can claim as peculiarly its own. "Brest," Lowell Mason's plain-song, has a limited range, and runs low on the staff, but its solemn chords are musical and commanding. As much can be said of the tunes of Dr. Dykes and Samuel Webbe, which have more variety. Those who feel that the hymn calls for a more ornate melody will prefer Madan's "Helmsley."

"LO! WHAT A GLORIOUS SIGHT APPEARS."

The great Southampton bard who wrote "Sweet fields beyond the swelling flood" was quick to kindle at every reminder of Fruition Day.

Lo! what a glorious sight appears
To our believing eyes!
The earth and seas are passed away,
And the old rolling skies.
From the third heaven, where God resides,
That holy, happy place,
The New Jerusalem comes down,
Adorned with shining grace.

This hymn of Watts' sings one of his most exalted visions. It has been dear for two hundred years to every Christian soul throbbing with millennial thoughts and wishful of the day when—

The God of glory down to men
Removes His best abode,
—and when—
His own kind hand shall wipe the tears
From every weeping eye,
And pains and groans, and griefs and fears,
And death itself shall die,

176

—and the yearning cry of the last stanza, when the vision fades, has been the household ?† of myriads of burdened and sorrowing saints—

How long, dear Saviour, O how long
Shall this bright hour delay?
Fly swifter round ye wheels of Time,
And bring the welcome day!

† Transcriber's note: This question mark is in the original. It is possibly a compositor's query which the author missed when correcting the proofs. The missing text could be 'word'.

THE TUNES.

By right of long appropriation both "Northfield" and "New Jerusalem" own a near relationship to these glorious verses. Ingalls, one of the constellation of early Puritan psalmodists, to which Billings and Swan belonged, evidently loved the hymn, and composed his "New Jerusalem" to the verse, "From the third heaven," and his "Northfield" to "How long, dear Saviour." The former is now sung only as a reminiscence of the music of the past, at church festivals, charity fairs and entertainments of similar design, but the action and hearty joy in it always evoke sympathetic applause. "Northfield" is still in occasional use, and it is a jewel of melody, however irretrievably out of fashion. Its union to that immortal stanza, if no other reason, seems likely to insure its permanent place in the lists of sacred song.

John Cole's "Annapolis," still found in a few hymnals with these words, is a little too late to be called a contemporary piece, but there are some reminders of Ingalls' "New Jerusalem" in its style and vigor, and it really partakes the flavor of the old New England church music.

Jeremiah Ingalls was born in Andover, Mass., March 1, 1764. A natural fondness for music increased with his years, but opportunities to educate it were few and far between, and he seemed like to become no more than a fairly good bass-viol player in the village choir. But his determination carried him higher, and in time his self-taught talent qualified him for a singing-school master, and for many years he travelled through Massachusetts, New Hampshire and Vermont, training the raw vocal material in the country towns, and organizing choirs.

Between his thirtieth and fortieth years, he composed a number of tunes, and, in 1804 published a two hundred page collection of his own and others' music, which he called the *Christian Harmony*.

His home was for some time in Newberry, Vt., but he subsequently lived at Rochester and at Hancock in the same state.

Among the traditions of him is this anecdote of the origin of his famous tune "Northfield," which may indicate something of his temper and religious habit. During his travels as a singing-school teacher he stopped at a tavern in the town of Northfield and ordered his dinner. It was very slow in coming, but the inevitable "how long?" that formulated itself in his hungry thoughts, instead of sharpening into profane complaint, fell into the rhythm of Watts' sacred line—and the tune came with it. To call it "Northfield" was natural enough; the place where its melody first beguiled him from his bodily wants to a dream of the final Fruition Day.

Ingalls died in Hancock, Vt., April 6, 1828.

CHAPTER XIV.

HYMNS OF HOPE AND CONSOLATION.

"JERUSALEM THE GOLDEN."
Urbs Sion Aurea.

"The Seven Great Hymns" of the Latin Church are:

* Laus Patriae Coelestis,—(Praise of the Heavenly Country).

* Veni, Sancte Spiritus,—(Come, Holy Spirit)

* Veni, Creator Spiritus,—(Come, Creator Spirit)

* Dies Irae,—(The Day of Wrath)

* Stabat Mater,—(The Mother Stood By)

* Mater Speciosa,—(The Fair Mother.)

* Vexilla Regis.—(The Banner of the King.)

Chief of these is the first named, though that is but part of a religious poem of three thousand lines, which the author, Bernard of Cluny, named "De Contemptu Mundi" (Concerning Disdain of the World.)

Bernard was of English parentage, though born at Morlaix, a seaport town in the north of France. The exact date of his birth is unknown, though it was probably about A.D. 1100. He is called Bernard of Cluny because he lived and wrote at that place, a French town on the Grone where he was abbot of a famous monastery, and also to distinguish him from Bernard of Clairvaux.

His great poem is rarely spoken of as a whole, but in three portions, as if each were a complete work. The first is the long exordium, exhausting the pessimistic title (contempt of the world), and passing on to the second, where begins the real "Laus Patriae Coelestis." This being cut in two, making a third portion, has enriched the Christian world with two of its best hymns, "For Thee, O Dear, Dear Country," and "Jerusalem the Golden."

Bernard wrote the medieval or church Latin in its prime of literary refinement, and its accent is so obvious and its rhythm so musical that even one ignorant of the language could pronounce it, and catch its rhymes. The "Contemptu Mundi" begins with these two lines, in a hexameter impossible to copy in translation:

Hora novissima; tempora pessima sunt; Vigilemus!
Ecce minaciter imminet Arbiter, Ille Supremus!
'Tis the last hour; the times are at their worst;
Watch; lo the Judge Supreme stands threat'ning nigh!

Or, as Dr. Neale paraphrases and softens it,—

The World is very evil,
The times are waxing late,
Be sober and keep vigil,
The Judge is at the gate,

—and, after the poet's long, dark diorama of the world's wicked condition, follows the "Praise of the Heavenly Fatherland," when a tender glory dawns upon the scene till it breaks into sunrise with the vision of the Golden City. All that an opulent and devout imagination can picture of the beauty and bounty of heaven, and all that faith can construct from the glimpses in the Revelation of its glory and happiness is poured forth in the lavish poetry of the inspired monk of Cluny—

Urbs Sion aurea, patria lactea, cive decora,
Omne cor obruis, omnibus obstruis, et cor et ora.
Nescio, nescio quae jubilatio lux tibi qualis,
Quam socialia gaudia, gloria quam specialis.
Jerusalem, the golden;
With milk and honey blest;
Beneath thy contemplation
Sink heart and voice opprest.
I know not, O I know not
What joys await us there,
With radiancy of glory,
With bliss beyond compare.
They stand, those halls of Zion,
All jubilant with song,*
And bright with many an angel;
And all the martyr throng.
The Prince is ever in them,
The daylight is serene;
The pastures of the blessed
Are decked in glorious sheen.
*   *   *   *   *
O sweet and blessed country,
The home of God's elect!
O sweet and blessed country,
That eager hearts expect!
Jesu, in mercy bring us
To that dear land of rest,
Who art, with God the Father,
And Spirit, ever blest.

* In first editions, "*conjubilant* with song."

Dr. John Mason Neale, the translator, was obliged to condense Bernard's exuberant verse, and he has done so with unsurpassable grace and melody. He made his translation while "inhibited" from his priestly functions in the Church of England for his high ritualistic views and practice, and so poor that he wrote stories for children to earn his living. His poverty added to the wealth of Christendom.

THE TUNE.

The music of "Jerusalem the Golden" used in most churches is the composition of Alexander Ewing, a paymaster in the English army. He was born in Aberdeen, Scotland, Jan. 3d, 1830, and educated there at Marischal College. The tune bears his name, and this honor, and its general favor with the public, are so much testimony to its merit. It is a stately harmony in D major with sonorous and impressive chords. Ewing died in 1895.

"WHY SHOULD WE START AND FEAR TO DIE?"

Probably it is an embarrassment of riches and despair of space that have crowded this hymn— perhaps the sweetest that Watts ever wrote—out of some of our church singing-books. It is pleasant to find it in the new *Methodist Hymnal,* though with an indifferent tune.

Christians of today should surely sing the last two stanzas with the same exalted joy and hope that made them sacred to pious generations past and gone—

O if my Lord would come and meet,
My soul would stretch her wings in haste.
Fly fearless through death's iron gate,
Nor feel the terrors as she passed.
Jesus can make a dying bed
Feel soft as downy pillows are,
While on His breast I lean my head
And breathe my life out sweetly there.

THE TUNE.

The plain-music of William Boyd's "Pentecost," (with modulations in the tenor), creates a new accent for the familiar lines. Preferable in every sense are Bradbury's tender "Zephyr" or "Rest."

No coming generation will ever feel the pious gladness of Amariah Hall's "All Saints New" in E flat major as it stirred the Christian choirs of seventy five years ago. Fitted to this heart-felt lyric of Watts, it opened with the words—

O if my Lord would come and meet,

in full harmony and four-four time, continuing to the end of the stanza. The melody, with its slurred syllables and beautiful modulations was almost blithe in its brightness, while the strong musical bass and the striking chords of the "counter," chastened it and held the anthem to its due solemnity of tone and expression. Then the fugue took up—

Jesus can make a dying bed,

—bass, treble and tenor adding voice after voice in the manner of the old "canon" song, and the full harmony again carried the words, with loving repetitions, to the final bar. The music closed with a minor concord that was strangely effective and sweet.

Amariah Hall was born in Raynham, Mass., April 28, 1785, and died there Feb. 8, 1827. He "farmed it," manufactured straw-bonnets, kept tavern and taught singing-school. Music was only an avocation with him, but he was an artist in his way, and among his compositions are found in some ancient Tune books his "Morning Glory," "Canaan," "Falmouth," "Restoration," "Massachusetts," "Raynham," "Crucifixion," "Harmony," "Devotion," "Zion," and "Hosanna." "All Saints New" was his masterpiece.

"WHEN I CAN READ MY TITLE CLEAR."

No sacred song has been more profanely parodied by the thoughtless, or more travestied, (if we may use so strong a word), in popular religious airs, than this golden hymn which has made Isaac Watts a benefactor to every prisoner of hope. Not to mention the fancy figures and refrains of camp-meeting music, which have cheapened it, neither John Cole's "Annapolis" nor Arne's "Arlington" nor a dozen others that have borrowed these speaking lines, can wear out their association with "Auld lang syne." The hymn has permeated the tune, and, without forgetting its own words, the Scotch melody preforms both a social and religious mission. Some arrangements of it make it needlessly repetitious, but its pathos will always best vocalize the hymn, especially the first and last stanzas—

When I can read my title clear
To mansions in the skies
I'll bid farewell to every fear
And wipe my weeping eyes.
* * * * *
There shall I bathe my weary soul
In seas of heavenly rest,

And not a wave of trouble roll
Across my peaceful breast.

"VITAL SPARK OF HEAVENLY FLAME."

This paraphrase, by Alexander Pope, of the Emperor Adrian's death-bed address to his soul—

Animula, vagula, blandula,
Hospes, comesque corporis,
—transfers the poetry and constructs a hymnic theme.

An old hymn writer by the name of Flatman wrote a Pindaric, somewhat similar to "Adrian's Address," as follows:

When on my sick-bed I languish,
Full of sorrow, full of anguish,
Fainting, gasping, trembling, crying,
Panting, groaning, speechless, dying;
Methinks I hear some gentle spirit say,
"Be not fearful, come away."

Pope combined these two poems with the words of Divine inspiration, "O death, where is thy sting? O grave, where is thy victory?" and made a pagan philosopher's question the text for a triumphant Christian anthem of hope.

Vital spark of heavenly flame,
Quit, oh quit this mortal frame.
Trembling, hoping, ling'ring, flying,
Oh the pain, the bliss of dying!
Cease, fond nature, cease thy strife,
And let me languish into life.
Hark! they whisper: angels say,
"Sister spirit, come away!"
What is this absorbs me quite,
Steals my senses, shuts my sight,
Drowns my spirit, draws my breath,
Tell me, my soul, can this be death?
The world recedes: it disappears;
Heaven opens on my eyes; my ears
With sounds seraphic ring.
Lend, lend your wings! I mount! I fly!
O grave where is thy victory?
O death, where is thy sting?

THE TUNE.

The old anthem, "The Dying Christian," or "The Dying Christian to his Soul," which first made this lyric familiar in America as a musical piece, will never be sung again except at antique entertainments, but it had an importance in its day.

Beginning in quadruple time on four flats minor, it renders the first stanza in flowing concords largo affettuoso, and a single bass fugue, Then suddenly shifting to one flat, major, duple time, it executes the second stanza, "Hark! they whisper" ... "What is this, etc.," in alternate pianissimo and forte phrases; and finally, changing to triple time, sings the third triumphant stanza, andante, through staccato and fortissimo. The shout in the last adagio, on the four final bars, "O Death! O Death!" softening with "where is thy sting?" is quite in the style of old orchestral magnificence.

Since "The Dying Christian" ceased to appear in church music, the poem, for some reason, seems not to have been recognized as a hymn. It is, however, a Christian poem, and a true lyric of hope and consolation, whatever the character of the author or however pagan the original that suggested it.

The most that is now known of Edward Harwood, the composer of the anthem, is that he was an English musician and psalmodist, born near Blackburn, Lancaster Co., 1707, and died about 1787.

"YOUR HARPS, YE TREMBLING SAINTS."

This hymn of Toplady,—unlike "A Debtor to Mercy Alone," and "Inspirer and Hearer of Prayer," both now little used,—stirs no controversial feeling by a single line of his aggressive Calvinism. It is simply a song of Christian gratitude and joy.

Your harps, ye trembling saints
Down from the willows take;
Loud to the praise of Love Divine

Bid every string awake.
Though in a foreign land,
We are not far from home,
And nearer to our house above
We every moment come.

*　　*　　*　　*　　*　　*

Blest is the man, O God,
That stays himself on Thee,
Who waits for Thy salvation, Lord,
Shall Thy salvation see.

THE TUNE.

"Olmutz" was arranged by Lowell Mason from a Gregorian chant. He set it himself to Toplady's hymn, and it seems the natural music for it. The words are also sometimes written and sung to Jonathan Woodman's "State St."

Jonathan Call Woodman was born in Newburyport, Mass., July 12, 1813. He was the organist of St. George's Chapel, Flushing L.I. and a teacher, composer and compiler. His *Musical Casket* was not issued until Dec. 1858, but he wrote the tune of "State St." in August, 1844. It was a contribution to Bradbury's *Psalmodist*, which was published the same year.

"YE GOLDEN LAMPS OF HEAVEN, FAREWELL."

Dr. Doddridge's "farewell" is not a note of regret. Unlike Bernard, he appreciates this world while he anticipates the better one, but his contemplation climbs from God's footstool to His throne. His thought is in the last two lines of the second stanza, where he takes leave of the sun—

My soul that springs beyond thy sphere
No more demands thine aid.

But his fancy will find a function for the "golden lamps" even in the glory that swallows up their light—

Ye stars are but the shining dust
Of my divine abode,
The pavement of those heavenly courts
Where I shall dwell with God.
The Father of eternal light
Shall there His beams display,
Nor shall one moment's darkness mix
With that unvaried day.

THE TUNE.

The hymn has been assigned to "Mt. Auburn," a composition of George Kingsley, but a far better interpretation—if not best of all—is H.K. Oliver's tune of "Merton," (1847,) older, but written purposely for the words.

"TRIUMPHANT ZION, LIFT THY HEAD."

This fine and stimulating lyric is Doddridge in another tone. Instead of singing hope to the individual, he sounds a note of encouragement to the church.

Put all thy beauteous garments on,
And let thy excellence be known;
Decked in the robes of righteousness,
The world thy glories shall confess.

*　　*　　*　　*　　*

God from on high has heard thy prayer;
His hand thy ruins shall repair,
Nor will thy watchful Monarch cease
To guard thee in eternal peace.

The tune, "Anvern," is one of Mason's charming melodies, full of vigor and cheerful life, and everything can be said of it that is said of the hymn. Duffield compares the hymn and tune to a ring and its jewel.

It is one of the inevitable freaks of taste that puts so choice a strain of psalmody out of fashion. Many younger pieces in the church manuals could be better spared.

"SHRINKING FROM THE COLD HAND OF DEATH."

This is a hymn of contrast, the dark of recoiling nature making the background of the rainbow. Written by Charles Wesley, it has passed among his forgotten or mostly forgotten productions but is notable for the frequent use of its 3rd stanza by his brother John. John Wesley, in his old age, did not so much shrink from death as from the thought of its too slow approach. His almost constant prayer was, "Lord, let me not live to be useless." "At every place," says Belcher, "after giving to his societies what he desired them to consider his last advice, he invariably concluded with the stanza beginning—

"'Oh that, without a lingering groan,
I may the welcome word receive.
My body with my charge lay down,
And cease at once to work and live.'"

The anticipation of death itself by both the great evangelists ended like the ending of the hymn—

No anxious doubt, no guilty gloom
Shall daunt whom Jesus' presence cheers;
My Light, my Life, my God is come,
And glory in His face appears.

"FOREVER WITH THE LORD."

Montgomery had the Ambrosian gift of spiritual song-writing. Whatever may be thought of his more ambitious descriptive or heroic pages of verse, and his long narrative poems, his lyrics and cabinet pieces are gems. The poetry in some exquisite stanzas of his "Grave" is a dream of peace:

There is a calm for those who weep,
A rest for weary mortals found;
They softly lie and sweetly sleep
Low in the ground.
The storms that wreck the winter's sky
No more disturb their deep repose
Than summer evening's latest sigh
That shuts the rose.

But in the poem, "At Home in Heaven," which we are considering—with its divine text in I Thess. 4:17—the Sheffield bard rises to the heights of vision. He wrote it when he was an old man. The contemplation so absorbed him that he could not quit his theme till he had composed twenty-two quatrains. Only four or five—or at most only seven of them—are now in general use. Like his "Prayer is the Soul's Sincere Desire," they have the pith of devotional thought in them, but are less subjective and analytical.

Forever with the Lord!
Amen, so let it be,
Life from the dead is in that word;
'Tis immortality.
Here in the body pent,
Absent from Him I roam,
Yet nightly pitch my moving tent
A day's march nearer home.
My Father's house on high!
Home of my soul, how near
At times to faith's foreseeing eye
Thy golden gates appear.
I hear at morn and even,
At noon and midnight hour,
The choral harmonies of heaven
Earth's Babel tongues o'erpower.

The last line has been changed to read—

Seraphic music pour,

—and finally the hymnals have dropped the verse and substituted others. The new line is an improvement in melody but not in rhyme, and, besides, it robs the stanza of its leading thought—heaven and earth offsetting each other, and heavenly music drowning earthly noise—a thought that is missed even in the rich cantos of "Jerusalem the Golden."

THE TUNES.

Nearly the whole school of good short metre tunes, from "St. Thomas" to "Boylston" have offered their notes to Montgomery's "At Home in Heaven," but the two most commonly recognized as its property are "Mornington," named from Lord Mornington, its author, and I.B. Woodbury's familiar harmony, "Forever with the Lord."

Garret Colley Wellesley, Earl of Mornington, and ancestor of the Duke of Wellington, was born in Dagan, Ireland, July 19, 1735. Remarkable for musical talent when a child, he became a skilled violinist, organ-player and composer in boyhood, with little aid beyond his solitary study and practice. When scarcely twenty-one, the University of Dublin conferred on him the degree of Doctor of Music, and a professorship. He excelled as a composer of glees, but wrote also tunes and anthems for the church, some of which are still extant in the choir books of the Dublin Cathedral Died March 22, 1781.

"HARK! HARK, MY SOUL!"

The Methodist Reformation, while it had found no practical sympathy within the established church, left a deep sense of its reason and purpose in the minds of the more devout Episcopalians, and this feeling, instead of taking form in popular revival methods, prompted them to deeper sincerity and more spiritual fervor in their traditional rites of worship. Many of the next generation inherited this pious ecclesiasticism, and carried their loyalty to the old Christian culture to the extreme of devotion till they saw in the sacraments the highest good of the soul. It was Keble's "Christian Year" and his "Assize Sermon" that began the Tractarian movement at Oxford which brought to the front himself and such men as Henry Newman and Frederick William Faber.

The hymns and sacred poems of these sacramentarian Christians would certify to their earnest piety, even if their lives were unknown.

Faber's hymn "Hark, Hark My Soul," is welcomed and loved by every Christian sect for its religious spirit and its lyric beauty.

Hark! hark, my soul! angelic songs are swelling
O'er earth's green fields and ocean's wave-beat shore;
How sweet the truth those blessed strains are telling
Of that new life where sin shall be no more.
REFRAIN
Angels of Jesus, angels of light
Singing to welcome the pilgrims of the night.
Onward we go, for still we hear them singing
"Come, weary souls, for Jesus bids you come,"
And through the dark, its echoes sweetly ringing,
The music of the gospel leads us home.
Angels of Jesus.
Far, far away, like bells at evening pealing,
The voice of Jesus sounds o'er land and sea,
And laden souls, by thousands meekly stealing,
Kind Shepherd, turn their weary steps to Thee.
Angels of Jesus.

THE TUNES.

John B. Dykes and Henry Smart—both masters of hymn-tune construction—have set this hymn to music. "Vox Angelica" in B flat, the work of the former, is a noble composition for choir or congregation, but "Pilgrim," the other's interpretation, though not dissimilar in movement and vocal range, has, perhaps, the more sympathetic melody. It is, at least, the favorite in many localities. Some books print the two on adjacent pages as optionals.

Another much-loved hymn of Faber's is—
O Paradise, O Paradise!
Who doth not crave for rest?
Who would not see the happy land
Where they that loved are blest?
REFRAIN
Where loyal hearts and true
Stand ever in the light,
All rapture through and through
In God's most holy sight.
O Paradise, O Paradise,
The world is growing old;
Who would not be at rest and free
Where love is never cold.
Where loyal hearts and true.
O Paradise, O Paradise,
I greatly long to see
The special place my dearest Lord,
In love prepares for me.
Where loyal hearts and true.

This aspiration, from the ardent soul of the poet has been interpreted in song by the same two musicians, and by Joseph Barnby—all with the title "Paradise." Their similarity of style and near equality of merit have compelled compilers to print at least two of them side by side for the singers' choice. A certain pathos in the strains of Barnby's composition gives it a peculiar charm to many, and in America it is probably the oftenest sung to the words.

Dr. David Breed, speaking of Faber's "unusual" imagination, says, "He got more out of language than any other poet of the English tongue, and used words—even simple words—so that they rendered him a service which no other poet ever secured from them." The above hymns are characteristic to a degree, but the telling simplicity of his style—almost quaint at times—is more marked in "There's a Wideness in God's Mercy," given on p. 234.

Horatius
Bonar, D.D.

"BEYOND THE SMILING AND THE WEEPING."

This song of hope—one of the most strangely tuneful and rune-like of Dr. Bonar's hymn-poems—is less frequently sung owing to the peculiarity of its stanza form. But it scarcely needs a staff of notes—

Beyond the smiling and the weeping
I shall be soon;
Beyond the waking and the sleeping,
Beyond the sowing and the reaping
I shall be soon.
REFRAIN
Love, rest and home!
Sweet hope!
Lord, tarry not, but come.
  *   *   *   *   *   *
Beyond the parting and the meeting
I shall be soon;
Beyond the farewell and the greeting,
Beyond the pulses' fever-beating
I shall be soon.
Love, rest and home!
Beyond the frost-chain and the fever
I shall be soon;
Beyond the rock-waste and the river
Beyond the ever and the never
I shall be soon.
Love, rest and home!

The wild contrasts and reverses of earthly vicissitude are spoken and felt here in the sequence of words. Perpetual black-and-white through time; then the settled life and untreacherous peace of eternity. Everywhere in the song the note of heavenly hope interrupts the wail of disappointment, and the chorus returns to transport the soul from the land of emotional whirlwinds to unbroken rest.

THE TUNES.

Mr. Bradbury wrote an admirable tune to this hymn, though the one since composed by Mr. Stebbins has in some localities superseded it in popular favor. Skill in following the accent and unequal rhythms produces a melodious tone-poem, and completes the impression of Bonar's singular but sweet lyric of hope which suggests a chant-choral rather than a regular polyphonic harmony. W.A. Tarbutton, and the young composer, Karl Harrington, have set the hymn to music, but the success of their work awaits the public test.

"WE SHALL MEET BEYOND THE RIVER."

The words were written by Rev. John Atkinson, D.D., in January, 1867, soon after the death of his mother. He had been engaged in revival work and one night in his study, "that song, in substance, seemed," he says, "to sing itself into my heart." He said to himself, "I would better write it down, or I shall lose it."

"There," he adds, "in the silence of my study, and not far from midnight, I wrote the hymn."

We shall meet beyond the river
By and by, by and by;
And the darkness will be over
By and by, by and by.
With the toilsome journey done,
And the glorious battle won.
We shall shine forth as the sun
By and by, by and by.

The Rev. John Atkinson was born in Deerfield, N.J. Sept. 6, 1835. A clergyman of the Methodist denomination, he is well-known as one of its writers. The *Centennial History of American Methodism* is his work, and besides the above hymn, he has written and published *The Garden of Sorrows*, and *The Living Way*. He died Dec. 8, 1897.

The tune to "We Shall Meet," by Hubert P. Main, composed in 1867, exactly translates the emotional hymn into music. S.J. Vail also wrote music to the words. The hymn, originally six eight-line stanzas, was condensed at his request to its present length and form by Fanny Crosby.

"ONE SWEETLY SOLEMN THOUGHT."

Phebe Cary, the author of this happy poem, was the younger of the two Cary sisters, Alice and Phebe, names pleasantly remembered in American literature. The praise of one reflects the praise of the other when we are told that Phebe possessed a loving and trustful soul, and her life was an honor to true womanhood and a blessing to the poor. She had to struggle with hardship and poverty in her early years: "I have cried in the street because I was poor," she said in her prosperous years, "and the poor always seem nearer to me than the rich."

When reputation came to her as a writer, she removed from her little country home near Cincinnati, O., where she was born, in 1824, and settled in New York City with her sister. She died at Newport, N.Y., July 31, 1871, and her hymn was sung at her funeral. Her remains rest in Greenwood Cemetery.

"One Sweetly Solemn Thought," was written in 1852, during a visit to one of her friends. She wrote (to her friend's inquiry) years afterwards that it first saw the light "in your own house ... in the little back third-story bedroom, one Sunday after coming from church." It was a heart experience noted down without literary care or artistic effort, and in its original form was in too irregular measure to be sung. She set little value upon it as a poem, but when shown hesitatingly to inquiring compilers, its intrinsic worth was seen, and various revisions of it were made. The following is one of the best versions—stanzas one, two and three:—

One sweetly solemn thought
Comes to me o'er and o'er,
I am nearer home to-day,
Than I ever have been before.
Nearer my Father's house,
Where the many mansions be,
Nearer the great white throne,
Nearer the crystal sea.
Nearer the bound of life,
Where we lay our burdens down,
Nearer leaving the cross
Nearer gaining the crown.

THE TUNE.

The old revival tune of "Dunbar," with its chorus, "There'll be no more sorrow there," has been sung to the hymn, but the tone-lyric of Philip Phillips, "Nearer Home," has made the words its own, and the public are more familiar with it than with any other. It was this air that a young man in a drinking house in Macao, near Hong-Kong, began humming thoughtlessly while his companion was shuffling the cards for a new game. Both were Americans, the man with the cards more than twenty years the elder. Noticing the tune, he threw down the pack. Every word of the hymn had come back to him with the echo of the music.

"Harry, where did you learn that hymn?"

"What hymn?"

"Why the one you have been singing."

185

The young man said he did not know what he had been singing. But when the older one repeated some of the lines, he said they were learned in the Sunday-school.

"Come, Harry," said the older one, "here's what I've won from you. As for me, as God sees me, I have played my last game, and drank my last bottle. I have misled you, Harry, and I am sorry for it. Give me your hand, my boy, and say that, for old America's sake, if for no other, you will quit this infernal business."

Col. Russel H. Conwell, of Boston, (now Rev. Dr. Conwell of Philadelphia) who was then visiting China, and was an eye-witness of the scene, says that the reformation was a permanent one for both.

"I WILL SING YOU A SONG OF THAT BEAUTIFUL LAND."

One day, in the year 1865, Mrs. Ellen M.H. Gates received a letter from Philip Phillips noting the passage in the *Pilgrim's Progress* which describes the joyful music of heaven when Christian and Hopeful enter on its shining shore beyond the river of death, and asking her to write a hymn in the spirit of the extract, as one of the numbers in his *Singing Pilgrim*. Mrs. Gates complied—and the sequel of the hymn she wrote is part of the modern song-history of the church. Mr. Phillips has related how, when he received it, he sat down with his little boy on his knee, read again the passage in Bunyan, then the poem again, and, turning to his organ, pencil in hand, pricked the notes of the melody. "The 'Home of the Soul,'" he says, "seems to have had God's blessing from the beginning, and has been a comfort to many a bereaved soul. Like many loved hymns, it has had a peculiar history, for its simple melody has flowed from the lips of High Churchmen, and has sought to make itself heard above the din of Salvation Army cymbals and drums. It has been sung in prisons and in jailyards, while the poor convict was waiting to be launched into eternity, and on hundreds of funeral occasions. One man writes me that he has led the singing of it at one hundred and twenty funerals. It was sung at my dear boy's funeral, who sat on my knee when I wrote it. It is my prayer that God may continue its solace and comfort. I have books containing the song now printed in seven different languages."

A writer in the *Golden Rule* (now the *Christian Endeavor World*) calls attention to an incident on a night railroad train narrated in the late Benjamin F. Taylor's *World on Wheels*, in which "this hymn appears as a sort of Traveller's Psalm." Among the motley collection of passengers, some talkative, some sleepy, some homesick and cross, all tired, sat two plain women who, "would make capital country aunts.... If they were mothers at all they were good ones." Suddenly in a dull silence, near twelve o'clock, a voice, sweet and flexible, struck up a tune. The singer was one of those women. "She sang on, one after another the good Methodist and Baptist melodies of long ago," and the growing interest of the passengers became chained attention when she began—

"I will sing you a song of that beautiful land,
The far-away home of the soul,
Where no storms can beat on the glittering strand,
While the years of eternity roll.
O, that home of the soul, in my visions and dreams,
Its bright jasper walls I can see;
Till I fancy but thinly the veil intervenes
Between the fair city and me."

"The car was a wakeful hush long before she had ended; it was as if a beautiful spirit were floating through the air. None that heard will ever forget. Philip Phillips can never bring that 'home of the soul' any nearer to anybody. And never, I think, was quite so sweet a voice lifted in a storm of a November night on the rolling plains of Iowa."

In an autograph copy of her hymn, sent to the editor, Mrs. Gates changes "harps" to "palms." Is it an improvement? "Palms" is a word of two meanings.

O how sweet it will be in that beautiful land,
So free from all sorrow and pain,
With songs on our lips and with harps in our hands
To meet one another again.

"THERE'S A LAND THAT IS FAIRER THAN DAY."

This belongs rather with "Christian Ballads" than with genuine hymns, but the song has had and still has an uplifting mission among the lowly whom literary perfection and musical nicety could not touch—and the first two lines, at least, are good hymn-writing. Few of the best sacred lyrics have been sung with purer sentiment and more affectionate fervor than "The Sweet By-and-By." To any company keyed to sympathy by time, place, and condition, the feeling of the song brings unshed tears.

As nearly as can be ascertained it was in the year 1867 that a man about forty-eight years old, named Webster, entered the office of Dr. Bennett in Elkhorn. Wis., wearing a melancholy look, and was rallied good-naturedly by the doctor for being so blue—Webster and Bennett were friends, and the doctor was familiar with the other's frequent fits of gloom.

The two men had been working in a sort of partnership, Webster being a musician and Bennett a ready verse-writer, and together they had created and published a number of sheet-music songs. When Webster was in a fit of melancholy, it was the doctor's habit to give him a "dose" of new verses and cure him by putting him to work. Today the treatment turned out to be historic.

"What's the matter now," was the doctor's greeting when his "patient" came with the tell-tale face.

"O, nothing," said Webster. "It'll be all right by and by."

"Why not make a song of the sweet by and by?" rejoined the doctor, cheerfully.

"I don't know," said Webster, after thinking a second or two. "If you'll make the words, I'll write the music."

The doctor went to his desk, and in a short time produced three stanzas and a chorus to which his friend soon set the notes of a lilting air, brightening up with enthusiasm as he wrote. Seizing his violin, which he had with him, he played the melody, and in a few minutes more he had filled in the counterpoint and made a complete hymn-tune. By that time two other friends, who could sing, had come in and the quartette tested the music on the spot. Here different accounts divide widely as to the immediate sequel of the new-born song.

A Western paper in telling its story a year or two ago, stated that Webster took the "Sweet By and By" (in sheet-music form), with a batch of other pieces, to Chicago, and that it was the only song of the lot that Root and Cady would not buy; and finally, after he had tried in vain to sell it, Lyon and Healy took it "out of pity," and paid him twenty dollars. They sold eight or ten copies (the story continued) and stowed it away with dead goods, and it was not till apparently a long time after, when a Sunday-school hymn-book reprinted it, and began to sell rapidly on its account, that the "Sweet By and By" started on its career round the world.

This seems circumstantial enough, and the author of the hymn in his own story of it might have chosen to omit some early particulars, but, untrustworthy as the chronology of mere memory is, he would hardly record immediate popularity of a song that lay in obscurity for years. Dr. Bennett's words are, "I think it was used in public shortly after [its production], for within two weeks children on the street were singing it."

The explanation may be partly the different method and order of the statements, partly lapses of memory (after thirty years) and partly in collateral facts. The Sunday-school hymn-book was evidently *The Signet Ring*, which Bennett and Webster were at work upon and into which first went the "Sweet By and By"—whatever efforts may have been made to dispose of it elsewhere or whatever copyright arrangement could have warranted Mr. Healy in purchasing a song already printed. The *Signet Ring* did not begin to profit by the song until the next year, after a copy of it appeared in the publishers' circulars, and started a demand; so that the *immediate* popularity implied in Doctor Bennett's account was limited to the children of Elkhorn village.

The piece had its run, but with no exceptional result as to its hold on the public, until in 1873 Ira D. Sankey took it up as one of his working hymns. Modified from its first form in the "*Signet Ring*" with pianoforte accompaniment and chorus, it appeared that year in *Winnowed Hymns* as arranged by Hubert P. Main, and it has so been sung ever since.

Sanford Filmore Bennett, born in 1836, appears to have been a native of the West, or, at least, removed there when a young man. In 1861 he settled in Elkhorn to practice his profession. Died Oct., 1898.

Joseph Philbrick Webster was born in Manchester, N.H. March 22, 1819. He was an active member of the Handel and Haydn Society, and various other musical associations. Removed to Madison, Ind. 1851, Racine, Wis. 1856, and Elkhorn, Wis., 1857, where he died Jan. 18, 1875. His *Signet Ring* was published in 1868.

There's a land that is fairer than day,
And by faith I can see it afar
For the Father waits over the way
To prepare us a dwelling-place there.
CHORUS
In the sweet by and by
We shall meet on that beautiful shore.
We shall sing on that beautiful shore
The melodious songs of the blest,
And our spirits shall sorrow no more,
Nor sigh for the blessing of rest.
In the sweet by and by, etc.

"SUNSET AND EVENING STAR."

Was it only a poet's imagination that made Alfred Tennyson approach perhaps nearest of all great Protestants to a sense of the real "Presence," every time he took the Holy Communion at the altar? Whatever the feeling was, it characterized all his maturer life, so far as its spiritual side was known. His remark to a niece expressed it, while walking with her one day on the seashore, "God is with us now, on this down, just as truly as Jesus was with his two disciples on the way to Emmaus."

Such a man's faith would make no room for dying terrors.

Sunset and evening star,
And one clear call for me,
And may there be no moaning of the bar
When I put out to sea,
But such a tide as, moving, seems asleep,
Too full for sound and foam,
When that which drew from out the boundless deep
Turns again home.
Twilight and evening bell,
And after that the dark,
And may there be no sadness of farewell
When I embark.
For though from out our bourne of time and place
The flood may bear me far,
I hope to see my Pilot face to face
When I have crossed the bar.

Tennyson lived three years after penning this sublime prayer. But it was his swan-song. Born at Somersby, Lincolnshire, Aug. 63 1809, dying at Farringford, Oct. 6, 1892, he filled out the measure of a good old age. And his prayer was answered, for his death was serene and dreadless. His unseen Pilot guided him gently "across the bar"—and then *he saw Him.*

THE TUNE.

Joseph Barnby's "Crossing the Bar" has supplied a noble choral to this poem. It will go far to make it an accepted tone in church worship, among the more lyrical strains of verse that sing hope and euthanasia.

"SAFE IN THE ARMS OF JESUS."

If Tennyson had the mistaken feeling (as Dr. Benson intimates) "that hymns were expected to be commonplace," it was owing both to his mental breeding and his mental stature. Genius in a colossal frame cannot otherwise than walk in strides. What is technically a hymn he never wrote, but it is significant that as he neared the Shoreless Sea, and looked into the Infinite, his sense of the Divine presence instilled something of the hymn spirit into his last verses.

Between Alfred Tennyson singing trustfully of his Pilot and Fanny Crosby singing "Safe in the Arms of Jesus," is only the width of the choir. The organ tone and the flute-note breathe the same song. The stately poem and the sweet one, the masculine and the feminine, both have wings, but while the one is lifted in anthem and solemn chant in the great sanctuaries, the other is echoing Isaiah's tender text* in prayer meeting and Sunday-school and murmuring it at the humble firesides like a mother's lullaby.

* Isa. 40:11.

Safe in the arms of Jesus,
Safe on His gentle breast,
There by His love o'ershaded
Sweetly my soul shall rest.
Hark! 'tis the voice of angels
Borne in a song to me
Over the fields of glory,
Over the jasper sea.
REFRAIN
Safe in the arms of Jesus (1st four lines rep.).
Safe in the arms of Jesus,
Safe from corroding care,
Safe from the world's temptations,
Sin cannot harm me there.
Free from the blight of sorrow,
Free from my doubts and fears,

Only a few more trials,
Only a few more tears.
Safe in the arms of Jesus.
Jesus, my heart's dear refuge
Jesus has died for me;
Firm on the Rock of Ages
Ever my trust shall be,
Here let me with patience,
Wait till the night is o'er,
Wait till I see the morning
Break on the Golden Shore.
Safe in the arms of Jesus.

—Composed 1868.

THE TUNE.

Those who have characterized the *Gospel Hymns* as "sensational" have always been obliged to except this modest lyric of Christian peace and its sweet and natural musical supplement by Dr. W.H. Doane. No hurried and high-pitched chorus disturbs the quiet beauty of the hymn, a simple *da capo* being its only refrain. "Safe in the Arms of Jesus" sang itself into public favor with the pulses of hymn and tune beating together.

Made in the USA
Las Vegas, NV
29 October 2021

33336116R00105